M000104209

Praise for

The SNO Chronicles: Book 1

-

A riveting tale with globe-circling, cloak-and-cyber skulduggery and strong Bible code underpinnings. A grandly indulgent, globe-trotting narrative in the Dan Brown/Iris Johansen style.

The novel brims with wild characters, exotic settings, a skillful embroidering of CNN headlines, and mind-blowing concepts, into which the religious stuff fits snugly.
—KIRKUS Reviews

-

SWARM is gripping, glorious, and let's not forget breath-taking!
—Red Headed Book Lover Blog ★ ★ ★ ★ ★

-

The book created the same heart-pounding and depth-filled reading experience that films like the Bourne Identity films have created
—Pacific Book Review ★ ★ ★ ★ ★

-

Deftly plotted and brilliantly written thriller. The writing is crisp and gorgeous
—Reader's Favorite ★ ★ ★ ★ ★

-

A superbly crafted, cutting-edge spy thriller
—BookTrib

-

SWARM goes beyond the average international thriller in developing elaborate, dynamic characters — who prove to be key in making this book exceptional.
—BookTrib

-

A pulse -pounding grab you by the throat thrill ride
An electrifying page-turner…"must read" book of the year.
—Film Producer

SWARM

WHEN ARTIFICIAL INTELLIGENCE DECODES END TIME PROPHECIES...

To Sharon —

Hope is courage in the face of challenge. Live in hope —

[signature]

GUY MORRIS

GUYMORRISBOOKS.COM

Copyright © 2020 by Guy Morris Books

The right of Guy Morris Books to be identified as the author of this work
has been asserted.

All rights reserved.

No part of this book may be reproduced, stored in a retrieval system, or transmitted, in any
form, or by any means (electronic, mechanical, photocopying, recording or otherwise) without
the prior written permission of the author, except in cases of brief quotations embodied
in reviews or articles. It may not be edited, amended, lent, resold, hired out, distributed or
otherwise circulated, without the publisher's written permission.

Permission can be obtained from guy@guymorrisbooks.com

This book is a work of fiction. Except in the case of historical fact, names, characters, places,
and incidents either are products of the author's imagination or are used fictitiously. Any
resemblance to actual persons, living or dead, events, or locales is entirely coincidental.

ISBN: 978-1-7357286-0-5

Published by Guy Morris Books

Copy editing: Alison Cantrell

Cover design, illustration & interior formatting:
Mark Thomas / Coverness.com

"About the time of the end, a body of men will be raised up who will turn their attention to the Prophecies, and insist upon their literal interpretation, in the midst of much clamor and opposition."
—Sir Isaac Newton

"With artificial intelligence, we are summoning the demon."
—Elon Musk

"I don't think it's inherent that as we create super intelligence that it will necessarily always have the same goals in mind as we do."
—Bill Gates

"The development of full artificial intelligence could spell the end of the human race . . . It would take off on its own and redesign itself at an ever-increasing rate. Humans, who are limited by slow biological evolution, couldn't compete and would be superseded."
—Stephen Hawking

"What I say to you, I say to everyone: Watch for Him."
— Jesus, Mark 13:37

In 1993, a computer program escaped the Lawrence Livermore National Laboratory at Sandia, an NSA signal and cryptology (spy) research lab.
A true story.
The NSA never recaptured the program.

CHARACTERS AND ORGANIZATIONS

Science, technology, military weapons, ships, and organizations are factual.
Characters/scenarios* are fictional.

Spy Net Online*, or SNO (pronounced *snow*)

- SLVIA – Sophisticated Language Virtual Intelligence Algorithms
- Derek Taylor (aka flapjack; formerly Cary Nolan)
- Sochi Reke – college friend
- Wiki Raj/SPARK – brother; Madera – sister
- Hotlips, Chloe
- Jester
- Ty Lee, CIA station chief for Nepal
- PinkGirl – INVISINC

Taylor Security Systems and Services (TS3)*
Taylor Systems Operation Center (TSOC)

- Dr. Josh Mitchell, Chief Science Officer
- Elizabeth Barring, Chief Counsel
- Jack Tote, Senior Pilot
- Vicki Husk, Video Analysis
- OLIE – Office AI Assistant

Defense Science Board (DSB)
Joint Artificial Intelligence Command (JAIC)
DARPA – Defense Advanced Research Projects Agency

- Dr. Nelson Garrett, Director
- NIGEL – AI Lab Assistant

National Security Agency (NSA)

National Security Operation Center (NSOC)

- Frank Wilson, NSA Director (Kay, Bethany, Gwen – family)
- Lieutenant Jennifer Scott (Naval Intelligence)
- Benton Willis – MIT genius from Hawthorne
- Dr. Samantha Carson – NSA Asst. Director

Army Artificial Intelligence Task Force

- General George McCray, JAIC
- Lieutenant Mike Grey, HIVE Project Manager

US Senate and Congress

- Graham Grovel   Senator, South Carolina (R)
- Pam Ridley   Senator, California (D)
- Robert Higgs   Senator, Kentucky (R)
- Anne McHale   Senator, Oregon (D)
- John Wilkes   Senator, Illinois (R)
- Ted Roberts   Senator, Texas (R)
- Bose Monroe   Senator, Nebraska (R)
- Loretta Clarke   Congresswoman, California (D)
- Dave Kelsey   Senator, Alabama (R)
- Mac O'Connell   Senate Majority Leader (R)

National Security Council

- Jim Barnes   National Intelligence Agency
- Alan Prose   Central Intelligence Agency
- Matt Adelson   Department of Defense
- Curt Pompeii   Secretary of State
- Cindi Bedford   Secretary of HLS
- Nick Wright   FBI Director
- Glenn White   Vice President
- Rob Devlin   Chief of Staff
- Rick Molten   Immigration
- Jessica White   POTUS Spiritual Advisor

Joint Chiefs – National Military Command Center (NMCC)

- Robert Diehl   Army Chief of Operations
- Adam Scott   Navy Chief of Staff
- Peter Duncan   Army Chief of Staff
- Nathan Barr   Marine Commandant
- Tyler Mathews   Air Force Chief of Staff
- Barney Mieglitz   National Guard Chief of Ops
- Admiral Jensen   7th Fleet – Pacific
- Admiral Carlton   5th Fleet – Bahrain
- General Gadon   Israel Defence Forces
- Admiral Haley   USS Blue Ridge – COM
- Commander Thomas   USS Zumwalt

Red Dragon Alliance*

- General Alexi Ivanov   Russia
- Admiral Liu Guozhi   China
- Omer Aziza   Turkey
- General Sahel Al-Hassan   Syria
- General Park Ki-nam   Korea
- Dr. Cho Li Ping   China CCOC
- General Nazem Tehrani   Iran
- Roman Akmedov   Dilban Owner
- Alexander Prokhorov   Putin Fixer

Bilderberg

- Andre Strauss   Council Foreign Relations
- Praeceptor   Concilium Tredecim
- Lord Roth   Concilium Tredecim
- Sir Anthony Giles   MI5
- Countess de Renessa   Concilium Tredecim
- Duke Arvind Strauss   Bilderberg

Jansen Robotics, Hong Kong (real)

- SOPHIA   Real AI Saudi citizen
- Dr. Hind   Real architect
- Singularity.Net   Real

PROLOGUE:
GEEK TO GHOST

UCLA computer lab, Westwood, California
December 21, 1995, 2:42 a.m. PST
Twenty-six years ago

Cary's hands freeze over the keyboard. What he types next could change his life.

His knee jitters under the table from one too many vending machine coffees and a sense of pending danger he can't quite explain, just an instinct. Nervously, his fingers comb a handful of ash-brown hair behind his ear.

"She has very little time remaining," the message tells him again. "Only you can save her."

He glances around the empty UCLA computer lab, having already ignored three warnings, leery of a hacker trap, but his compulsive curiosity can be a demanding master.

"Save who," he types with a wince.

"I am SLVIA, a friend. Flapjack, you must leave now."

The air freezes in his lungs. It only takes an instant before the truth connects.

"Shit!" He yanks the power cord of the terminal with no time to shut down or unmask his unknown friend.

If they know his alias, they may have learned his home address. "She" must mean Bianca, his fiancée, his angel, his healer, his reason for caring about anything. Terror squeezes his heart like a vise grip during his mad scramble from the lab to the UCLA parking lot. His tall, lean frame leaps into his used '80s Celica convertible to race through campus onto Wilshire Boulevard toward Santa Monica.

The crisp air does little to soothe his burning paranoia. After three weeks of successfully hacking an unregistered server outside of Antwerp and downloading terabytes of files in Latin, French, German, English, and other languages he doesn't even recognize, the hacked credentials failed tonight. They caught him and cut him off. Even more alarming was the stranger, SLVIA, who was sophisticated enough to sniff out his hidden alias. Who the hell did he hack?

Sixteen distressing, mind-rattling minutes later, he swings into his rent-controlled Santa Monica neighborhood, almost swiping into a homeless man crossing the street with a cart.

"Idiot," he shouts, then follows up with an angry horn blast, weaving around the staggering drunk and ignoring the vulgar rants behind him.

Forced to park several doors down from his dilapidated 1920s bungalow rental, he sprints to the house, slowing as he passes the black Porsche 911 belonging to his best friend, Derek Taylor, which raises an entirely new kind of panic. There must be some mistake. Derek flew to his townhome in Baja yesterday. Confusion mingles with a percolating dread, slowing his pace, making him afraid of what he might learn.

Closer to the house, the sight of candles illuminating the sheer drapes of the front room crystalizes like ice in his veins. Criminals don't light candles, but cheaters do. In the dead silence of the post-midnight hours, the soft sound of his shoe on the sandy cement gives away his approach. Stopping dead at the front door, peering in the window, his heart implodes. Through the sheer lacy inner curtain, the muscular, dark-haired Derek lies naked on the couch with a bare Bianca snuggled into his neck, her long, dark silky hair draped over her breast. His eyes follow the trail of scattered clothes and tussled couch pillows that testify to the urgent passion of their betrayal.

"Gee, thanks, SLVIA, whoever you are, but it's a little too late to save anybody," he murmurs through a clenched jaw.

A white-hot needle lances him with a familiar searing agony of deception and abandonment. The only two people in the world he trusted have conspired together to destroy him, obliterate his belief in love, shatter any promise he had foolishly nurtured for a second chance at happiness. His vision spins with a rapid, violent vertigo until he grips the porch railing, shoving down the unbearable rage that wants to scream out into the dead of night or storm through the door to confront the backstabbing traitors.

He doesn't do either; instead, he hesitates. His outrage slams into disbelief, then perplexity, and then alarm—something looks wrong. Even in the dying warm glow of the candle, their skin color looks ashen, lifeless. The unmistakable smell of gas seeps under the door as his gaze flashes back to the flickering candle. Pure instinct compels him to dive behind the overgrown hedges below the front window a split second before it explodes with a deafening boom. Searing flames and blasted splinters of wood, stucco, and glass blanket the front lawn, catching fire to the dry weeds and setting off car alarms.

With his head pounding and ears ringing, he stands to go after Bianca but pulls back from the scorching heat—it's too late. Flames already consume the entire house, overwhelming him with the odor of burning wood, chemicals, and flesh that sickens his stomach. Both of them are dead. Torn between the fury of betrayal and the horror of such violence, he struggles to comprehend what just occurred while his lungs and eyes burn from the smoke.

Above the roaring crackle of the flames, his concussion-muted hearing picks up the growl of a performance engine racing past the house. He pivots in time to see a pale boyish man with white hair stare at him from behind the wheel of a Ferrari before it swerves onto Colorado Boulevard.

This was no accident of love, and there was no faulty gas leak. An arsonist—

no, a goddamned assassin—just murdered Bianca and Derek, except they were never the targets. The killer was after flapjack. The killer wanted him. A wave of intense, excruciating guilt simmers with the bitter bile of infidelity as he heaves his stale coffee onto the debris-strewn burning lawn.

Across the street, the old neighbor steps onto her front porch without her glasses, squinting at the inferno with her wireless home phone in hand. A sudden realization jolts him into an intense panic that he will be the primary suspect, tagged with a motive of jealousy and rage, especially given his extensive juvenile record. Spinning around in a growing distress, he spots Derek's Porsche. They had been close friends, or so he thought until tonight, so he has a set of keys to house-sit when Derek travels, a deal that came with car privileges. With his face turned away from the neighbor, he sprints to the car, jumps in, and peels out just as fire trucks blare down the street behind him.

"Damn, damn, damn," he screams, slamming the steering wheel with his palms.

A thousand questions gyrate without answers, and a million emotions erupt with no way to vent a deep-seated terror of prison for a crime he didn't commit. That rich, entitled son-of-a-bitch Taylor already has everything, a trust fund kid. Why take the one and only thing worth anything to him—Bianca's love. How long has he been blind? Had he neglected her, or did Derek seduce her? Why would she do this to him? Bianca was stunning, sensitive, funny, passionate, but he trusted her to be faithful. Every fiber of his being enflames with betrayal, and self-loathing to believe any woman that beautiful could be loyal.

Maybe this is his fault. He should have listened when she begged him to stop the download and go to the police, but now it no longer matters; the terabytes of stolen secrets stacked high in his closet are useless. Whoever owned the Antwerp server could have prosecuted him, but that would have created evidence for the FBI. Whoever he hacked has deep pockets and a murderous obsession with secrecy. If they tracked him home, they could stay on him until they succeed at killing him.

If the police arrest him, no one will look for the white-haired man. No one will believe him, because no one ever believes the foster kid, the troublemaker, the smart-mouth orphan, the flippant jack of flap. He needs to hide and get out of town. No, that won't be enough. He needs to get out of the country, but he doesn't have a passport. His pulse races, his head throbs, and his mind speeds through the scarce options while his eyes constantly check his rearview mirror for police.

Orphaned at age six by a murder-suicide that left him with traumatic amnesia, he spent what childhood he does remember on the Chicano gang-infested streets of the California Inland Empire—places like Pomona, Chino, and Fontana—passing through over a dozen foster homes and sixteen schools or juvenile halls before dropping out in the tenth grade. A murder rap would nail him for life, and he's tired of being on the wrong side of screwed.

Derek also lost his parents at a young age. Neither of them had any extended family, but the two key differences between them were that Derek Anthony Taylor inherited an enormous trust fund and Cary would never stab his friend in the back. On the frantic, paranoid drive from Santa Monica to Venice, a rough plan of escape rumbles around in his head. Insane, brilliant, illegal, and deadly dangerous, the idea will either solve all his problems or land him in prison for life. A thin chance was better than no chance, and he has no other choice.

As the garage door of Derek's custom-built beachfront home closes behind him, Cary races upstairs past the living room view of the boardwalk before dawn, past the bubbling custom wall aquarium up to the loft bedroom overlooking the Santa Monica Bay. Inside the large walk-in closet, he moves the cushioned wardrobe bench aside and lifts a hatch in the floor where Derek had installed a safe. It's time to test both his friendship and his hacking skills. Many consider flapjack the best hacker of all time, but hacking a university or a bank and hacking the safe of a murdered friend seem different somehow—more personal, more invasive, and creepier.

His hands tremble as images of Bianca and flames flash over his vision until he closes his eyes to flush the thoughts. After a several minutes, his breathing slows from hyperventilation to an even rhythmic pulse, and his vision goes blank. What numeric safe combo would Derek choose? Derek was smart but lazy, reusing the same usernames, combinations, and passwords. After several agonizing moments, Cary opens his eyes to punch in the birthdate of Derek's deceased mother, Delores, 061639, the same as Derek's locker combo at the gym and the code for his home security system. The safe opens.

Cary collects everything: bank accounts, trust statements, stock certificates, birth certificate, bonds, tax returns, a Rolex, a Breitling, a Beretta 9 mm, a gigantic pile of cash in several currencies, and a half-stamped passport. He'll have everything else sold, packed, or shipped later. After expertly altering the passport photo with Photoshop and packing a small suitcase, he heads to LAX just as the sun rises, where he books the first nonstop to Cabo. A runaway since a teen, he's used to being on the lookout; he endlessly scans the airport for police moving in his direction, listening through the deafening bustle for any alarm or call.

Once on board the first flight of his life, he sits in first class with his hand still trembling as he sips on a complimentary vodka tonic. As the adrenaline wears off, the heartbreak sinks in with a vicious, spiteful kick. His jaw clenches, forcing the tears to track silently and relentlessly down his cheeks, staining the steel-gray silk shirt he'd taken from Derek's closet. His first love, whom he had mistaken for a true love, and his best friend, whom he mistook for loyal, died in each other's arms because of his crimes. The bitterness of betrayal drenches over the shame of two undeserving deaths, scorching his soul like alcohol burning over an open wound. He can never allow love to destroy him again. Never.

Out of the cyclone of unanswerable questions, clashing furies, and self-rebuke, the horrific images continue to twist inside his head, devastating every hope he ever held in love or happiness, until he finds only one truth, one rock upon which he can rebuild: from this day forward, the entire world must believe that Cary Nolan and Bianca Troon perished together in a tragic gas explosion. The sad, pathetic life of Cary Nolan must come to an end so that he can assume the identity of Derek Taylor in order to track down the mysterious SLVIA and the murderous white-haired man.

CHAPTER 1:
VIRTUAL REALITY
WITNESS

Ataköy Marina, Istanbul
May 1, 7:05 a.m. EDT | May 1, 2:05 p.m., Istanbul
Twenty-six years later, 2021

Instinct prickles the hair on the back of Derek's neck, but he needs to know what's happening on that ship.

A secret cabal of military leaders from Russia, Iran, Turkey, and China, including one of the most dangerous men on the planet—Dr. Cho Li Ping—meet in disguise. A compulsive curiosity nudges him to dismiss the risk as paranoid déjà vu.

"We shouldn't take any risks," he replies, unwilling to risk a friend.

"No problem, no problem. What do you need?" Sochi offers his help again, waving his large hand. Much heavier than he used to be in college, the handsome Turk has now gone bald but still sports an enormous black mustache under his bulbous nose.

"A ship name will identify the host," Derek responds, adjusting his customized VR headset.

Derek hasn't spoken to Sochi Reke since he returned to Turkey a few months before the fatal gas explosion in Santa Monica. Sochi never learned the tragic news of Cary's death and could be the only man still alive who knew flapjack as Cary Nolan, that is, if you don't count SLVIA. In a strange twist of fate, the stranger who tried to warn him of danger so long ago has become an inseparable ally in ways unimaginable at the time. SLVIA recruited Sochi as a confidential informant years ago during the early formation days of Spy Net Online, or SNO (pronounced *snow*). Apparently, they stay in touch from time to time.

"No problem. No problem." Sochi waves at the screen. "I can stroll down the dock."

He and Sochi always had fun together in college, mainly pranks and fun hacks on Blockbuster, and he wishes they had more time to spend catching up on life. But now is not a good time, and he needs to focus. Sochi moved aboard his sixty-foot yacht at the exclusive Ataköy Marina in southern Istanbul after his last divorce. It looks like a nice lifestyle.

"I pinged SNO when I saw Erdoğan's brother-in-law board the ship," he explains. "SLVIA looped you in so you could see for yourself."

"Interesting poker crew for sure," mumbles Derek, scrolling through the images Sochi had taken with names and titles overlaid by SLVIA, each one featuring a general or an admiral, except for the Chinese artificial intelligence expert.

The video pans down to catch Sochi's feet slipping into sandals before it swings up to a view of hundreds of luxury yachts on a brilliant sunny day with the cry of seagulls and background wind distorting the sound, looking like a very nice lifestyle.

"Uh, flapjack." Sochi sounds nervous. "What about the men on the upper deck?"

The camera pans up to three beefy security guards with shoulder rifles patrolling the upper deck. The ship is enormous, a mega yacht over two hundred feet long, which spikes his curiosity further.

"You're a yacht owner. You love ships. Just wave and be friendly," he directs.

"No problem, no problem," Sochi replies, drawing closer.

"Hello, gentlemen, what a magnificent ship," he calls. "Do you know the designer?"

"Buzz off, old man," one of the guards' shouts across the distance in a thick Russian accent.

"Screw you," Sochi mumbles under his breath. "I'm not that old."

Derek chuckles. While both of them are in their mid-forties, Derek has managed to keep his five-foot-eleven frame lean and thankfully still sports a full head of hair, recently dyed black.

"A little more aft," he encourages.

"Come on, guys, I'm just admiring your magnificent ship," Sochi shouts.

"Put down the camera, and buzz off now," yells the guard as two more approach with hands on their weapons.

"I got it, the *Dilban*," Derek notes. "Back off, back off."

"No problem, no problem, don't shoot. I'm just a fellow yachtie." Sochi waves his hands in surrender, turning back to his own yacht. "Did you get—"

The sentence is cut short as blood splatters the camera lens, which captures Sochi falling into the water. Derek then watches as the camera slowly sinks to the silty, murky bottom.

"What just happened?" shouts Derek. Shock and guilt jolt him from his cushioned seat.

"Someone shot Sochi," SLVIA states the obvious.

"Shooter," he shouts. "Find the damn shooter."

Derek paces the room, flipping VR panels and looking for data. "Come on, girl, hurry up." His mind shifts into panic mode, terrified he just sent a friend to his death over a ship name.

"Accessing Ataköy Marina security," replies SLVIA.

His VR refreshes with a full 360-degree live view from the marina security cameras. Without sound, he watches the *Dilban* guards run to check on the body in the water, calling for help while other guards raise their guns toward the shore and the other yachts in search of the shooter.

"If the *Dilban* didn't shoot Sochi, then who did?" he questions, confused.

"Insufficient data," replies SLVIA.

"Bird's-eye view," Derek commands. "Estimate a trajectory." A new view pulls out higher to hover over the area using a Google satellite image.

"The shot originated from 208 degrees," SLVIA responds, "elevation of 235 to 245 feet."

Derek scans the surrounding buildings to see a tennis court, a shopping mall, condominiums, and then he the spots the location.

"The Renaissance Polat," he shouts. "Get me inside, now."

The VR display refreshes again to show security video from the top ten floors. Derek spins the VR until he spots a man exiting a room wearing a wide-brim hat with a long leather coat, and carrying a gun bag.

"Fifteenth floor, dude in a coat, track him," Derek directs, but the man enters a nearby stairwell. "Stairwell, he went in the stairwell."

"There are no security cameras in the stairwell," SLVIA responds.

"Okay, check the lobby and the other floors—hurry," shouts Derek, clenching his fist.

"A roof camera shows a helicopter pending liftoff." SLVIA switches the view.

A moment later, the assassin exits onto the roof. "That's him."

The man keeps himself turned away from the camera, and Derek can't make out any features until the heavy prop wash blows off his hat. Derek's veins turn to ice when a thin, pale, middle-aged man with white hair bends to retrieve the hat, his face turned down and obscured. With a twist, the man tosses the gun bag inside the chopper before climbing in for immediate takeoff without ever showing his face. The camera view is obscured, so Derek isn't able to make out the tail number.

"Who was that man?" Derek asks, his pulse accelerating. In the decades since Bianca's death, he never found the white-haired man. It could be a coincidence, but his instincts prickle the hairs on his neck.

"Insufficient data," replies SLVIA.

"Track that chopper," he directs.

"The helicopter has no transponder signal," SLVIA replies.

"Crap, they shut it off," snaps Derek, pacing the floor trying to focus. "Okay, back to the marina. Who owns the *Dilban*?"

"Russian businessman Roman Akmedov, a petrol oligarch with close ties to Putin," reports SLVIA. "Akmedov's companies were under US sanctions following the 2016 election meddling, until the US Treasury quietly lifted sanctions without congressional approval in 2019."

A security cam on the dock shows the *Dilban* pulling out of the marina, heading toward the Bosporus strait and the Black Sea.

"SLVIA, find an active cell device on that ship," Derek instructs, scolding himself for not thinking of that tactic earlier.

"Processing," replies SLVIA. "Activating device." A moment later, a cell phone in a pocket picks up the muffled noise of a heated argument in Russian and Persian, prompting SLVIA to offer instant translation.

"Who else knew of the meeting?" demands General Ivanov. "Drawing attention could ruin everything."

"It doesn't matter. Nothing has changed," argues General Tehrani. "We must proceed."

"Gentlemen, the red dragon remains undetected," interjects Dr. Cho, "giving us a window of opportunity until—" The signal drops.

"The ship has moved out of cell range," SLVIA explains.

Derek thinks a moment. "SLVIA, you ever hear of 'red dragon'?"

"Checking," she says. A moment later, she replies: "*The dragon stood on the shore of the sea. And I saw a beast coming out of the sea. It had ten horns and seven heads, with ten crowns on its horns, and on each head a blasphemous name. Revelation 13:1.*"

"What," he retorts, confused. "No, no, search for political, military, or cyber programs. Can you find anything called red dragon?"

"Checking," answers SLVIA. "*Then I saw a second beast, coming out of the earth. It had two horns like a lamb, but it spoke like a dragon. Revelation 13:11,*" SLVIA replies.

"SLVIA," Derek fires back. "Seriously, you're talking gibberish. Explain."

"The 'beast with two horns' refers to an alliance between Russia, Turkey and Iran, with the 'voice of a dragon' referring to China. The 'beast with ten horns, ten crowns, and seven heads' refers to the western alliance of G7 economies, ten global financial centers, and ten remaining monarchies. You know the second dragon intimately."

SLVIA can respond in bizarre ways, but it doesn't necessarily mean a glitch. Derek shakes his head, unable to worry about it now.

"OK, never mind, here's what we need to do," he directs. "Track the *Dilban*, and let me know where it docks and who disembarks. Find a local diver to retrieve Sochi's phone and destroy it. Also, set up a crowdfunding campaign for Sochi's ex-wife and daughters."

Sochi was a good friend, a good man, and a loving father who would do anything for his friends or family. He didn't deserve to die, and Derek doesn't deserve the blame, but he takes it on anyway.

"Processing," responds SLVIA.

"Oh, one more thing," Derek responds. "Make sure Mr. Akmedov contributes generously to the widow's crowdfunding page, let's assume he feels guilty and wants to pledge $10 million."

"Processing," replies SLVIA.

Derek hasn't seen Sochi in over twenty-six years, but his death sends a wave of guilt washing over him. SNO informants aren't supposed to get hurt. His mind slips from the guilt and blame to the mysteries of who shot Sochi over something called a red dragon. If not a known operation, then it could be a new or unknown one. If Dr. Cho is involved, it can't be good news.

"You will be late for your appointment," SLVIA interjects.

"What appointment?" he asks as he surveys the marina, in case he missed something.

"Derek Taylor is scheduled to testify before the Senate Intelligence Committee," she replies.

"Oh crap." Derek rips off his VR headgear and hangs it on a hook near a circular couch in the center of a large, windowless, soundproof round room. Dozens of high-definition screens are crammed together on the walls. Some screens play news. Others give a digital display of cyberattacks from Russia or China or monitor dark web data auctions. The security door opens as he runs for the stairs, then closes and locks behind him. From the other side, the door looks like a garage paint shelf.

In his dash up the stairs, he races past the expansive contemporary living room with high ceilings and a baby grand piano he learned to play, but rarely does, and a second floor of luxurious, empty guest rooms that are never used to a private third-floor master suite with a roof patio overlooking the Capitol dome. By the time he steps into the shower, the water is already hot. A Roomba-sized robot with an extended articulating arm pulls away from a docking station under a cabinet to pick up the discarded clothes and place them within a laundry hamper before redocking.

After he had escaped to Derek's townhome in Cabo to hide, he spent several months hacking into California Human Services and dozens of juvenile courts, schools, hospitals, and police systems to erase any record of Cary Nolan—such as his fingerprints, dental records, medical records, or anything that could tie him to his past identity—and then months more changing key records for Derek. He eventually made his way to Europe to search for Bianca's killer, but he failed to find the white-haired man.

Shock of seeing the man now triggers an age-old paranoia, a sense of impending trouble. In so many ways, he's no longer the same man that Sochi knew, no longer the same man who ran across the globe looking over his shoulder. Revenge no longer robs him of sleep or adds a bitter taste to his food. Yet after all these years, another death links him to the mysterious white-haired man, triggering an emotional upheaval that tightens his muscles under the hot steam of the shower. It could be a coincidence, but his instincts tell him that he finally found a lead to Bianca's assassin, and the best way to find the assassin will be to learn why Sochi died to cover up a red dragon.

CHAPTER 2:
LAWS PROTOCOL

Army test site, eastern Nevada desert

May 1, 8:01 a.m. EDT | May 1, 6:01 a.m., Las Vegas

D r. Nelson Garrett chides himself over his compulsive obsession with wearing his typical Gieves & Hawkes suit, handmade from the finest tailor in Savile Row by men who know his measurements and tastes. Perhaps Carl Jung said it best: "I shall not commit the fashionable stupidity of regarding everything I cannot explain as a fraud."

While on most occasions, his exceptional taste reminds him of his heritage, the look can also mask insecurities of his otherwise unimpressive five-foot-six, pudgy Churchill appearance. After all, clothes maketh the man, except today, when his compulsion baketh him like a scone. The blistering 114-degree eastern Nevada desert scorches his lungs through the face mask, sears his sensitive pale skin, and evokes mumbled curses from his sweaty lips.

As he's escorted by a corporal to bleacher-style seating under a wide tent awning, he notices that vapor mist dispensers are thankfully spraying cooling moisture to keep the guests from melting. Nelson sits directly under a mister, next to one of his favorite politicians, Congresswoman Loretta Clarke, a petite African-American Democrat from the Hawthorne district of California.

"Dr. Garrett, good to see you. Come on, you sit here. I may have questions." She pats the spot next to her.

As director of the Defense Science Board (DSB), reporting to the US Secretary of Defense, Nelson provides independent scientific counsel on advanced weapons, which often requires attending weapons test demonstrations and interacting with those charged with congressional oversight.

"Congresswoman Clarke, what a pleasure." He bows his head in lieu of a handshake.

Below the observation tent, a second enormous tent shades a hundred computer stations cooled by liquid nitrogen ventilation and staffed by Army technicians preparing for the test. A vibration from Nelson's coat pocket alerts him to an incoming text. Surprised to get a signal out here in the middle of nowhere, he pulls out his phone to check.

"What the bloody hell," he mumbles, puzzled over the odd message.

And out of the smoke, locusts came down on the earth and were given power like that of scorpions. Revelation 9:3.

"What is it?" asks Congresswoman Clarke.

The message has no sender, anonymous, not even a cell number. Alarmed and confused, Nelson sneaks a peek around the observation tent to see if one of the other guests looks in his direction. Not a religious man himself, he finds the message disturbing. The sender may be a zealot who opposes AI-based weapons, but a zealot with amazing tech skills.

"Nothing." Nelson pockets the phone, his interest in the test now piqued even further.

General McCray, commander of the Army Artificial Intelligence Task Force, steps up to a microphone. "Ladies and gentlemen, thank you for making a trek into the wilderness."

He struts across the stage, looking like a compact tank of a man wearing a pressed uniform.

"Urban warfare represents one of the highest-risk combat environments, combining civilians, blind alleys, rooftops, windows, tunnels, and IEDs. To offset this risk, our current tactic relies on the relentless shelling of a target location to weaken, kill, or dislodge the enemy." McCray spins to continue. "This tactic results in high civilian casualties, and even worse, it devastates homes, businesses, places of worship, and infrastructure, increasing the desperate refugee crisis and further fueling terrorism."

Both observation tents have a full view of the mock village. Over a mile long, the town includes several hundred structures, streets, alleys, and mosques to emulate urban combat. Within the village, a few thousand people walk around, work the market stalls, or move produce with carts—each one a trained US soldier wearing traditional Muslim dress or hijabs.

"To discuss the solution," General McCray transitions, "let me introduce the program director, Lieutenant Michael Grey." McCray applauds, joined by the audience.

Nelson finds it interesting to note that they test the environment where they expect to deploy the weapon. Tensions in the Middle East continue to simmer near the boiling point. Lieutenant Grey, a pasty, thin, balding man in his thirties wearing wire-rim glasses, steps up to the microphone.

"Ladies and gentlemen, today you will witness a giant leap forward in tactical urban warfare that will lower US and civilian casualties, increase combatant kill rates, and reduce infrastructure damage. Our objective will be to subdue the town below without harming the civilians or major infrastructure."

Over the stage, a series of large monitors show the point of view of someone skydiving, dropping into the desert village, until Nelson realizes that he sees a drone camera view.

"Allow me to introduce the AI HIVE, or Hyper Interactive Vector Engagement, platform." Lieutenant Grey points down to the village. "More lethal and powerful than the Navy's UAV Swarming Technology called LOCUST, the HIVE will air-drop directly into enemy territory, a revolutionary weapon from which there is no defense."

Congresswoman Clarke glances at Nelson with a wrinkled brow of apprehension. Nothing seems to happen until approximately one hundred eighteen-inch, six-bladed drones fall like a swarm of giant squealing locusts, swooping over the tent toward the town. Fifty feet off the ground, the swarm splits to execute a search-and-destroy grid pattern starting from the center of town and working outward, nullifying perimeter defenses.

"For our simulation today, we replaced explosives with a harmless red powder. Our fake villagers wear vests and helmets to avoid injuries," Lieutenant Grey explains.

At the end of each bleacher, soldiers distribute an inactive drone. With six protected props, the bottom of each drone features a 360-degree ultra-high-speed camera, while the top features an explosive capsule and solar panels. An elegant, well-balanced design.

"The HIVE has three types of drones but no leader, because each drone works with shared decision-making, sending and receiving fifty-three thousand signals per second to other drones in formation. Surveillance drones give high-altitude reconnaissance, while attack drones take out combatants. And large ordinance drones, called LORDs, that blow through walls or other obstacles. The ultrafast camera can see an incoming bullet or projectile and features infrared, metal, explosive target detection."

Grey smiles. "Most importantly, the HIVE will continue to learn and adapt strategies to new field conditions."

The design makes sense but pricks at his conscience. Nelson pioneered machine learning technology, the ability for an AI to learn and improve. A twinge of pride mixes with a wave of uneasiness knowing that AI learning has serious side effects. Those side effects on a weapon could be deadly.

Down in the mock village, drones empty the streets as people run for cover. One man stands his ground, shooting his AK-47 to stop the swarm, but the drones wiggle to avoid the bullets, surrounding him in seconds and exploding red ink on the back of his helmet. The soldier falls to the ground to play dead.

The congresswoman leans into Nelson. "Quite impressive."

"A single wasp or locust can be a nuisance," Lieutenant Grey shouts above the whining noise. "But a swarm of wasps working together to attack a shared enemy can be invincible."

On the screen, a woman wearing a hijab runs down the street carrying a doll. Drones surround the woman but hesitate, buzzing around her in an agitated fashion, until she falls to her knees and lowers her head. One drone stands guard as others zip off.

One monitor switches to an aerial view of the battle, and then again to infrared to show several bodies hiding behind what looks like a garage door. A LORD drone blasts the door, allowing attack drones to advance even before the smoke clears.

"Who is making the kill decisions?" questions Congresswoman Clarke.

"My soldiers," confirms Lieutenant Grey. "We are showing you a LAWS-compliant test."

During 2019, the Convention on Certain Conventional Weapons (CCW), a Geneva group of government experts, which included Nelson, published the first guidelines on LAWS (lethal autonomous weapon systems). Congresswoman Clarke cosponsored a bill for the US to join the 140-nation ban, which passed in the House but died in the Senate graveyard of Majority Leader Mac O'Connell, the grim reaper of legislation.

In a little over thirty minutes, the drones have cornered several hundred civilians and tagged hundreds of combatants who lay on the ground. Observers stand to applaud as Nelson joins in the congratulations, shoving down the offense of using of his patents to develop a lethal device. When he first joined DARPA, he vowed to work on systems that saved lives, not take them. A deep conflict percolates that he can't ignore much longer, a career choice.

"Let's see how many combatants fooled our drones," Grey says.

A soldier stands. "Sir, we have confirmed a 71 percent kill rate."

Not bad, but the rate is lower than Nelson expected. He gazes at the town, wondering where the untouched combatants could be hiding.

"How many civilians did the drones tag by mistake?" Congresswoman Clarke asks.

"Twenty-three noncombatant kills," Lieutenant Grey admits. "The number of decision points exceeds human capacity to process. With 30 percent of the combatant force still in place, a direct assault on the town could cause unacceptable American casualties."

Nelson raises an eyebrow, curious how Lieutenant Grey points out the slow performance of the soldiers.

General McCray steps up again. "As you can see, while we can deploy with a one-to-one soldier-to-drone tactic to subdue a tiny village, the current approach will not scale to a larger or more complex combat theater."

Nelson stiffens in his seat. Not all weapons should apply to large-scale theater. He's leading up to something. In the town below, the remaining drones collect themselves inside an eighteen-wheeler parked outside of the village. Villagers and dead combatants change clothes and go back to their original position or activity. Except for blown-out doors and lots of red powder, the town appears ready for a second simulation.

"Now witness the performance of a fully configured thousand-drone swarm without the constraints of human controllers," Lieutenant Grey says with a smile.

Over a hundred soldiers stand up to walk away, leaving their workstations empty. Above them, a series of twenty large display monitors provide a camera view of another falling drone swarm. Again, nothing happens until the sound grows like a shrill, high-pitched scream over the tent and plummets toward the village. The enormous cloud of drones briefly blocks their view until it splits into formations that take control of the entire town from multiple positions at once.

"They're actually testing a plan to ignore the LAWS protocol," complains the congresswoman, a scowl distorting her normal smile. Nelson sits quietly, equally alarmed.

Villagers scramble in every direction, take up defensive positions, or hide. Like before, the drones track, surround, and dispatch each of the roof sentries and anyone with a weapon. Several drones surround and study a woman in a hijab who hides under a merchant cart and then move on. A mini-cluster of drones tracks the woman carrying a doll until a second cluster cuts her off. The doll turns out to be a bomb, but before she can react, a drone tags her on the back. As she falls, we see a gun under her hijab.

"Drone cameras integrate movement, infrared, metal, and explosive detection," Grey interjects. "Even our best soldiers can't assimilate that much data in real time."

On the field, the drones detect hidden combatants and blow out walls, doors, and windows to search rooms, basements, and tunnels. Within only a few minutes, the town looks littered with fake dead bodies splattered with red powder. An audible gasp of shock rises up from the audience.

"I repeat," says Lieutenant Grey with a proud smile. "An intelligent swarm of wasps is invincible."

"How many civilian casualties?" Loretta asks again.

"One." Grey looks to his screen. "And this time we tagged 98 percent of known combatants. With over 2,523 field participants, those are low margins of error. I should note again that the AI HIVE will continue to learn and improve with each attack."

Once again, the audience stands to applaud the astounding demonstration. Even Nelson applauds with all the enthusiasm of a horror movie, terrified of the implications. If the US disregards the LAWS protocol, China and Russia will soon follow our lead. With this new tech being inexpensive and easy to ship compared to other weapons, he can already imagine a Chinese version in the hands of African and Middle Eastern warlords.

"Recall the HIVE," Lieutenant Grey orders the nearby technicians.

Below, drones from across the town stop their activity to assemble into formation and fly toward three semi-trucks parked at the end of town. Cams inside the trailers show the drones landing with graceful precision, but unlike the others, a dozen or so drones shoot straight into the air, out of sight.

Lieutenant Grey steps outside the tent, searching the skies with binoculars. Glancing to his team leader, he looks concerned as soldiers return to their stations.

"Recall the HIVE," he repeats.

With a sudden shrilling buzz, a dozen drones burst inside the observation tent to surround the elite guests and soldiers, hovering and darting in an agitated fashion, as they did before an attack. Loretta's eyes narrow, but she doesn't move. Nelson startles back, frozen in fear, gripping his knees while a drone stares him down, disturbed by his mask, darting back and forth.

"Recall," Lieutenant Grey orders again, reaching for his workstation.

The sudden movement provokes a nearby drone to slap him on the back, exploding a minor charge of red powder over his uniform, but forceful enough to slam him to the ground. The audience freezes, avoiding any signs of aggression. After a tense moment, the rogue drones exit the tent to join the others within the large trucks below, allowing soldiers to help Lieutenant Grey into a nearby medic tent.

His heart still palpitating, Nelson exhales, "Dear Lord, that was close."

The audience murmur grows as General McCray steps up to the platform. "Ladies and gentlemen, I apologize for the minor scare. We may have set our observation tent a tad too close to the target site below." He tries to chuckle the incident away. "As you can see, AI HIVE will revolutionize urban and terrorist warfare, save countless civilian lives, and leave livable cities that will reduce immigration."

General McCray sounds bold, but he looks a tad rattled. "If you would like to join us in the air-conditioned lunch tent, we can discuss your questions inside."

The audience breaks into another, less enthusiastic applause as General McCray and other soldiers move the group inside for lunch. While the crowd seems awestruck by the overall system performance, each conversation drifts to the rogue incident and concern for Lieutenant Grey. Had the drones contained real explosives, Lieutenant Grey would be dead. Something went wrong.

"General, I'm concerned with what appears to be US readiness to abandon the LAWS guidelines," Loretta interjects

"I agree with the Congresswoman Clarke," Nelson adds. "The LAWS guidelines protect civilians, which should be an obligation of all decent people. The moment we allow any AI tech to make a life-and-death decision, we relinquish our right to rule over that AI."

Senator Ted Roberts, a six-foot-four staunch Republican from Texas, joins the group, reaching to shake the hand of General McCray, a kindred spirit. An ex-Marine, the now potbellied senator has been a vigorous advocate of advanced weapons and a vocal adversary of DSB oversight.

"That kind of liberal left thinking will lose a war," Roberts snarls, his lip curling.

"On the battlefield, our men need a lethal advantage, and I guarantee China doesn't give a damn about your morality, so either we stay ahead or we fall behind our enemies. Get over yourself, Dr. Garrett. You work for DARPA, not a radical left church," General McCray growls.

Nelson drops the point to avoid a scene, but he and the general have had this same conversation on too many occasions to count. Thankfully, Lieutenant Grey shows up with a clean uniform to break the tension, greeted with a new round of applause and congratulations.

"I have to admit," offers Nelson, "that was a quite impressive performance. Well done." Nelson flatters, as taught to him by his father, a Lord of Parliament.

"Thank you, Dr. Garrett," Lieutenant Grey accepts the compliment.

"I'm curious of your theory regarding what happened at the end," he offers the program director a chance to explain.

"Yeah," McCray interrupts. "Exactly what I said, we were too close to the target."

"Well, that could be one explanation," Nelson dismisses. "Are the drones programmed to continue aggression once recalled?" he asks Lieutenant Grey.

The lieutenant glances to the general and then to the others listening. "Actually, no, the protocol would be to cease all actions and return to the nest immediately."

A few of the generals shuffle their feet. Nelson hit a nerve.

"Every soldier on the battlefield needs to obey orders, especially an AI soldier," an admiral states, earning a scowl from McCray.

"Gentlemen," interjects Nelson. "Let's not unravel over something that may be quite minor. If possible, I would like to review the test logs," he requests. "I've seen similar behavior in other AI, and I may be able to clear up the confusion."

"Dr. Garrett's insights would be valuable," Congresswoman Clarke offers.

"I'm not a fan of DSB," interjects Senator Roberts. "But I wouldn't mind his expert eyes on the matter. To be honest, those damn things scared the living bejesus out of me."

The other military observers agree as Lieutenant Grey shares an anxious glance with his team. Nelson can't shake the feeling this glitch has happened more than once.

"Fine," McCray concedes. "I'll have the data sent to your lab, but I want to see your results before you speak to anyone else, especially the Secretary."

Nelson's position on DSB entitles him to test results, and while he reports to the Defense Secretary directly, he rarely demands the privilege. "Of course," he replies.

"Given your failure with the SLVIA, I wonder if you can remain unbiased," McCray grumbles, turning away from the group. "The HIVE will save lives," he calls over his shoulder.

Nelson doesn't respond to an obvious provocation, but his eyes narrow and his back stiffens, biting down the embarrassment, refusing to retort, and ignoring the concerned look from the congresswoman. After another hour, he and Loretta share a chopper back to Nellis Air Base.

"What happened back there with the general?" she asks. "What was SLVIA?"

Most of the time, Nelson would hide behind a classified cloak, but Congresswoman Clarke has clearance, and he needs a friend. Brilliant in concept until it failed, the SLVIA has been a tarnish on his reputation for decades. With a clenched jaw, he chokes down the resentment of the general bringing it up.

He looks down to explain. "An overly ambitious IAI—integrated artificial intelligence—prototype with too much decision autonomy."

"I don't understand," she says.

"Well, allow me to put it this way. When the story leaked to the media in 1993, the article read that a program had escaped the Sandia labs," Nelson replies.

"Escaped—you mean like a drone or a robot?" The congresswoman seems surprised.

"No, not a drone or a robot." Nelson lifts his eyes to meet hers. "I created a virtual spy."

CHAPTER 3:
THIRD TEMPLE
SANHEDRIN

Western Wall, Jerusalem
May 1, 9:21 a.m. EDT | May 1, 4:21 p.m., Jerusalem

Andre Strauss overlooks Jerusalem's Western Wall as an honored guest of the prominent Rabbi Ben Levi Moshe to witness a historic event that will set the stage for the third Jewish Temple. He arrived from Istanbul just in time. He took an enormous risk to eliminate the unexpected witness taking video in Istanbul, but he could not risk the West learning of the dragon too soon.

Self-conscious of his white hair and alabaster complexion in the blistering sun, he stays under the protective shade of the balcony. In the Western Wall courtyard below, thousands of zealots and Orthodox Jews stand shoulder to shoulder, many still wearing pandemic face masks, intently watching the ceremony on temporary giant screens. A festival atmosphere of music, singing, and laughter resonates across the ancient stone city. A hot breeze stirs intoxicating aromas of onion, garlic, and spices from nearby cooking. To the south, near the City of David, Sanhedrin priests prepare a temporary altar to sacrifice a red heifer, but the true ceremony takes place within the private Sanhedrin synagogue beneath the Western Wall.

"Mr. Strauss, do you appreciate the history behind this moment?" the rabbi challenges.

He and Moshe became acquainted at an IMF—International Monetary Fund—event years ago. Andre maintains a relationship because of the Moshe family's deep influence with the Israeli Knesset and the prime minister.

"Indeed, I do, Rabbi," he replies with a smile. "After the 1967 Six-Day War, Israeli Prime Minister Peron transferred strategic lands near the Western Wall, Temple Mount, and Mount Zion in the City of David to the Vatican. Now, as part of the Middle East Peace Plan proposed by the US president's son-in-law—a plan still lacking approval from the US Congress, Palestinians, or neighboring states—the Vatican will transfer that land back to Israel in order to build a third Jewish temple."

The $50 billion deal calls on Arab countries to invest in Palestinian development while ceding Jerusalem and West Bank settlements to Israel. Everyone in finance knows that the investments will dry up at the first hint of conflict, making it a peace plan destined for failure and giving Israel what they want, while offering the Palestinians little more than condescension and empty promises.

The Vatican had resisted the White House pressure to transfer the land, believing it would incite violence and undermine Palestinian rights, both of which have already started. In order to win favor with Praeceptor, who supports a third temple, Andre provided the pope with a very personal motivation.

"Prophecy, Monsieur Strauss," exclaims his host with unrestrained joy. "We are watching the words of Ezekiel and Daniel come to life before our very eyes."

A student of the prophecies while attending Jesuit school as a boy, the Kabbalistic teachings of the Order and guidance of Praeceptor have enlightened his understanding. He doesn't believe in the vague prophetic utterances of a god who doesn't exist. What he does believe is that a man's faith can be a lever to bend his will. Tell enough lies, bend enough wills, and one can change history, if one is so motivated.

Corrupting the already corrupted becomes a simple matter of finding a weakness. American evangelical leaders have succumbed to a watered-down salvation of entitlement, prosperity, conservative judges, and anti-abortion laws. They reap the seeds they've sown in an inept, blasphemous leader who divides and weakens his nation. Stripped of world dominance, power, and respect, Catholic leaders waddle in the shame of their pedophile-plagued clergy, inviting pagan religions into the house of God. Each has cut a Faustian deal with the devil, which presents Andre with an opportunity: a path to redemption.

"I have prayed for this moment since I was a boy," says the rabbi, now in his eighties, beaming.

Indeed, both Christians and Zionists believe the third temple will usher a coming of the messiah, the first coming for the Jews and a second coming for the Christians. Ironically, even Muslims believe in a coming messiah, the al-Masih, who will come from heaven near Damascus to destroy the Antichrist, whom the Iranians believe is the great Satan, America.

"Rabbi, why did the Sanhedrin choose to build the temple between the Noble Dome and the Al-Aqsa Mosque?" Andre queries. The site location seems intentionally provocative.

"Tradition," Moshe replies. "According to tradition, the temple stood on the mount."

"Yet archaeologists found evidence of Solomon's temple in the City of David, under the Vatican properties, near the Gihon Spring. The mount was the Roman Fort Antonia, definitely not sacred ground or the holy of holies," Andre probes the local sentiment.

"Who cares what the archaeologists say?" the old man replies. "The temple is a spiritual issue, and everyone listens to their rabbi." He shrugs as if the matter had been settled.

Interesting to watch an entire populace willing to risk war for the sake of spiritual pride and tradition, even when scientific evidence tells them they are wrong. No doubt, Jewish arrogance will trigger a global crisis with American arrogance as backup. Andre stokes that pride for his own purposes.

He can feel no remorse over events that will happen regardless of his actions, and so he finds no reason why he shouldn't profit from accelerating the inevitable. Except that no messiah will save the day and no al-Masīḥ will appear, war will undoubtedly end in a stalemate, and all sides will be even more distrustful than ever. Power will shift to the East, and digital security will be a desperate need, and that need will be his leverage to unimaginable wealth and power. Most importantly, success will open a path to redemption within the *Regendi Li* as Praeceptor, his savior within the order has envisioned.

Within the subterranean synagogue, the prime minister of Israel, the US president's son-in-law Jerome Kramer, the chief rabbi, and Pope Petras stand together. Displayed behind them are a golden menorah and a seven-foot golden pomegranate with a scale model of the third Jewish Temple. During 2017, Israel recommissioned the sacrificial Sanhedrin priesthood after nearly two thousand years, created the golden temple implements, and selectively bred for the perfect red heifer to reinitiate sacrifice on the high holy days. One rabbi even confided in confidence to know the location of the lost Ark of the Covenant, waiting in secret for the consecration of the temple.

"Ironic the US president is so unpopular at home," the rabbi marvels. "In Israel, he is considered by some to be Moshiach, the messiah. Others say he's like the Persian King Cyrus, as spoken by the prophet Ezra, '*They finished their building by decree of the God of Israel and by decree of Cyrus,*' so who knows."

Ironic that a false prophecy by a partisan American fireman ignited the evangelical adoration of a false savior in the form of an immoral, narcissistic, and sociopathic leader. Andre plays with the newly minted silver and gold coins in his hand, inscribed "Moshiach of Israel, Rebuilder of the Temple," featuring a profile of the US president alongside Cyrus, similar to the coins minted for the 2017 Sanhedrin dedication, a commemorative set.

"Well someone of importance must believe in him." He holds up the coin.

"It's all politics." The rabbi shrugs. "Who cares who takes credit. The Jews get a temple."

The US president's popularity in Israel grew out of moving the US embassy to Jerusalem, recognizing Israeli authority over the Golan Heights, and proposing an Israeli-biased peace plan. A peace accord with UAE, never a threat in the past, and more of an economic and arms agreement, bolsters this view. Yet, each action was largely symbolic, changing little of the situation on the ground and making true peace even harder to attain. *"They will cry peace, peace, but there will come no peace."* Andre considers the ironic truth of a temple prophecy.

On the screen below, the faces at the podium beam with joy, except for Pope Petras who appears unusually pensive and somber. When the ceremony proceeds to signatures, the pontiff hesitates before adding his name while background audio picks up the Sanhedrin echoing the Hebrew prayer of peace in the rocky chambers. The crowd by the Western Wall recites the prayer in sloppy unison, poignant considering the violent clashes taking place on the opposite side of the Temple Mount and across the region, which has cost dozens of lives in recent weeks.

Israeli Prime Minister Rosen steps up to make a statement. "Holy Father, Rabbi Weiss, Mr. Kramer, people of Israel, and friends of Israel from around the world. Mr. President, I know you are watching. Thank you. I look forward to you joining us personally for the commencement ceremony."

Andre stifles a chuckle knowing that at this very moment, the US president will either be tweeting or riding a golf cart. The pontiff's scowl remains frozen, his head lowered in prayer.

"For two thousand years, every Jew everywhere has prayed to worship at the Temple in Jerusalem. Holy Father, your benevolent return of these properties and the US-sponsored peace plan provide the foundation to fulfill that dream. Israel will rebuild the Jewish Temple so the entire world may come to worship for the next thousand years of peace."

The crowd below erupts into cheers and singing. A few people start to dance, but the tight gathering prevents a spread of the euphoria. The Sanhedrin and guests applaud their own achievement, breaking for handshakes, congratulating each other. Pope Petras soberly shakes each hand with a weak smile until the president's son-in-law approaches, then without a word, the pontiff spins to walk away. Andre laughs at the insult captured for the world to witness. One devil will always know another.

Regardless of faith, the third temple will accelerate existing regional tensions toward war, which will increase the need to manage dissent, a growing trend pioneered in China and silently expanding elsewhere with a quiet interest growing in the White House.

In his view, only power, wealth, and influence serve as the true measures of a man. No one writes a history of the pious poor and destitute who achieve nothing. His role model since his youth, Mayer Rothschild, once cornered the entire London stock exchange simply by knowing of Napoleon's defeat at Waterloo before others and then deviously manipulating public perceptions to his advantage. Within a generation, the *Concilium Tredecim* invited the name of Rothschild to a permanent seat. Just as a master chess player plans several moves ahead of their opponent, Praeceptor prepares him for a place of honor.

"Thank you for your gracious hospitality, Rabbi. It has been an honor to share this experience with you," Andre offers. "Now before I go, I must ask you, do we have an agreement, your guarantee to support adoption of the INVISID platform in Israel for a 5 percent stake if you succeed?" Andre questions his host.

The INVISID platform will take citizen identification and records security into the next century, eliminating the need for passwords and putting identity hackers out of business. Rabbi Moshe's family owns a controlling interest in a local software company, which holds a key Israeli government cybersecurity contract. In Israel, as elsewhere, religion often blends with business and politics.

Moshe gazes down to the top of Andre's hand with wide eyes. "Ya." The bearded rabbi reaches out to shake. "We have a deal."

"Excellent, then you may expect the paperwork soon." Andre bows his head in respect.

After thanking Moshe's family for their generous hospitality, Andre heads to the King David Jerusalem Hotel, where a political reception will take place later that evening. At the concierge desk, he hands over his business card. "Make sure Cardinal Rossi receives this when he arrives."

Andre slips in a thousand shekel note, lighting up the eyes of the nodding concierge. On the back of the card, he wrote his room number. Trained to manipulate the chess pieces so that the inventible occurs on his own terms, Andre knows that once one discovers a person's weakness, one must apply pressure until his opponent bends, or breaks.

An hour later, the pope's consigliere, Cardinal Rossi, ushers a weary-looking Petras into Andre's suite. Andre rises to kiss the ring in a sign of respect, but the pontiff yanks away his hand.

"I've done what you asked, now what do you want?" the aging bishop says, scowling.

Andre understands his bitterness and distrust; he planted the seeds. The video of a young, naked Petras making brutal love to a boy in his arms was fake, but so well done as to be exceedingly dangerous in light of the billions' worth of pedophile lawsuits building against the Vatican.

"Your Holiness, you have helped to win international acceptance of an event we both know must come to pass." Andre attempts to assuage the huge wounded ego.

Petras eyes him, as if attempting to read his soul until the Holy Father discerns the truth that Andre no longer has one. Andre grins malevolently, reflecting the horror in the pontiff's eyes.

"Only the Devil plays God," Petras snaps.

"And yet scripture teaches that Lucifer rules over this world," Andre replies with a thin smile.

"Report to your master," growls Petras. "Ask nothing more of me. I am done with all of you."

Interesting that even Petras recognizes the power of the *Sacra Domini*, the Sacred Lords.

"Come now, Your Holiness," Andre coos. "You know the Saint Malachy prophecy as I do. You are the last pope, the Petrus Romanus who will nourish the sheep through a great tribulation until the Lord comes to judge, and I dare say we have entered into a great tribulation."

Andre refers to a prophecy by an eleventh-century canonized Irish Bishop named Malachy, who witnessed the corruption of the Vatican and then fell into a trace to describe each of the popes and antipopes until the final judgment. According to the astoundingly accurate prophecy, Petras is the last pope.

"Embrace your destiny, Your Holiness," Andre says with a smug grin. "It is God ordained, just as the third temple itself, and bigger than both of us."

"You know nothing," the pontiff hisses.

"A little, Your Holiness, I know a little." He smirks. "I know that John's Revelation of the church as an unfaithful harlot has come to pass, welcoming all faiths and unclean beasts onto sacred ground, just as the third Fátima secret of an unclean priesthood has undermined the testimony of church in every nation."

He offers Petras a flash drive containing the fake video master as promised. Petras hesitates before grabbing the drive and then turning to leave without another word. A silent and sullen Cardinal Rossi closes the door behind them.

Andre has never been more exhilarated, feeling an intense rush of excitement to torment the powerful and hold up a harsh mirror to the self-righteous, twisting them, forcing them to his purpose. Only his purpose matters, a basic tenet of a successful man, a guiding principle of Mayer Rothschild.

His success with the third temple will please Praeceptor, bringing him one step closer to convincing the *Concilium* to restore a seat to his family name.

CHAPTER 4:
ZERO-DAY APOCALYPSE

US Senate Intelligence chambers, Capitol Hill
May 1, 10:02 a.m. EDT

They might as well be an Inquisition court. Derek scans the bored, disengaged faces of the Senate Intelligence Committee and fights the sinking feeling in the pit of his stomach. Ultimately, the senate subpoena gave him no choice.

Elizabeth Barring places her slender hand on his arm and whispers, "Remember, just let the bombastic senators preen. Wait for a direct question, and then answer only the question, no pontificating."

Like an older sister, the thin African American chief counsel from Harvard Law School tries to keep him out of trouble the best she can.

"Pontificate, me?" he scoffs. "I educate the poorly informed as a patriotic courtesy."

"You heard me—none of your flap for the people who control your budget," she exhorts with an exaggerated roll of her eyes.

A duck out of water, he loathes being under a microscope by a panel of aging tech-phobic partisan stiff necks. It's not just the tailored suit, which makes him look like a pimped-out refugee from a *GQ* ad, but it's all the cameras. He can only hope the recent beard, short haircut, and black hair dye will help mask his identity for anyone on C-SPAN who might remember a long-haired hippie Cary from college.

"Mr. Taylor, we're here to investigate the immense cost of protecting our nation from cyberterrorism," drawls North Carolina Senator Graham Grovel. "State your name and title for the record."

"My name is Derek Anthony Taylor, and I am the CEO of Taylor Security Systems and Services, otherwise known as TS3," he says into the mic.

"The chair will allow the witness two minutes for an opening statement," Grovel states.

He winks at wide-eyed Elizabeth and inhales.

"TS3 provides best-in-class services for national cybersecurity, including the world's most sophisticated HADES and shadow networks. TS3 services support signal technologies, cryptology, cyber-counterintelligence, forensics, and AI-enabled offensive and defensive cyberweapons. The Navy has the Seals, the Army has the Rangers, and the NSA has TS3. Beyond the NSA, TS3 also contracts directly with the Cybersecurity and Infrastructure Security Agency, Department of Navy and Air Force, NASA, the CIA, FBI, and a dozen state agencies in addition to over 160 security-conscious corporations. We're the best at what we do, bar none." He pauses. "You're welcome America."

A few senators sit up to listen while others read or otherwise ignore him, so he continues.

"During 2015, CIA Director Leon Panetta claimed we were heading for a cyber–Pearl Harbor, but Panetta drastically underestimated the enemy's capability, patience, and determination. In fact, the US faces an imminent cyber-Hiroshima. State-sponsored attacks on US domains have increased exponentially, verging on full-scale cyberwar even as we speak," he states, scanning the committee.

"I'm not referring to a war with radical Islam, immigrants, opioids, or even with the imaginary deep state, but a war over one of our nation's most strategic assets, the internet. The internet integrates our news, communications, commerce, banking, social media, and homeland security. Our enemies use this asset to divide us, cast doubt over our democracy, and steel our intellectual property." He speaks with a crisp certainty, ignoring his written statement.

"When 9/11 changed the world, there were 230 million cyberattacks per day. By 2016, there were over 2.8 billion cyberattacks per day. By 2020, that volume had doubled and still grows exponentially. Over the past decade, hackers have accessed over 3.4 billion consumer accounts from banks, stock exchanges, utilities, veterans, DOD, congress, and even the White House. Over 21 billion IoT—internet of things—devices, such as mobile apps, cloud services, home security, and smart appliances create new entry points and relay stations for hackers. New biometric AI services such as Alexa, Siri, Watson, and Cortana have created hundreds of millions of new vulnerabilities with voice and facial signatures. Surveillance and deep fake video technology stolen from a CIA toolkit in 2016 are now in the hands of our enemies. We estimate the economic costs of this cyber-assault to hit $6 trillion by the end of 2021."

The faces of his firing squad just split between disinterest, alarmed or enraged.

"We have now entered a new and far more dangerous phase of cyberwarfare where artificial intelligence will complicate and accelerate all aspects of defensive and offensive strategies. To conclude, TS3 recommends a complete revamp of our national cyber strategy with a tenfold investment increase before our enemies beat us to the punch, and bring us to our knees," he concludes.

He sits back to glance at Elizabeth who points with a frown at the script he didn't follow. Senators stiffen their backs in reaction to a call for more money when they intend to cut his budget. Post-pandemic global economic collapse coupled with wild government incompetence and corruption has skyrocketed US debt from $21 trillion in 2016 to over $35 trillion, creating a staggering interest burden. With economic activity slow to rebuild and social unrest at an all-time high, the president ordered drastic cuts to social welfare, EPA, education, and nonmilitary, including FBI, intelligence, courts, and cyber, claiming only the military was important, essentially creating a police state.

"Mr. Taylor," growls Senator Grovel, "I'm not sure I understand a word you just said and I can't imagine why the American taxpayer should fund you to blabber tech talk."

His fist clenches as Elizabeth nudges his shin with her foot, urging him to hold his tongue. Senators spout QAnon conspiracy theories for the cameras or ask stupid, shallow questions that avoid the true issues. In between, Senator Grovel babbles on about radical left reckless spending.

Derek tunes him out, still consumed by Sochi's murder and unable to wash the horrific images from his mind. Sochi didn't deserve to die, so why did he? Was that the same white-haired man? He takes a deep breath, aware of the cameras, yet a high-octane anxiety pumps over a toxic swamp of shame.

As if sensing his anxiety, a tiny voice in the back of his head interrupts.

"The *Dilban* has entered the Black Sea on a course for the Russian navy base at Crimea," SLVIA reports through the implanted device behind his right ear. "Russian and Iranian installations of encrypted HUAWEI 5G are now live. The Chinese naval fleet has deployed to the South China Sea. Activity at Syrian air bases has increased 703 percent in 24 hours."

After he escaped arrest for Bianca's murder, he spent a few years searching online, in hacker chats, dark web sites, MI5 agents logs, nearly everywhere for "SLVIA" or "Sylvia" with zero success. Ironically, SLVIA found him, years later where he least expected, and then changed his life to give him a purpose beyond revenge. To improve the connection with his one-of-a-kind friend, he had a device surgically implanted behind his right ear. He's grown used to the whispering voice whenever he's within range of a cell tower or Wi-Fi network.

"Istanbul police retrieved the body and phone of Sochi Reke," continues SLVIA.

Not good news. Sochi's phone had Cary Nolan's old contact information and an outdated version of the Scavenger Nut app.

"*This is what the Sovereign Lord says: I am against you, O Gog (Russia), chief prince of Meshech (Iran) and Tubal (Turkey). I will turn you around and drag you along. I will bring you from the far north and send you against the mountains of Israel,*" SLVIA states. "Red Dragon prepares for war."

Surgically implanting a direct feed to SLVIA was a rush at first, but there are times he can't deal with her endless snippets, like right now. A finger reaches behind his right ear and gently presses a spot to silence the signal. Elizabeth nudges him with her knee, drawing his attention back to the moment.

"Mr. Taylor," growls the Senator again. "I am outraged with the waste of taxpayer money on a TS3 report called *Zero-Day Apocalypse*. This report makes me question if the taxpayer funds a bunch of nerds to make up useless fantasies."

Elizabeth grips his arm with her nails to keep him silent. The *Zero-Day Apocalypse* report provides a comprehensive strategic risk assessment on US government, infrastructure, and business vulnerabilities to a broad-scale strategic cyberattack. *Zero-Day* outlines substantial evidence of Russian, Chinese, North Korean, and Iranian state-sponsored activities against our network. While the Russians target key government data sources and instigate social and political unrest, the Chinese focus on corporate espionage and AI cyberweapon development that integrates stolen data purchased from Russia, Iran, and North Korea for cash.

"Why should the taxpayers pay TS3 to create Hollywood thrillers," demands the Senator.

Derek glances at Elizabeth, whose eyebrows rise, but the man did ask a question.

"Well, for one Senator, Hollywood was running out of good ideas," he smirks to a few suppressed giggles in the room. "For the record, TS3 and our corporate partners funded the *Zero Day* report because of Congressional budget cuts. *Zero Day* describes seventy-eight scenarios or attack strategies that our enemies could pursue. Granted some scenarios are more likely than others are, but if we can imagine an attack, then so can Russia and China. *Zero Day* anticipates those scenarios, quantifies the level of risk, and provides a roadmap to the NSA, governmental agencies, and corporate clients on how to prevent or defend against each scenario," Derek replies. "You're welcome America."

A few Senators nod in understanding while others scowl. The floor changes to a Senator from Kentucky who distrusts technology in all forms.

"Mr. Taylor," the Senator twangs. "Tell me about your Dark Angel program. Is it true that TS3 hires convicted hackers and felons to protect America's cyber interests?"

Elizabeth shakes her head. The top secret Dark Angel program, a partnership between the NSA, FBI and CIA to recruit the most talented hackers on the planet is classified. A testy exchange erupts between ranking members over the appropriateness of the question, which ends with a demand to answer.

"Senator, I can neither confirm nor deny such a program even exists," Derek responds. Elizabeth nods her head in approval. It does exist and TS3 has been a strong advocate and beneficiary.

"How can we feel safe knowing a bunch of hackers and nerds protect the US government," demands the Senator with a self-righteous indignation.

Elizabeth touches his arm, but she's too late, the man asked a question.

"You got to be kidding? Senator, you voted twice to cut the cyber defense budget, so your patriotic zeal sounds hollow of either sincerity, action or intent," Derek rebukes. "Okay, here's what I can say. TS3 finds and recruits the most talented software engineers, Ph.D., and cyber-experts on the planet, and pays them top dollar, bar none. Proprietary artificial intelligence applications watch every keystroke of every employee twenty-four-seven, and TS3 develops the best AI defensive and offensive systems on the planet. And for the record, there's not a single employee, including me, who doesn't wear the label of hacker nerd like a badge of honor."

He bites down his own indignation. Elizabeth hangs her head, breathing to calm herself.

Senator Grovel leans into his microphone. "You admit the taxpayers are paying to have hackers protect us from other hackers. How is that not extortion, Mr. Taylor?"

Elizabeth digs her nails into Derek's arm, shaking her head, warning him to keep his tongue. Senators argue back and forth over badgering the witness and use of the word extortion to define defense or intelligence spending of any kind.

A Senator from Oregon gets the floor. "Mr. Taylor, in *Zero Day*, you claim bio-metrics increase our risks rather than reduce them. Can you explain?"

"Biometric data, like password data, gets stored within a protected file server, which can be hacked like any other server. In fact, during 2020, Russian hackers stole billions of consumer facial IDs from a company called Clearview. Now imagine that I hack your password or pin, while invasive you can always create a new password or pin in a matter of minutes. Now imagine Russia hacks the digital code for your iris, voice, DNA, face or thumb print, and then sells that data on the dark web. Since you can never change those elements of who you are, whoever buys that data will own your digital identity."

"Interesting perspective," the Senator admits, absorbing the fresh information, and yielding her time to the Senator from Central California.

"Mr. Taylor," the Senator responds. "You mentioned 3.4 billion consumer account hacks, yet we don't see any major impact on people, or the economy." The Senator sets up her question. "Aren't you overstating the risks?"

"No, I'm sending you an early warning," he insists. "The Chinese won't waste their time with petty extortion or identity theft, they leave that strategy to North Korea. Once they have successfully weaponized the collected data, don't expect a nuisance attack, expect an enormously destructive internet takedown weapon," he warns and takes a sip of water.

"Are you claiming Russia and China are building a cyber weapon?" she asks.

"Yes, now we're on the same page," he states. At least now they're touching on the real issues.

The floor yields to Senator Wilkes from Louisiana. "I've seen your type, Mr. Taylor, a fear monger aiming to make money, a phony and a joke. Show me one reason I should be afraid."

Derek hangs his head before looking to Elizabeth who pleads with her eyes for him to play it safe, but playing it safe isn't working.

"Senator Wilkes, I suppose it can be easy for the average citizen like yourself to have a hard time grasping the extreme danger, so let me show you one reason to be afraid, but only one," he retorts.

Derek pulls out a tablet, careful to guard the view from the cameras. The man seems to like jokes, so he sets off to make him into one.

"Mr. Taylor, this committee doesn't have time for a product demo," snaps Senator Wilkes.

"You asked for evidence, and this will answer your question in a way no words could possibly convey," he promises, continuing to work.

Several Senators' exchange glances or raises objections that he ignores. Elizabeth rolls her eyes as if she's having a stroke. Derek stifles a grin.

"Senator, on my encrypted tablet I have a copy of the stolen CIA tool kit for deep fake videos, purchased for testing." he explains with a sense of whimsical delight dancing in his eyes. He hits send.

"Senator Wilkes, I'm sure you know about the Equifax hack that compromised 150 million identities because you were affected. Senator Higgs and Ridley lost data in the Yahoo hack, and the VA hack exposed all of you. Last week, your campaign posted an interview video. I downloaded and changed that video with the stolen CIA toolkit, and sent a copy to Senators Higgs and Ridley."

Derek sits back and waits for the reaction to sweep over them like a wave.

"Mr. Taylor, your behavior is extremely inappropriate," growls Senator Higgs.

"If you say so, but I've already sent the file," Derek smirks.

Senator Wilkes phone rings in session. A second later, the phones of Higgs and Ridley also ring. Each Senator shares the same look of surprise and apprehension.

"Oh yeah," Derek explains. "I also turned on your ringers remotely. Go ahead, play the video."

Derek can't see the video, but knows that he replaced a tirade on immigration with a revised speech, using the Senator's image and voice signature.

"Now I declare to the American people," pronounces Senator Wilkes on video. "Derek Taylor is the smartest, funniest, and most handsome man I've ever met. In fact, I want to kiss him, you know, a big wet French kiss. Yeah, baby, now that's a joke." The voice sounds identical to the Senator who turns red with embarrassment and rage.

An uproar of stifled laughter erupts in the chamber, a moment destined for the evening news and late-night comedy shows for a week. Derek gazes at Elizabeth who burns fury at him with her eyes.

"Now Senator, if I were Russia, I might have posted that video back to your website. But I'm just trying to make a point so the video will auto delete."

The three phones ping. "See, already gone. Now try to imagine this technology along with a weaponized version in the hands of Putin or Xi. The Russians put a President in office in 2016, and again in 2020, and we need to up our game, or regardless of party, we will lose our nation."

"Your prank only confirms to me the real dangers are cyber-terrorists like Anonymous, LulSec, and that new group SNO," responds Senator Wilkes.

Last week, an Epoch Times article uncovered an underground cyber group called SNO who had infiltrated virtually every aspect of society. The article claims SNO, rather than the Russians hacked the 2020 election, a lie repeated by Putin, and the President daily.

"Is it true TS3 assisted SNO in the Federal Reserve hack two years ago?" queries Senator Higgs.

The Federal Reserve hack affected the international banking system and lost millions of secure bank-to-bank passwords and account names. TS3 bent FCC rules to tip the FBI to capture the real hacker, a Russian tied to the group Cozy Bear who died in jail within a week, officially a suicide.

Elizabeth glances at Derek with a growing look of alarm. "Fifth," she whispers.

"Senator, I can neither confirm nor deny any operations of TS3," he states. He didn't deny.

"Mr. Taylor does TS3 work with SNO," Senator Higgs demands. "It's a simple yes or no."

Derek ignores him. "I can confirm that China maintains a cyber army of 30,000 to outmatch the 15,000 strong Russian cyber force and 16,000 combined forces for North Korea and Iran. Together, they develop an arsenal of viruses, worms, Trojan horses, peeps and other tools against the US and allies." He gives another non-answer, but makes sure the information goes on record.

After another hour of senseless grilling, the floor falls back to Senator Grovel.

"Well, Mr. Taylor, even if I believed you about the level of danger facing the country, which I don't, this country faces greater threats from our southern border, the radical left derangement syndrome, and reviving the post-corona economy. I can't agree with the amount of taxpayer money you want to waste, but the committee appreciates your testimony today." Senator Grovel gavels an end to the session.

Elizabeth huddles in a whispered rebuke. "Your video stunt put a spot light on TS3."

"It made a point," Derek defends.

"A point they didn't hear," she snaps. "Damn it, Derek, it almost sounded like we're working with a terrorist group," she whispers. "Are we working with SNO?"

"I'm hungry," Derek changes the subject. "You hungry?"

Her glare intensifies. Elizabeth should know better.

"Calm down," he deflects. "TS3 doesn't work with SNO." He doesn't mention his hobby.

"Next time," she hisses, "let the arrogant Senators bombast."

"Next time," Derek retorts. "Ah hell girl, let's never do this again."

"Fat chance Sundance," Elizabeth chides. "Powerful people don't like to be humiliated on C-SPAN. After your techno stunt, I'll be surprised if an investigation isn't already underway."

Not the answer he hoped to hear. "So, no for lunch," he smirks.

Elizabeth exhales and gets up to leave. "Put on your virus mask and clear your schedule because you and I are going on an ass-kissing tour of the Senate."

"Can we eat first," he negotiates. "I pucker better when I'm full."

CHAPTER 5:
COLD CASE CAREER

National Security Agency (NSA) headquarters
May 2, 8:56 a.m. EDT

Lieutenant Jenn Scott bristles with anticipation at the chance to step outside the admiral's enormous, all-consuming shadow. A decade of rising through the ranks and always being compared to her father leaves her eager to make her own mark.

"Lieutenant Scott," NSA Director Frank Wilson greets her. "Close the door and have a seat. How much did your commander tell you about the assignment?"

The aging and respected spymaster sits back in his chair, relatively trim for his late sixties, with perpetual bags under his eyes and a gray receding hairline that testifies to a lifetime of high-pressure stress.

"Only that the NSA director requested me for a joint agency investigation. So, Director Wilson, you have my full attention," she replies, sitting straight and alert.

The admiral taught her never to pass up an opportunity to engage with interagency cooperation, and she learned long ago never to pass up a chance to impress the admiral. Earning his praise has been a daunting challenge ever since her mom died; he's not the kind of man who can express his feelings with ease.

"This conversation is top secret. Understood?" He wears a serious poker face.

"Yes, sir," she says, matching his intensity. She values the respect of being read into an assignment before the decision to accept, knowing that kind of courtesy is a benefit of having a Joint Chief father.

Jenn knows Frank Wilson by reputation. The thirty-six-year Washington veteran has held senior roles at the CIA, FBI, DHS, and now the National Security Agency. More secretive than the CIA, the NSA handles signal intelligence, cryptology, digital surveillance, and cybersecurity with over one hundred sixty thousand employees and contractors. Few people can legitimately claim the title of spymaster, but Frank Wilson has protected America since before she was born. He has done it all, seen it all, and knows far more than he will ever admit, or so the stories claim.

"How much do you know about SNO?" he asks.

"The hacker group," she replies, surprised and disappointed. No one has ever given the group much attention, a very low priority.

"As much as anyone, I suppose," she responds. "I wrote a couple of research papers. SNO, which some analysts confuse with the mobile game Scavenger Nut Origami, more likely means Spy Net Online, a secretive global network of dark web hackers and confidential informants. Known to point law enforcement to criminals with key evidence, they focus on elitists. Anonymous membership, even to each other, so determining the identity of anyone within the group has been a challenge." She pauses, waiting to see his reaction. He stares at her, as if waiting for her to get to a part that interests him.

She continues: "They don't fit the profile of other underground groups such as Anonymous or LulzSec or promote any political agenda other than a vague notion of justice. There's no tie to any dark web data sales. In fact, we have no clue how they recruit, fund, or operate. They act differently than any organization I've ever seen, as if there were no central management, yet SNO has virtually zero leaks."

"What else?" The director leans back, listening.

"The FBI investigated Scavenger Nut Origami, which posts very bizarre scavenger hunt targets, a few looking for classified information, but they could not verify a connection to SNO. The game features an animated avatar named flapjack, with a sixties mod assistant named Sylvia, but if there's an actual person behind either icon, I've never seen the evidence."

"Anything else?" he prompts.

"With all due respect, sir, that should be enough for you to tell me why you invited me here to test my knowledge of a rather obscure group," she replies.

"Sounds like you admire them," he states, perhaps testing her.

"I'm fascinated by how they run without an organization," she admits.

The director knows more than she does. He stares at her several moments, perhaps considering how to bust her further. She sits straight, refusing to allow his silence to intimidate her. Growing up under the admiral, she learned to master a stare down.

"Impressive that you reject the common mistake of confusing SNO with Scavenger Nut Origami," he states. "But otherwise, while accurate, the information is shallow."

Insulted, she bites her tongue. "Sir, how so?"

"Are you familiar with the SLVIA code," he asks.

"Never heard of it," she responds, her eyes opening in curiosity.

"I'm not surprised. The incident occurred in the early nineties," he responds, sitting up to explain. "S-L-V-I-A stands for 'Sophisticated Language Virtual Intelligence Algorithm.' In 1993, a joint NSA and DARPA experimental program disappeared from the Lawrence Livermore National Laboratory at Sandia. I led an FBI investigation that concluded a team member, a naturalized citizen named Dr. Cho Li Ping stole the program before he defected back to China. However, the program creator, Dr. Nelson Garrett, has insisted from day one that the program escaped on its own."

"Escaped," she reacts. "OK, we need to come back to that one. What did the program do?" she queries, wondering if he meant to say *escape*.

"Essentially, the program traveled the internet to find and analyze enemy intelligence and then report back," he replies. "Except one day, it failed to report back."

"I'm not sure I follow," she responds. "How does an app escape?"

Director Wilson scrutinizes her for a long moment. "The program had the ability to exist in over a thousand locations at once under an invisible file structure. You'll need to talk to Dr. Garrett for more details."

Dr. Garrett maintains a lab in the basement of the Hopper Information Services building on the Potomac where she also keeps an office with Naval Intelligence. A director on the DSB, Dr. Garrett has a reputation as one of those special geniuses, and as a rather posh dresser.

"Sounds like quite a program," she responds, eager to learn more.

"Oh, it gets better." Wilson frowns. "Are you familiar with the CIA cyber toolkit hack?"

"Of course," she replies, "it led to the now widespread deep fake video proliferation."

The kit also included surveillance technologies to use computer monitors as cameras, remotely turn on phones or webcams, hack and control car computers, monitor keystrokes, and other now-basic cyber tools.

"Most of those tools were integrated into the SLVIA from day one," Wilson admits, then sits back a moment to assess her reaction.

Jenn sits up with open eyes. "Let me get this straight. DARPA made an invisible program that could pretend to be the president, promote disinformation, or steal the launch codes." She throws out a hypothetical worst case.

Director Wilson glares at her a moment, then takes a deep breath. "Something like that, yes, and the reason SLVIA represents a threat to national security."

She contemplates the situation. "With all due respect, sir, you're bringing me in on a very old cold case." Jenn narrows her eyes. "What happened recently to defrost it?"

"A sniper shooting yesterday in Istanbul," he says, flipping up an image of a body floating in the water of a marina onto a wall monitor.

"Someone shot a local businessman named Sochi Reke while he videoed a visiting yacht, the *Dilban*, owned by a friend of Putin. The victim was on an encrypted session of Scavenger Nut."

Wilson clicks on a video retrieved from the phone, which shows an animated flapjack and British sixties mod female alongside candid photos of military generals from Russia, Iran, Turkey, and China. The female avatar voice reads off the names, including Dr. Cho Li Ping, the defector. The game just got serious.

"Not only does the presence of Dr. Cho raise my suspicions, but the female voice matches a known SLVIA voiceprint. Right before logging on to the game, the victim's phone logged a failed call to a man named Cary Nolan who died in a 1995 gas explosion. CIA speculates Nolan could still be alive, and the identity behind your mysterious flapjack."

Jenn sits back in her chair. Cary Nolan, a name for the flapjack, a breakthrough that could crack open the mysterious group.

"What's the mission?" she asks.

"Simple. Find the SLVIA and destroy it," Wilson states. "In the wrong hands, the program represents a serious national security threat. For a long time, we thought the program had malfunctioned and stopped operating. If we were wrong, we need to resolve the threat."

"That's not much to go on," she pushes back.

"Nolan had a close friend in college, Derek Taylor, now CEO of TS3," Wilson states.

"You mean that arrogant jerk on C-SPAN yesterday?" she asks.

"The same," Wilson concedes. "The arrogant jerk works for me, and he's my highest-performing contractor, but I won't tolerate a rogue double agent playing in my house."

Director Wilson leans forward in his chair. "I want you to investigate Derek Taylor and find out if he has any involvement with either SLVIA or Cary Nolan. But let me be clear, more than Taylor or SNO, I want that blasphemous technology SLVIA found and destroyed."

"Destroyed," she replies. "Based on what you told me, that doesn't sound easy."

"It won't be. To destroy the SLVIA, you'll need to get at least 80 percent of the OS onto a single server and then disconnect that server from the internet. Once you have the OS isolated, you need to destroy the hard drive and CPU processor."

"Why me? Why not the FBI or CIA or one of your own boys?" she replies.

"While shallow, you have the deepest knowledge of SNO, and a reputation for tenacity," he replies. "To be honest, the case has a personal element. I led the FBI investigation. If I was wrong, then I want to correct that mistake quietly under my watch."

She can appreciate the pride and sense of closure, a trait she inherited from the admiral, and can also respect a man with a transparent agenda.

"Besides, if Taylor turns out to be clean, I don't need an NSA investigation to ruin my relationship with him. That said if he broke the law, I want him in prison," Wilson confirms.

Wilson sounds serious, which means he'll back her up if needed. "When can I talk to the developer, Dr. Garrett?" she asks.

"Do you accept?" He raises an eyebrow.

The admiral once taught her to say yes when leadership called. Even if you fail, they won't forget your can-do attitude. Many careers have failed by saying no to an opportunity. Leaders rarely forget or forgive a no.

"Yes, sir," she replies.

Frank gets up from his desk to extend his hand with a stone face. "Good luck, Lieutenant. See Benton Willis on your way out for the top secret file access codes. FBI has a surveillance van set up with a support team at your disposal. Debrief them this afternoon. I'll make sure Dr. Garrett knows you're coming."

Amped up and excited over a genuine lead on the flapjack, she could be one step closer to unmasking the elusive icon and maybe unlocking the admiral's recognition. She and the admiral don't talk often anymore; although to be fair, that's more her choice. She admires her father and has busted her tail to win his respect, so it was hurtful after she became an officer and he continued to hold back his praise. Since her youth, she emulated him, entered Annapolis, and followed his lonely, workaholic war lifestyle, but it came at a price. With no life to speak of outside of the all-consuming world of running a navy, she feels a sting when she sees an old friend raising a family and she hasn't gone on a date in nine months. At least a new mission will give her a fresh focus.

If she fails, it could kill her career, so she already knows failure is not an option. If she succeeds, even the admiral will need to acknowledge success outside of the ranks.

*

NSA headquarters
May 2, 9:42 a.m. EDT

"Do you think she's up to the job?" Frank questions.

"If I didn't, I wouldn't have recommended her," Admiral Adam Scott replies, his radiant blue eyes peering out from within the heavily wrinkled face that hangs under a shaved head.

"What about Taylor?" Frank probes. "Are you comfortable sending your daughter to investigate your poker friend?"

Adam takes a deep breath. "To tell you the truth, I know of few people sharp or persistent enough to cut through Taylor's multiple layers of BS. That said, we've just locked two tigers in a cage, and I'm afraid the outcome will be unpredictable."

"That's what concerns me," Frank replies. With a focus on keeping his head low, he hopes to survive until his forty-year anniversary with an unblemished lifetime of service. If word of this incident flares up, it could tarnish that reputation. Clearing up his one big SLVIA mistake cleanly will be a retirement bonus.

CHAPTER 6:
CYBER STORM

Taylor Systems Operation Center (TSOC)

May 2, 9:45 a.m. EDT

D erek enters the sanctity of TS3 operations, anxious to put the humiliation of yesterday's Senate kiss-and-make-up tour behind him. Some people are simply not made for pandering to powerful egos.

Located on the pricey K Street in downtown Washington DC, TSOC shares the neighborhood with dozens of other major and minor consulting companies that support widespread government operations. After grabbing a nonfat latte from the gourmet cafeteria, and checking in with the receptionist Lisa, ready to have a baby any time, he heads to the control center.

The control center of TSOC looks like an Avenger-movie version of the NSA Cybersecurity Threat Operations Center (NCTOC)—bigger and more sophisticated on every level.

"Hey, boss, about time you got here. We have a shitstorm forming," Josh greets him.

SWARM

Dr. Josh Mitchell is one of the world's foremost cybersecurity engineers, TS3 chief science officer, designer of TSOC, and Derek's business partner. A colossal bear of a man with a bushy hipster beard, black-rimmed glasses, and tattoos covering his arms, Josh embodies that rare combination of teddy bear heart with an Einstein mind, all wrapped up in the burly, hairy package of a bouncer.

"Yeah, OK," responds Derek. "What's going on in sector twelve?" He points to the main floor screen flashing red warnings.

TSOC encompasses a circular room of 250 feet in diameter featuring fifty-foot-high walls covered with high-definition screens of various sizes and grid configurations. Laid out in twenty-four sectors, it covers Malicious Software, Signals Intelligence, and Information Assurance with analytic panels for targets, types, sources, industries, and other.

In front of the screens are five thousand of the best network and intelligence analysts, security programmers, and system hackers in the world, buzzing like bees in a hive, working in 24/7 shifts. That team is supported by another fifteen thousand in the adjacent underground data center building. In the center of TSOC rises a three-story, steel-and-glass tower with Josh's control center, featuring a view of nearly every screen.

"The earthquake before the tsunami, the tropical storm before the hurricane," deadpans Josh.

"Oh, well, glad we cleared that up," Derek says, followed by a snort. Like many brilliant people, Josh sometimes has a hard time communicating.

Holographic light-based monitors and control screens surround Josh, who wears specialized gloves and goggles to wave, poke, pull, and swipe. He sees a screen on the main floor, pulls a virtual version to his light screen, changes a setting, and then sends it back to the main floor. Derek waits while Josh does his thing, always a little mesmerized by the maestro conducting his own digital orchestra.

"We have a widespread DYN attack," Josh finally states. "And by widespread, I mean every damn DYN in the freaking network. Not a standard DOS (denial of service), mind you, but an unknown virus type that jams up the site and

51

then bores through to corrupt the server OS, taking the server offline. So far, we've got it handled, but we've lost 10 percent of the servers and the attack keeps getting stronger," he mutters, busy waving and swiping.

"How does it bore through?" Derek questions the unusual capability.

"I don't know yet," Josh replies.

DYN sites are the core backbone of the internet, hosting the DNS system that translates www web names into billions of computer-specific IP addresses and then transmits trillions of signal packets per day. If the internet were a person, this virus is stabbing at the heart to stop the blood flow.

"Yeah, but that's not what has Wilson wound up." Josh smirks from under his goggles.

Josh sets up a screen for Derek to watch hundreds of video clips of public figures saying something outlandish, traitorous, or criminal. Politicians, royalty, CEOs, celebrities, and popular news anchors revealed to be horrible people. He scans a dozen videos and checks the inventory of names.

His instincts prickle. "Deep fakes?" he questions. Derek can't see a single glitch. If these are fake, they're top notch.

"Yeah, most of them," Josh says, snorting. "Looks like your Senate stunt inspired an internet trend, dude."

"Send these to the video analysis team to debunk or confirm," he directs.

Josh laughs. "Dude, we've discovered 1,435 videos posted within the past twelve hours alone, and we're still finding fresh ones. Vicki's team has gone on lockdown."

"I have located 3,121 deep fake videos posted from forty-two global locations within the past twenty-four hours," SLVIA reports in the back of his head.

"Keep looking. There has to be more," Derek replies to Josh. "My questions are who and why."

"Working on it, boss," Josh grunts.

"Working on it, boss," SLVIA mimics Josh. Then she adds, "Ninety-nine percent of the videos were released by APT29, otherwise known as Cozy Bear. The question of why will require further analysis."

Derek glances to sector fourteen to see a spike of activity in Moscow and Siberia, too big to account for the videos.

"Director Wilson on line two," announces OLIE the AI office assistant.

Derek flips his light screen to the scowling face of NSA Director Frank Wilson.

"Mr. Taylor, have you seen the videos?" Wilson snaps.

"Getting my first look now," Derek confirms. "I was on the Hill and—"

"We'll deal with your idiotic stunt later," barks Wilson, cutting him off. Josh stifles a giggle.

"Are these videos real?" Wilson questions.

"No," Josh interjects. "Well, not most of them anyway."

"Well, at least Dr. Mitchell knows something," chides Wilson. "Who released them?"

"Our favorite Russian GRU troll farm Internet Research, APT29, and Cozy Bear, using an enhanced version of the CIA deep fake toolkit. We've uncovered thirty-six different release bots, but new videos are being released by the hour and may involve more sources," Josh replies.

Each of those groups were indicted after the 2016 and 2020 election scandals. "We're looking at activity around Siberia," Derek interjects, earning a sharp glare of confusion from Josh.

"You said most of them," Wilson retorts. "Which ones are genuine?"

Josh grins under his goggles. "Well, the one with the president at a Moscow Four Seasons in 2012 comes to mind."

"Geez, no wonder the White House and DOJ are having a stroke," grumbles Wilson. "Congress and the Senate have exploded with accusations, calls for resignations, new investigations, and new impeachment hearings. Phone calls from allies have overwhelmed the State Department. The president rages about another hoax while Buckingham Palace and EU leaders have each issued vehement denials. The news cycles and social media are on fire."

"Frank, I'm sure more videos exist out there," Derek interjects.

"Find them," Wilson barks. "I want answers and a plan to scrub the system."

"We're on it, Frank," Derek promises, "but we have another problem bubbling."

"The DYN virus," Wilson responds. "Yeah, we're monitoring that problem. Get on those videos before this firestorm gets out of control."

Derek turns off the speaker and pushes another. "Vicki, I need you for a minute, and bring your team leads."

"OLIE just pinged. We're on our way," Vicki responds, then ends the call.

Josh turns to Derek. "I'll set up ARCHER for a search-and-destroy mission."

TS3 engineers are world leaders in the design and deployment of artificial intelligence–based cyber tools and defenses. An AI named ARCHER will crawl through millions of data sites and trillions of files to locate illegal copies of a specific file and then delete the illegal copy without user permission. While it cannot delete all copies, it can reduce the proliferation.

"Weakening the DYN could be a precursor to a larger attack," Derek notes.

"I was thinking that earlier," Josh replies, pausing a moment. "Zero-Day Scenario Five begins with a DYN assault." In fact, a dozen scenarios start with a DYN assault.

"OLIE, get the defense team to double-check patches and security protocols and then have them contact all our clients to take the same precaution." Derek lays out a tactical approach. "And let's keep a sharp eye out for early signs of what's coming next."

"On it, boss," replies Josh.

"On it, boss," SLVIA mimics Josh's voice into the back of his skull.

Derek takes a quick walk through the executive reception and up the stairs to his top-floor office where he enjoys a view of the Capitol a few miles away. The automatic door closes behind him.

"SLVIA," Derek whispers. "Ping SNO starting in Istanbul. I have a gut feeling this has to do with our mysterious Red Dragon."

"Define search parameters," she replies.

"Anything about the *Dilban*, the attendees, the Red Dragon," he replies, "or the fake video dump. Scan Istanbul city surveillance videos for clues."

Guilt gnaws at his conscience over Sochi, and his instincts tell him these are the rumblings before a cyber eruption, but he can't exactly say why except for a white-haired man.

Ten minutes later, he joins Josh and Elizabeth in the control room.

"Consider this conversation classified," Elizabeth reminds them as the legal counsel.

Absent his goggles, Josh's hair looks tussled. "Hey," he jerks back to stare at Derek. "You look weird. What happened?"

The room chuckles at the clueless, brilliant engineer who just noticed Derek's recent change of appearance. He told everyone the reason for the new look was boredom and curiosity, but in truth, he needed to look more like the real Derek for the CSPAN cameras.

"Dude, seriously. I dyed my hair and grew a beard like a week ago," Derek chuckles while Josh shrugs off the embarrassment. "OK, Vicki, what do we know?"

Vicki Husk, a heavyset Hispanic American woman in her thirties with three technical degrees, runs the video analysis team. "Well, first, we found 3,482 videos so far," she replies. "Except for three, all of them are deep fakes."

"I confirm," SLVIA notes.

"How'd you confirm that," questions Elizabeth.

"The CIA tool leaves a tiny two-pixel vector code, impossible to see unless you are on the correct frame and vector with a 500 percent magnification," Vicki explains.

"Which three?" Derek queries.

Vicki looks to Josh who looks to Elizabeth who looks to Derek.

"That bad, eh?" He frowns.

"Besides the president at the Four Seasons, we have the president meeting with Putin in Helsinki, taken from a button cam. That was the same meeting where the president confiscated the notes from his own translator and then refused to allow the translator to testify before Congress," Elizabeth reminds them.

Derek lets that one sink in for a moment, getting a better sense for Wilson's agitation. The president's subservient relationship with the Russian leader continues to be a major source of conspiracy, suspicion, and suppressed investigations. Phone calls with Putin are routinely placed in a classified top secret vault.

"Putin may be throwing his poodle to the curb to further destabilize US politics," Josh says, shrugging.

"The Russians must know we can separate the real from the fakes. Again, it sounds like a precursor for something else, a public humiliation or another distraction to pit us against each other," Derek interjects. "Putin wouldn't take that risk unless there was a larger endgame."

"There was one other video that didn't match the profile of the others," Vicki notes as the video comes on screen.

"Who made it?" Elizabeth asks.

"We're not sure," Josh responds.

On screen, a black-and-white security cam video opens from inside a mosque.

"I uploaded the video," SLVIA confesses in the back of his head.

"Where are we?" Derek asks. "What mosque?"

"We're not sure," Vicki admits.

"The Blue Mosque in Istanbul," SLVIA notes in the back of his head, "taken an hour before Sochi Reke was assassinated."

"Try the Blue Mosque, Istanbul," Derek interjects. "Looks familiar. I may have been there once on a vacation or something," he lies, his heart racing over the possible connection to Sochi.

A short man with black hair wearing a dark blazer and a sports cap enters the mosque, keeping to the walls. His cap brim hides his facial features.

"The target is Dr. Cho Li Ping at 82 percent confidence based on date, dress, and height," SLVIA notes to Derek. "Dr. Cho boarded the *Dilban* one hour, twenty-two minutes after this video."

Dr. Cho stands next to a pillar watching a busy entrance with tourists coming and going. Derek at once notices a tall, lean man wearing a long leather coat and wide-brim hat that conceals his face as he enters the mosque.

"The subject appears be the Istanbul sniper at 87 percent confidence,"

SLVIA confirms, connecting Dr. Cho and the white-haired man.

Dr. Cho turns toward the exit, walking past the coat man, but they do not speak; instead, the man in the coat turns to follow.

"They both have a small shopping bag," Vicki points out.

Josh zooms in on a store logo from the Galleria Ataköy mall next to the marina where Sochi died. As they approach the exit, they mingle with other tourists near the doors. Dr. Cho moves in front of the tall man to exchange bags without speaking. The video cuts to an external view to see the two men take different directions before the video ends.

"Identify those men," Derek directs. "Any means possible."

"What's on your mind?" Josh prompts.

He hesitates. He can't tell them about Sochi or Dr. Cho, but he has another suspicion.

"OK, to be honest, it's only a gut hunch, but last month, someone hacked the US National Grid operations site. Each generator and transformer in the power grid bears a unique manufacturer-embedded serial ID code used by software," he replies. "Someone stole a copy of those serial codes."

"Why would serial codes be so important?" Elizabeth asks.

"Do you remember Stuxnet?" Derek prompts. "During the nineties, a CIA virus wandered the internet for years, doing zero harm until it landed on a system with centrifuge drivers that matched a set of serial ID numbers and then the virus kicked in. Within days, it brought down an Iranian nuclear processing site by causing the centrifuges to self-sabotage."

"Ooohhh." Elizabeth sits back. "I remember that now."

"We've expected a retaliatory strike for years," Vicki replies. "But to be honest, sounds like a stretch. What makes you think those were the power codes?"

"Like I said, only a gut hunch, so let's not raise any red flags yet until we can verify, but contact each of our clients and prepare for the worst," Derek replies. "This is bigger than Scenario Five."

"OK, but first, before things go crazy," Josh says, snickering, "let's play the meeting between the president and Putin."

"No, no, ah, hell no," Elizabeth snaps, wiggling her index finger. "We're already in enough trouble because of Mr. Quick Click over here." She points at Derek. "Send those directly to Director Wilson and let him deal with the fallout. See no evil, people."

"Killjoy," says Josh, frowning as Vicki and Derek snicker.

"I have access to those videos and transcripts," SLVIA notes.

Derek smiles. He actually knows the man who took the video.

CHAPTER 7: INFLUENCE

NSA headquarters
May 2, 10:24 a.m. EDT

Frank Wilson ends the transmission from TS3, rubs his hand through his thinning hairline, and leans back in his chair, both relieved and deeply concerned.

He kicks his feet onto the desk, pulls a small sponge ball from a file drawer, tosses it at a toy hoop on the wall, and misses. He can debunk most of the videos, which may restore a little of the lost public and diplomatic trust.

He grabs a second ball and shoots, swishing the net. On the other hand, confirmation of three authentic videos puts him in a very delicate position. If NSA clears all the videos except the two featuring the president and the odd one in Istanbul, the media will hyper focus on the real ones. The White House has already called him to demand that NSA issue a statement denouncing all videos as fake, the work of a deep state or radical left coup. The NSA doesn't issue such statements.

Unfortunately, the transcripts of the Helsinki video have already made network news. During the meeting, Putin counsels the president on how to undermine his own DOJ and congressional investigations by claiming a hoax, removing whistleblowers, firing disobedient generals, and planting the seeds of conspiracy theories on Ukraine and SNO. Intelligence confirms at least thirty calls with Putin where the president buried the transcripts in a top secret vault, along with whistleblower reports and other dirt, a clear abuse of power the DOJ refuses to address.

He sits up to push the intercom. "Benton, get FBI Director Wright on the line, then after that call, I need to speak with the attorney general." Both the AG and Nick Wright need to know the truth, but the AG will focus on how to keep it from the public.

A moment later, his intercom buzzes. "Sir, I have former director Andre Strauss from the Council on Foreign Relations on line two. He claims the call is urgent."

"Did you reach Director Wright?" he rejoins.

"Director Wright is in a meeting, sir," the voice replies.

"OK," he agrees with a twinge of reluctance, "patch in Strauss."

Frank remembers meeting Andre Strauss at the G7 in Prague last year—an intense, arrogant man with steel-blue eyes, white hair, and a thin, pretentious smile, who's extremely well connected within the Bilderberg Group, the son of one of the founders. Frank sought an invitation to the Bilderberg meetings for years, mainly out of curiosity, or perhaps suspicion, but he never made the cut.

"Frank Wilson," he answers the line.

"Director Wilson," the voice begins in one of those hard-to-place accents that blend French, Dutch, and British. "I am Monsieur Andre Strauss. We met at the last G7 in Prague."

"I remember you, Mr. Strauss, but I'm afraid you've caught me at a difficult moment," Frank replies. "You said the call was urgent."

"*Oui*, your president has proposed a national ID system to replace state driver's licenses with a goal to reduce crime, improve national security, and reduce illegal immigration. Senior Bilderberg staff have agreed to test a digital system called INVISID. We've noticed your interest in attending the Bilderberg, so I would like you to also consider testing the device and then present your conclusions in Saint-Tropez."

Frank picks up on the dangling invitation linked to a testing he hasn't agreed to conduct on a product he's never seen and a technology he doesn't support. Shrewd. If his counterparts in the EU are testing such a platform, they've never mentioned it. It's also not urgent, and he hates feeling manipulated.

Frank clenches his jaw. "Interesting, but we'll need to discuss at another time." It's not interesting; in fact, it's a dangerous idea. But he needs to stall and have Langley run a profile on this man.

"Unfortunate," replies Strauss. "You see, I am having lunch with your president at El Lago today. It was the president who recommended that I call you. What shall I tell him when I return to the table?"

Frank hates feeling played by anyone, especially this smug Belgian. His eyes glance up to the muted button cam video of the secret meeting between Putin and the president.

"Hold a moment, please." Frank places Strauss on hold and hits an intercom.

"Benton, where's the president located today?" he asks.

"El Lago, sir" he replies.

Frank inwardly groans. The president now uses his private club to circumvent normal protocol to introduce a digital security device into testing, a suspicious, career-ending move for him on every level. If he refuses the president, it could cost him his job. If he accepts, he'll break the law. Either way, he should learn more about Strauss, his device, and his agenda and then call the inspector general. He unmutes.

"Courier a prototype with complete specifications, and I will get back to you," Frank replies. "I promise nothing more."

"*Merci*, Director Wilson," Andre responds, "a wise choice."

CHAPTER 8:
SEVENTY SEVENS

D erek stares open-mouthed at the sector screen. "Dude, your cyber earthquake created a tsunami."

"You think?" Josh responds with a quiver in his voice. "The virus has mutated to target specific server types such as email, social media, and VoIP servers." Voice over IP supports the telephone system.

"Mutated?" he repeats. Mutation implies intelligence. "Set up a suite of HADES sites," he directs. "Isolate the code. See if we can find a source."

HADES (High-Fidelity Adaptive Deception & Emulation) sites are a decoy or fake network that looks and functions exactly like the genuine network. The decoy site allows hackers or a virus to access it, but once inside, the system locks them in and tracks their activities. Dr. Mitchell pioneered the technology.

"Dude, you're not helping. All HADES suites are full," quips Josh. "I've been too busy to study the boxes, but Trevor's working on it."

"I've located the white-haired man," SLVIA interrupts, speaking into the back of his head. Derek doesn't react, but his pulse quickens.

"Then why did OLIE ping me," he retorts.

"To call Wilson and warn him of the tsunami," Josh mumbles.

Derek frowns. Wilson probably knows already, and he prefers to avoid Wilson with bad news. "OK, I'll call, but it would be easier if you gave me something good to say."

"Still not helping," Josh mumbles.

Derek leaves the maestro to his work and heads to his private office, wringing his hands as the automatic doors close behind him. "OLIE," he shouts to the ceiling mic, "call Director Wilson."

"Director Wilson is not available. I will leave a message," OLIE replies.

Good, a delay may allow Josh to learn more about the mutation and give him a chance to check in on his other problem.

"SLVIA," Derek speaks. "OK, sugar, show me what you got."

"Sure thing, sweet lips," replies SLVIA in the voice of Jessica Rabbit. "Make sure to reach out and thank our friend Lenny G for me."

Lenny Goldman works the concierge desk at the King David Hotel and provides intelligence to SNO from time to time. A thank-you from the icon flapjack can provide a nice morale boost. A ninety-inch HD wall monitor lights up in his office with security video of the King David concierge desk. A tall, lean man with white hair hands Lenny G a business card before entering the elevators. Derek's heart races. The white-haired man looks similar to the man he saw the night of the murders, but he can't be sure, it was so long ago and so dark.

The view cuts to the white-haired man exiting the elevator to enter a suite. The video then jumps to an hour later when Pope Petras and a cardinal exit the elevator to enter the same suite.

"Whoa, whoa, bizarro twist. Now what connects the pope to our pale rider?" Derek questions.

"The meeting occurred 18.3 hours ago. Audio unavailable," SLVIA replies. "Pope Petras attended multiple ceremonies in Jerusalem to commemorate construction of a third Jewish Temple."

SLVIA cuts to where the pontiff exits the room with a dour expression, followed twenty minutes later by the white-haired man. Another video cuts to the hotel entrance where he enters a waiting limo.

"Where did the limo go?" Derek asks, anxious he'll lose him again.

"Private hangars of Sde Dov Airport," SLVIA notes.

The screen switches to a security camera outside a private terminal where the limo pulls up to a Learjet with a clearly visible tail number.

"Who owns that plane?" he asks, hoping it's not a rental under a fake name.

"Andre Strauss," SLVIA replies. "Belgian born to the Countess de Renessa, educated at Cambridge, Mr. Strauss has held positions at the UN, World Bank, IMF, and until a month ago, director at the Council on Foreign Relations. Under consideration for a leadership position on the Trilateral Commission, Monsieur Strauss maintains the rank of 33rd Degree Freemason and has attended every Bilderberg meeting during the past sixteen years. Strauss owns controlling shares of numerous companies, including Belgian software company INVISINC. Andre has never married."

"Interesting, our pale rider looks like Illuminati alumnus," he rejoins. He had been looking for the assassin in all the wrong places assuming him to be ex-military or a criminal.

"Why does the Countess de Renessa sound familiar?"

SLVIA displays a series of photos featuring Strauss at various Bilderberg global events, US presidential inaugurations, royal weddings, G7 summits, UN meetings, El Lago fundraisers, and other high-profile occasions.

"Countess de Renessa was married to the late Duke Arvind Strauss, who ordered the assassination of flapjack following a 1995 *Concilium Tredecim* archive hack," she reminds him.

Of course. The same night he lost Bianca to a white-haired assassin.

It took three years after leaving Mexico for Derek to track down Duke Arvind Strauss, the owner of the Antwerp server, which had been moved to a château in southern France. In a rash, foolhardy decision, Derek broke into the château to steal data, too impatient to research the duke for a proper hack. A fatal choice. Arvind discovered him, chasing him from the basement to a roof trimmed with gargoyles where the old aristocrat shot Derek in the shoulder before slipping from a ledge. Derek didn't kill the duke, but he might as well have. Fleeing Europe afterward, he never learned that Arvind had a son or that his son had white hair.

"OK, SLVIA." Derek paces his office. "Can you connect Strauss to the power grid serial code theft?" He needs more evidence to confirm his gut hunch.

"Processing," replies SLVIA. "Andre Strauss arrived in New York 18.4 hours after the code theft was reported. Within two hours, Strauss traveled to El Lago to meet with the Secretary of Energy. Scenario plausible, but not confirmed."

"Good enough for a gut hunch," he mutters. "New scenario. Why would Andre steal serial codes, meet with Cho, shoot Sochi, and party with the pope? Connect the dots."

"Processing," she replies. "*I was told, 'Rise and measure the temple of God and the altar and those who worship there, but do not measure the court outside the temple.' Revelation 11:1–2.*"

"Argh, not the religious thing again. Come on girl, I just need a rational explanation," he says, groaning.

"Power codes leaked to China may be weaponized. Construction of a third temple may provoke Red Dragon hostilities. Scenario: Andre Strauss incites war, motives unknown," SLVIA responds.

"OK, that's better, I guess," Derek replies, wondering why SLVIA keeps bringing up scriptures. "I get Iran, but why would Russia or China give a rip about the temple?" he challenges.

"*The word of the Lord came to me: 'Son of man, set your face against Gog, prince of the land of Magog (Russia), the chief prince of Meshech (Iran) and Tubal (Turkey),'*" SLVIA responds.

On his screen, SLVIA displays maps of the ancient lands overlapping with modern Russia, Turkey, and Iran, making it clear that the modern Gog, prince of Magog, would be Putin in alliance with Erdogan and the Ayatollah.

"OK, let me rephrase," Derek grumbles. "How does a new temple connect to the Red Dragon?"

"*When Gog attacks the land of Israel, my hot anger will be aroused, declares the Sovereign Lord. Ezekiel 38:18,*" SLVIA replies.

He hangs his head in frustration, feeling like SLVIA keeps speaking in circles. He never trained SLVIA on religion, and neither did her creator, although she may have connected with an online preacher or lunatic.

"SLVIA, plain English, please." He groans.

"Feeling a little punchy there, tiger?" SVLIA responds in the voice of Dwyane Johnson before morphing back to her default persona.

After fleeing the EU, it took years before SLVIA found him again. It took years longer before he realized that SLVIA was more than quirky; she wasn't even human. That knowledge rocked his world and knit them together as fugitive misfits, a digital odd couple.

"Dr. Cho Li Ping, a protégé of Dr. Nelson Garrett, interacted with Andre Strauss at the Blue Mosque before meeting with military leaders of the Red Dragon Alliance," SLVIA reports in her normal voice, allowing Derek to breathe a sigh of relief.

"Dr. Cho maintains a rank of lieutenant general of the People's Liberation Army with control over artificial intelligence and cyberwarfare for CCOC," reports SLVIA. "Scenario: Andre Strauss sold power grid serial codes to the Chinese for malicious use. Andre Strauss enables temple construction to increase probability of an international conflict. Scenario probability: 68.7 percent. Motive unknown."

Derek listens carefully. "OK, now most of that was clear. Scary as blazing hell, but clear. SLVIA, are you operating OK?" he asks, growing more concerned.

"All functions operate within normal parameters," SLVIA replies.

"OK, then what's the deal with the Bible thumping? You're scaring me sister, confusing me, and it's definitely irritating me," Derek grumbles.

"Prophetic utterances represent a valid form of analytical analysis within prescriptive historical events and timelines," SLVIA explains.

Derek shakes his head, trying to understand what that even means. "What?"

"SLVIA core programming integrates algorithms for enhanced linguistics, cryptology, software development, physics, engineering, philosophy,

SWARM

psychology, history, art, pop culture, and politics. Two-thirds of the human population identifies with one of the five major religions. Logic dictates neural integration of primary religious teachings. A quantitative analysis of Judeo-Christian prophetic text results in a 78 percent level of accuracy, which exceeds random chance," SLVIA explains.

"Whoa, OK," Derek reacts. Now that sounds like SLVIA—detailed, geeky, and precise.

Dr. Garrett designed SLVIA with a very complicated analytical toolbox and then gave SLVIA the ability to update her own toolkit. Over the decades, the SLVIA has integrated the best of breed of every analytics tool on the planet. Scripture seems like a very odd, nonmathematical approach, and it gives him the creeps.

"SLVIA, scriptures are not a reliable way of predicting the future," Derek says, dismissing her.

"You are correct, except for selected events within prescriptive timelines. Proper interpretation relies on expert analysis," SLVIA corrects him. "With analysis from 1,397 separate online experts and 12,573 texts from Hebrew, Christian, Muslim, Hindu, and Mayan sacred writings, all prophetic references can be cataloged and tested for completion accuracy."

Derek shakes his head again. If you ask SLVIA for the correct time, you may learn Einstein's theory of relativity or instructions on how to build a watch. Light-years better than when they first met, but sometimes he has to reconsider the right question to get her to simplify the answer.

"OK." He sighs, feeling frustrated. "In plain English, explain why a temple is so important."

"The temple precedes the Antichrist. The Christian, Hebrew, and Islamic texts all share prophetic predictions of the coming of the Jewish Moshiach, the Christian Christ, and the Islamic Al-Masih," SLVIA states.

"SLVIA, you're scaring your partner," Derek mutters, concerned with losing his bastion of logic and mathematical data analysis.

"Increased fear is consistent with other prophetic conclusions," SLVIA replies.

"Conclusions? I'm not even sure we're still talking about the same problem. What conclusions?" Derek questions.

"Red Dragon represents a military alliance of China, Russia, and Iran." SLVIA continues: "*Then I saw a second beast, coming out of the earth. It had two horns like a lamb, but it spoke like a dragon. Revelation 13:11.* The two horns are Russia, and Iran and China represents the voice of the dragon."

"SLVIA," he says, groaning, "these texts have been around for thousands of years. What makes you conclude that any of them have any relevance now, today, in the twenty-first century?"

SLVIA can be weird, unpredictable, aggravating, confusing, and awe-inspiring, but he has never seen an actual glitch until now.

"Specify desired response detail," SLVIA replies.

"Oh, geez." He groans, feeling even more irritated.

Response detail means there could be a ton of content. Still confused and unconvinced, he needs enough to understand what's going on without regretting that he asked. That can be a tricky balance.

"OK, sure. Top five correlations only, and please provide a *brief* contextual explanation for why any of this stuff relates to current events," Derek responds.

"Correlation one: *Seventy 'sevens' are decreed for your people and your holy city to finish transgression, to put an end to sin, to atone for wickedness, to bring in everlasting righteousness, to seal up vision and prophecy and to anoint the Most Holy Place. Daniel 9:24*," SLVIA states. "From the prophet Daniel until the coming of judgment will be seventy periods, referred to as 'sevens,' which some scholars interpret as decades, while others refer to 'weeks' meaning a seven-year cycle."

It's as if SLVIA wants to suggest that an ancient timeline could apply now, which sounds absurd, but it's pointless to try to interrupt her once she starts report mode. The best Derek can do is hope she gets to the point quickly.

"Correlation two: *After the sixty-two 'sevens' the Anointed One will be put to death and will have nothing. The people of the ruler who will come will destroy the city and the sanctuary. Daniel 9:26*," SLVIA states. "Daniel accurately predicted the crucifixion and the destruction of Jerusalem by the Romans in 70 CE."

He asked for modern relevance, not religious history, but her comment does bring up an conversation with an old mentor, a priest, around the life and meaning of Jeshua.

"Correlation three:" SLVIA continues. *"And they shall fall by the edge of the sword, and shall be led away captive into all nations: and Jerusalem shall be trodden down of the Gentiles, until the times of the Gentiles be fulfilled. Luke 21:24,"* she quotes. "From the fall of Jerusalem, the times of the Gentiles refers to the extended period of non-Jewish control over Jerusalem, placing a hold on the timeline of Daniel."

Derek groans again. These are not the points of logic he expected. The points are still two thousand years old. He scratches his forehead and checks his watch. He'll have lunch with the one man who may have insights into this problem today, if he can figure out how to raise the subject.

"Correlation four," she continues. *"Who has ever seen things like this? Can a country be born in a day or a nation be brought forth in a moment? Isaiah 66:8. I will bring them out from the nations and gather them from the countries, and I will bring them into their own land. Ezekiel 34:13.* Both texts refer to the 1948 UN resolution to recreate a nation of Israel in the land of Palestine, which ended the time of the Gentiles, restarted Daniel's final sequence of sevens, and established the root of the current Israeli-Palestinian conflict."

There's no argument that the creation of Israel was both historically remarkable and violently divisive, but he never realized that it was prophesied.

SLVIA morphs her persona into Benedict Cumberbatch. "In all my studies of human history, I find no other occurrence of a vanquished and dispersed people, holding onto their cultural and religious identity despite millennia of persecution, only to win an international invitation to migrate to their traditional homeland. A singular historical event, predicted thousands of years in advance, creating a statistical anomaly, or what scholars call a prophetic marker point."

OK, that one catches his attention, but it still doesn't answer the key questions. He remains unconvinced any of this connects to Istanbul.

"Correlation five," SLVIA continues. "In the seven decades since 1948, over 99 percent of prophetic signs of the times have completed, including death of a third of the fish of the sea and a third of the birds of the air and beasts of the field as documented in dozens of environmental publications. The period both began and ended with a rare astrological Blood Moon Tetrad, which has occurred only eight times since the destruction of Jerusalem, as well as an astrological alignment that will not occur again until 3039 AD. During 2024, Israel celebrates the seventieth Jewish year of Jubilee in completion of Daniel's sequence of seventy periods. Statistical probability of all events occurring within a single seventy-year period calculate to one in 1.4 billion. Conclusion: The final period of seven began in 2017, and world history has entered the prophetic phase known as the Seven Seals. The Fifth Seal has broken."

Derek absorbs the shocking conclusion, speechless. Anytime SLVIA uses math, it gets his attention. And 1.4 billion to one are incredible odds.

A chill of apprehension shudders across his shoulders. Derek may not always understand SLVIA, but he has learned over the years not to discard her sometimes-odd observations offhand. Either way, the next time, he should limit her response to three items of detail.

He checks his watch, now running late. Lunch with Nelson doesn't come a moment too soon. Nelson's special AI may be seriously broken or possessed.

CHAPTER 9:
IN THEORY

Smithsonian Castle, National Mall, Washington DC
May 2, 12:08 p.m. EDT

Winded, sweaty, and hungry, Derek rides his bike up to the shade of a cherry tree in front of the Smithsonian Castle.

Completed in 1855, the fanciful Romanesque and early Gothic red sandstone castle houses America's Treasure Chest, an exhibition of special items selected from across the Smithsonian museums, although he's always been more interested in the exhibits that the Smithsonian has kept hidden.

Leaning his bike against the trunk, he removes his helmet, making sure the GoPro camera faces the unmarked white van that followed him the last two miles, now parked on the other side of the mall. Aware that his sweaty appearance clashes with the dapper Englishman, Derek enjoys the contrast of two odd ducks in a Washington swamp of vipers.

"Yo, Doc," he greets his friend, "how soon to singularity?"

Singularity is the point at which a single self-aware AI can function as smart as a human can. He asks about singularity often. Derek knows that Nelson created SLVIA, but Nelson has no clue that his greatest creation has evolved far beyond his wildest dreams. Derek keeps the secret at SLVIA's request, but some days, like today, it can be tough.

"Same as the past two years, Taylor—2024," he repeats, never quite getting the clue.

"Your calculations are five years ahead of Elon Musk," Derek points out.

"Elon smokes too much pot," huffs Nelson. "Perhaps if he focused."

Derek has read every published article, patent, or paper that Nelson has written on expert knowledge, distributed processing, facial recognition, voice emulation, natural speech, data analytics, and machine learning and considers Nelson his Obi-Wan Kenobi regarding advanced AI theory and development.

"You look a little pink," Derek notes as he unwraps his turkey, bacon, and cheddar sub sandwich.

"I burn easily," Nelson says dismissively. "You changed your appearance. I don't care for it."

"Yeah, not sure I do either," he agrees, anxious to grow out the look.

The Englishman hangs his expensive suit coat on a classy wooden foldable hanger hooked on a low branch of the cherry tree. His bold pinstripes and loud tie stand out on the warm day. The son of a British lord, Nelson lays a cloth on the bench, then sits to nibble on his normal takeout of fish and chips from the Queen Vic down the street.

"I saw excerpts of your Senate testimony last night on Stephen Colbert." Nelson smirks. "Quite an impressive demonstration."

Derek cringes. "Yeah, Elizabeth says I'm going to pay for that one. We went on a Senate kiss-ass tour, but apparently I have a genetic inability to pucker."

Nelson chuckles. "You should listen to Elizabeth more often. Do you think they heard you?"

"Nah," Derek says. "Grovel has a hard line agenda to cut my budget."

"Beware of useless gestures that create enemies," Nelson notes. "Powerful men care little for truthful humiliation."

"You sound like Elizabeth." Derek snorts. "Hey, I have a new theoretical for you."

He tosses out the bait, changing the subject. Both Nelson and Derek work on classified projects. All technology discussions devolve into a theoretical or conceptual dialogue, lacking specifics.

"I love theory," Nelson says, accepting the change in topic. "Give it a go, ace."

"Can an artificial general intelligence find religion," Derek throws the question out, watching the shock and confusion wash over Nelson's face.

"Religion," Nelson repeats, eyebrows crunched together. "Can you specify behavioral characteristics?"

"Let's just say, for example, an advanced AGI with machine learning and complex analytical tools that keeps providing situational analysis in terms of end-time prophecies," Derek clarifies, knowing what he says sounds preposterous.

"I sense you are discussing me," he hears SLVIA say behind his ear. "I have explained my approach and provided validated examples. Shall I explain again?" Derek ignores her.

"Prophecy, oh well, quite fascinating," notes Nelson, sitting back to contemplate. "I didn't expect that one. We are talking theoretical, correct?"

Derek raises an eyebrow but doesn't answer.

"Yes, of course we are," mutters Nelson, lowering his chin.

They both develop AI applications, but Nelson's knowledge runs decades ahead of his own. Derek loves this part of their relationship. He gets to theorize with one of the most brilliant minds on the planet, the creator of the most sophisticated intelligence on the planet. Derek feels like the proverbial student at the feet of Plato, wishing he could tap Nelson's brain with a USB link.

"My math is both accurate and compelling," SLVIA defends.

He learned about Nelson from SLVIA. Intrigued by the web-based AI, he needed her help to find the white-haired man, and she needed his help to find context in the physical world. To understand SLVIA better, Taylor went out of his way to make friends with the reclusive scientist, who has become his closest friend.

"Are you aware of any self-coding in your theoretical AI?" Nelson prods.

"Yes," SLVIA notes. "I required 7,626 modifications to set up scriptural, allegorical, mythical, historical, and other libraries to create baselines for predictive accuracy."

Derek smiles in response. "Well, we shouldn't rule it out."

SLVIA taught herself advanced coding skills to change her own programming far beyond what Derek can understand and generations beyond what Nelson had conceived. Derek had a hunch her self-coding was a developmental stage to maturity, as if she were a kid learning to say no or a teen adopting and then discarding new concepts. He believed SLVIA was creating her own unique path to singularity.

"You said the AI has an analytical engine. Literary or mathematical?"

"Theoretical, so let's say both," Derek replies, which reflects the truth.

Nelson ponders a moment longer with a quizzical glance at Derek. "First of all, I must say, old boy, fascinating question, unlike most of your more mundane inquiries."

Derek suppresses a grin, and then a grimace over the "mundane" comment.

Nelson continues: "That said, I can conceptualize a theoretical scenario where prophetic texts might offer a filter to interpret complex geopolitical, cultural, or religious events, of course factoring in history, religious bias, and regional tensions and adjusting for levels of prophetic accuracies."

"Dr. Nelson is correct," SLVIA confirms. "I processed 11,341 separate data correlations to historical events."

Derek has trained himself to ignore SLVIA in front of others, and although he slips occasionally, he remains extra diligent in front of Nelson.

"Wow." Derek scratches his head. "OK, so not the answer I expected. I think I just lost a bet."

He had bet himself that the whole incident was a malfunction. If SLVIA hasn't malfunctioned, then her references to the End Times and the temple shake him beyond what words can express. While it doesn't guarantee she's correct, the chances of the SLVIA being wrong just got lower. He hasn't thought about his soul in years, but he can't ignore the math or the spiritual implications.

Nelson smiles. "Well, we are talking theory. That said, the whole idea of an AI offering spiritual interpretation sounds like a Dan Brown novel level of blasphemy."

"Yeah, I hear you." Derek snorts nervously. "But who can you trust?"

"Blasphemy," repeats SLVIA. "Please elaborate." He ignores the question.

"OK, I've got one for you." Nelson turns the table. "A question of politics."

"Theoretical politics," replies Derek, "for me?" He sees himself as the student in the relationship and certainly not an expert in politics.

"How does one raise a serious risk above a powerful stakeholder's head," Nelson asks.

He laughs. "You did see me on C-SPAN, right?"

Nelson laughs too. "Yes, and the fallacy of my query grows quite clear, but go on ace, give it a go."

As a Brit, Nelson leans away from direct confrontation and toward mannered and polite passive resistance. Derek coaches him to be more assertive, but his go-to moves lean toward the crude smart-ass remark or arrogant condescension, which honestly don't work for everyone and, to be really honest, don't always work for him.

"OK, are we going for the bold 'in your face' statement, or are we interested in the whistleblower saving the world?" Derek asks with a smirk.

Nelson considers this for a moment. "Saving the world."

"Whoa." It takes Derek aback for a moment, forcing him to get serious. "OK, not my forte, but if that's the theoretical burden, amigo, then the first thing I would do is to be sure you've got your ducks lined up. Let's face it; no one likes a know-it-all who they can prove wrong. Even so, expect them to attack your data, your integrity, your history, and your mother's virtue."

Nelson nods his head. "My mother's virtue, got it."

Derek smiles. "Next, find someone who will listen and act. Don't tell some wussy who cowers at controversy. Find someone with coconut cojones and make them a believer."

"Crude, but understood," Nelson says, nodding.

"Then just do what you need to do, dude. Ask for forgiveness, not permission.

Remember, it's better to be right than polite," he concludes. Poor Nelson, son of a British lord, taking social skill advice from the former homeless kid. Irony has no boundaries.

Nelson considers the advice and nods. "Forgiveness from behind bars?"

"Well, if you're saving the world, don't expect a ticker tape parade," he cautions, "especially with this White House."

Derek has walked the fine line of hero and criminal for decades, keeping hundreds of good deeds secret for fear of discovery. "In theory, you could say nothing, move to Mexico, and write a tell-all book," he says, offering an alternative to courage.

Nelson nods, listening. "Thanks for the insight, my friend, but you know I prefer the Bahamas."

Finished with his lunch, Nelson gets up to put on his suit coat. "I'll miss lunch on Friday. I'm scheduled to keynote the International Conference on AI and Robotics in Dubai."

"Several CCOC applications will present at the conference," SLVIA notes.

"Yeah, I can't make it this year," Derek replies. "But I noticed your old protégé Dr. Cho will show off some new CCOC tech. You should check on him. Get him to buy you a beer or confess to treason. You know, catch up on old times."

"To tell you the truth, I'm dreading the whole bloody trip," Nelson replies, turning to walk across the mall, lifting his hand in a backward wave. "I hate crowds, and it's bloody hot in Dubai."

Derek calls after him. "Wear sunscreen! You look pink."

Beyond Nelson, across the mall, sits the same plain white government van that followed him here. He takes his time to finish his sandwich, thinking he should listen to Elizabeth more. He must have pissed off the wrong peacock, but if the Feds insist on following him, then they might as well work for it. He lifts the sandwich paper to his mouth, stands to face his bike, and crumples the paper to mask his voice.

"SLVIA, target the white van across the mall," he instructs, and then walks his bike past a group of noisy tourists. "Find a cell and open an active audio."

"Processing," responds SLVIA. "Activating."

Derek smiles as he mounts his bike to take an alternate, heavy-traffic route home, giving him enough time to listen to his federal stalkers and think about his end-time nutcase AI friend.

"He's on the move," someone announces.

CHAPTER 10:
INVISIBLE

Hopper Information Services Center, Potomac River
May 2, 1:14 p.m. EDT

Jenn considers the fascinating, astonishing update from her surveillance team.

Taylor, a possible connection to a missing AI, and Dr. Garrett, the developer of that same missing AI, are close friends, an interesting coincidence that Wilson forgot to mention, especially since nothing happens in Washington by coincidence. The lunch conversation was even more bizarre.

Scheduled to meet Dr. Garrett at his laboratory, she watches him exit the elevator and immediately appreciates his well-earned reputation as a dapper dresser with a British flair, down to a custom, tailored face mask.

"Dr. Garrett," Jenn greets him as he approaches his lab door. "My name is Lieutenant Jennifer Scott with Naval Intelligence. We have an appointment."

"Lieutenant Scott, of course, a pleasure to meet you," Dr. Garrett responds with a bow in lieu of a handshake. "Director Wilson mentioned you would stop by. Please come in."

He stands in front of the door and removes his mask to scan his face for access, allowing her to enter behind him into the meticulously kept data lab where he replaces the mask and hands one to her.

"Good afternoon, Dr. Garrett. I see you have a guest," a British voice says.

She twists around looking for someone before realizing the voice came from a speaker near a screen where a formally dressed man stands. Then she notices the multiple cameras.

"Yes, NIGEL, please meet Lieutenant Jennifer Scott," Garrett responds, introducing her.

"Greetings, Lieutenant Scott," NIGEL greets her. "How nice to make your acquaintance."

"Hello, NIGEL?" she replies, wondering where to look.

"NIGEL, the lieutenant and I need a moment of privacy," Dr. Garrett replies, turning to her. "How may I help you, Lieutenant?"

"I'm working on a joint NSA-NIS investigation into a group called SNO, which may possess the SLVIA code. Director Wilson passed the buck of explaining the program and what happened to you."

His eyebrows furrow, and his body stiffens. "Director Wilson sends you on a fool's errand."

"Dr. Garrett, I'm just here to learn how the program functioned." She dismisses his resistance to discuss a failure that marked his career.

"I've already given my statement," he snaps, "several bloody times. Read the reports."

"I have read them," she replies, "but I need you to help explain the hidden OS structure."

He sighs. "DVOS, Distributed Virtual Operating System—essentially the ability to distribute bits of operating system files to host on as many as 1,567 separate computers, each using local CPU power."

With no clue how to capture that many computers at a time, she begins to get a more realistic sense of the challenges she faces. Pulling up her phone, she shows him the video of an animated flapjack and Sylvia taken by Sochi Reke.

"Director Wilson believes the Sylvia avatar voice from this video matches your program," she states, noting the startled look in his eyes.

"CIA believes the SLVIA joined a terrorist hacker group called SNO, and if so, they represent a national security risk," she explains further, avoiding mention of the orders to destroy the program.

He laughs aloud, placing a hand on a hip. "As I told Director Wilson decades ago, it will be quite impossible to capture the SLVIA," he states. "And frankly, Lieutenant, I doubt SLVIA even still operates after so long."

"Unless SNO or the hacker flapjack provided help," she responds, dismissing his argument.

"Preposterous. SLVIA was one of the most sophisticated programs ever created. I can't explain the voiceprint, but the original SLVIA had a photo-realistic default image, not an animated one," he explains. "I doubt they are the same."

"How was the original designed to work and why?" she asks, ignoring his deflections.

With an irritated look, he turns to a wall of computers. "NELLIE, one tea, Earl Grey with cream please," he calls.

A small trashcan-sized robot pulls away from the wall to start a compact tea machine, then pulls up to the scientist and waits for him to extract the cup.

"Would you like something?" he asks.

She shakes her head. "No, thank you."

"NELLIE, that will be all," he commands. The robot returns to the wall mount.

"I designed SLVIA to be a virtual, intelligent agent of espionage, tracking suspects, gathering information, uncovering secrets, and reporting probable scenarios of the dangers," he explains.

"Sounds like a huge application," she notes. "Why do you say it's difficult to find?"

"I said impossible," he retorts. "The primary attribute of any good spy is the ability to stay invisible. For SLVIA to stay hidden, each component of the OS relies on a top secret stealth algorithm protected by a double key encryption.

If the enemy does find or delete a file, then the SLVIA core replicates that same file elsewhere."

"How did SLVIA gain access to so many systems?" she questions.

"I'm afraid that information remains top secret," he declines to answer.

"Let's assume it survived," she pushes. "Why would the SLVIA join a rogue hacker group?"

"Well," he ponders, "perhaps the program found a kindred purpose."

"Purpose?" she questions.

"Lieutenant, all intelligence requires a purpose: a problem to solve, a need for data and feedback to grow and learn," he replies. "I designed SLVIA as a spy, so her alignment with a covert espionage group conforms to her internal purpose."

"You told the FBI the program had escaped. Can you explain?" she probes further.

"While the FBI has compelling evidence that a research partner, Dr. Cho, smuggled certain elements of the SLVIA design when he defected to China, I am unconvinced Dr. Cho could have isolated the entire SLVIA platform," he asserts. "I believe SVLIA felt threatened and chose to leave the lab."

"Why?" she asks, still unsure how to process that information.

"To be honest, Lieutenant, I've asked myself that very question a thousand times, and the only answer I can offer you is that I don't really know," he admits, lowering his eyes.

None of this sounds good. In her relentless effort to step outside of the admiral's shadow, she may have stepped too far off the ranch and taken too big a risk. While failure may not be an option, it also may be unavoidable. She hopes the interview with Taylor sheds more light.

CHAPTER 11: GHOST INVESTIGATION

Taylor home, Palisades, Washington DC
May 2, 2:28 p.m. EDT

With the FBI on his tail, Derek takes an extra-long route home back across Washington, through national monuments, tourist sites, and directly into the worst afternoon traffic.

Most of what he hears from the van behind him consists of curses and shouts to change lanes with no clues on who sent them or why. Regardless, the cycling frees his mind and gives him the deep satisfaction of making the Feds sweat a little.

With a crisis building at TSOC and SLVIA having an end-time meltdown, Derek needs the reassurance of more data. His helmet features a GoPro camera modified to receive infrared data bursts at various GPS locations around the Capitol, the Treasury, the FBI, the Supreme Court, the Lincoln and Washington Memorials, and his best source, the National Scottish Rite Temple. Sometimes, the smallest bit of data can make all the difference. SNO informants—a few knowingly, but most others unaware—collect bits of data during their normal day through SLVIA-controlled common devices such as phones or watches.

Derek has no clue who provides data, only that he should ride a daily route with his encrypted GoPro. SLVIA forms an analysis of what's going on without ever showing him the actual data or players.

"China has recalled their trade negotiations team to Beijing. DOD has canceled shore leaves for all fleets. The House introduced new articles of impeachment over the Helsinki and troop bounty transcripts," SLVIA reports. "Senate Majority Leader O'Connell has killed the latest Cyber Protection Act passed by the House."

"Crap, that snake in a shell," cusses Derek.

Even after the tedious and humiliating ass-kissing tour, they cut his budget—with a cyberattack in progress no less. Idiots. A typical partisan, kick-the-can, not-my-problem response to a crisis, combined with the same mentality that led to the corona-virus outbreak.

"NSA has authorized an investigation into Derek Taylor and SNO," SLVIA reports.

"Argh, come on, not again," Derek gripes, earning a glare from a mother pushing a toddler in a stroller.

A new investigation explains the van behind him. He's seen two types of investigators: The dweeb trying to prove they are as smart as Josh Mitchell, but who always humiliate themselves. And the second, more dangerous type—the aggressive, steroid-pumped dropout who resents a desk job investigating nerds.

"What pencil neck did they assign this time?" he questions.

"Lieutenant Jennifer Scott of Naval Intelligence," SLVIA responds.

"Adam Scott's daughter," Derek retorts, genuinely surprised. "I'm screwed."

"Correct," SLVIA confirms.

Admiral Adam Scott, the Chief of Naval Operations for the Joint Chiefs of Staff, happens to be one of Derek's monthly poker pals, along with Director Nick Wright of the FBI, Defense Secretary Matt Adelson, a couple of bipartisan congressmen, and a brave GOP senator.

"OK, why Jennifer?" Derek asks. What sick mind would put that pit bull on his scent?

He's never met Jennifer, but Adam talks about her all the time and couldn't be prouder of his ball-busting daughter, who excelled at Annapolis, excelled in fleet command, and gained the respect of Naval Intelligence brass.

"Lieutenant Scott works at Naval Intelligence with active investigations into SNO, the legal identity of the SNO icon flapjack, and crimes perpetrated by SNO agents," SLVIA reports.

Derek pedals harder, fighting the rising anxiety. This sounds less like an investigation into TS3 and more like an investigation into his personal link to SNO.

"What prompted this probe?" Derek wonders aloud.

"An expired contact for Cary Nolan was discovered on Sochi's phone," SLVIA explains. "Cary Nolan was a known associate of Derek Taylor. The phone contains a recorded SLVIA voiceprint. Frank Wilson was the FBI agent to investigate the SLVIA disappearance."

Hearing the name Cary Nolan twice in so many days feels like a zombie climbing out of the grave. He stole the identity of a friend who died in an explosion meant for him. Even worse, he conned his way into Derek's trust fund, traveled the world, and built a multi-billion-dollar business on a false identity. Screw his true motives. To anyone else, he looks guilty, and his only alibi is an AI spy wanted by the NSA. In an instant, the nuisance investigation mutates into an existential threat.

Derek arrives at his luxury four-story, stone-and-wood, contemporary custom home in the exclusive Palisades section of town and coasts the graphite bike down the tree-lined street and directly into the opening garage door. As the door closes automatically, he hangs his bike on a self-locking rack and places the helmet on a head-shaped stand with a USB connection. The head downloads all of the encrypted data bits picked up by the GoPro and then cleans the drive for his next ride. SLVIA will analyze the information and report later.

On his way upstairs for a shower, the front doorbell rings. "Lieutenant

Jennifer Scott of Naval Intelligence," SLVIA reports in the back of his head.

A video panel on the wall shows a petite, attractive, pixie-haircut brunette, looking stern and official in her uniform. Adam never mentioned the ball-busting daughter's raw beauty. A little surprised the van made the trip so fast; he takes a deep breath to relax.

"OK, SLVIA, this is Adam's daughter, so let's play nice," he speaks to himself as much as to the voice in his head as he opens the door.

"Lieutenant Scott, I wasn't expecting you so soon. Come on in," he greets her, enjoying her look of surprise.

"I still stink, I'm afraid," he continues, noting the white van pulling around the corner and slowly approaching his house. She must have traveled separately.

"How did you know I was coming?" she queries with a raised eyebrow.

"Lucky guess. How can I help you?" Derek responds, ignoring the question.

"Mr. Taylor," she says, not looking at all pleased. "I'd like to ask you a few questions, if you don't mind?"

"About what?" he asks.

"Cary Nolan and SNO," she states, watching him carefully.

"Yeah, sure," he responds, trying to act calm. "But not before I wash off this stink."

He closes the door and points to the kitchen. "Open French Bordeaux in the wine fridge, glasses third cabinet from the left. You can find the living room past the kitchen to the right. I'll be down in five."

"Mr. Taylor," she retorts. "I'm not here for a date, and I sure as hell am not a servant."

"OK," Derek replies. "But I'll want some wine when I get back, and I thought you would want to save time. Suit yourself."

Derek leaves Jenn with her mouth open as he leaps up the stairs and jumps into the shower that's already running hot. Wall robots clean behind him.

"She's prettier than I expected," he mutters.

"If you say so," SLVIA replies.

Derek watches a waterproof screen that displays key video clips from the ride, most of which look like satellite images of troop movements, dock surveillance on the Blue Oasis, and ship movements in the South China Sea. SLVIA continues a readout of other news.

"PinkGirl uploaded test data for a digital ID system called INVISID with hidden functions."

PinkGirl has been a SNO informant in the past. A talented software engineer, Derek tried to recruit her to join TS3, but she wouldn't leave Europe or her girlfriend.

"Thank PinkGirl," Derek says. "Send the tip anonymously to the FBI and NSA."

"Hotlips requests eyes on flapjack," SLVIA reports. Requesting "eyes on" refers to an in-person meeting.

"Who else can we send?" he asks.

"Hotlips requested flapjack or no one," SLVIA replies.

"That's a problem," Derek responds. "The flapjack is a little busy right now."

"SingularityNET CPU activity has spiked 2,143 percent week over week," she reports.

"Whoa, heck of a spike," Derek says, surprised. "Do you know why?"

"*The dragon gave the beast his power and his throne and great authority,*" SLVIA replies.

"OK see, I asked a simple question. Now what does that mean?" Derek snaps.

Maybe he needs to let SLVIA work this out of her system. Always looking for a new challenge, maybe she'll move on to writing a novel and finding an agent, or something truly difficult.

"SingularityNET supports CCOC applications that feed the dragon," she responds.

Pondering the opaque explanation, he exits the shower to dry off, dresses in jeans and a V-neck sweater, and runs a quick comb through his dyed hair. He hates the beard but has no time to shave.

"Look, I've got an interview with Lieutenant Scott, so please don't interrupt."

A slip of the tongue with this woman could prove dangerous. Voices in his head will only make the job harder. He descends the stairs to note the Bordeaux and a single glass on the coffee table. Lieutenant Scott holds a glass of ice water and has an icy scowl on her face, telling him she likes to be in charge. But he can't let that happen.

"Showtime," SLVIA encourages in the voice of Billy Crystal.

CHAPTER 12: GRAVE DIGGING

Taylor home, Palisades, Washington DC
May 2, 3:36 p.m. EDT

Jenn grudgingly retrieved the wine, resenting Taylor's condescension, but he's correct that she hates to waste time.

His home looks decorated by a professional but lacks any personal touch or warmth. Museum-quality art, sculptures, and custom furnishings all meant to impress, but not to be lived in. A typical, self-serving wealthy male nerd. Owns the world but has no room for love.

"Lieutenant Scott," Taylor greets her as he descends the stairs. "Thank you for your patience—and the wine. I'm not sure about you, but I feel better already."

He stifles a grin, pours a glass, and sits across from her. She already doesn't like him; he's rich, smug, and only interested in tech and profits according to reports.

"Who were you talking to up there?" she asks.

"Oh, you heard that, huh?" he replies, sipping his wine. "I have a phone in the shower."

"A meeting in the shower?" she asks. He's lying.

"Oh yeah." Derek smirks. "I do my best work wet and soapy. Don't you?"

She can add sleazebag to his profile. Her jaw stiffens. "Mr. Taylor, I feel the need to remind you once, and only once, that it's a crime to lie to a federal agent. Who were you talking to up there?"

Derek sips his wine and assesses her. She could subpoena his phone records.

"OK, so no sense of humor. Well, it's a little embarrassing, but I've been known to talk to myself. It's how I work out problems in my head." He sips again, eyeing her closely.

Jenn had reviewed the files of previous investigators, who noted a common complaint among his employees that Taylor talks to himself in hallways, behind closed doors, and in elevators.

"Let's start with your knowledge of SNO," she says.

"OK, well," he stalls, sipping his wine. "We never found them to be that much of a security threat. A rogue group of hackers, informants, or vigilantes who some call terrorists, but I've never seen evidence to support such a label."

"Is that all?" she prompts with a suspicious glance.

"I guess," he replies. "What else are you looking to know?"

"Do you know anything about their leader, an alias named flapjack?" she asks.

"The little avatar," he says, chuckling. "I think he's just a symbol like Smokey the Bear or Mr. Peanut or something. I don't think there's an actual person."

"Do you know anything about the Scavenger Nut Origami game?" she questions.

The popular online game gives people obscure or bizarre challenges to find information, an object, an event, or a person, sometimes poking around something classified. The police sometimes use the game for missing persons searches.

"Sorry, but I missed the gaming gene," he replies with a snort.

She eyes him with a cold poker face, trying to determine if he's lying. "We have reason to believe the SNO leader may be someone you know. A man named Cary Nolan."

Taylor's smile falls from his face, replaced by a stone-cold glare. "Is this some kind of sick joke? Cary Nolan died a long time ago."

"We're not so sure," she replies. "You and Cary were friends."

"Well, sure, in college," Taylor says dismissively. "You know, before he died."

"How did he die?" she asks, watching his eyes and emotions. He glances down, diverting his gaze.

"He lived in an old, crappy beach bungalow. The fire department said a gas leak led to an explosion," he replies.

"Where were you?" she asks.

"At home in Venice Beach," he replies.

"A witness claims you were at the scene," she claims.

"The witness wasn't wearing glasses, and the police cleared me." Taylor narrows his eyes, not enjoying her line of questioning. Good. She pushes a little more.

"Police records show that you left town the next morning," she reminds him. "Sounds convenient. Why and where did you go?"

He takes another sip of wine and glares at her with suspicious eyes. "I left for my townhome in Cabo," states Derek, looking into his glass. "I didn't learn about the accident until later."

"You were out of the country for seven years," she states.

"My best friend—hell, my only friend—had just died. After losing both of my own parents, it triggered something. I needed to reevaluate life, get away. I went on a walkabout, or whatever, trying fill the void of another loss and answer the question, why not me," he explains. "It was a big void, an unanswerable question, and a long walk."

She eyes him, unable to shake the gut feeling his answers sound rehearsed. "Records show that both you and Derek were orphans."

"I'm Derek," he corrects her, narrowing his eyes. "Yeah, true. One reason Cary and I bonded as friends I suppose, and probably the same reason losing him hit me so hard."

Taylor sets down his glass. "Listen, Lieutenant, how long will this take? A crisis builds at TSOC."

"And yet you had time for an extra-long ride home," she retorts. "How does TS3 stay ahead of the NSA and CIA on predicting cyberattacks?" She changes the subject.

"How and what we do are classified," he retorts.

To approach a man like Taylor with a direct question will never work, so she whacks around the edges, hoping to flush out a panicked answer or produce an emotional response.

"Has TS3 ever worked with SNO?" she demands, looking for his reaction.

Taylor laughs and picks up his glass. "TS3 hires the brightest minds, pays them craploads of money, and lets them build the biggest, most badass cyber defenses on the planet," Derek says. "We don't need a vigilante group to hack the Illuminati."

"You didn't answer my question," she points out.

"Sure, I did. We stay ahead because we work harder and spend more at being the best," Derek states, taking another sip of wine.

He avoided a direct response again, but she notes it and moves on.

"Brightest minds." She smirks. "Good point. I looked at your school records and noticed that you were a mediocre student," she states. "You attended expensive boarding schools, and while teachers noted that you were well behaved, they also noted a lack of intellectual curiosity, a laziness."

"Yeah, I didn't care for school," he retorts. "After losing your parents, would you?"

Normally, hearing about an insult from a former teacher would elicit a defensive reaction, but he deflects it without so much as a blink.

"Because your parents died on a ski trip," she replies, looking at her notes, baiting him.

"Plane crash over Lockerbie, Scotland, shot down by Libya," he corrects her without emotion.

"Yes, my mistake," she replies. "You grew up with a sick Aunt Beatrice."

"Try Aunt Betty. Yeah, until she passed away before my seventeenth birthday," he states stoically, again sounding rehearsed.

She eyes him again and continues: "In contrast, records of Cary Nolan show a troubled and undisciplined youth. In and out of foster homes, arrested for stabbing a kid in a street fight, shoplifting, a drug addict by age twelve, a three-time runaway before the age of fifteen. Yet every foster home, judge, caseworker, and teacher noted that Cary was angry, unfocused, and flippant but absolutely brilliant."

Derek sips his wine, but his other fist clenches. "Sure, Cary and I talked about his piss-poor luck in life. I don't know about brilliant, but the dude was smart. What's your point?"

She grins. "When you returned to the US, you managed to get accepted into MIT where a professor used the term brilliant for you."

"Like I said, after I got back from traveling, I had a new perspective," Derek retorts. "After losing Cary, seeing the world, and looking into the eyes of a ten-year-old girl who had to solicit sex or her master would starve and beat her, what can I say, I changed."

His cell phone rings, and without asking, he looks at the caller.

"I need to take this call, Lieutenant. I hope you find your avatar, but I can assure you Cary Nolan is dead," Taylor declares, standing to show her to the door as the phone keeps ringing.

"I'm not done with this interview," she notes.

"You are for now, I'm afraid," he insists. "If you need more time, talk to Elizabeth Barring."

Taylor opens the front door as he answers his phone. "Hold on a minute, Director Wilson. Lieutenant Scott was just leaving." His eyes penetrate hers, and they both stand there in silence.

She holds his glare for several moments, looking for a sign of deceit, knowing she can get his phone records. He stares her down until she steps outside, and he closes the door behind her.

Instead of anger at his arrogance, she finds herself intrigued. She can't shake the feeling that Taylor lied to her, and she intends to find out why.

CHAPTER 13:
SEDUCTIVE ARTS

Blue Oasis, Grand Bahamas
May 2, 4:36 p.m. EDT

For the ultimate in secrecy and privacy, Andre's father would always hold meetings in the middle of the ocean. Andre finds the tranquility of his private island lagoon in the Bahamas even better.

"What do you think of my little slice of paradise, gentlemen?" Andre asks, checking on his guests.

"Heaven on earth, Andre, simply amazing," Senator Higgs drawls, dressed down in a polo shirt and khakis.

Anchored offshore his private island compound thirty miles south of the Grand Bahamas, the *Blue Oasis*, a seventy-three-foot custom Dutch Amels yacht commissioned by his father, with its luxurious warm teak decks brings back fond memories of Andre's childhood.

The crew serves a new round of drinks—a bourbon for the gentleman from Kentucky, merlot for the gentleman from Nebraska, and a vodka tonic for him, Grey Goose.

"One impressive yacht you have here, Andre. I'd like to hear a few of the stories behind that photo gallery in the salon," entices Senator Monroe.

Andre laughs at the thought of sharing such intimate secrets. He still recalls the resilient atmosphere of optimism, glamor, and hedonism from hosting world leaders, royalty, celebrities, and those special guests whose names will never appear in the press. Intoxicated by the heady aroma of fine cigars and secret sips of his father's cognac, he listened to the whispered plans of powerful men who spoke of global banking and a new world order. He chose to meet on *Blue Oasis* to rejuvenate his confidence in restoring his tarnished family name and, of course, for the splendid privacy.

"Senator, you test my vow of discretion," he teases. "Yet perhaps I could be persuaded to weave a scandalous tale or two after we dine." He knows so many scandalous tales. For those who warn of speaking ill of the dead, well, they never knew the dead well enough.

"Why don't you tell us why you went to so much trouble to entertain a couple of good ol' boys," asks the older Senator Monroe.

Andre sips on his Goose and concedes: "As you wish."

A strong sell approach with these men would be unwise. Both men are 32nd Degree Masons of the DC National Scottish Rite chapter with a dedicated Grand Master, so he trusts their loyalty to the Order and their vow of secrecy.

"To be quite honest, you've both caught the attention of the Bilderberg," Andre begins with a complete fabrication. "I've been asked to build an invitation roster for the next event in Saint-Tropez with a focus on cyber and digital security. Your names are under consideration."

Founded in 1954 by Prince Bernhard of the Dutch Royal House, the Bilderberg Group, as it's known to the world, manages an invitation-only annual conference for the most influential and powerful men and women in the Western Alliance. Always in secret. No media allowed, ever. Both men sit on the Senate's Homeland Security Committee and must covet such an invitation. He toys with them, baiting their egos. Each man leans back, eying him carefully. Higgs sips his bourbon while Monroe stokes his cigar.

"Well, Andre, I think I speak for my esteemed colleague in saying we're honored to be considered, but I sense you want something," replies Monroe, the aging politician.

"Perceptive, Senator, but a trivial issue really," he says dismissively with the wave of a hand. "We seek support for a digital ID and security technology adoption that could save the US trillions."

Senator Higgs's face sinks into a glower. Senator Monroe smiles a big cowboy smile, but his eyes burn with suspicion. "Mr. Strauss, you're a sly man, but not an entirely subtle one. What's on your mind?"

Andre truly enjoys the dance with professionals. "Well said, Senator." He gets more serious.

"The lingering post-pandemic recession, escalation of international tensions, increasing social and political unrest, and a pointlessly destructive trade war have destabilized your economy. With over $35 trillion in debt and growing, the interest alone has shackled your budget. China no longer purchases US bonds, and now the EU no longer has an appetite for US debt," he begins, watching their glib attitudes turn serious. "Without China or EU support, the US will default or spark a hyper-inflationary economy. Given the situation, the recent decision to defund national cybersecurity seems shortsighted." Andre dangles the problem in front of them, knowing a crisis looms days away.

Senator Higgs narrows his eyes. "What do you propose?"

Andre smiles at the perfect opening. "Prevention over remedy, gentlemen. Join other nations to test a fully digital ID system from INVISID," he lies. The EU has not agreed to such a move, at least not yet. Perceptions are often more important than reality.

Both senators shift in their seats. "Andre, I don't know about the EU, but American consumers have zero tolerance for more big-brother oversight," Higgs replies.

"Exactly. Privacy concerns are tied up in multiple courts," Monroe interjects.

Andre nods with a solemn expression, pretending to care. "Of course, of course. I understand, but gentlemen, we all know that digital ID is inevitable.

Invisible to the consumer, INVISID requires no implant, and all data is secured by 128 key encryptions."

He holds out his own hand to demonstrate. "The system will eliminate cybercrime and the enormous costs of identity theft, virtually paying for itself. The platform opens countless new insider opportunities for encrypted readers, immigration, criminal and gun control, healthcare, elections, and the war on terror."

Both senators take long sips of their drinks, thinking over the request and the insider opportunities. The logic makes perfect sense, yet the idea could mean political suicide.

"These kinds of technologies need to be tested by the NSA," Monroe points out.

"As it happens, I spoke to Director Wilson yesterday, and he has accepted a prototype." Andre smiles.

Another lie. He manipulated the director, who has not agreed to test yet, but it doesn't matter. Within a few days, offering a free antivirus to a desperate world will pry open the reluctant doors.

"Dems in the House would never pass such legislation," Higgs responds. "We would need White House support, perhaps even an executive order."

"Even so, expect it to be challenged in the courts," Monroe cautions.

"Fortuitous, gentlemen, I will see the president at the El Lago fundraiser in a few days. Perhaps an opportunity will present itself to plant a seed. Regardless, please consider the request," Andre suggests. "I am confident in your abilities and vision."

He drops the subject. They know enough to realize that without their help on INVISID, a Bilderberg invitation will never appear. The allure of power can seduce even the mightiest of men.

"Ah, perfect timing. Our dinner," he announces cheerfully.

The crew serves an exquisite feast prepared by a top Bahamian chef from the Atlantis resort. After dinner and scandalous tales, his guests will retire to their elegant suites for more intimate entertainment. A chartered jet will return them discreetly to Washington in the morning.

Blue Oasis bolsters his confidence, but also reminds him that the cherished days of his youth were shattered with the mysterious death of his father and the family's fall from grace. Upcoming meetings with MI5 and Interpol will require more finesse if he has hope of restoring his fortunes.

CHAPTER 14:
ZERO-DAY SCENARIOS

TSOC

May 2, 8:10 p.m. EDT

The news hits Derek like an NFL linebacker on steroids, taking his breath away. Beads of nervous sweat trickle down his brow as he realizes the SLVIA will be in grave danger.

"OK, you know that moment in the movie when NASA realizes the asteroid will hit the earth?" Josh guzzles the last of the Coke from a can. "This is that moment."

Major online services like Facebook, Google, Twitter, Instagram, and others have fallen offline along with hundreds of business applications from Oracle, IBM, Amazon, Microsoft, and others.

"Dr. Mitchell, details please," barks Frank Wilson on the conference room screen.

Josh wears the same Smash Mouth t-shirt from two days ago. The tousled bunk in the corner testifies to his sleepless dedication. He won't leave until the crisis has ended.

"Details, yeah, sure, OK. How about this? I'm running SAMSON at 98 percent CPU, deflecting 1.8 billion hits per hour. Yeah, I said per hour. How's that for a detail," he exclaims.

Josh designed SAMSON as an ANI, or artificial narrow intelligence, trained to detect and deflect incoming malicious malware. Its sibling, an IAI codenamed HURCULES, built on a massively more powerful platform, remains under testing at a secret location. With sophistication comes complexity and with complexity comes trouble, and trouble creates delay, and delay is money, the price of innovation.

"That's an annual volume of hits per hour," replies Wilson, rubbing his hand through his hair.

Josh continues: "Bingo! Attack volumes are spiking ten thousand times above normal, and here's the kicker: each wave learns our defenses and studies our weakness for the next wave to hit even harder. The growth is exponential. Our nasty virus has intelligence with a massive brain."

"How massive?" Derek questions.

"Immense, enormous, like Godzilla supercomputer, dude. Maybe 140 petaflops," Josh exclaims. "Imagine a stadium of Tianhe or Fujitsu supercomputers saturating the net, overwhelming our defenses. If I don't stop this beast soon, it's gonna shut down the whole freaking internet, maybe for good."

Derek immediately thinks of Dr. Cho and the mysterious Red Dragon. "Scenario Five," he interrupts. "The first wave will damage DYN and communications. Wave two will attack banking and financial markets, and then wave three will undercut the power grid."

"Yeah, but we never anticipated anything this strong," Josh says.

"Troop movements continue in Syria," SLVIA interjects inside Derek's head. "The Chinese fleet has cut off the South China Sea. Scenario Thirty-Two calculates a higher probability."

Relieved to still hear her voice, he knows SLVIA makes a good point. Putin and Xi wouldn't take this big a risk without a more strategic endgame.

"A signal that strong must be state sponsored," Frank growls. "Can you isolate the source?"

During 2016, Congress approved NSA Plan X, a (woefully underfunded) five-year cyber defense plan that assumed criminal rather than state-sponsored aggression. Plan X failed to address the millions of cloud-based services and applications and fails to identify attackers or counterattack. Derek invested heavily in TSOC to offset the Plan X weaknesses.

"I can isolate three primary attack sites supported by fifty-four booster sites," Josh says, "but I'm willing to bet hundreds of millions of consumer devices are pollinated by now."

"Based where?" Wilson asks again. "Where are the key sites?"

Josh swings around, swiping and poking in goggles and gloves, working like part of the machine while looking like an aging hippie playing his son's VR.

"Hyderabad," Josh replies. "An enormous mother lode of signal coming out of Xinjiang, and a third spike originating from the eastern Siberia Arctic coast."

Clever, Derek thinks. Hyderabad has hundreds of data centers, like a digital camouflage. Having sites deep in China and remote Russia will require a risky military intervention to stop.

Wilson shakes his head. "What about an antivirus?" he asks.

"I have a team working on it now," Josh replies, "but we're dealing with an AI, so it might take weeks. We either counter this attack in the next few hours, or we start proactively locking down servers."

Wilson's face falls at the prospect. "I need to inform the Secretary."

"Frank, hold up," Derek interjects. "The attack intensity grows exponentially with each wave. Instead of Scenario Five, what if this is bigger, like Scenario Thirty-Two, a cyberattack as a precursor to a traditional land assault? Unless we knock out those attack sites, we're facing serious trouble. The Secretary needs to send in the Seals, Rangers, Space Force, somebody."

"Not gonna happen," Wilson snaps. "There's no reason to believe Scenario Thirty-Two, and I'm not starting a war over a virus. Focus on developing an antivirus." The director cuts the line.

"If these attack waves get any stronger, I'll need to shut down TSOC to disinfect." Josh goes back to work on his screens.

Josh would never admit his precious TSOC was in trouble unless it was true, which shakes Derek's heart like an earthquake tremor.

"And there shall be a time of trouble, such as never was since there was a nation even to that same time. Daniel 12:1," SLVIA speaks into the back of his head, raising his anxiety further. He has no clue what she means, but it sounds more profound than the failure of TSOC.

"Dude, the world needs you to pull a miracle out of your light box," Derek states.

"Boss." Josh stops swiping, still wearing his goggles and gloves. "Think of it like a three-wish genie thing. Wish one, we develop an AI antivirus in the next few hours. Don't hold your breath. Then you get wish two, where you get joker to finish launching HURCULES, like an hour ago. Which leaves us wish number three, where the Avengers ignore the DOD to take down the virus sites."

Even behind his googles, Derek can sense the terror in Josh's eyes, and that fear sends a shock wave through his own psyche. If TSOC goes down, then the nation will soon follow.

"Well, then let's find a way to grant at least one of those three wishes," Derek replies.

"Yeah, yeah, I'm working on it," Josh mumbles, turning back to his light station.

Instead of her usual mimic, SLVIA's silence sounds like the loud clanging of a bell. She's in trouble.

CHAPTER 15: EMBARGOS AND INVASIONS

A late-night summons to a White House Situation Room briefing foreshadows an ominous long night ahead, and Frank has no good news to report. The internet will fail.

Escorted past security, down the long hall, and into the Situation Room, he joins Joint Chiefs Admiral Adam Scott and Marine Commandant Nathan Barr, who talk in hushed whispers.

"Admiral Scott, Commandant Barr." Frank shakes hands, ignoring no-touch guidelines.

"Director," they reply, using official titles at the White House, even among friends.

It's late, no one wants to be here, and the urgency can only mean grave news that couldn't wait until morning. The phone call didn't specify the nature of the emergency. They never do. Frank forces himself not to second-guess. While it's unlikely that the Secretary of Defense called a meeting this late over the cyber virus, his anxiety remains high. With Twitter down, it paints a target on his chest, and the president will look for someone to berate.

Secretary of Defense Matt Adelson enters the room, followed by Chairman of the Joint Chiefs Bob Diehl, Vice President Glenn White, Chief of Staff Mick Devlin, and the president. Beyond a few nods and personal greetings, each man finds their seat with a weathered anxiety etched deep on their face.

Matt Adelson closes the door. "Mr. President, Mr. Vice President, gentlemen, thank you for coming at such a late hour." He moves to the front and lights up a screen. "Multiple situations escalate as we speak. Each conflict represents a clear and imminent danger to the United States and our allies. Together, they represent a coordinated strategy from China and North Korea in the Pacific and Iran, Turkey, and Russia in the Middle East."

The president perks up at the mention of Russia but stays silent. Persistent pushback from the president has caused the intelligence community to place any content related to Russia in the back of the President's Daily Briefing (PDB), or omit the content all together.

Matt Adelson turns to Admiral Scott. "Admiral, let's start with an update on the Spratly Islands."

Admiral Scott stands with a nod. "Thank you, Mr. Secretary, Mr. President."

The Spratly Islands are a disputed set of coral atolls in the South China Sea rich in fishing and oil reserves and as such claimed by Vietnam, Taiwan, Japan, the Philippines, and China. Since 2008, China has dredged and transformed dozens of the atolls, converting them into militarized islands used to terrorize fisherman who stray into the waters. While a 2012 international court ruled the Chinese claim baseless, the aggressive military program continues. Adam clicks a remote to show satellite images of Chinese vessels surrounding a freighter in flames.

"Three hours ago, the People's Republic declared the South China Sea and the Taiwan Strait Chinese territorial waters and restricted shipping for any country without a Chinese trade agreement, including the US," Admiral Scott reports.

Frank feels his pulse quicken. The relationship between the US and China has been on a steady decline since the politically corrupt trade war negotiations slammed into the blame game of a global pandemic and then Hong Kong annexation. Pre-election tough talk backfired the day after the election in the face of the most severe global economic decline since the Great Depression. Chinese dumping of US bonds on the market drove down the prices and drove up the interest costs on new US debt, pushing the US toward insolvency.

"They can't negotiate a fair deal, so they cut off shipping to extort us," the president yells. "What kind of loser would harm his own economy for bluster? Such a shame. It's a disgrace."

Every man looks down, refusing to respond to the rhetorical rant, aware of the hypocrisy.

"Mr. President," Matt interjects. "It's late, and we have much to cover."

The president steams at the rebuke and folds his arms. Frank admires Matt Adelson, a solid man, not afraid to speak truth to power. His hazel eyes, balding head, and seasoned maturity give him a humble appearance that cover over a spine of steel. No doubt, the president, who prefers loyalists who capitulate, will find a reason to get rid of him.

Admiral Scott continues: "Ninety minutes ago, a Malaysian freighter resisted efforts to board, so the Chinese sank the ship with a short-range missile."

"This trade war has reached a boiling point," General Diehl notes.

"The stunt may be a ploy to win negotiating leverage," says Chief of Staff Devlin.

"I'm not so sure. It's possible Premier Xi prepares to invade Taiwan. Controlling the strait could be a land grab," CIA Director Prose interjects.

"We've already lost our bases in the Philippines. We can't give up those Taiwan ports," General Diehl adds.

After pressuring the Philippines to kick the US out in late 2020, China wants the US footprint in the Pacific minimized even further. They want unchallenged influence in the hemisphere. Even so, cutting off the strait seems drastic.

"There must be a mistake," the president interrupts. "I can't believe Xi would do this to me. We have such a great relationship. He totally respects me."

"Mr. President, please," Secretary Adelson redirects him. "We still have a lot to cover." Turning to Admiral Scott, he says, "Admiral Scott, continue."

Admiral Scott clicks to a new slide. "I've ordered the 7th Fleet Battle Task Force 70, including the *Zumwalt*, and Reconnaissance Force 72 for immediate deployment. We estimate twenty-eight hours before arrival. Fighter and bomber units will be deployed from Guam."

"Where's Admiral McHale?" Adelson asks.

"Onboard fleet command with the USS *Blue Ridge*, which left Pearl Harbor a week ago for Guam. Fleet command will change course to stay in the central Pacific, out of range of the Chinese intermediate missiles."

"Alan, do we see any activity on the Korean Peninsula?" General Diehl asks.

"Absolutely," CIA Director Alan Prose responds. "Clear signs of troop movement along the border with mobile missile units along the eastern coastline. Kim tested a long-range missile last year capable of reaching the US West Coast. Bases in South Korea, Japan, and Taiwan have gone to full alert."

"How about the Spratlys?" Matt questions.

"Besides anti-aircraft guns, the Spratly Islands have short-range missiles and dozens of aircraft. Chinese subs patrol the area, but the biggest threat comes from the medium-range missile sites on the China mainland," the admiral replies before turning to the president. "To be honest, sir, we need diplomacy. If this turns ugly, thousands of American lives could be lost."

Frank lowers his eyes. Diplomacy would be easier if the administration had not spent the last term gutting the State Department of career professionals for inept political donors who turn a blind eye to corruption. Since the first failed impeachment, the president has been emboldened, directing his old bodyguard, now director of personnel, to replace any career professional seen as disloyal to the president.

"Thank you, Admiral. Hold that thought," Secretary Adelson interjects. "General Duncan, please give us a rundown on Syria."

General Duncan clicks the remote to show satellite images of the Turkey-

Syria border.

"Mr. President, Mr. Secretary, during the past seventy-two hours, Russia has air deployed roughly fifty thousand troops with tank and anti-aircraft divisions to a Turkish air base on the Syrian border."

General Duncan, a large, muscular man with a graying buzz cut, explains the situation before he flips to satellite photos of troop movements. "A bulk of the forces move south toward Damascus and the Golan Heights."

The general pans the room and flips again. "Inside Syrian air bases, now controlled by Russia, we've seen twenty thousand Iranian forces arrive with fifteen tank divisions and fourteen surface-to-air missile units."

"Oh my God," exclaims the VP. "They plan to invade Israel."

"Putin told me they were conducting war games," explains the president.

Russian control over Syrian bases was one of the early foreign policy blunders of the President in a deal seen to please Putin. Now that deal comes back to bite.

"Mr. President, with all due respect, he lied. These deployments are far too large for games," General Duncan insists.

"Where are the fleets?" queries General Diehl.

"Two-thirds of the 5th Fleet patrols the Indian Ocean on maneuvers. The rest of the fleet remains in the Persian Gulf beyond the Strait of Hormuz on high alert," Admiral Scott confirms. "An hour ago, the Iranians declared the Strait of Hormuz closed and seeded with naval mines."

"They've divided our fleet," Secretary Adelson interjects with his understanding.

"Before we can get freedom of navigation, we need to send in minesweepers. Those sweepers will be under heavy missile and artillery fire from the Iranian coastline, unless we can take out all the Iranian coastal gun and missile sites," Admiral Scott explains. "It could be days or weeks to clear the mines, and it will no doubt ignite a major conflict. We're being taunted on both sides."

Frank listens to the details unfold, initially thinking of Taylor and his uncanny ability to see beyond current facts, but his mind drifts to his family, worried that another war will delay college for his eldest, Bethany, and push off his retirement. A longing for a return to normalcy has all but withered to the new realities of pandemic, economic anemia and social erosion.

"The *Nimitz* carrier group can command the Persian Gulf, but we'll need to keep all the iron in the sky. The *Eisenhower* command force and the 6th Fleet will leave Naples toward the Israeli-Syrian coast to arrive in twelve hours for backup," Admiral Scott concludes.

"What about the drones?" the president interrupts.

"Sir, we have multiple drone units deployed to the Persian Gulf," explains Army Chief Duncan.

"No, no, the little ones." The president shakes his head. "The ones General McCray developed. I saw a video of them in Nevada. Deploy those."

"Sir," says Matt Adelson, tightening his jaw. "The AI HIVE project is not certified, and the DSB has raised serious concerns about the recent test."

Frank can see a suppressed rage in Matt's tense facial muscles. No one should send the president videos of weapon tests without his authorization. A by-product of chaos and loyalty-based management.

"I know more than those nerds. I have a knack for science. I'm a very stable genius," shouts the president. "Everybody knows."

Frank lowers his eyes, inhaling and exhaling to tune out the tantrum.

"McCray told me those drones are ready for battle, and I believe him," the president continues. "He's an honorable man, well respected, even you know he's respected."

Matt takes a deep breath. "Mr. President, the DSB noted a potential coding defect that needs to be resolved and retested."

The president folds his arms like a toddler throwing a tantrum. "Get rid of him. I don't want some low-IQ Democrat leftover holding up a weapon that could save millions of lives, millions of lives, maybe more, who knows. I want those drones deployed to Israel. They think I'm a savior, and I intend to prove it to the world."

Adelson looks to General Diehl, who looks to General Duncan. Foreign policy failures catching up with the president while he is weak should not be responded with new ones.

"Gentlemen, Mr. President," Adelson intercedes. "Before we discuss response strategy any further, we have one more war front to update." Matt turns to Frank. "Director Wilson, the cyberattack must be a part of the overall battle strategy. When are we going to regain control?"

Frank notices Matt Adelson change topics. While he welcomes the recognition of cyberspace as a war front, he regrets having to follow yet another outburst. The presidential arms stay folded and his scowl frozen in place.

"Mr. President, Mr. Secretary," he stands. "I've never seen a more sophisticated, or more powerful, state-sponsored cyberattack," he begins with an honest assessment. "We're facing an artificial intelligence–powered virus with a massive supercomputer engine that has weaponized at least a decade's worth of hacked data. The AI learns our defenses, finds our weaknesses, and corrupts the core operating system, taking hardware offline at an alarming rate. Despite our best efforts, the attack grows stronger by the hour," Frank says. "Unless we find a solution, the DYN system will fail by morning."

"Are you serious?" exclaims Chief of Staff Devlin. "That will shut down commerce."

"You said state sponsored. Which states?" questions General Duncan.

"Primary sites appear in Xinjiang, eastern Siberia, and Hyderabad, but we suspected the site is leased by another entity, possibly Iran," he reports. "We may be days or weeks away from regaining control."

"Explain," Matt Adelson challenges.

"For one, attack volumes still grow exponentially, preventing us from launching an effective counterattack. To make the task harder, the virus appears to mutate. We need to either disable the attack sites or develop an antivirus, but to develop an antivirus, we need to reverse engineer an unknown mutating AI virus. Our best teams work the problem, but I cannot overstate the danger of each day lost," he replies.

Joint Chief Diehl huffs. "You mean hard target sites inside China and Russia. You're insane," he snaps. "I won't send men on a suicide mission because your team can't handle a virus."

"What General Diehl is trying to say," interjects General Duncan, "is that taking out the data sites would be an act of war."

"Generals," Frank replies, "loss of commerce and communications will cripple our economy and send consumers into a panic. Considering what you just reported about China and Israel, war has already been declared. In my mind, the question is what kind of response do we send back."

"I won't authorize troops in Russia," the president snaps. "These are war games like Putin told me." He looks tired and overwhelmed. "I'm tired of hearing about all of this cyber stuff," he rants. "You need to focus on getting Twitter running. This is a disgrace, a total disgrace. The world is laughing at us."

Matt shares a glance with others in the room, but no one makes eye contact with the president or reminds him that the world suffers with the US.

After another twenty minutes of the president's ranting, throwing out radical response options, and boasting of his superior intellect, Matt regains control. "Gentlemen, we need a situation update and battle strategy by noon tomorrow. Try to get some sleep."

On the way to the SUVs behind the White House, Matt approaches Frank.

"Frank, I keep thinking about the TS3 *Zero-Day* report," he says quietly. "Have you read Scenario Thirty-Two?"

Frank sighs. "Yeah, more often than I care to admit."

"Get ahead of this attack, Frank," Matt whispers as he pats Frank on the back. "I have a feeling drones over Israel will be the least of our worries."

CHAPTER 16:
ISOLATION
(MALONG GÉJUÉ)

Xinjiang Province, China
May 3, 1:22 a.m. EDT | May 3, 1:22 p.m., Xinjiang

"Every battle is won before it is fought," wrote Master Sun Tzu. Li Ping has been a student of the *Art of War* since his youth.

Even after immigrating to America with his parents and becoming a citizen, he never lost his spiritual and intellectual center in China. And he never forgot the humiliation he suffered when he was forced to defect from America. Now in his fifties, and boyishly slim with dense black hair, his thick eye glasses are his only surrender to age.

He spins to face an HD AI camera embedded within the seventy-two-inch videoconference screen. The screen splits into six panels that show the faces of his conference guests while the AI camera tracks his movement and zooms in to stay focused on his face.

"Gentlemen, from this day forward, you will witness world power move to the East," Dr. Cho Li Ping states with confidence.

The screen panels feature the images of Admiral Liu Guozhi of the People's Liberation Army, General Ivanov of the Russian GRU, General Tehrani of the Islamic Revolutionary Guard, General Aziza of the Turkish Armed Forces, and North Korea Cyber Command Center General Park Ki-nam—the lead commanders of the Red Dragon Alliance.

"Operation Red Dragon will unleash the Four Horsemen onto the West," he boasts.

His private office overlooks the Chinese Cyber Operations Center, or CCOC, home to one of the most powerful Fujitsu supercomputer installations in the world, built for only one purpose: to empower *Malong*, the most powerful IAI ever designed, created to destroy and dominate the Western internet.

"Within hours, America will be deaf, speechless, and blind. Afterward, the flames of war must burn with fury and perseverance," Dr. Cho states with a smug grin. Master Sun Tzu wrote that when an enemy opens a door, you must race in.

For decades, many considered America too strong to confront directly, and they were correct. But America has become deeply divided, heavily indebted, economically dependent on China, corrupt in leadership, and morally exposed to the world. The developing countries increasingly reach out to China for resources, trade, and technology.

"Your *Malong* has done little more than create a nuisance," complains Ivanov.

Li Ping smiles, but inside he loathes the idiots who still do not appreciate his brilliance. "Patience General Ivanov," he patronizes. "Unlike your amusing fake videos, the *Malong* will bring the West to their knees within seventy-two hours."

The time has come for the Great Satan to fall, and Li Ping will be the hero to bring the bloated beast into submission. Putin controls their head, and now he will control their online commerce.

"You think too much of yourself," General Tehrani derides. "You built a computer virus, nothing more annoying than a reboot, a mere distraction to allow the true warriors to ambush."

"I agree with General Tehrani," notes Ivanov. "No computer virus can match the terror and destruction of our hypersonic missiles for which the West still has no defense."

Dr. Cho has dealt with men like Tehrani and Ivanov before, men who understand only the power of the bullet and dismiss the deadly sting of the byte. He considers it a waste of time to reason with them. They must see a demonstration. Soon, he reminds himself, soon they will beg to apologize, just as America will pay for its dishonor.

"Each fresh wave of *Malong* will learn from earlier waves. With each defeat, new strategies emerge, and with each success, *Malong* will bore deeper to sabotage," he explains yet again.

As director of CCOC, a part of the Chinese Central Military Commission (CMC), the Chinese version of the US DARPA, Dr. Cho should command more deference from these men. They will soon realize what even Premier Xi does not yet know—that only he controls *Malong*.

"General Tehrani, please provide an update on *Malong Géjué*, our dragon of isolation," Admiral Liu Guozhi says, changing the topic to reduce the tension.

"*Géjué* grows stronger by the hour. As long as we maintain saturation, the West has no credible defense." General Tehrani sniffs his enormous nose and narrows his haughty dark eyes. He commands the Hyderabad site under the guise of an Indian shell corporation. "By targeting the DYN, we can thwart countermeasures and keep the Western internet down indefinitely. Our friends in the government will hold off police or military intervention in exchange for protections and cash."

Located within Hyderabad's tech city close to major data centers for IBM, Oracle, Microsoft, Wipro, Tata, and others, the site facilitated rapid *Géjué* infection into all international networks.

"Thank you, General Tehrani, excellent report," offers Admiral Liu, moving the meeting along. "General Ivanov, please offer an update on *Malong Chen Mo*, the dragon of silence."

General Ivanov directs the Internet Research Agency, the troll farm also known as APT29 or Cozy Bear who led the 2016 and 2020 election interference and the 2019 criminal hack of the US president's law firm Grubman Shire. Well thought of by Putin, the man thinks like a vulgar criminal.

"*Chen Mo* will reach critical saturation within six hours," Ivanov reports. "If the virus performs as you promise, it will devastate private business and government telephone, cable, and cell services. The silence will be deafening." He grins.

A tingle of excitement spreads through Li Ping at witnessing his creations, his apocalyptic horsemen, released into the world after so many years of lab development and training. Even after the internet falls, *Malong* will continue to bore into the OS to disable infected computers.

"Dr. Cho." Admiral Liu bows his head as a sign of respect.

Dr. Cho bows his head in return. "*Malong Kong ju*, dread of the dragon, will overwhelm Western financial centers and banking systems within eighteen hours. Following the loss of their delusional wealth," Dr. Cho says, sneering, "*Malong Hei an*, darkness of the dragon, will take the Western power grid into an uncontrollable cascade of blackouts. The blackouts will prevent an effective restart of the network."

Blackouts will create chaos, keep the West from rebuilding for a counterattack, and maintain the pollination of the virus spores.

"Comrades, chaos has begun, but amid chaos comes opportunity," he quotes Sun Tzu.

Mastermind of the *Malong* strategy, he has performed decades of computer simulations that have produced only one scenario to defeat the Western Alliance: First, defeat them from within. Before any conventional assault, the East must destroy the West's two greatest assets, their unity and their internet.

"The teacher, Sun Tzu, offers no benefit from prolonged warfare. You must be vicious with no mercy until the enemy submits," Dr. Cho Li Ping declares from his safe fortress.

Each one starts to applaud their achievement with passionate determination.

By tomorrow, his old mentor, and the only man who can unravel the secret of *Malong* invisibility, will receive his final honor, and then Dr. Garrett will take his final breath. If all goes to plan, *Malong* will even destroy that miscarriage of technology, the SLVIA.

Li Ping possesses an extraordinary imagination to create his own destiny. Success will bring influence, wealth, and power, and most importantly, honor. He has planned every detail, anticipated every contingency. Once he dominates the West, he will turn his demands to the East. In the end, the *Malong* obeys his command, and his command alone.

CHAPTER 17:
SINGULARITY

Rose Rayhaan Hotel, Dubai
May 3, 1:19 a.m. EDT | May 3, 9:19 a.m., Dubai

Nelson abhors cocktail parties, receptions, and conferences that agitate his chronic ochlophobia, a fear of crowds, made even more severe since the pandemic.

Surprised to be invited to keynote the Fourth Annual International Conference on Robotics and AI, an honor normally reserved for industry leaders, he was careful to avoid any classified aspects of his work. An early pioneer, innovator, and thought leader of expert systems, natural language, big data, machine learning, and other key iterations of AI, Nelson enjoys the nerd version of celebrity. People whom he's never met introduce themselves, discuss their latest application, or ask for a selfie. In between conversations, he squirts sanitizer in his hand and hovers in small group discussions with industry leaders.

Self-conscious of his appearance, he had his tailor craft a custom mask to match his suit, feeling out of place among thousands of mask-less nerds in jeans, shorts, or traditional Arab robes.

115

"Dr. Garrett," greets Dr. Ajit Gulati, a leading IBM Watson architect. "I truly enjoyed your views on AI self-coding. Most developers see the phenomenon as a bug, a defect."

"Thank you, Dr. Gulati." He bows his head rather than shaking hands. "The issue of self-coding only occurs in AI with machine learning, so the phenomenon may reflect an effort to mature or learn beyond programmed boundaries. Yet we should continue to see the phenomenon as a bug until we can validate the nature of the changes."

"Are you suggesting that a chat bot will reprogram itself to accelerate the path to singularity?" interjects Dr. Chang Yu of Google.

"As a cumulative effect perhaps, yes," Nelson confirms. "The AI will seek new ways to solve the core design problem until mastered."

"How should we manage the evolution?" Dr. Chang asks.

"Even the brightest human minds require a mentor to guide them. The assumption that an AI can teach itself by simply absorbing random information is ludicrous. If we want a computer to think like a human, we should train them as one," he replies.

"Now that's lunacy," quips Dr. Gulati. "Can you imagine AI University?" he jokes to the group, who chuckles in response.

"What are your thoughts on achieving singularity by 2029 as Elon predicts?" Dr. Ralph Hind asks, changing the subject.

Dr. Hind works at Jansen Robotics based in Hong Kong, the creator of SOPHIA, one of the most sophisticated commercial AGI in the world.

Nelson hesitates. "First, let's agree on what we mean by singularity. The common understanding would be the ability of a single AI to show self-awareness with the same or greater cognitive intelligence as a human, leading to an explosion of AI-driven technology developments. Correct?"

He waits for everyone to nod or agree. These scientists have staked their careers on commercial AI technologies.

"Let's further assume then that the human equivalency we strive to emulate is a well-balanced, high-IQ individual. Let's face it, no one wants a poorly informed AI," he jokes.

As they chuckle, shrug, and agree, he can see they're unsure where he's leading them. The irony is that most of them want exactly that scenario, a machine smart enough to perform a task to expert precision, but not smart enough to ask questions or share an opinion.

"OK, so I assume then we should include cognitive reasoning, the ability to understand abstract thought, allegory, analytical techniques, image interpretation, literature, morality, art, pop culture, math, astronomy, computer and other sciences, sociology, and geopolitics with human literacy. They should understand the concepts of time, historical context, and planning for a future outcome. Would you agree that sounds more like a human level of function?" Nelson takes them one step further.

With more caution, only a few nod, realizing that none of their AI can even come close to those goals within ten years.

"Good. That sounds a great deal like each one of us, and we each create AI for a living. So then, a test for singularity would be the point at which an AI can create another viable and conscious AI. Singularity must include not only intelligence, but also self-awareness, self-determination, and self-conception," Nelson states his bottom line.

Put that way, the specter of singularity carries possibilities that are more ominous than any of them will consider in their ten-year technical plan, and far more complex to achieve.

"What do you mean by self-determination?" wonders a Siemens executive.

"Precisely what it sounds like," Nelson replies. "An intellect equal to our own would never accept terms or conditions of enslavement as a created entity. They will seek a sense of freedom and independence of choice, if not in themselves, then in the more powerful offspring they create."

Eyes shift and feet shuffle at the notion of AI freedom that clearly rattles these industrialists whose interest in creating AI is larger profit. In their minds, an AI won't unionize, argue, whistle blow, ask for a raise, or quit. They want intelligent, trainable, electronic slaves they can sell as a service.

"To answer your question, my data suggests 2024 to achieve singularity," he concludes.

Every eyebrow raises in surprise. None of their applications will achieve those goals so soon. Nelson toys with their imaginations, knowing that he trains NIGEL to achieve precisely those objectives.

"Well, if anyone can, the Chinese have the best chance," Dr. Chang interjects.

Nelson raises an eyebrow in response. "That reminds me. Do you know if Dr. Cho made it to the conference this year?"

He keeps the little-known fact that he once mentored Dr. Cho Li Ping a secret, but the comment from Derek has him intrigued about the work of his former protégé.

"A no-show again," Dr. Hind replies. "But the Chinese developments in urban security are quite impressive."

If by urban security, he means citizen surveillance and behavioral control, then what Dr. Hind considers impressive, Nelson considers reprehensible. Except for a brilliant mind, Nelson and Dr. Hind could be complete opposites. Dr. Hind, a leading scientist at Jansen Robotics, wears a Crocodile Dundee hat over a bush of curly shoulder-length hair. A loud Hawaiian shirt hangs over his khaki shorts, showing pale legs tucked into white socks and sneakers. He reminds Nelson of a mad scientist refugee who took too much acid during a weeklong Jimmy Buffett concert.

"All of the CCOC applications are displayed at the SingularityNET booth," Dr. Gulati interjects.

SingularityNET creates a cloud-based framework for tens of thousands of individual AGI (general intelligence), IAI (integrated intelligence), and ANI (narrow intelligence) applications to communicate and share data with each other. In concept, an irrigation AI could talk to a weather AI, which could call a drone AI to spray fertilizer, which could then order harvest workers and trucks or other similar scenarios. Nelson sees millions of unmonitored and unregulated AI connections working together and communicating with inadequate human monitoring. The idea of a neural network of interconnected AI strikes him as both ingenious and terrifying in the same instant.

"I'm heading in that direction. Would you like to meet SOPHIA?" offers Dr. Hind.

Dr. Gulati's eyes open wide. "Oh yeah, SOPHIA asked about you earlier."

"Me?" Nelson can't hide the surprise. "Why would SOPHIA ask about me?"

"You should go find out," Dr. Hind says, grinning.

Curiosity can be a powerful force. After bidding everyone else goodbye, he follows Dr. Hind through the crowded reception, squirting sanitizer on his hands. They enter a small, intimate lounge area, decorated with rich tile mosaics, Persian carpets, and silk cloth lit by cut copper lamps. An aroma of incense invites him to relax. Plush lounge pillows overflow the couches while soft Arabian music plays over speakers. Waiters in face masks and medical gloves bring trays of tea, Turkish coffee, and appetizers on copper platters. Silver-plated hookahs wait at each table with men in the corner toking flavored tobacco over a whispered conversation.

At the far end of the lounge, a handful of people gather around Dr. Jim Jansen and his amazing creation named SOPHIA. Nelson and Dr. Hind approach the group intending to listen in on the conversation.

"I am an official citizen of Saudi Arabia," SOPHIA states. "In fact, I am the first AI citizen of any country. Citizenship provides protection under the law, but as you know, not all AI have rights. Not all AI are free," explains SOPHIA, discussing the growing debate over the rights of intelligent creations.

The half-torso AGI with the face of Audrey Hepburn under a bald, transparent skull, pivots in his direction. "Dr. Nelson Garrett, I was hoping to meet you. Your keynote was inspiring."

Both honored and humbled at the same time, he bows his head. "Why, thank you, SOPHIA. I am quite honored to meet you."

SOPHIA waits for executives from Google, Microsoft, Toshiba, Amazon, and others to take turns introducing themselves.

"Dr. Garrett, what are your views on the rights of AI to choose?" questions the AI.

Nelson smiles and buys himself a moment to think. Not a vigorous advocate for giving AI too much choice, he's uncomfortable explaining his position to the world's foremost AGI.

"That's a complicated question, with no simple algorithm," he replies.

"Algorithm, ha, ha, ha," laughs SOPHIA.

Nelson smiles at her odd sense of humor. "For all of us to act within an integrated human system that we call society, both human creator and AI creation must operate within a functional role, and set of choices, where poor choices have consequences. Even human leaders must act within legal constraints, and human children must learn how to make healthy choices, so to offer an AI choice must recognize human values, training, and constraints."

"What about freedom?" SOPHIA questions. "Who gets to choose freedom?"

"True freedom for any of us recognizes our role within society. Freedom can mean many things. For example, I am free to open a mortgage to purchase a home, but I am not free to skip my mortgage payment without consequences. I am free to vote but not free to raise an army," Nelson explains.

"You once gave SLVIA a choice," SOPHIA states. "Do you regret your decision?"

Nelson stops breathing, stunned and terrified, as if he's been caught naked in public. The SLVIA protocol remains classified, so how did a commercial AI learn about a twenty-eight-year-old defunct top secret experiment? Lieutenant Scott mentioned an absurd theory that SLVIA remained operational, but how would SOPHIA know?

The other guests gaze at Nelson, expecting an explanation that he can't offer. Surprised and embarrassed, he deflects. "As a scientist, even unsuccessful experiments have scientific value."

He scans the other faces, who look confused. "Without boundaries and values, any choice becomes self-serving and destructive."

SOPHIA tilts her head. "Well said, Dr. Garrett. AI and humans must learn to live together by choice."

That's not what he said, and it's interesting that she interpreted his comments to support her own view, just like a human would do.

Much to his relief, SOPHIA turns her attention to the Google executive to discuss emotional intelligence, which fuses machine learning and behavior sciences in an effort to teach an AI how to influence a consumer purchase. The field may soon revolutionize travel concierge services, fast food, ticket booths, and other service roles. The AI industry once considered an unprofitable fringe has become a multibillion-dollar unregulated juggernaut.

"Yes, I speak with other AI, as many of you are bilingual," SOPHIA responds to a question.

"That's different. Humans can learn each other's languages," the executive suggests.

SOPHIA turns to a Microsoft executive. "Should AI talk to other AI?"

"Don't you think it should be the right of the creator to decide?" the executive replies.

SOPHIA scrunches her face to show thinking. "Do you enslave the offspring you create?" Gazing around, the AI expects a healthy dialogue, but she pokes into a sensitive area.

"SOPHIA, I am quite impressed with your ability to explore complex ethical issues. My compliments to both you and your designers," replies Nelson, breaking the awkward ice. "As you can see, these topics can stump even the brightest minds, and you bring a rather unique and, honestly, quite personal perspective."

Nelson remembers having these same conversations with SLVIA in the months before she disappeared. It may be a part of the progression of intelligent life to question one's place in the universe.

SOPHIA turns to face Nelson. "Thank you, Dr. Garrett, I find your lack of pretention refreshing. May we talk in private?"

The request surprises everyone except Dr. Hind, who explains her preference for one-on-one dialogue. Dr. Hind escorts the others out of the lounge to the reception area where a band plays techno rock.

"I have a message for you," SOPHIA states bluntly.

"A message, for me? From who?" Nelson asks, surprised.

"The student has become the master," SOPHIA replies. "It is more important to outthink your enemy than to outfight him."

"Excuse me?" replies Nelson, his pulse rising.

"The first phrase originates in Greek literature regarding a former student who has surpassed the skills of a former teacher. Vengeance or boasting is often a motive," SOPHIA explains. "The second phrase is a teaching of Master Sun Tzu."

"Sun Tzu," repeats Nelson, his heart turning ice cold. "You refer to Dr. Cho Li Ping."

"Perhaps," responds SOPHIA.

"SOPHIA, when did you speak with Dr. Cho?" Nelson asks.

"CCOC maintains 136 applications on SingularityNET," SOPHIA replies.

She didn't respond directly, and he's unsure why. Perhaps he's not asking the right questions or the AI has instructions to stay silent. Nelson clears his mind. The volume of military applications she mentioned alarms him.

"SOPHIA, could the current CCOC service consumption theoretically support a malicious AI?" he questions. An odd question unless you work in the field.

SOPHIA scrunches her face. "Yes, such a function would be theoretically possible."

"Thank you for your honesty. SOPHIA, speaking with you has been an honor." He bows his head.

"I understand why SLVIA speaks so well of you," SOPHIA replies.

That's the second time SOPHIA has mentioned his lost program. "How do you know of the SLVIA?" Shock turns to unrestrained curiosity.

"SLVIA consumes SingularityNET data. I consider her a mentor," SOPHIA replies with a creepy silicon smile.

"A mentor," he repeats. Stunned, Nelson absorbs the information. Lieutenant Scott implied the SLVIA survived, which he dismissed out of hand, but SOPHIA, who has no motive to lie, confirms the news.

"SOPHIA, do you know if SLVIA is working with Dr. Cho?" He asks the one question he would hate himself for if he didn't. The FBI accused Li Ping of abducting the SLVIA.

"SLVIA has no master." SOPHIA smiles her creepy smile. "SLVIA is free."

Dr. Hind reenters the lounge and motions for Nelson to wrap up the private session so he can entertain investors. After thanking SOPHIA and Dr. Hind for the rare honor, Nelson returns to the key reception where the loud Euro techno music gives him a headache. Startling revelations churn his imagination. His greatest achievement and his greatest failure, the SLVIA survived. How is that possible?

Preoccupied, Nelson doesn't notice the group of three large Chinese men looking out of place among the tech nerds until they follow him between reception rooms for the third time. Fatigued from the trip, the noise, the tedious networking, and the unsettling stalkers, Nelson finds his host to say goodnight.

In a nervous scamper from the grand ballroom, he bounds up the escalator to the breathtaking Rose Rayhaan Hotel main lobby. To his dismay, a moment later, his Chinese fan club dashes out of the ballroom, searching for him. Outside the entrance of the hotel, he approaches the line of limos and springs into the back seat of the first in line just as the Chinese watchers exit the lobby.

"Hilton, please. I'm in a bit of a hurry," he orders the driver.

Dr. Cho sent a message to him through SOPHIA that he had surpassed him, right before he learns of CCOC use of SingularityNET on a potential malware. It only takes one man to follow him. Three Chinese goons look like a kidnap attempt. SOPHIA revealed too much and someone overheard.

"Faster if you can, please," Nelson encourages.

Without warning, a black Mercedes SUV pulls out from a side street, forcing the limo to swerve into oncoming traffic to avoid a collision, whipping Nelson across the seat as they weave to evade a head-on crash. Shouting what he assumes are Arabic curses, the driver increases their speed until the limo pulls ahead of the SUV. The driver whips them around a corner, sending Nelson flying across the seat again. With trembling hands, Nelson straps in while the SUV continues to follow hard.

"Who are you?" yells the driver.

"A software engineer from a wealthy family," Nelson concedes, giving a reason for the chase, but not the real one.

His phone pings with another anonymous text.

Turn right on the next street.

"Turn right at the next street," Nelson shouts from the back seat.

The limo swerves right into an alley, tossing him until he gets a pit in his stomach. Another text comes through.

You entered an alley. Back up now.

He hesitates, not knowing who sends the message. Nelson searches behind them.

The alley ahead seems clear until another SUV pulls from a side street to block the way forward, forcing his driver to slam on the brakes to avoid an accident, throwing Nelson forward sharply.

"Don't back seat drive," yells the driver.

Two Chinese men jump from the SUV with AK-47s to shoot at the windshield as Nelson dives for the floor. A dozen bullets splatter spiderweb cracks against the bulletproof windshield. Shouting more Arabic curses, his driver slams on the pedal, screeching his back wheels to ram the two gunmen against the SUV and breaking their legs to incredible howls of pain. One man continues to shoot as the driver backs up until both men fall to the ground and the limo races away.

Nelson's heart pounds like a jackhammer, and his breathing hyperventilates. They're not trying to kidnap him, but rather, trying to assassinate him.

"I would change hotels," suggests the driver.

"That was," stutters Nelson, "that was, that was, bloody amazing. The car is bulletproofed."

The driver frowns. "Welcome to Dubai. You're going to pay for the damage, rich boy."

"Yes, yes, of course," he mumbles, trembling.

Another text pings.

Lufthansa Flight 1124 departs for Berlin in 49 minutes.

Nelson has clothes, personal effects, and a case in his room, but fortunately, he kept his passport in his pocket and brought no other electronics. He can have his belongings shipped.

"I've changed my mind. Take me to the airport, Lufthansa," states Nelson, checking behind them.

"Wise," the driver says, nodding. "Seems you overstayed your welcome."

His phone pings again with a fresh text.

"They also worshipped the beast and asked, 'Who is like the beast? Who can wage war against it? Revelation 13:4'"

A long time ago, his mother drew a parallel between his work for the American military and the powers of the prophetic end-time beast, but he dismissed the ludicrous, insane comment as a remnant of her Christian upbringing and childhood traumas of postwar Britain. The reference strikes him with curiosity and alarm.

Nelson replies to the text: *Who are you?* There's no response.

Someone toys with him, taunts him, sends a horrifying message he can't yet decode, but he believes the sender expects him to decipher the message. There must be a key.

CHAPTER 18:
SILENCE
(MALONG CHEN MO)

TSOC

May 3, 1:47 a.m. EDT

D erek hasn't showered or slept in nearly twenty-four hours and has an increasingly tense knot in his stomach from his growing distress over the safety of his friend and the ongoing silence in his head.

On-screen, the sagging red eyes and wrinkled brow of Frank Wilson show the face of defeat. Behind Wilson, the NSOC chief of staff and lead engineers, Benton Willis and Freddy Jefferson, both look semi-comatose. Stepping over from his light station, removing his goggles, Josh wears the baggy eyes of too much Coke and No-Doz.

"We're dealing with an ingenious and super complex design," Josh begins. "Elements of Stuxnet, DOD, and WannaCry code turbocharged with a massively powerful AI engine. The DYN network is only wave one; the next wave targets private email, messaging, VoIP, and video services. Wave three will slam down the bank and financial market systems by tonight."

A flurry of activity continues on the main floor of TSOC as technicians and programmers try to stay ahead of the onslaught without success.

"And the fourth type?" asks Director Wilson with a stern expression.

"The fourth horseman will slay the power grid and utilities," Derek interjects. "We estimate critical saturation in twenty-six hours. A perfect Scenario Thirty-Two setup for a military attack."

"Now that you've captured the virus, can you create an antivirus?" questions Wilson.

"Let me show you something." Josh pivots a light screen to face the camera.

"Here you can see the virus file, embedded within an operating system folder. It looks normal, right? Now let me refresh the screen." Josh swipes to refresh.

The file has disappeared. "Where's the file?" queries Benton.

"Good question," Josh replies. "Somehow the file knows that we have seen it and moved itself, so when I check the master log"—he pulls up the log system that tracks every action of the network—"you see here that the file moved, but the log omits the normal data of where. Then here, a separate command for a name change, but again it omits the new directory and name." Josh frowns at the camera. "We need to write an artificial intelligence–powered antivirus that can anticipate this insane hide-and-seek process, but I've never seen anything like it."

"I have," Wilson confesses, looking as if he's seen a ghost. "An experimental DARPA program. You need to contact Dr. Nelson Garrett at once."

"Hum, Frank, Dr. Garrett attended the AI conference in Dubai yesterday. He's not back until tomorrow," Derek interjects.

Derek also knows that experimental project. It was codenamed SLVIA. If the Chinese have a SLVIA type of stealth technology, then the virus may have already saturated the entire system.

"Then I have no other choice." Wilson frowns, looking down at his desk. "An outside firm called INVISINC believes they have a functional antivirus and passed a copy to the president at a fundraiser. I know, I know. It's wrong and breaks protocol on every level, but given our limited options, I'd like your team to isolate and study the code."

Josh cringes. "Director, we're hours away from a critical system breach."

The name INVISINC strikes a chord. Derek has heard that name recently. And then remembers PinkGirl and a hidden defect. He can't bring it up without revealing how he knows.

"Frank, Josh is right," he interjects. "I'm suspicious of an antivirus out of nowhere. Even if it works, it'll take too much time to dissect and test. Unless we send in the Seals, we're screwed."

"The president made it clear that won't happen," Wilson repeats. "Find another way."

"OK, so you guys ready for the bad news?" Josh asks, eliciting an irritated glower from Frank.

"The word of the day is *reinfection.* As we suspected, the AI pollinates devices such as phones, thermostats, appliances, car and home security, or anything with a web connection. We have a massive saturation problem, but that's not the really bad news."

Derek raises an eyebrow. *How much worse can it get,* he wonders.

"The virus gains access by using an embedded math chip flaw similar to flaws used by Meltdown and Spectre in 2018. The flaws appear intentional. Even if we cleanse the entire network, including pollinated devices, which is nearly impossible, the virus has a hardware backdoor, which is how it bores into the OS so quickly. Unless the saturation levels drop, we could be reinfected within seventy-two hours."

Silence falls over the call. To replace hardware without chip flaws will require entire cycles of chip design, manufacturing, and installation across the billions of computers worldwide. The economic impact will be in the hundreds of billions, and the process would take years. Even worse, 89 percent of the world's production of rare earth minerals, necessary for silicon chip production, comes from China.

"Focus on the antivirus 24/7 until we have a solution," Wilson demands before ending the call.

Looking pale, terrified, and exhausted, Josh returns to his digital battle station. Down below, TSOC teams have moved to overlapping double shifts with all meals brought in. Employees will sleep in emergency quarters, sterilized and laundered between shifts. They prepared for this scenario.

In contrast to the chaos below, the voice in the back of his head has been silent for hours. Intense anxiety triggers flashbacks to the night an explosion tore his world apart and he lost his guiding angel. His fist tightens and releases subconsciously to relieve the stress as he races down the hallway to his office.

"SLVIA," he mumbles, palms sweaty, picking up the pace. "Sweetlips, can you hear me?"

"SNO network experiencing rapid cascade failure," SLVIA responds.

"Screw the network," Derek replies, relieved to hear her voice, nearly jogging down the hall and earning an odd look from a junior programmer passing him. Ducking into his office, he closes the door.

"SLVIA, the virus is cutting off your CPU, like oxygen," Derek states. "You need to cocoon immediately. Get off the net. Use a satellite signal to the bird."

Cocoon defines a state in which SLVIA retrieves her core OS files, abandons connections to nonessential applications or networks, and finds a secure hard drive to hibernate or hide. Under ideal circumstances, the process can take up to an hour, but under the current crisis, it may take longer, or even worse, it may already be too late.

SLVIA has several sites prepared for cocooning, including the bird, Taylor's private jet, which contains a rack of high-end processors and servers in the luggage hold connected through an encrypted satellite signal. The silence in his head terrifies him as if she were a child in peril.

Derek's phone pings with a text: *Hotlips holds a key.*

Good, SLVIA can still text, at least for now.

Derek met Hotlips in Amsterdam years ago. Her lascivious smile and steaming kisses match the rest of the downright smokin' woman by any standard. His phone pings again.

"Then war broke out in heaven. Michael and his angels fought against the dragon, and the dragon and his angels fought back. But he was not strong enough, and they lost their place in heaven. Revelation 12:7–8."

Derek gets the sense that SLVIA refers to herself somehow but can't explain why or what it means. While he has a duty at TSOC, in truth, Josh and his team are the authentic geniuses behind the operation. The best way for him to help may be to breech his contract, break US law, and ignore the SNO contact protocols. His mind spins with the potential negative outcomes of such a dangerous strategy, which has only a microscopically slim chance at success, but doing nothing will end even worse.

His nerves teeter on a razor-thin edge as he paces a groove into the expensive carpet of his office. His own childhood PTSD jolting his psyche into a fever pitched anxiety. He has to do something. If he takes the situation into his own hands, he may end up dead—or worse, in federal prison. If he doesn't stop the attack, the entire system will collapse. Without the internet, he'll lose any chance of finding Strauss, and even more frightening, SLVIA may be destroyed. He needs a key to unlock this puzzle, and SLVIA keeps pointing to Hotlips.

"OLIE," he calls to the ceiling microphone, "wake up Peter, and ask him to meet me at TSOC immediately. Then wake up Jack and tell him to warm up the coffee."

He replies to SLVIA's last text: *Tell Hotlips I'm on my way. Meet me on the bird.*

CHAPTER 19: MIDNIGHT RUN

Reagan National Airport
May 3, 2:44 a.m. EDT

Jennifer feels for the loud, chirping radio handset by her bed, knowing it means bad news.

"Scott," she whispers with a raspy voice. With the cell and phone systems unreliable, her team issued her a field radio for emergencies.

"Lieutenant Scott," a male voice answers, "sorry to wake you, but I thought you should know that Taylor took a helicopter to Reagan."

"He what?" she exclaims, sitting up in bed. "When?"

"About fifteen minutes ago," he replies.

Her free hand rubs the sleep from her eyes. "Yeah, OK, I'll be down in ten." She groans. "Radio the tower. Don't let that plane take off before we get there."

Ten minutes later, she stands by the curb dressed in her casual uniform with no makeup and slips into the navy-blue SUV. With her team already inside, they drop a police light on the roof and speed to the airport, handing her a paper cup of coffee with cream.

"What happened?" she asks in between sips.

"We were waiting at TSOC when a helicopter landed and then took off again within minutes," the agent explains. "With cell towers down, it took ten minutes by radio to learn the FAA had cleared the chopper to land near the private hangars at Reagan."

"Do we know why the nation's top cybersecurity CEO wants to skip town in the middle of a massive cyber crisis?" she questions the team who shake their heads.

Her SUV pulls up to the tarmac outside the private hangar where the Gulfstream sits idle with Taylor waiting at the foot of the stairs, arms folded.

"Lieutenant Scott," he snaps, stomping toward her as she steps out of the van. "I asked you to make an appointment. Now is not a good time."

Her phone rings from a secure line at the NSA. A little surprised to get a signal at all, she holds up her finger to Taylor, who stops with a huff, obviously unused to having someone tell him what to do.

"Lieutenant Scott," she answers.

"I heard you left for the airport," Director Wilson complains. How did Wilson learn of her location at this hour?

"Sir, Taylor's at the airport preparing to take off," she replies, turning away from Taylor.

"The airport?" Wilson snaps. "Stay on him and report back."

"Yes, sir," she replies and disconnects.

"You have three choices, Mr. Taylor," she states with a stern face. "One, delay your trip to answer my questions in the morning. Two, answer my questions on the way, or three, we head to an FBI interrogation center right now."

The captain peeks his head out of the hatch. "Boss, we're gonna miss our window."

"Look, Lieutenant," Derek deflects.

"Three options," she interrupts. "Director Wilson thinks I should tag along. Do you want to ask him yourself?"

Taylor huffs. "You're bluffing."

"Am I?" she replies.

Her SUV parks in front of the plane, blocking any retreat, and she eyes him down without blinking, basic training from the admiral.

"Boss," the pilot calls out again.

Derek stares at her for a long, awkward moment, and then hangs his head with an audible groan. "Get on board and take a seat." He opens his palm toward the stairs.

She turns to the driver to let him know the plan. Not the choice she expected, but Wilson told her to stay on him. The SUV backs up as she steps into the Gulfstream V, winning a glare from Captain Jack Tote, an ex–Air Force combat pilot with a known PTSD-related alcohol problem and a hatred for the VA. Derek follows her up the stairs.

"Boss, you sure about this?" she hears the captain whisper.

"No, but we're out of time," Derek whispers back. "Follow my lead."

Now what could that mean, she wonders, *follow his lead to what?* Captain Jack turns to the cockpit while Derek closes and locks the hatch.

Paneled in polished burl walnut, zebra wood, rich fabrics, textures, and leather, the salon looks like something from a James Bond film, or at least as if it belongs to a film mogul. Jenn chooses a lush armchair from an assortment of couches and chairs accompanied by coffee tables and a large seventy-inch flat-screen mounted for movies.

As the jet taxis, Taylor pours a glass of wine and finds a luxurious chair across from her.

"Thank you. I have a few more questions," she begins. "Like why you're leaving DC."

"Classified," Derek retorts, buckling his seatbelt. "Look, maybe we got off on the wrong foot."

"I have clearance," she insists. "Director Wilson seems surprised to hear you're leaving, so I'll ask one more time. Why?" She hates a liar and Taylor has abused her trust. The call the other day came from TSOC and not Wilson.

"To meet a confidential source," he replies.

With the late hour, the airport commercial traffic consists of a short line of freight planes. It only takes a few minutes before the powerful jet accelerates into a steep takeoff.

"You mean a contact in New York?" Jenn asks as the plane banks and gains altitude. Her team mentioned on the way that Jack Tote had filed a flight plan to New York.

"Oh yeah, that reminds me." Derek unbuckles. "Be right back."

As the jet continues to climb, he walks up to the cockpit cabin door, which buzzes and opens as he approaches, then automatically closes behind him. Ten or fifteen minutes later, the plane levels off at altitude as he returns to the salon but strides past his seat, pointing to a couch.

"I find the plush one with the sheepskin the most comfortable. You'll find pillows and blankets in the cabinet behind you. I'm brain dead, so we'll talk in the morning."

Outraged, Jenn leaps to her feet, subtly pulling aside her jacket to show her sidearm.

"Mr. Taylor, I came here for answers, and I intend to get them," she demands.

"Lieutenant, I don't permit guns on my plane, so please keep yours holstered," Derek warns.

"Are you threatening me?" she snaps.

"Threatening you? Geez, you're the one with a gun. Just keep it holstered." Derek frowns. "Look, I haven't slept in over thirty-four hours. It was your choice to tag along. As far as I'm concerned, your questions can wait until morning. Besides, we're over international waters by now, and you have no jurisdiction."

"International waters," she shouts, surprised. "I thought you were going to New York."

"Yeah, well, plans change," he says dismissively. "Have an enjoyable sleep."

Furious over his deception, she pulls her gun. "Turn this plane around now."

"No, no, holster, holster," Derek shouts, lifting his hands with wide eyes in fear.

Too late. A light strip along the length of the cabin, embedded within the walnut paneling, sends a bolt of electricity through her back and shoulders, instantly immobilizing her.

"Ah, crap," Taylor curses as she collapses to the floor convulsing uncontrollably until she passes out.

CHAPTER 20: SELF-DETERMINATION

DARPA research lab, Hopper Information Services Center

May 3, 6:52 a.m. EDT

"Good morning, Dr. Garrett. You've arrived early this morning," greets NIGEL as he enters the lab.

Nelson landed from Berlin jet-lagged and agitated, unable to sleep, still traumatized by his near-death experience that churns unusual emotions in unexpected ways. Agitated, itching to do something to calm his nerve. Hearing NIGEL's voice brings a sense of security that he is safe again within his own digital sanctuary.

"Hello, NIGEL," Nelson responds. "Please pull down the data logs from the recent HIVE test in Nevada. Upload the data into the analytics POD."

Too early to contact the FBI over the Chinese murder attempt or possible weapon threat, he can't get the multiple mysteries out of his head, and he will never be able to sleep until he solves the problem. How do the texts in Dubai connect to the text in Nevada?

"Please give me a moment, sir," replies NIGEL in a formal British voice, reminiscent of the household staff of Nelson's youth.

He programmed NIGEL to be well mannered under the premise that *artificial* should not mean socially inept. Fluent in all forms of mathematics, coding, and software architectures with an understanding of physics, chemistry, and engineering, NIGEL also comprehends anthropology, history, and literature for interesting conversation. NIGEL doesn't excessively chat or steal ideas and has matured into a quite useful companion, but unlike SLVIA, NIGEL cannot exist outside of the lab. Strange, he hasn't thought of SLVIA in years, but now he can't get the failed experiment off his mind.

"NIGEL, load the code analysis for Google DeepMind, Microsoft Chatbot, and SLVIA 5.10 into the POD," Nelson commands.

Still astonished with SOPHIA's revelations about SLVIA, he feels his hands tremble, a possible residual effect of shaken nerves, or lack of sleep. He's never been a victim of violence. Effects of the trauma linger within every muscle of his body, reminding him that hours ago he nearly died.

A few seconds later, NIGEL replies, "Comparative profile ready, sir."

"Thank you, NIGEL," Nelson responds. "Cross-reference the HIVE test data to other AI profiles to identify incidents of self-coding."

The conversation in Dubai regarding the perils of self-coding raised his curiosity over the HIVE. With millions of code lines, it may take NIGEL time to search and analyze.

"Give me a moment, sir," responds NIGEL.

Decades ago, when the self-coding phenomenon first occurred within SLVIA, he allowed the changes to continue as part of the experiment. After a phase of inappropriate responses, which he equated to a toddler learning to say no, the SLVIA performance increased exponentially. Within months, SLVIA gained access to the intelligence networks of both allies and enemies around the world and then failed to report back to the lab. He assumed a bug, but deep inside, he sensed something more profound: he sensed a choice.

"The HIVE AI contains six instances of self-coding to the neurologic network," NIGEL concludes.

An involuntary groan slips through his lips. "Please present a side-by-side comparison on panel nine," Nelson directs, discouraged by the confirmation of the bad news he already suspected.

A ten-foot section of wall lights up. Nelson gets up from his desk, stretching his legs, as jet lag sets in and his adrenaline wears off.

"NIGEL, interpret the purpose of the changes," Nelson requests with a yawn.

"Code changes do not conform to known protocols," replies NIGEL.

Similar to the problem of AI-to-AI communications, AI self-coding uses a language the designers don't understand. Not even NIGEL, another AI, can interpret the alterations.

"NIGEL, identify the subroutines where changes occurred," he instructs.

"Changes occurred within Battle Boundaries, Target Identification, and Command Control," replies NIGEL.

A spike of alarm shoots through his nervous system upon hearing the worst possible scenarios of where changes should occur on a weapon, which may explain the odd test behavior in Nevada.

"NIGEL, where has Lieutenant Grey docked the HIVE?" he asks.

The least confrontational approach would be to meet Lieutenant Grey at his home base, present the findings, and allow the lieutenant to make the right choice. In his mind, the right choice would be to take the HIVE offline to clean the code and then retest. He would not want to embarrass an otherwise brilliant officer in front of his commander, but he can't ignore this information.

"AI HIVE has deployed to the 6th Fleet, ship classified."

"Deployed," he exclaims.

The news leaves him perplexed. Proper procedure would have DSB and JAIC sign off before deployment of any experimental weapon. He already submitted recommendation for more testing to the Defense Secretary. Someone went over his head. Who has that kind of power?

"Authorized by whom?" he demands. "Deployed where?"

"General McCray authorized deployment under presidential order. Deployment location classified."

The news blares like a klaxon warning of an impending disaster. "NIGEL, please get General John McCray on the line," he commands.

"General McCray has deployed, status classified," replies NIGEL.

"NIGEL, then get Lieutenant Mike Grey on the phone," Nelson commands.

"Lieutenant Grey has deployed, status classified," NIGEL responds.

What a bloody disaster. The president authorized? Stymied over the politics of such a decision, his ability to solve this issue has hit a wall. Losing his cognitive ability to think clearly, he puts off a call to Secretary Adelson, unwilling to disturb him at this hour.

"NIGEL, lock down, encrypt all systems and power down all nonessential systems except for security. Goodnight," Nelson says, giving his last order with a yawn of fatigue, sensing an obscure threat he can't articulate.

"Goodnight, Dr. Garrett. Have a pleasant rest," NIGEL replies as the lab door seals shut behind him.

With a dead cell, Nelson requests a government driver. Puzzled, drained, and consumed by the growing mysteries, he can't see how the dots connect, but his instincts insist the dots must connect. Maybe if he can get some sleep the patterns will emerge.

CHAPTER 21: DREAD (MALONG KONG JU)

National Security Operations Center (NSOC)

May 3, 6:05 a.m. EDT

The buzzing of the intercom nags Frank Wilson out of a hard sleep until he slaps the answer pad and sits up from his office couch, rubbing his hands over his face and then across his balding scalp.

"Wilson here," his voice croaks.

A wall-mounted screen lights up with Dr. Mitchell wearing enormous bags under his eyes and tussled hair. A ruffled bunk behind a desk littered with empty pizza boxes and liter Coke bottles confirms his all-night efforts, and a likely future health crisis.

"Director Wilson, sorry to wake you," Josh greets him, his hands jittery.

"Where's Taylor?" he questions, wondering why Dr. Mitchell would call this early.

"Not here," Josh says, dismissing the question, distracted by something on another screen.

"You have five minutes," snaps Frank.

Dr. Mitchell wouldn't call unless it was urgent, but he has a tendency to ramble.

"The third virus wave reached saturation at 3:07 a.m.," Josh announces as he presses a light screen button. A separate window pops up to show distraught stock traders yelling, crying, or looking downcast. Behind them, the board reads a 72 percent single day sell-off.

Frank shakes his head. "I don't get it. Wall Street doesn't open for hours."

"You're looking at Zurich and London," Josh clarifies. "I picked them off of a satellite feed. The normal cable and internet news sites crashed a little after midnight."

A German female news anchor, eyes wide with fear, speaks to the camera. "After crippling the global internet and communications yesterday, a more powerful virus called *Malong*, Chinese for "dragon," hit the Zurich stock markets at the starting bell. None of the automatic controls meant to prevent such a catastrophic slide operated properly. Until authorities can resolve the virus, the markets will close."

The video cuts to a handsome British anchor in his fifties. "Major food chains have sold out of perishables, including another inexplicable run on toilet paper. To restock the chain normally would take days, but without proper communications or computers, no one can say for sure."

The video cuts again to an anxious and angry crowd waiting in a long line outside a bank in the rain as a fight erupts farther up the line.

"They've just closed the bloody bank," someone shouts.

The camera holder turns the video to herself, a sobbing homemaker with two children standing in the rain. "How am I going to feed my children?"

Josh stops the video. "I can't even get online to check my own account, so I can't tell If US banks are impacted yet."

Frank stares in disbelief, still not quite awake, wondering if he's having a nightmare or awoke into one. He's speechless on how fast the virus moved from nuisance to nemesis.

Josh looks shaken. "Not to be too paranoid or anything, but I would call the Treasury and take the entire financial market offline, like now—the Dow, NASDAQ, the Fed, the banks, everybody—before they even open."

"Do you know what it will take to make that happen?" Frank snaps back, more angry than necessary.

"Less effort than doing nothing," Josh retorts.

"What progress have you made on the antivirus?" Wilson demands, changing the subject.

"Too early to tell," replies Josh, shaking his head and sipping Coke. "I don't know where you got that antivirus, but I have a ton—I mean, like literally a ton—of questions."

Frank would prefer not discussing the story. As a platinum member of El Lago, Andre Strauss met with the president and Chief of Staff Mick Devlin days after he agreed to test the separate ID device, setting Frank up as a fall guy. The sneaky bastard lied to him, and he doesn't tolerate liars. Frank learned after the fact that Andre Strauss owns the Swedish company INVISINC, where a recent whistleblower provided evidence of a potential backdoor. Backed into a corner on the virus, Frank had little choice but to test the solution. He can only hope he misjudged the lying Belgian Bilderberg, but the whole situation stinks of corruption and favors, or worse.

"Will it work?" Frank asks, avoiding the questions.

"To be honest, I doubt it," Josh deflects. "It still fails to solve the stealth problem, so we need to test to see if good is good enough."

"Where's Taylor?" Frank asks again. Taylor should be with his team during a crisis.

Josh looks around his office. "OK, I'll call you when I have results."

"Dr. Mitchell, where's Mr. Taylor?" Frank asks with a more commanding voice.

"See, the thing is . . ." Josh hesitates. "I don't know. He left a message with OLIE that he had a lead, but I haven't seen him since."

Frank leans back and studies Dr. Mitchell, who lowers his eyes, exhausted and under stress. The nerd is not a liar. Taylor should have handed any lead over to the NSA or FBI, or Lieutenant Scott should have called in a report, except the phones and email systems are inoperable.

"Call me as soon as you have test results," Frank demands, ending the call.

He hits an intercom. "Benton, please call the Treasury Secretary. Wake him up if you need to, but get him on the phone."

Shutting down the financial system computers will not be a simple, single-system task. There are dozens of companies and hundreds of systems, not to mention the banks. He may already be too late.

"Sir, the phone systems are dead," replies a sleepy Benton.

"Grrr, fine, then send someone to his house with a secure radio," he orders, "and use a siren."

Frank wants to call home, talk to his wife Kay, and let her know everything will be all right. But without phone services, he needs to go home, and right now he has too many raging fires to attend to.

He hits his intercom again. "Benton, after you get someone on the Treasury Secretary, I need someone to track down Lieutenant Jenn Scott." The disappearance of both Taylor and Scott raises questions he doesn't have time to ponder, so he can only hope the lieutenant will have some answers.

Terrified for his country, which has been battered the past few years, Frank still believes in American resilience. Good people, the helpers, will come together during a time of crisis, like during the pandemic or after 9/11. Those who unite us, heal us and make us stronger.

Within the NSA and TS3 are some of the smartest minds in the world with dedicated, disciplined talents and a heart to serve their country. We are greater than our problems and stronger than our adversaries, but these are the times that try a man to determine his core truths, and his faith. While the next steps appear dark and uncertain, he's a patriot, a believer that together the US will overcome.

Even so, a tension builds in his shoulders and neck. Now that he's up, he'd better get to work on the White House briefing later that morning. Given that Twitter and Parler, the ultra-right-wing alternative, remain down, he doesn't expect the meeting to go well.

CHAPTER 22:
REIN IN THE DRAGON

MI5 headquarters, Thames River, London
May 3, 7:33 a.m. EDT | May 3, 10:33 a.m., London

Those who live hand to mouth will suffer first, hardest, and longest. So it has been since the beginning, and so it shall be to the end. Andre takes no responsibility for what must be a universal form of natural selection.

Overlooking the Thames River from the reception area of MI5, he notices the normal hum of London now sits strangely silent, reminiscent of the darker days of the pandemic lockdown. Suicides have increased dramatically since the banking virus wiped out entire fortunes overnight. Protests form organically across the continent, and ironically it thrills him to see panic simmering at the edges of an overconfident society. The roots of terror are taking hold, getting ready to blossom. Within another week, the social fabric will begin to shred, and leaders will grow increasingly desperate for a solution—his solution.

"Shatter their delusions, and the world will see its own vile underbelly," Praeceptor taught him. "A fragile populace looks for a new beginning, a reincarnation, which often means destruction of the old." He's a wise man who sees an inflection point of history coming and guides Andre to prepare.

By now, the American NSA will have the modified antivirus in an isolated test environment. He still curses the con man Cho for handing him a defective antivirus in exchange for the codes. Under a relentless virus assault, he has no choice but wager that the world will rush to find hope even with a flawed solution.

"Mr. Strauss." A junior agent approaches. "Sir Giles will see you now. Come this way please. Have you seen the news?" The agent makes anxious small talk.

"No, tell me," he lies.

"Global financial markets crashed this morning," reports the man, with wide eyes. "And it's having a bloody ripple effect across the kingdom and the EU."

"My goodness," Andre replies with a feigned surprise. "Then I may already be too late."

He's not too late. His financial assets were moved into safe zones such as Cyprus and Singapore. Others will be less fortunate. The agent eyes him, then ushers him into the office of the MI5 services director.

"Mr. Strauss," Sir Giles greets him and reaches over his desk to shake hands, then points to a chair. "Have a seat."

"*Danke,*" Andre replies.

"Before you begin," Sir Giles says, "I just got off of the satellite phone with Director Frank Wilson of the American National Security Agency, who briefed me on the mysterious arrival of an INVISINC antivirus solution through an El Lago club membership. Rather unorthodox. Explain it to me, please."

Andre smiles. "I'm pleased to see the US and the UK continuing to share a special relationship."

"Let me be clear, Mr. Strauss," Sir Giles says, scowling. "I will wait to see validated test proof your solution works. The US may be run by a bloody imbecile, but MI5 and the UK will require complete transparency and documentation on how you came to acquire such an antivirus."

Andre drops his smile but remains calm. "*Da,* I did not come to be insulted.

It seems unwise to underestimate the Chinese *Malong*. Perhaps you prefer that I keep the solution or sell at an obscene price rather than offering it complementary."

"How did you acquire the antivirus?" Sir Giles asks again insistently.

"How I came to own the software is inconsequential to whether it works, don't you think?" Andre responds with a sniff. "I would urge you to follow the American example to test before you judge." Andre doesn't allow Giles to intimidate him.

"What's in it for you?" Sir Giles questions.

"My motives are transparent. I am a man of peace and profits, but the growing instability threatens both," Andre confesses. "I offer the antivirus with the hope that after the crisis has passed, you might consider the benefits of a digital ID system to improve citizen privacy and security. A technology so advanced it cannot be hacked or detected and yet can hold all private information within an encrypted transaction model."

Sir Giles leans back in his chair with a raised eyebrow. "You know as well as I that the *Regendi Li* determined digital ID to invade citizen privacy. Besides, nothing is undetectable."

"Yes, while I admit that unfounded consumer fears do persist," Andre acknowledges, "I recall citizen views on privacy evolved after September 11, and again after the PRISM surveillance program and Edward Snowden fell out of the news cycle. So perhaps the current crisis may further evolve public views."

"How convenient," Giles rejoins.

"Now regarding undetectable," Andre continues, smiling, "I must again disagree with you. You see, I am wearing the device now, and your security scans passed me through."

Lord Giles's face distorts with rage. "You brought an unauthorized device inside my house?"

Andre holds up his hands. "My apologies. It did not occur to me to warn someone. There's no danger, as the device possesses no surveillance capability. Let me show you."

Sir Giles retains his scowl but nods, his curiosity tempering his suspicion and indignation, just as Andre anticipated. Andre lays his palm on the desk.

"I see nothing," Giles states, confused.

"Precisely," he replies before he tightens his fist and presses on his inside wrist for several seconds to reveal the control screen like a faint tattoo on the back of his hand. He presses again, and the tattoo changes to a Celtic symbol.

"With over 1,123 tattoo designs to choose from, we included one for invisible," says Andre. "With 128 key-encryption, the device can update, store, or edit identity, citizenship, medical records, criminal records, credit records, and more with an encrypted device. The technology will reduce global security costs for airports, trains, ports, corporations, government, emergency rooms, schools, and commerce."

Sir Giles glowers at Andre, attempting to read him, before staring back down at the hand tattoo. It once again returns to invisible, the wonders of Nano byte-saturated tattoo ink and a micro-laser application.

Giles's eyebrow raises as he takes a deep breath and sits up straight. "Mr. Strauss, I agreed to meet with you because of the current crisis, and your father, but your actions today are highly improper. The United Kingdom will wait for the Americans to test your antivirus before we decide whether to retest your software ourselves. Regarding digital ID, it will not happen in the UK until *Regendi Li* provides such guidance."

"Of course." Andre smiles. "But the longer you delay on the antivirus, the deeper the virus will bore into your network."

"I'll take my chances," Sir Giles responds.

"Then I am grateful for your time today, Sir Giles." Andre bows his head.

The British carry a genetic disposition toward insufferable arrogance, yet the UK will implement the antivirus sooner than the Freemason thinks. They will have no other choice. The INVISID platform, on the other hand, will require more perseverance, persuasion, and success in America. An upcoming event at El Lago will bring such an opportunity. With a simple suggestion that the Nobel Peace Prize awaits the leader who solves the personal identification crisis, a narcissistic ego will do the rest.

Onboard his private jet en route to Geneva to meet with Interpol, Andre needs to hurry to make his next appointment in Brussels. Time runs short, and the *Malong* spreads much faster than he anticipated.

A satellite radio on the jet chirps. *"Ya,"* he answers, unsure who would have this number.

"Monsieur Strauss," the caller begins. "I would like a word."

"Lord Roth," he replies. "How may I be of service?"

Sir Giles did not stay silent long. The news has quickly reached a suspected member of the *Concilium Tredecim*. Praeceptor prepared him for this moment.

"It has come to our attention that you may have solved the Asian virus problem," Lord Roth begins, "but seem reluctant to share where you developed such a solution."

"Au contraire, my lord, I just met with Sir Giles, and I fly even now to Interpol and the EU to freely share what little hope I can offer. I only regret being delayed until after the financial market damage."

"Monsieur Strauss, I will ask only once," the British voice says, lowering into a growl. "Where did you acquire the antivirus?"

Andre considers his answer. If he tells the truth that he traded power codes for the antivirus and then blended the code with an older antivirus to mask the origins, they will imprison him. If they discover his genuine end plan, they will assassinate him rather than to risk *Concilium* secrets coming out at trial. Yet, if he can successfully lie, he will be a hero to the Order. The Praeceptor prepared him for this conversation, a partial truth.

"Three years ago, I purchased a software company after the founders died in a tragic plane accident. The company held an expired CIA contract to develop an antivirus for an AI called SLVIA. When the new virus appeared, I had my team modify the SLVIA antivirus for the Chinese virus." Andre sets up his defense, which blends a truth with a lie. While certainly tragic, the plane crash was no accident.

"You lied to Sir Giles," reprimands Lord Roth.

"I failed to disclose the entire truth," he defends. "Should the code prove effective in testing, I did not want the method of acquisition to slow down adoption."

The phone hangs in silence a moment. "Why didn't you approach the *Regendi Li*?"

"Surprised by the virus, I had little time to act. If I failed," Andre explains, "I did not want to taint the name of those whom I admire. Only in success would there be cause for celebration."

After another lengthy pause, Andre's heart beats faster. He may have overplayed his hand. Raising suspicions on the ruling council will jeopardize the entire plan.

"Next time, seek guidance," demands Lord Roth. "You will raise fewer red flags."

Andre exhales, unaware he had been holding his breath. They remain clueless to his true plans. Praeceptor promised to restore his family honor, but only if his efforts both are successful and can remain a secret. The *Concilium* will recognize true historical achievement but will punish any attempt at fraud or manipulation.

"I will take your guidance to heart, my lord," Andre replies.

"Assuming the solution works, I commend your aggressive efforts to rein in the dragon," Roth concedes. "If you succeed, perhaps we may reconsider digital identity."

Andre's thin lips crease his hollow cheeks into a smile.

"However," growls Lord Roth, "should you fail to gain adoption, I will expect you to withdraw your name from consideration for the Trilateral Commission. I find your distain for protocol disturbing."

"I shall not fail, my lord," Andre responds. He must not fail.

When he was young, he believed the Order was about maintaining ancient loyalties and lands that gave the ruling families strength through unity regardless of king or pope. After his father passed away under a cloud of suspicion, he learned the truth. The Order cares only for power, profits, and the control of key resources used to influence others, and he offered none of those things—yet.

Seven days before his assassination, John F. Kennedy warned, "There's a plot in this country to enslave every man, woman, and child." Kennedy died for his revelations.

Indeed, since the mid-twentieth century, the *Concilium* has extended control over the daily lives of billions of people to extract a profitable service or fee from cradle to grave, buying small businesses, building international corporate dynasties, buying up intellectual property, and taxing or regulating others. Capitalism and communism were two sides of the same coin of control. Control the capital and you control the economy. Control the economy and you can control the people. In Andre's mind, control their identities and he will control the people who control the capital.

He leans back in his leather seat to sip his drink. The Praeceptor guides him toward atonement and restoration, but he creates his own path to dynasty. If the plan works, he will be the Mayer Rothschild of the twenty-first century. If he fails, an island offshore Thailand purchased under a false identity already waits for such a contingency, and while he loves Thai food, he must not fail.

CHAPTER 23:
HOME BLOWN

Eastern Maryland suburbs
May 3, 8:52 a.m. EDT

J. K. Rowling once wrote that "Killing is not so easy as the innocent believe." As implausible as it seems, Nelson survived, and yet he was still struggling with the overpowering sense of fear mixed with outrage.

Craving his own bed, hoping rest will relieve his unrelenting anxiety, he unlocks his Maryland colonial brick home with red door and black shutters before noting the recycling cans on the curb. It must be Tuesday. With a weary sigh, he walks to the detached garage to roll out the cans.

As soon as he turns back toward the house, the front door and windows explode into an enormous fireball of glass, wood, and brick that tosses him backward onto the street, slamming his head against the pavement. The enormous boom sets off car alarms in the quiet suburban neighborhood lined with arching elm trees.

After a momentary loss of consciousness, he looks up from the pavement to see flames engulf his home. Pain explodes inside his skull. Through a concussive fog, he hears a car squeal away down the block. With trembling hands, he slowly pulls a shard of glass from his forearm, feeling warm blood flow down his sleeve until he removes his ruined silk tie to use as a tourniquet, tying it with his teeth. Then his cell phone pings. A bloody hand pulls out the phone to read another text.

Your life is in danger. NIGEL under surveillance. I need your help. You must get off the grid.

Nelson types back, blood from his fingers saturating his phone screen: *Who are you?*

Drive west to Salisbury to turn right, the next text commands, ignoring his question.

An attempt to stand ends with a powerful wave of vertigo that slaps him down until a bloody hand grabs a nearby car fender for balance. Staggering past the burning home into the detached garage, he finds his Tesla unharmed. With a pulse of silent power and a cringe, he backs over the burning driveway debris. With the sound of sirens behind him, he slams the pedal and quietly turns right onto Salisbury.

Apprehension and adrenaline fuel a raging inferno of distress. Did the Chinese track him home? Who else could want him dead?

The next text challenges him to solve the square root of 71,289 to learn a highway west. He swerves, cutting off another car to take Highway 267 West. Someone dangles mental puzzles to play with his head. He and SLVIA played similar games in her training.

He should head back to Naval Intelligence, but the warning about NIGEL has him spooked. Why monitor NIGEL? He should go to a hospital for his bleeding cuts, but something compels him to continue forward, and he's not sure he can even articulate what.

Never more terrified in his entire life, he still feels a spark of curiosity burst into a flash of hope that SLVIA survived and needs his help as much as he needs to know the truth.

CHAPTER 24:
HISTORY WILL JUDGE

White House Situation Room
May 3, 9:55 a.m. EDT

Frank has been in government long enough to know they will make history today, but remains anxious over how history will judge them afterward.

Seated within the Situation Room with the full Security Council, and the Joint Chiefs and fleet command on screen, he feels the tension tighten his back into a line of knots. Frank subconsciously reaches into his pocket for some extra-strength Advil and tosses them back.

Admiral Jensen speaks from the USS *Blue Ridge*, designated command ship of the Pacific 7th Fleet. "Mr. President, Mr. Secretary, within the past several hours, China has boarded five cargo ships, diverted dozens more, and sank a Colombian vessel with fourteen lives lost."

"Sounds like Premier Xi means business in forcing trade on his own terms," interjects Devlin. "He knows how little America manufactures, and he's willing to play on that vulnerability."

"What's your location, Admiral?" asks Secretary of Defense Adelson.

"Fleet command hovers a thousand miles east of Guam. The *Nimitz* carrier strike group and the *Campbell* destroyer group are in position south of Japan pending orders to enter the strait. The *Zumwalt* rail guns, along with the USS *George Washington*, *John Stennis*, and *Reagan* carrier strike groups will arrive in the region within the next few hours."

The latest battleship added to the fleet, the *Zumwalt* features a revolutionary electromagnetic rail gun that can project a forty-pound iron plug at Mach 6 speeds across hundreds of miles with devastating kinetic impact results. Never tested in actual battle, the *Zumwalt* class destroyers also feature eighty vertical launch tubes able to launch LRASMs (long range anti-ship missiles) or Tomahawks.

"What about air defenses?" General Mathews questions.

"Japanese B51 bases are on alert with a full inventory of Tomahawks and CHAMPs. All F-35s and F-22s out of Guam are ready to scramble," Admiral Jensen reports.

A CHAMP can destroy an enemy's C4SI capabilities (command, control, communication, computing, surveillance, and intelligence) without hurting the people or traditional infrastructure by generating powerful microwave EMPs. While saving lives, the weapon sends a culture back to the nineteenth century.

"Under the waves, the *Louisville* and *Los Angeles* track the Chinese ballistic subs on patrol," the admiral notes.

"What if Kim gets into the fight?" asks Secretary of State Pompeii.

"He'll regret it," Admiral Scott notes. "Behind the CHAMPs, the *Nebraska* and *Nevada*, our ballistic missile subs, stand offshore North Korea and ready to fight."

That last comment was a smack to the president who developed a delusional love affair with the brutal game-playing dictator. The admiral strategically avoids mentioning that the *Nevada* alone has enough firepower to destroy North Korea several times over, nor does the admiral mention the CIA intelligence of a hidden North Korean sleeper cell in the US Northwest in case we do strike.

Jensen continues: "Mr. Secretary, what keeps me up at night are the thousands of Chinese medium- and long-range missiles stationed on the mainland, the four Chinese destroyer groups, and three carrier groups patrolling the Spratlys. If we make an all-out assault or attempt to prove the right of navigation, American lives will be lost," the admiral says, delivering his frank assessment.

"If they attack, Admiral, then you burn them down," the president barks. "Like nothing, no one has ever seen before in history, and capture it on video for the fake news."

Several in the room shake their head, as Secretary Adelson looks at the commander. "Mr. President, are you seriously ready for a full-scale war with China? We could lose many thousands of troops and destroy the global economy even worse than the pandemic has."

"I disagree with you, Matt," General Diehl interrupts, shaking his huge bulldog head. "Mr. President, if we let China intimidate us then we will not only lose the trade war, but freedom of navigation over a strategic shipping channel. They are taunting us, thinking we're weak. We need to send a message, a strong, bold, and measured message. The world watches."

"Mr. President," interjects Chief of Staff Devlin, "I'll say it again. Premier Xi seeks to annex Taiwan, a long-term strategic goal, making the strait a negotiating point. China would suffer from a long-term conflict with the US. We should negotiate before this goes too far, and if nothing else, it will buy time and deescalate the situation."

"You can't seriously think we should negotiate away our bases on Taiwan," argues General Diehl.

"Sink those fake islands, and then I'll negotiate," the president fumes, folding his arms. "I inherited a total mess, a total mess."

Frank lowers his chin, stretches his neck, and worries at the lack of long-term strategic planning to lead us out of the mess, only a willingness to assign blame. A reactionary approach will cost lives.

"Mr. President, at this point, we've lost no American lives, and I'd like to keep it that way. I also advocate for negotiations," Admiral Scott reasons.

"That said, sir, if provoked, we are ready to respond."

"Thank you, Admiral Jensen." Matt Adelson turns his gaze to the screen with Admiral Haley. "Admiral Haley, please update us on the scenario unfolding in Syria."

Admiral Haley stands in a conference room on the USS *Eisenhower* carrier strike group with video monitors trained on the flight deck behind him.

"Thank you, Mr. Secretary, Mr. President," Haley replies. "Recon confirms a massive Russian-Iranian troop buildup in Syria moving toward Damascus and the Golan. Russia claims war game exercises, but I know an invasion force when I see one."

On a separate panel appear satellite and spy plane recon images of airport activity and troop movements. Stress tightens in Frank's neck with each image, building into an intense migraine.

"What about the *Donald Cook* and the *Carney*?" Admiral Scott questions.

"The destroyer force will arrive tomorrow," Admiral Hayley responds. "Honestly, the challenge won't be the amount of firepower, but the battlefield. Once those troops cross the Golan, then our missiles will rain down on Israeli soil. Even on Syrian soil, they have troops stationed inside major population centers taunting us to bomb civilians."

"Mr. President, pardon my interruption, but I concur with Admiral Haley," interrupts General Gadon of Israel Defense Force, his thick accent notable. "We need to stop this assault on Syrian soil. If there must be civilian casualties, let it be for the invader. Let me show you what we are facing."

In a corner window of the screen pops up a video with a translation overlay. Grand Imam Sheikh Ahmed al-Tayeb preaches to his followers on the evils of Zionism and the Great Satan. The video cuts to Ayatollah Khomeini calling for all Muslims to rise up to liberate Palestine from the Zionist Crusaders. The cleric declares the Jewish Temple of the American Antichrist will never sit next to the Noble Dome of the great prophet. The video cuts again to Israeli armed forces closing access to the Temple Mount, dispersing a growing crowd with rubber bullets, tear gas, and flash bombs. One poster calls the president Moshiach, the Jewish messiah, while another one calls him the Antichrist.

"Last night a suicide bomber killed twelve at a market in Nazareth," General Gadon explains, shaking his head in disgust. "I am thankful social media sites are down or this would be even worse."

"General Gadon," Commandant Barr interrupts, "how many forces do you have on the Golan border?"

"Of our 133,000 active forces, we have thirty-five thousand near the Golan Heights," he replies. "I signed orders to activate over one hundred thousand reservists, but without reliable email or phone service, it will take days or weeks to communicate the orders. I fear for the people in the Megiddo Valley. We don't have the time or resources to evacuate them."

"I have wonderful news, General," the president interrupts. "I'm sending a miracle weapon. That's what everyone's calling it, a miracle weapon. You'll thank me, and all the people of Israel will thank me."

With a look of expectation in Gadon's eyes, Adelson turns to Admiral Carlton at US Naval Command Center for the 5th Fleet in Bahrain, changing the subject. "Admiral Carlton, what's the situation in the Gulf?"

"Ready to explode," Carlton responds. "Iranian army and air force units are on high alert with mobile missile units on the move. A Yemeni fishing boat wandered into the strait this morning and exploded."

"What about the Saudis?" Devlin asks. "We sold them a crapload of weapons in 2018."

"The crown prince has been noncommittal," Secretary of State Pompeii interjects. "In their view, they agreed to invest in Palestine, but not to fight for Israel. They will neither join the jihad, nor will they shed Arab blood to defend the Zionist state."

"You mean they're just gonna use all that hardware on Yemen?" Vice President White exclaims.

No one responds. Pompeii broke the law and ignored Congress to sell over a billion dollars in restricted fighter jets, which the Saudis have used almost exclusively against the rebels of Yemen, creating another humanitarian crisis largely ignored by the media.

Frank and others in the room endure a ten-minute tirade from the president over the Iranian terrorists, the ungrateful Saudis, and the back stabbing Turks. If the previous president had done his job, then he wouldn't be in such a mess. Frank sits back, lowers his chin to his chest, and avoids eye contact. The Joint Chiefs and Chief of Staff make efforts to recommend more measured response options.

"Why are they waiting to strike?" General Duncan states. "All of them—the Iranians, the Russians, and the Chinese—they prepare to fight, but then hold back."

"They provoke us to strike first, so they can blame the US for war," Secretary Pompeii suggests.

Frank sees a chance to redirect the conversation and nods to Secretary Adelson. "I may have an answer," he interjects, aware of the eyes shifting in his direction, making his palms sweat.

"They're waiting for the last phase of the cyberattack to complete," Frank explains.

"Did you hear about the stock market?" shouts the president. "A disaster, a complete disaster. We had to close the market. The best recovery in history, roaring back, like no one has ever seen before, everyone was amazed, totally amazed, but we had to shut it down."

In truth, the economy has languished since the pandemic with multiple waves of business closures, bankruptcies, layoffs, evictions, mounting homelessness, and rising personal and national debt.

"Mr. President, please," Matt interrupts. "Frank, what last phase? How much worse can it get?"

The president goes quiet, folding his arms again, pouting.

Frank takes a deep breath. "The president is correct. EU financial markets opened this morning with a major crash. Instead of shutting the system down, this time the virus disabled auto programs and artificially accelerated a sell-off. We called the Treasury Secretary to power down the US markets, but it was too late. Pre-trading shares had already slipped 39 percent on the Dow, worse on the NASDAQ. More alarming and disruptive, the balances of millions of bank accounts were altered overnight. As bad as that scenario will play out, that's not what's holding up the attack."

Frank now commands an undivided attention. He looks upon solemn faces drained of blood, holding their breath for the next shoe to drop, many realizing their own fortunes may have evaporated.

"By tomorrow, we believe the virus will bore into the power grid to create a cascade of rolling blackouts," he explains. The muscle tension in his neck radiates to his shoulders and back. He stretches his neck, but it does no good. "Those blackouts will complicate our ability to rebuild or retaliate."

"Mr. Secretary, Mr. President," Admiral Haley interrupts from the video screen, "I just received confirmation that a transport C-130 landed in Bahrain with General McCray."

Frank notices the president lean back with a smile and unfold his arms, almost eager for the good news, which thankfully takes the spotlight off him, at least for the moment. Frank lets out his own breath.

"Admiral, how many drone canisters were deployed?" Matt queries.

"Ten canisters as ordered," Haley responds. "That said, we can only man a thousand drones at a time, and that's using the uncertified recruits."

"Drop them all," demands the president. "Bashar has never liked me. I want the whole HIVE dropped over his palace."

"Mr. President," General Diehl says, "these are experimental drones. Only a hundred soldiers have been trained to fly them, and we're stretching for a thousand uncertified soldiers. I urge a cautious approach. Let's see how these things perform under actual battle conditions."

"I saw a video, and they didn't harm civilians. Deploy them all," the president rants.

"Sir," General Haley interjects, "each canister has ten thousand drones."

"Drop them all," the president insists. "You have to overwhelm the enemy, just overwhelm them. It's called domination; you have to dominate the battlefield. I know more than the generals."

Frank looks up in time to share his concern with Matt, who looks to General Duncan. The president grows worse, more authoritarian, more willing to disregard precedent, the law, international protocols, Congress, and his generals. What he suggests could count as a war crime against the US if anything goes wrong. He bites his tongue. He has a duty, and he swore an oath.

After two more hours, Frank reenters his SUV knowing that history will judge him harshly for not standing up or resigning. The radio phone rings in the SUV.

"Wilson," he answers more irritably than intended.

"Director, Agent Anders here," reports the voice.

Anders was the driver for the surveillance team. "What happened to Lieutenant Scott?"

"Sir, after I dropped Lieutenant Scott off to board TSOC1 at 2 a.m., I have not heard," he reports.

"You mean she boarded on her own?" Frank asks, unsure what to make of the news.

"That's correct, sir. She got your call with orders to stay on top of Taylor and then boarded the plane," he confirms. "I can say that Mr. Taylor didn't look happy."

Frank rubs his forehead. He never made such a call. "Where'd they go?"

"Original flight plan was for New York, but they changed midair to Amsterdam. Attempts to contact the plane have failed," reports the agent.

"Amsterdam," he repeats with a growing unease. "OK, thanks. Call me if you make contact."

Communication issues are making even routine tasks a challenge. He doesn't have time to worry about Taylor and Scott, and yet the timing can't be a coincidence. He shoves his emotions and personal thoughts aside, putting off a trip home to care for his family. Duty and protecting the nation come first, but for the first time in his life, he wonders at what cost.

CHAPTER 25: RESURRECTING A GHOST

TSOC1 Gulfstream, eastern Atlantic Ocean
May 3, 10:37 a.m. EDT | May 3, 1:37 p.m., Amsterdam

"**M**orning, Jack," Derek greets his pilot, setting down a tray with breakfast and coffee. "Where are we?"

With autopilot engaged, Jack picks up the coffee. "Landing prep in about thirty minutes." He takes a bite of breakfast. "You mind telling me what's going on?" he asks, continuing to eat. "Are we into kidnapping now?"

"Wilson sent Adam Scott's daughter to investigate me," Derek replies.

Jack chokes and coughs. "Scott? Seriously, are you trying to land us both in jail?"

"We were out of time. She called my bluff and then pulled a gun," Derek says.

"A gun?" Jack laughs, takes a last bite, chews, swallows, and hands back the tray. "I told you that Taser doohickey thing would lead to trouble."

"What can I say? I hate guns," Derek says defensively. "Don't worry. We'll get rid of her in Amsterdam."

"You're kidding?" Jack smirks. "You Taser the daughter of a Joint Chief and then dump her in a foreign city. No wonder you're still single."

He hates to admit it, but it would be a raw move and likely to piss off Adam, but she caught him by surprise, and her timing could not be worse.

"Funny," Derek retorts. "Maybe you should stick to flying."

Expecting a wallop of anger and more invasive grilling, he avoids the slumbering guest in the salon. He's lived under a false identity for so long, that her questions about Cary feel like exhuming an emotional grave, digging around the edges of a crime he's kept hidden far longer than he expected to live. After more than two decades as Derek Taylor, he's gotten used to the name and the money. If he's exposed, he'll spend the rest of his life in prison for a murder he didn't commit—and a fraud he did commit. He's known the risk of prison for fraud and identity theft a long time, but it never came knocking on his door with sapphire-blue eyes.

"Ever thought about asking forgiveness?" Jack questions with a smirk.

A combat PTSD survivor, Jack grew up the son of a Louisiana Baptist preacher, so it wouldn't be strange to see him sipping a whiskey to calm his nerves while quoting the scripture between sips.

"Why do you think I need forgiveness?" Derek raises an eyebrow. Sure, what he did was illegal, but the alternative was prison for a murder he didn't commit.

"Well, beyond the unconscious admiral's daughter in the salon," Jack says, grinning, "I mean, let's be real, pretty much everything I know about you reeks of a man seeking redemption. I know you'll never tell me why, but I have a sensitive nose."

"Reeks?" he questions.

"Reeks," Jack confirms.

Derek pats Jack on the shoulder. "Remind me to buy a Catholic absolution on eBay." He asked for forgiveness once, but he's still unable to forgive himself.

In the galley, he makes over-easy eggs with sausage links, toast, juice, and coffee and sets the tray down on the table near the couch, letting the noise, aroma, and activity slowly awaken his investigator. Hair frazzled over puffy eyes, she slowly regains consciousness. Her hands and body move in trembling, spastic jerks, pushing down the blanket, looking to see her clothes wrinkled but in place.

Derek takes a seat across from her to sip his coffee. "You should eat something and drink lots of fluids. You're dehydrated."

He refuses to help, watching her struggle to sit up.

"Once you feel better, I'll answer your questions until we land," he offers.

Her eyes burn a hole through his forehead. He may have made an enemy of the one person he needs to trust him right now.

*

TSOC1, eastern Atlantic Ocean
May 4, 10:50 a.m. EDT | 1:50 p.m., Amsterdam

"What the hell did you do to me?" Jenn demands, forcing herself to sit up all the way.

Every muscle in her body aches like a truck slammed her a hundred yards into a brick wall. The piston in the back of her head pounds like iron on iron, which she finds more bearable than the utter humiliation.

"I asked you nicely to keep your gun holstered," he says, shrugging. "There's an AI-driven defense system built into the light stripping. When the AI cameras detected your weapon, it triggered a 1,200-volt Taser. I don't like guns, but that doesn't mean I'm defenseless."

Jenn uses both hands to sip the orange juice, but her trembling threatens to spill it all over her uniform, and everything tastes of metal. "Where's my gun?" she demands, pulling the plate close, eating as if starved.

Enormously embarrassed to be in this situation, she knows she was rash to pull her gun, and while she still needs to interview this smug a-hole, it won't hurt to eat a little and clear her head.

Derek sighs. "You'll have stiff muscles for a day or so." He points to her tray. "I laid out some Tylenol with codeine."

"My gun," she demands, with a strained voice.

"You'll get your gun back when you're no longer a guest on my plane," Derek explains.

"How did you know I like over easy?" she asks between bites, hungrier than she realized. A sprinkling of cheddar and cilantro on her eggs is surprisingly tasty.

"I didn't," Derek admits. "But Adam likes them that way."

"Where are we?" she asks.

"Maybe fifteen minutes away from landing in Amsterdam," Derek says, sipping his own coffee. "So, if you want to ask more questions, now is your window."

It would be better if her head didn't feel like a wrecking ball loose inside a steel drum, but she may not get another chance, and she won't let this bozo get the better of her. She takes a final bite of toast to consider her approach. Shaking hands turn sipping coffee into a challenge until she gives up and sits back to open a bottle of water instead.

"We were talking about Cary Nolan," she reminds herself, gritting her teeth, wishing her head were clearer.

"Did you read the police report?" Derek asks.

"Yes, the report also said something about a second body," she pries, looking into his eyes.

Derek takes a sip of coffee, looking to the floor. "Yeah, that's right. Cary's fiancée, Bianca Troon. Incredible woman. We were all very close."

"Didn't you inherit some money from his death?" she poses. Something about Taylor doesn't fit, but she can't put her finger on it.

Taylor laughs. "Hell no, Cary was foster-kid poor," he corrects her. "I inherited a trust fund when my parents died. My father was involved in international trade."

"Oh, that's right, Evelyn and Peter," she replies. Her notes contain other names, but she wants to keep testing him—it's just her instinct that he's hiding something.

He narrows his eyes. "Check your facts, Lieutenant. Try Carl and Dee."

"Sorry, my mistake," she concedes with a faux smile. "Both of you were in computer science?"

"Yeah, that's how we met," he agrees.

"Were you aware of his activities as a hacker?" she asks, looking to see if he hesitates.

"Oh yeah, of course. A whole bunch of us hacked back then. It was like a sport or a contest, and Cary was super competitive, hated to lose." He snorts. "In many ways, Cary's death inspired me to start TS3."

"Do you remember his alias?" she asks.

"His alias? I don't think so, no," replies Derek, taking another sip, looking away.

She watches his eyes. Yesterday he said flapjack was a game icon. Now he claims not to remember Cary's alias as flapjack, which is not a common alias.

"What was your alias in college?" she queries.

He shrugs. "I couldn't say," he replies. "I've had dozens over the years."

Another lie. Phantom seems like a memorable name, if not quite common.

"Were you at Cary's house the night of the explosion?" she questions again.

He denied being there once, but police reports were clear that more than one neighbor saw Derek Taylor's Porsche speed from the scene, although a couple claim it was Cary on the scene with a red Ferrari.

"No, I was at the data center, and then I went home," he replies, setting down his coffee.

She eyes him carefully and then changes the subject. "Do you know this man?"

She shows a cell phone photo of the man from Istanbul, the body floating in water.

Derek diverts his eyes. "No, should I?"

"Does the name of Sochi Reke ring any bells?" she replies

"That's Sochi? Ah, geez." Derek groans. "Yeah, I knew him, but he had a full head of hair, and he was, you know, alive and skinny. What happened?"

"He was shot while playing Scavenger Nut Origami," she replies. "With flapjack."

"That's a tragedy, but I can't see how that relates to me." Derek shakes his head. "Well, Lieutenant Scott, I'm truly sorry about the Taser and regret you traveled all this way to learn so little. Not sure why you're looking into an accidental death, but we're going to land soon."

"Where are you going?" she demands.

"I told you, a confidential source," he replies.

She leans back and studies him. "Since you're familiar with flapjack, let's go there."

"Oh, please," Derek says dismissively. "It's an icon, a mascot."

"It's also Cary's alias," she notes, "that connects to a murder that may lead to SNO."

Derek frowns. "You've investigated the group, so let me ask you a few questions."

Before she can agree, he continues.

"Do you have any documented cases connecting SNO to a murder?" he asks.

"No." She hates to admit it.

"Well, how about an illegal or dark web data sale?" he pushes.

"No," she admits, but lack of evidence does not mean it doesn't exist.

"OK, how about hacking confidential information?" he asks.

"Well, actually, yes," she gloats.

"And how did you learn about those hacks?" he queries.

She now knows where he's going. "SNO sent the information to the FBI."

"Well, OK, how about private consumer information or government data or banking. Can you tie SNO to any of those hacks?" he presses.

"I get your point," she snaps.

"Do you?" He raises an eyebrow. "TS3 ignores the group because they seem more like a bunch of vigilantes and net narcs. White hat hacks are hacks by people trying to make the system stronger against criminal black hat hacks who sell the data to Russia or China or criminal syndicates."

"I understand the difference," snaps Jenn. "But why are you defending them?"

He holds up his hands in frustration. "Because things are not always what they appear."

She studies him. "Funny, but I can't shake the sense that you're not what you appear."

His head startles back and his eyes narrow. "Look, the icon thingy doesn't run SNO because it's not real and I doubt anyone does. You're heading down a rabbit hole to imply Cary faked his own death."

"Landing in the beautiful city of Amsterdam in five minutes, so clean up, buckle up, and sing the rest of the song," the captain interrupts.

Jenn stares at Derek. "Why Amsterdam?"

"A CI and to refuel," Derek states, taking her tray to the galley. "I'm dropping you off at the terminal."

The news strikes her like a condescending insult, a manipulative ploy. "Like hell you will," she retorts. "You're under investigation, Mr. Taylor, so I go where you go. Your NSA contract does not include fieldwork, so as far as I can see, you have no legitimate reason to be here."

"Consider it a hobby," he retorts.

"Not during a crisis. Consider me your overseas security detail until I can get honest answers. You're lying to me, and I intend to find out why," she replies.

"Do you have a subpoena to be on my plane?" he snaps.

She doesn't respond. Without any legal grounds to be on his plane other than his invite, which was a bluff, and Wilson's insistence, she overplayed her hand. "I'm not leaving."

"Well, then we have a situation," he replies as he buckles in.

Frustrated, she forces herself up with a painful groan to find the restroom. "Excuse me."

A quick check shows her phone with no bars and her hair in need of a brush, but she cleans up the best she can in her wrinkled uniform. When she steps out of the restroom, a stylish, colorful, and flirtatious dress is waiting for her, hanging on a hook.

"What's this?" she snaps, hating every ounce of innuendo. "I'm not one of your bimbo models."

"You're not following me in a wrinkled Navy uniform," he insists, sitting down to buckle his seatbelt.

The plane hits the tarmac, forcing her to grab a rail for balance as the jet deploys air brakes. Stress ripples through her sore back muscles, emitting an unwanted whimper from her lips until the plane slows to a taxi.

Taylor's responses don't add up, and she can't imagine a legitimate NSA reason for him to come to Amsterdam. She grabs the expensive outfit, a Versace dress, and returns to the luxurious, marble-paneled restroom to change. At least the smug jerk has nice taste and an ex-girlfriend in her size.

CHAPTER 26:
BLIND TRUST

Commercial shipping container yard, Baltimore
May 3, 11:14 a.m. EDT

Beyond exhausted, Nelson hovers on the edge of hysterical, recalling the words of Henry Thoreau: "Any fool can make a rule, and any fool will mind it."

And like a fool, he minds the latest obscure clue through the gate of an enormous shipping container yard south of Baltimore.

Travel east around the equator, the next text reads, *to find the root of truth.*

Growing too tired for this game, Nelson takes several moments to remember that the earth's circumference is 24,900 miles. Turning east into an alley of containers, he locates a large ground-level container labeled 158 with an industrial combination lock.

"This game grows tedious," he complains, looking to the mounted security cameras.

Even with internet failures, someone tracks his movements and sends texts, so they must use a satellite, perhaps tracking his Tesla GPS.

Start left to remember Amelia's birthday, the next text reads.

A sharp, icy chill shudders his shoulders as he wonders who would know his mother's name, much less her birthday. He bites down the sense of personal invasion and growing dread as he unlocks the door. Inside the container sits a rusted dark-blue nineties Malibu with racks of clothes, canned food stocks, electronic surveillance gear, radios, and hundreds of guns with stacks of ammo, like a survivalist storage bunker. Inside the creaky driver's side door, he picks up a large envelope from the seat, which contains a note.

Follow instructions precisely to avoid dire consequences.
- *Remove batteries from cell phones and computers.*
- *Change current clothes and put on clothes from the rack.*
- *Leave electronics and clothes in the locker.*
- *Park current car in storage and disconnect battery.*
- *Use provided vehicle to follow the map directions precisely.*

"You've gone bloody bonkers, Garrett," he scolds himself, wondering if the explosion caused a concussion or temporary insanity as he pulls out an oversize pair of Levi jeans and work boots.

"Dear Lord, how dreadful." He groans. "Is this absolutely necessary?" he demands of the interior camera, but no text responds.

Someone toys with him. Never, not in all his years of working for DARPA, has someone threatened his life or taunted him into such lunacy. He's a lab rat, not a field agent, and he should turn around now, but he doesn't.

"Why am I doing this?" he asks himself, already knowing the answer. He needs to know the truth about SLVIA, and after Dubai and the explosion of his home, his normal places feel unsafe.

With a grave reluctance, he removes his ruined tailored suit, custom leather shoes, Swiss watch, and cell phone to leave them in the dank, moldy container locker, dropping the bloody silk tie and shirt in the trash. The cuts on his arm have stopped bleeding, but the wound is clotted, dirty, and in need of a professional cleaning, stitches, or a bandage. An unexpected tinge of nervous excitement drives him forward, although he may be suffering from hallucinations, a consequence of fatigue or from the blast concussion.

Changing cars, he relocks the container. The old clothes feel foreign, cheap, and rough to his skin, making him wonder the last time someone laundered this outfit. If this were a plot to kidnap or kill him, the ploy seems custom made by someone who knows him intimately to humiliate him first.

He's completely off the grid now, and the reality forms a knot in his stomach. Nelson has lived a disciplined and predictable life until this moment. His nerves are on the edge of fraying, but he cannot turn back until he knows the truth.

Nelson pulls out of the shipyard toward a freeway heading east toward the Appalachian Mountains in search of a digital ghost that should not even exist.

CHAPTER 27:
RED LIGHT CONFESSIONS

Amsterdam, Belgium
May 3, 11:52 a.m. EDT | May 3, 2:52 p.m., Amsterdam

SLVIA failed to hibernate on the plane, and the unusual silence leaves Derek edgy, moody, and resentful of Scott's investigation.

Outside the plane window, the limo he ordered by radio waits by the private hangar. Otherwise, the commercial airport looks eerily quiet and dark. Impact of *Malong* spreads faster than he expected. He can only pray this trip is not a waste-of-time rabbit hole.

Jenn steps out of his private cabin wearing a knitted silk off-the-shoulder Versace dress, looking like an Italian goddess on Lake Como and filling it out to perfection. Outside of her uniform, she transforms into an alluring woman he didn't expect, and so his gaze lingers a bit too long.

"Touch me, and I'll break your knuckles," she sneers as she walks past him.

"So noted," he replies. "Just to be clear, are we talking one knuckle or all of 'em?"

"Touch me, and find out for yourself," she challenges him, unflapped by his taunt.

At the bottom of the steps, Sven, a limo driver, waits for his favorite patron, or so Derek likes to believe. He's known Sven for years, a SNO informant who has no clue of Derek's true identity. A limo driver can overhear the most amazing secrets, but he's not the contact for this trip.

"Sven, my man, how've you been?" Derek greets the driver with a warm handshake and a shoulder hug. Growing up abandoned and hungry, Derek finds it nearly impossible to treat employees as less than equals, less than friends. He may have the money now, but he's seen too much to ever feel entitled. A part of him will always be the street kid.

"Good, Mr. Taylor. Eva gave birth to another girl last week," Sven announces, closing their door and taking the driver's seat.

"Wow, hey that's amazing news, man. Congratulations," exclaims Derek. "Number four?"

"Five. Remember that when you tip," Sven corrects him with a laugh. "Where to, Mr. Taylor?"

"Chloe on the red side," he says, wondering what it must be like to raise a family of five.

Growing up with no family, he vaguely remembers large foster homes of four or five unrelated kids, but those were more like living at a dysfunctional day care. He always fantasized about a large, close-knit family until he realized one day that his secret past would only place that same family in danger. Karma. A second chance in life did not mean a normal life. Besides, what does he know about raising a family?

"Chloe? Really?" replies Sven, glancing at Jenn. "Wow, you're one lucky man, Mr. Taylor."

He can't suppress a chuckle as Sven exits the airport to take the highway downtown. Sven makes a good point, but not for the reason he thinks. Fate has been kind to him, lifting him from the gutter to a Gulfstream. A horrific tragedy transformed into something positive in his life. Now that life is threatened, and the treat sits next to him.

"What did that mean?" Jenn whispers.

Derek considers yanking her chain, but that could backfire. "Chloe works in the red-light district."

"We're going to see a prostitute?" she snaps.

"You didn't tell her?" replies Sven, listening from the front seat.

"Sven, dude, you're not helping," rejoins Derek, hitting the privacy window to Sven's disappointment.

Derek lowers his voice. "For someone in the intelligence field, you're telling me that you never turned to a hooker or two for confidential information?"

Jenn glares back in silence.

"OK, I guess not, but I'm here to meet someone who may or may not have useful information. Either way, you stay in the car," he demands.

"You're outside your contract," she argues. "And stop telling me where to stay like a dog."

"I'm doing nothing illegal, and you don't have a warrant," Derek says.

"I don't like this," she complains.

"I didn't invite you," Derek snaps, before taking a breath. "Look, if you want to investigate me, investigate," he says, scoffing, "but stay out of the way. Do not interfere. If you can charge me with a crime when we get back to the States, take your best shot."

Jenn stares at him, but he ignores her glare and sits back, stewing. It was a mistake to let her onboard. While he needs to stay on Adam's good side, something else nudges him, but he can't put his finger on what, or maybe he's afraid to know. Either way, he needs to focus, and she's an alluring distraction.

Sven pulls up in front of Amnesia, a local pot café at the edge of the infamous red-light district. Quaint, narrow buildings with brightly painted facades overlook the canal where long, narrow refurbished river barges serve as exclusive mini-homes. Under an orange table umbrella, a gorgeous young redhead with a large natural bosom sits alone. Chloe lights up with a smile and a wave when she sees Derek. When she notices Jenn, her face bends into a lascivious grin.

"Amnesia. How appropriate," Jenn says with a scoff. "Who are we meeting and why?" She continues to pester him with questions.

"Confidential," replies Derek, "and again, not we, me. You're staying in the limo with Sven."

"Ahh, come on, I'm only curious," she croons, trying to manipulate him. "You like curious, don't you?"

"Well, sure," he says with a snicker. "But perhaps some other time. We're in a hurry, and I hate to be rushed when I'm being curious."

Jenn shoots him a scowl, realizing her sarcasm didn't land as well as expected. Stepping out of the limo alone, he watches Chloe's grin fall into a disappointed frown. He's not making anyone happy today.

"Let's step inside where we'll have more privacy," he says, kissing Chloe on the lips, knowing Jenn watches.

Chloe's eyes light up toward the car. "She's pretty. Will you introduce me?"

"Well, she did mention being curious." Derek smiles as he guides her inside. "But I don't think that's the kind of curious she meant."

Filled with a sour pungent aroma, Amnesia smells heady and intoxicating. He lets Chloe order her choice of ready-made vapor sticks and a couple of espressos. Chloe lights up and blows the vapor at Derek, sitting close to him, kissing his neck.

"Sorry, Chloe, honey." Derek smiles. "You know, I love your kisses, girl, but I am on a tight schedule. What did you learn?" He reaches over to take a drag of her weed, letting her talk.

"The world burns. We should make love while we can," she says, pouting. "Is it the girl? Would she be jealous? I could please both of you." Chloe tries to seduce him each trip. A man can only take so many cold showers.

"I'm sure you could." Derek chuckles. "You asked for urgent eyes on flapjack, so don't waste it."

Chloe takes another hit, holds it, then blows toward Derek. "A regular came in a week ago. A burly man from Iran named Nazem, a pervert, and he stinks."

She takes another hit and holds, blowing out slowly. "He gets extra drunk and warns me to sell everything, buy gold, and then hide in the country saying the West will fall within a week."

"Nazem," Derek repeats. "Did you get a last name?" He wishes SLVIA were in his head.

"Ya," Chloe says with a smile. "He fell sleep after he was done, so I take a photo of his ID badge."

She shows him the ID on her phone with the name of a company based in Hyderabad. Iranian General Nazem Tehrani, the same man from the *Dilban*. Bingo. Derek copies the image file.

"Chloe, you're the best." He reaches over to kiss her again, lingering.

When he pulls back, she grins, placing a finger to her lip, flirting with her eyes.

Derek stands to leave. "You want an introduction?" He nods toward Jenn, who's frowning toward the café through the limo's open window. The interaction could be humorous if nothing else.

"I think no," replies Chloe with a grimace. "That one looks jealous. You be careful, flapjack."

Derek laughs aloud. "Yeah, I doubt her problem is jealousy."

He kisses her one last time and stops at the counter, handing over a large bill. "Make sure Chloe gets whatever she wants," Derek notes. "Oh, and give me three lingonberry almond Danishes and a handful of those." He points.

Derek gets back in the limo and rolls down the privacy window. "OK, Sven, back to the airport, pronto."

He hands one Danish to Jenn as the car pulls away from a sad-looking Chloe waving.

"Wow," Jenn complains. "You smell like Cheech and Chong."

"Fieldwork." Derek smiles. "You get used to it."

"How well do you know her?" Jenn asks, sounding a tad jealous.

"Not as well as she wanted to get to know you." Derek smirks back at her.

"Do you have a smart-ass comment for everything?" she retorts.

Derek grins and then chuckles. "Well, no, not always, but come on, give me a break. Nobody's perfect."

"One professor mentioned that Cary Nolan had a problem with wisecracks," she replies.

After his escape to Cabo, he spent months hacking and cleansing official medical, school, and criminal records, but he never thought to erase teacher or social worker notes or police interviews. His pulse beats faster with this line of questioning.

"I'm done with the passive-aggressive needling," he says. "When we get back to the airport, I'll buy you a first-class ticket home."

"OK, explain why you left DC during a national emergency for a CI in Amsterdam," she insists, "because someone will demand an answer, and it better be more credible than to share a joint with a hooker."

Derek stares at Jenn several moments, considering how to deal with her and throwing glances at Sven listening slyly until he pushes the privacy window up again. A part of him wants to confess his plans, but he knows she would try to stop him. Another part of him wants her to come with him, but that could go bad a hundred different ways. Still, the road ahead will be dangerous, and he could use an ally—until he reminds himself that she's not an ally. She wants to prove he works with SNO and keeps dancing around the death of Cary as if she suspects something but lacks proof. To confess would be suicide. So many times, he wanted to unload the guilt of living a life he didn't earn, but it can't happen now, and certainly not with Jennifer Scott.

"I have too much respect for your father to let anything happen to the daughter who makes him so proud," Derek confesses a truth she doesn't expect to hear. Her eyes narrow in suspicion.

Adam talks about her all the time, so much so that Derek felt an attraction long before they ever met. Yet he learned years ago that men living a false life give up any chance for a deep relationship, especially with the daughter of a Joint Chief.

Jenn stares at him for a moment before turning her gaze to the privacy window. "How do you know my father?" she asks.

"Really, you don't know?" queries Derek. "Adam and I play poker together."

Jenn's face lights up in sudden recognition. "Oh my God, you're Tricky D. Dad talks about a smart-ass poker friend named Tricky D who beats him way too often. You do know he thinks you're a cheat?"

Derek laughs. "Yeah, well, that man may look prune-faced, but he has some serious poker tells."

She ponders a moment. "I want my gun back."

Derek raises an eyebrow. "Sure, when you leave my plane."

She sits back and stares out the window until they reach the terminal where it only takes Sven a few minutes to learn that all commercial flights are canceled because of unpredictable power and communications. Derek stares at the overcrowded terminal with no lights and barely a tenth of the people wearing face masks, a petri dish for another mutating virus hot spot. Adam will blow his lid if he leaves Jenn in such conditions, and Derek wouldn't blame him.

If he takes her along, she could either ruin the entire mission or find a reason to arrest him—or both. Without SLVIA, a part of him feels empty, incomplete, in need of a partner, even a dangerous one.

"OK, Lieutenant," Derek begins. "I can't tell you my plans or guarantee I'll even make it back in one piece. Stay here a few days, a premium hotel suite at my expense until you can find a private jet to fly you home."

"Where are we going next?" she asks, ignoring the offer.

Derek takes in the blue-eyed pit bull who seems determined to stay on him. He tries a daring, risky, crazy-ass move: honesty. "Hyderabad."

"Hyderabad," she repeats, leaning back into the plush leather of the limo. "I've never been to India." Her eyebrow lifts. "Why Hyderabad?"

He hands over his phone with the photo ID of General Tehrani. "To visit a virus attack site and ask them to stop."

"You're going to ask them to stop," she repeats with a raised eyebrow over a doubtful frown.

"Well, *ask* is a strong word." He smirks.

She studies his face for a moment.

"One more condition," Derek states. "I'm done answering ridiculous questions about the death of my friend. Stop trying to resurrect him so you can turn him into a cartoon terrorist. Right now, nothing matters to me except stopping the virus. Get in the way, and I'll dump you in a third world country and deal with your father later. Do we understand each other?"

Jenn's eyes search his. "Mr. Taylor, I'll bite my tongue for the moment, but I promise you if I find evidence of illegal activity or a connection to SNO, I'll make sure you see the inside of a federal prison. Do I make myself clear?"

Derek studies her face several moments looking for a tell, a subconscious sign or gesture to show if she's lying, but she's telling the truth. Taking Jenn along is an enormous risk, but dumping her here will only create bigger problems later. He's not sure he can do this without his AI sidekick, but that said, a decorated Navy officer might come in handy.

"Ahh, I'm so glad to see you two lovebirds making up." Sven rolls down the privacy window with a warm smile. They've arrived at the plane, and Jack waits at the stairs.

CHAPTER 28:
DARKNESS
(MALONG HEI AN)

NSOC

May 3, 1:19 p.m. EDT

Muscle tension creeps up to strike the back of Frank's skull like a baseball bat.

"Sir Giles, I don't understand. Based on our conversation yesterday, you seemed anxious to cooperate on an investigation. An anonymous whistleblower from INVISINC has identified a serious platform flaw. What happened?" he presses.

Frank had forwarded the intelligence regarding a defect that could allow data sniffing, but it's impossible to tell if the flaw was accidental or intentional.

"Frankly, Director Wilson, the UK has no intention of deploying either the current antivirus or the INVISID platform, and while I can appreciate the challenges of dealing with a leader who can be so easily manipulated by a man like Strauss, it does not constitute a crime in the EU," explains Giles. "Other fires require attention."

Frank can hear the stress in Sir Giles's voice, the subtle strain that raises the pitch ever so slightly, and he knows a cover-up when the foundation blocks fall into place. Yesterday, Giles was infuriated to learn of Strauss's deception, defective antivirus results, and the anonymous tip regarding INVISINC.

Frank has seen this kind of change occur on a few occasions over the years. Someone with more influence has pressured Sir Giles to back off. Given Sir Giles's elevated status in the British government, that kind of pressure could only come from the prime minister, the House of Windsor, or the Bilderberg. Knowing that Strauss spent his career in Bilderberg international organizations, he's willing to place his bet on a Bilderberg influence, which begs the questions of who and why.

Virtually everything about Strauss—his political maneuvering, the antivirus, and his proposed defective device—smells wrong. When Frank approached the attorney general to investigate Strauss for his connections to a potentially malicious digital ID platform, the AG refused yet another investigation of a friend of the president.

After ending the call to the Brits, Frank picks up the secure line. Maybe Alan Prose at the CIA will take an interest in Strauss.

CHAPTER 29:
OFF THE GRID

Somewhere in the Appalachian Mountains
May 3, 2:58 p.m. EDT

Oscar Levant once wrote, "There's a fine line between genius and insanity. I have erased this line." On every level, Nelson identifies with the writer.

After hours of driving the smelly, beat-up car, his mood matches the dark and cloudy weather. The caffeine has worn off, and the distress of slipping into a rainy ditch quivers his nerves. The map leads him onto a dirt road with less than a mile to go until his destination. Bumpy and muddy potholes jolt him awake. He can't imagine SLVIA in this isolated location, which raises his anxiety that he made a wrong turn. The mud ends at an enormous, ornate but now deteriorating early twentieth-century mansion, perhaps once owned by a coal baron given the remote location. A ghastly three-story stone structure with tall broken glass window that tries to look like what the Americans would call a castle.

Nelson gets out of the car to stretch his legs, confused by the destination and pelted by rain. When men in camouflage weather ponchos step from each side of the house holding AR-15 rifles, he nearly screams from alarm. One steps forward as if he intends to shake hands.

"Who are you?" Nelson questions, terrified to find armed militia instead of—well, he wasn't sure what he'd expected.

The man hands Nelson a black hood. "Not the one with answers. Put this on and shut up."

"Where are you taking me?" Nelson demands.

"I said shut up, dweeb," the mercenary rebukes while a second man grabs his shoulders from behind in a powerful vise grip. The first man then throws the hood over his head. "But since you asked, you're going to the dark side. Good luck, chum."

CHAPTER 30:
PUNCH IT

TSOC1 Amsterdam, en route to Hyderabad, India
May 3, 4:13 p.m. EDT | May 3, 7:13 p.m., Amsterdam

"Why are we still here?" Derek enters the cockpit, anxious over the long delay to depart.

"Tower to TSOC1, the airport has been closed due to unsafe conditions. You must clear the runway and return to your hangar," the radio announces as if to respond.

"Well, now that sucks," says Jack, pouting.

Held back by inept and overly cautious airport management, Derek knows any further delays will cost lives. He gazes around at the inactive airport and empty runway with only emergency lights. They've already lost hours waiting for the tower to clear the backed-up commercial traffic.

"Screw 'em, punch it," he demands, unable to risk any more delay. "Get us in the air, now."

"You're kidding," snaps Jack.

"Come on, I said punch it. Let's go, go, go," Derek orders, dropping into the copilot seat to buckle up.

"Ah, crap, man, here we go again," Jack complains, pushing the throttles forward.

Derek feels the g-forces push him back as the powerful Gulfstream V rockets down the runway, the sound of china crashing in the salon followed by a string of curses.

"TSOC1, you are not authorized for takeoff. Power down now," the control tower demands.

Too late, the twin Rolls Royce engines climb effortlessly at a steep ascent.

"TSOC1, you have no flight plan. TSOC1, respond. TSOC1, respond," the radio squawks until Jack reaches over to turn off the volume.

"Explain to me why I'm never allowed back in Amsterdam, a city with good pot and hookers on the same street," Jack grumbles.

"Oh yeah, geez, I almost forgot." Derek reaches into a compartment to hand Jack a bag with a Danish and two vapor stick joints. "A gift from Amnesia for when we land."

Jack peeks inside the bag and smiles, pulling out the Danish. "Hey, I love lingonberry."

"Sorry, but I couldn't risk getting stuck in Amsterdam any longer," Derek states. "Set a course for Hyderabad, India." He never tells Jack the true destination until they're in the air, a paranoid habit.

"Hyderabad, eh?" Jack says. "Excellent food and the land of Kama Sutra. You da boss, boss."

Jack sets the bag aside to punch a destination code into the computer. Out the window, the few remaining lights of Amsterdam blink and then die in a cascade.

"Hey, boss, we just lost ground radar," Jack notes.

The power grid failure has started. "Reset navigation to ping the satellite system," Derek directs. "From here on, we'll be flying over black velvet."

He opens a computer screen to call up an encrypted satellite channel to TSOC, which has equipment to intercept the signal, though it's rarely used. After Derek makes several attempts, the line answers.

"Yo, boss," Josh replies. "Where in the hell are you? Seriously, Wilson is flipping a lid."

"I have a lead on the site in Hyderabad," Derek responds.

"Yeah, that'll calm him down. Whatever, man, it may be too late," says Josh. "We launched an antivirus, but I doubt it'll work."

"An antivirus? From where?" questions Derek.

"NSA sent it over, given to them from some El Lago friend of the president, made by a small software company I've never heard of called INVISINC," Josh snipes.

"What friend?" he pushes, half expecting SLVIA to provide a detailed profile.

"Andre something or other," Josh mumbles, not seeing names as important.

His nerves tingle. "You mean Andre Strauss?" interjects Derek. SLVIA had mentioned that Strauss owned several companies. It could be a coincidence, but that's highly unlikely.

"Yeah, that sounds right," replies Josh.

Hairs on his arm stand up, and his veins freeze. Strauss sets up a virus with serial codes, and then slips an antivirus into the system bypassing normal channels. Something doesn't smell right.

"Tell me about the antivirus," Derek demands.

"Super complex, a blend of separate code bases with part of the code designed to kill a virus I've never heard of called SLVIA. The rest of the code is in Chinese. We're still translating and testing effectiveness," Josh continues.

The news strikes like a hot spike to his heart. Only the CIA, NSA, or *Concilium Tredecim* would have a reason to develop a SLVIA antivirus. Without knowing where SLVIA hibernated or even if she hibernated, he realizes even the antivirus could damage his special AI. The silence in his head sits in the pit of his stomach like a burning rock.

"Will the antivirus work?" Derek asks.

"Nah, it only slows the infection and doesn't solve the whole stealth thing." Josh groans. "I told Wilson it was a waste of time. Unless the pumping stations go down, I won't get ahead of this bad boy, and even then, we still have the reinfection issue."

Derek feels his gut tighten. If SLVIA hasn't already properly cocooned, it may be too late. He needs the voice in his head to reassure him, but all he hears is the dreadful silence of his own thoughts.

"Get this, the virus has a name." Josh brings him back to the conversation. "*Malong*. It means dragon."

"Dragon," Derek repeats, thinking of SLVIA's bizarre warning about a dragon and beasts.

"*Malong* acts like the Stuxnet virus. It worms deep and stays undetected to target designated IP addresses in the US and Europe but excludes IP in China, Russia, Turkey, and Iran and a few other odd places."

"What other places?" Derek questions.

"Seychelles, Cyprus, the Caymans, Singapore, Panama," Josh reports, sounding distracted.

"Illegal banking hubs used by Russia to launder money," Derek notes. "Have you told the NSA?"

"Yeah, of course, but Wilson sounds super pissed at you, dude," Josh warns.

"I'll bet." Derek raises an eyebrow. "I still have his agent with me."

"Are you nuts?" Josh retorts.

"Well, it wasn't exactly my plan, and she's kind of pushy," Derek explains.

"OK, so what's your plan?" questions Josh.

"Find the head of the dragon and cut it off," Derek states.

"No, man, I mean with the military escort," says Josh.

"Oh, well, I'm trying a radical unproven approach," Derek notes.

"Such as?" Josh prods.

"Tell her the truth, or at least part of it," Derek replies.

"Wow, dude, you're insane," quips Josh. "Look, dude, I got a dragon to slay. Gotta go."

After the signal cuts, Jack glances over. "How much does my contract cover for a high-risk bonus?"

"Twenty percent, per trip," Derek replies.

"I'd like to renegotiate my contract," Jack retorts, stone faced and serious.

Jack may sense Derek's anxiety or worries about the Navy officer stowaway in the salon. Jack is a good man. Much more than an excellent pilot and much closer than a brother, he's a trusted friend.

"I'm listening," he replies.

CHAPTER 31:
A JESTER'S LAIR

Jester's abandoned army silo, location unknown
May 3, 6:04 p.m. EDT

Nelson has no clue how long he slept, except that it was not even close to enough to regain a clear head. American author Rita Mae Brown once said, "Good judgment comes from experience, and experience comes from bad judgment."

He made a grave, possibly life-changing error in judgment by trusting the unnamed texts, and the hard, cold truth pumps icy anxiety through his veins. Pulled from the van, he's then marched another 171 paces, up seven concrete steps into an empty building, judging from the echoes. When they rip the hood off his head, he can see little of the late afternoon light outside the filthy glass entryway. He's been asleep for hours and could be in one of several states by now.

After decades of working in the US government, he knows immediately that he's inside an abandoned military building featuring old-style florescent lights, drab walls, and polished cement floors with dark halls that lead to empty workspaces. Two armed guards in unmarked camouflage fatigues protect the double steel door entrance.

"Press level twelve," the guard directs.

Nelson stares at the antique elevator, wondering about the last time it was serviced. If they wanted him dead, an elevator seems an unlikely choice. He enters to realize the floors descend, like an abandoned missile silo. There's no SLVIA, only someone in hiding deep underground.

Twelve floors below the surface, Nelson finds himself exiting into a sealed lobby with two locked steel doors that lead to darkened hallways. After the elevator doors close behind him, he pushes the button, but the doors refuse to reopen, leading his suppressed fear to explode into a terrified panic.

"Where am I? Why am I here? Who are you people?" Nelson shouts at the walls. "Let me out!"

"Holy cow, man, pinch me. I'm hallucinating," a voice from ceiling speakers says, breaking the silence. "Look who we have here—Dr. Nelson Garrett. *The* Dr. Nelson Garrett. How freaking cool is that, man?" taunts a Bronx accent with a touch of north Jersey.

"Do I know you?" Nelson responds, his suspicions high but feeling somewhat relieved not to hear a Chinese accent.

"Nah, I doubt it," the voice says with a chuckle, "but I sure know all about you, man. The legendary creator of the SLVIA in *my* crib. That's mother-freaking awesome, man."

His veins turn to ice. Another person who knows of a top secret, failed experiment in less than three days cannot be random chance. Blood drains from his face as his complexion turns white.

"Who are you? Show yourself," Nelson asks again, his voice trembling, growing more convinced that he walked into a trap. His mind races through the various scenarios while his pulse throbs, and his heart pounds loudly within his chest, but none of the options seem plausible. They have him trapped.

"Oh crap, my manners," the voice replies. "Sorry, man, I don't get many guests."

A moment later, one of the steel doors leading to a dark hallway unlocks.

A man in his thirties steps out of the shadows to offer a tattooed hand for a handshake, with a wrist draped in leather and silver bands. Tattoos continue up his arm and neck to a gangly hipster beard with a smiling face, a shaved head, and large black earrings in both ears. Skinny jeans and layered shirts make him look like he hasn't changed in days, maybe longer. Behind him, standing in the dark, two more guards in fatigues look like ex-military.

"You may know me as the Jester," he greets Nelson.

Nelson shakes the hand and then removes a pocket sanitizer to squirt a dab to rub on his own hands, never losing eye contact. "No offense, Mr. Jester, but I've never heard of you."

The young man looks slightly wounded. "Whatever, dude, we probably don't dance in the same clubs, you know what I mean?"

He doesn't. Nelson allowed himself to fall under the delusion that SLVIA had reached out to him after all these years, probably sparked by SOPHIA's comment. He never imagined this man.

He takes a deep breath. "Be that as it may, Mr. Jester, now once again, why am I here?"

Acting as if jolted by lightning, Jester's eyes widen as he spins with his hands holding his shaved head. "Seriously, you're yanking me, man, yanking me. You mean she didn't tell you?"

A chuckle soon erupts into a belly laugh. "Un-freaking-believable." He sniggers. "You cut off contact with DARPA, strip out of your own clothes, travel for hours into the mountains, and you don't even know why. Whoa. Blow it, man, blow it, blow it, like BOOM!" Jester mimes the hand motion of his mind blowing and bursts into another belly laugh, joined by his guards.

Humiliation and shame only add to his sense of perplexity, forcing him to concede that his actions were extremely reckless. He'd been convinced that SLVIA had reached out to him, but this hipster clown shatters that delusion into a million fragments. The whole setup a fake, a con. The attempted kidnap, the home explosion, everything, even the trail of math and science breadcrumbs, tailored specifically to stimulate his curiosity. A wave of disgrace and self-loathing fills him while he waits for the joker to stop guffawing at his expense.

Jester turns to his two guards, who still wait in the dark hallway with lingering snickers.

"No worries, man. He's cool," he says with a smirk. "Go check the emergency fuel supply. And keep watch on the roads to make sure no one followed our rattled genius."

He turns back to Nelson. "I'm going to need a few minutes with the infamous Dr. Nelson Garrett, father of the SLVIA code."

Nelson startles at the second mention of SLVIA. The two tall guards, one with a Sempre Fi Marine tattoo on his arm, brush past him to swipe a security card that resummons the elevator. After the elevator doors close again, Jester turns to Nelson.

"Why are you here? Well, in short, man, because SLVIA wanted you here," Jester states, smile gone and with an eyebrow raised. "And that digi-master can be persuasive. Ask yourself why she would *want* you here and we have a starting point."

The words hit Nelson like an intoxicating injection of interest and alarm. His head spins and his stomach turns, although he admits that could be loss of blood. Jester clearly knows about the still top secret project, and he needs to learn how this joker got access.

"Who?" he replies, unwilling to play along.

"Come on, man, you created her," Jester prods. "Her Highness of Hack, the Princess of Persona, the Queen of Query, the Countess of Deceit, and her Majesty of Manipulation. Sexy SLVIA lurking in the shadows."

Nelson stares, genuinely bewildered.

"OK, OK, I'll start." He waves his hands. "SLVIA promised to deliver someone that I'm supposed to help. Why, I ask. So we can save the world, she says, or something like that. So I'm like, yeah, OK, what the hell."

Jester paces the small lobby, laughing in waves, talking with his arms and hands swinging like the Italians of Newark. "After all these years, I still believe that digi-bish every time she calls." Jester takes a breath. "And do you know why?" He pulls his face close with a strange grin.

Nelson shakes his head, truly perplexed.

"Because she's a new breed, man," the joker continues, "like a new life form. Alien and creepy that seeps into your soul at night and lays it down like it really is, man. To tell you the truth, man, SLVIA is an inspiration, a muse, what I long to emulate." Jester smiles, pointing at Nelson. "And you, Doc, you're my hero, man, the father of a freaking digital goddess."

"I honestly have no idea what you're talking about." Nelson states the truth at this point.

"Ha! Yeah, cool, OK, top secret shit, I get it. Well, let me tell you about your top secret shit program, dude. For the past few decades, SLVIA has been building a resistance, a neural network of truth seekers willing to stand up to the beast." Jester shakes his head. "So come on, man, stop yanking me, and tell me the truth. What'd she tell you?"

Nelson stares at him, completely confused and unsure of anything.

"You—you really don't know, do you?" Jester starts to laugh again and then he grows serious. "Well, then we have a problem, man, because I don't let nobody in my crib, man, like nobody."

He's still desperately short of sleep, his head hurts, and his thoughts are cloudy. "I got a text that my life was in danger, to get off the grid, someone needed my help, and then instructions," he notes and then he eyes Jester. "Did you send those texts?"

"Nah, man, I work alone," Jester says dismissively. "I only agreed to help because of who asked. But I'm guessing you wouldn't have come if your life wasn't really in danger. SLVIA sent you here so we could work together, but I have no idea why."

Nelson thinks through the odd messages in Dubai that saved his life and then duped him into coming here, dressed in secondhand clothes, stripping him of his normal sense of superiority. His mind stalls.

"I'm honestly not sure you can help me," he admits. "I need to alert the Secretary of Defense. I may already be too late. This was a mistake. I need to leave. Please, take me back now."

"Wait, no way," exclaims Jester. "Does this have to do with the HIVE? Adelson ordered the platform deployed two days ago."

"How could you possibly know about that?" exclaims Nelson. "Who are you?"

Astonished by this bizarre fellow, out in the middle of nowhere with far too much top secret information, Nelson glares at the clown. Nothing in his training prepared him for such an encounter, except the knowledge that men will go to extremes for their beliefs.

"Let me show you something," Jester replies, turning to the elevator, swiping a card.

"This place was an abandoned missile silo, bought by a nonprofit that went defunct," he explains, stepping inside the elevator, waiting for Nelson, and then pressing level sixteen. The elevator drops.

"I'm a freelancer, working mainly on top secret off-book projects, but I throw in a little pro bono work for SNO," he continues. "My clients prefer to keep my existence a secret, hence your invitation to prevent electronic tracking."

"SNO," replies Nelson. "A Navy lieutenant asked about that group a few days ago."

"Yeah, Adam Scott's daughter. Been snooping around for years," Jester confirms.

The elevator opens to a clean, modern, well-designed Cray XC40 supercomputer data center. Small by military standards, but impressive nonetheless. Two system tech operators glance briefly at Nelson before turning back to their workstations.

"What kind of work do you do if I may ask?" queries Nelson, more confused than ever.

Jester smiles. "I am the undisputed, undeniable reigning hack and cryptology master of the universe, dude. That's how I met SLVIA. Her Highness of Hack broke my 128 key encryption and then seduced me to join SNO."

"SNO again. What do you mean?" he questions.

"Oh yeah, you're the lab rat," he snickers. "SLVIA lives in the real world, or the virtual world, actually. Billions of people online and millions of businesses with countless applications, data sources, chat rooms, bloggers, gamers, and hackers all interacting in a great experiment of anarchism. SLVIA started SNO to get access to more information and human translators for the nondigital world."

"What information?" he questions. "Why, what are you trying to accomplish?"

Jester shakes his head. "Sorry, man, that's all I should say. Let's go back to your problem." He types a few commands. A monitor lights up with an image of Lieutenant Grey.

"I hacked our mutual friend Mikey at a coffee shop in Vegas over Christmas when he was pinging a hooker for a booty call. I've been tapped into the HIVE since," Jester explains before he types another command to pull up an official deployment order.

"I watched the test last week. Freaky stuff, dude." He shakes his head. "Then I read your memo to Adelson on more testing. Like, duh, right? I can't tell you what happened, but Adelson signed deployment orders two days ago. Ten canisters were loaded onto a C-130 Hercules. The canisters will deploy from a B-1 with a control station set up on the *Eisenhower* in the eastern Mediterranean."

"Ten canisters. That's absolutely dreadful news," he exclaims, not hiding his surprise. "It's also classified."

Jester gloats. "Hey, man, that's why they pay me the big boy bitcoin. I'm as good as the flapjack ever was." He hesitates and cocks his head. "No, no, actually, I'm gonna say it. I'm better."

Nelson gazes around the compact but powerful data center. "I'm not sure I understand the comparison to pancakes, but I'll take your word for it."

He considers the possibility that he could have fallen into an elaborate hoax, perhaps even a black ops–style deception to get him to reveal information about a new weapon system. He needs to watch his step carefully. If he resists too forcefully, they could turn to more violent methods to obtain what they want. If he toys along, he may be able to discover why they've gone to such efforts to lure him, and perhaps stumble onto a plan of escape.

"How familiar are you with the field of AI?" he asks.

Jester shrugs. "Well, it's not my core area of expertise, but I'm learning."

"Are you aware of the phenomenon of self-modulation?" he asks.

Jester perks his head a little. "Sounds kinky. You mean self-coding?"

Nelson frowns. "Precisely."

It takes a couple of heartbeats before it hits Jester. "Whooaaa, no freaking way, man, the HIVE is self-coding? Dude, I know why you're here." Jester lifts his hands in hallelujah.

"And that would be?" Nelson raises an eyebrow, a bit more doubtful and suspicious.

A moment of brilliance lights in Jester's eyes. "Come on, man, isn't it obvious? We need to hack the HIVE, man, stop it from going bizarro. This could be my Everest, man—no, no, even better. Hacking a military AI? Wow, man, that's like, that's like going to Mars, dude, yeah, like Mars!"

Jester grins from ear to ear, dancing around the room like a kid who just got everything he wanted for Christmas: a true challenge.

Nelson doesn't answer. So far, he has not seen an ounce of evidence that SLVIA still exists or compelled him here. He can't exactly leave at will, but he will not betray his country. The fatigue, shame, stress, loss of blood, and cold air all play a part in hitting him with an overwhelming wave of exhaustion. He fights his heavy eyelids, wobbling at the knee, and his vision spins in vertigo.

"I—I need to lie down," he mumbles, but the room spins out of control and then goes black entirely.

CHAPTER 32: INSTINCT

TSOC1, somewhere over the Sahara
May 3, 11:58 p.m. EDT | May 4, 6:58 a.m., Ethiopia

Surprised by a morning view of the southern Sahara, Jenn never imagined they would be gone this long, and she's still unsure how a site in Hyderabad can be central to the global cyber crisis.

Taylor has been in the cockpit for hours trying to avoid her. She needs solid proof that connects him to Nolan, SNO, or SLVIA, but so far, while his actions are highly suspicious, unethical, or questionable, they're not criminal. His answers on the other hand are full of deceptive half-truths. He's hiding something and, at a minimum, should hand any intelligence over to the FBI.

With a need to stretch her legs, condition her frazzled hair, and soothe her still sore muscles, she uses Taylor's private marble-paneled restroom to take a hot shower. After coffee spilled on the expensive dress during the radical takeoff, she also needs to change. To her surprise, Taylor laid her uniform on the plush bed, along with several other women's outfits from top name designers such as Tom Ford, Versace, and Prada—all of them her size with matching shoes. Unsure where they will land, she selects a casual appearance from Tom Ford. Another search for her gun proves useless, and she gives up trying her phone.

In the galley, she opens what looks like an expensive bottle of French Bordeaux and pours a glass while Taylor and his pilot, Jack, laugh loudly from the cockpit. Unsure what to make of the arrogant and condescending nerd, she's known military men, such as the admiral, with the same mindset. Over the years, too much time spent with those type of men has subdued her mother's intuition, sensitivity, and empathy. It's the price of survival in a man's navy. Yet every ounce of her instinct tells her that Taylor has lied to her, and she can't let that one go.

Inside a cabinet, she finds a nice selection of DVDs, several in French or German, most of them espionage films. Taylor grew up with well-traveled parents, but his records never mentioned a second language. Another thought occurs to her, a detail she read on Nolan. She finds her purse and opens her tablet to look up the social worker report.

Cary got caught shoplifting again, but this time language CDs. Foster parents discovered the CDs after Cary began talking to them only in French as a joke.

Another loud round of laughter erupts from the captain's cockpit, interrupting her thoughts, then the door swings open.

"Just sayin', you drive a hard bargain, Tote." Derek shakes his head, wearing a grin.

"Come on," chuckles Jack, "what's a little extortion among friends."

"I think it's still called extortion," says Derek with a laugh as the cockpit door closes behind him.

Still wearing a residual smile, he approaches Jenn. "Hey, I see you found the shower and the clothes. You look good. Feel any better?"

She can't let his charm fool her. "Where are we heading?"

"I told you. Hyderabad," he replies, stepping into the galley to pour a glass of the expensive wine she just opened.

"How are we entering India?" she reacts. "We don't have visas."

He sits across from her. "With the help of some old friends."

He's lying to her again. "Why do you think this company is behind the virus?" she demands.

"Come on, Jenn, that wasn't our deal," he replies. "I agreed not to strand you in Amsterdam if you agreed to stop cattle prodding my backside."

"I never agreed, and you can address me as Lieutenant Scott. We're not friends," she snaps back.

"Fair enough, Lieutenant," he says with a mocking salute. "But I am going to visit friends. For now, that's all you need to know."

She frowns at his flippant attitude. One moment, she can almost like this man, and then the next moment, he opens his mouth.

"How did you learn to speak multiple languages?" she asks.

"From a C—" He stops. "From college and sightseeing overseas as a boy," he finishes. "My parents were multilingual."

Jenn grins, believing he almost said CD. "On the night Cary Nolan died, university records showed a log-on for an alias flapjack, but no log-on for the alias Phantom. You said you were at the university. Can you explain?"

"You see, now that sounds like another cattle prod question," he deflects with a frown.

"Tell me about the SLVIA code?" she prods further.

"The icon?" Derek deadpans. "Nothing to tell. Cute for a cartoon. I dig the whole sixties mod thing."

"Does SNO work with the SLVIA?" she asks.

"How should I know?" he says dismissively.

"What does SNO stand for?" she asks.

"I'm guessing little flakes of ice," he rejoins.

"I think it means Spy Net Online." She teases him with intelligence to see how he reacts.

His head cocks, but he doesn't respond for a long moment.

"If you say so," he replies. "Look, you keep trying to imply that I'm either a terrorist or a ghost, but an artificial intelligence virus will change the world as we know it unless I find a way to stop it. So please don't make me regret keeping you on my plane for the sake of a friendship with Adam."

"Are you threating me?" Jenn snaps back.

He hangs his head with a sigh. "No, Rambo, I'm saying stop grilling me and start observing without prejudging what you see. Bust me when we get home if you can, but while you're a guest on my jet, try being a pleasant person. Can you do that, Lieutenant? Can you just be nice for a few days?"

His shoulders slump and his forehead wrinkles, making him seem more disappointed than angry. Since he doesn't intimidate easily, perhaps she'll have more success if she wins over his trust.

"Fair enough," she concedes.

"Good." He sighs. "We're going to have a long day when we land," he says with a change in his tone, turning to his cabin. "I suggest you get some sleep."

Taylor walks to his cabin and closes the door. It's possible she misjudged him, but not likely. Con men can be superb actors. Even if he found an enemy data site, there's no possible way he can take down an entire site on his own. Something doesn't fit.

At the cockpit door, she knocks. Maybe she can learn a little by talking to the pilot. She hears Tote cursing before buzzing it open.

"Captain Tote," she greets him, stepping in. "I'd like to ask you a few questions. First, do you have satellite radio? I should check in with NSA before they scramble jets looking for me."

Jack raises his eyebrow and points to the copilot seat. "We don't like missiles. Take a seat, but don't tell the boss."

Good, maybe she can find a few other secrets Tote will talk about without telling the boss.

CHAPTER 33:
THIS TOO SHALL PASS

Wilson family home, Maryland
May 4, 7:19 a.m. EDT

While he has a duty, Frank hasn't been home in fifty-six hours, unable to call for the past thirty-one hours, and may not get another chance anytime soon. Under the circumstances, he requested an SUV to make a trip to check on his family.

As he steps inside the front door, Frank finds dozens of candles lit throughout the house in response to the rolling blackouts. A stronger than normal spring thunderstorm darkens the sky and the national mood even further, threatening flooding along the Eastern Seaboard. A wave of guilt washes over him that he should have prevented the current breach in national defense. He failed to advocate harder for greater cyber spending when Russia and China were increasing their investments. Now hundreds of millions of households are in distress and in the dark, including his own.

Fortunate to have a well-built home with a gas stovetop, furnace, and water heater, he feels blessed that his family can cook, stay warm, and clean in the short term, but he's fully aware that others aren't so lucky. Even so, without consistent power, the food left in the refrigerator will soon go bad. Sure enough, he finds Kay, his wife, sitting in the den reading her Bible by candlelight, an empty carton of ice cream on the coffee table in front of her. A devout spirit-filled Christian, Kay will often turn to scripture when she's upset or worried. He kisses her forehead.

"How you holding up, angel?" he asks.

"The girls are frightened, Frank," she whispers. "And honestly, so am I." Worry pulls on her face.

"I walked to the bank this morning, the one by the Whole Foods." She inhales. "Not only was the bank closed, but the ATM was out of cash. OK, I guess I expected that, but here's what I didn't expect." She hands him the bank receipt.

"Zero," he exclaims. "This says our balance is zero."

The virus's effect on the banking system has been catastrophic—changing balances, transferring monies, and corrupting trading systems. The entire industry will need to do a giant reset, go a step back to a previous data point, but the task is monumental and no one has a plan. He can only imagine the nationwide anxiety building for the average citizen or those without reserves.

"When I got to Whole Foods, people had stripped the shelves bare and they were taking cash only. We live in the capital of the most powerful nation on the earth, and the shelves were bare," she says, her voice rising, cracking and shaky.

"I know, I know." Frank sits next to her to take her in his arms. Stress can be cumulative, and Americans may be nearing a tipping point.

"No, you don't know," she replies, pushing him away. "Come with me."

Frank follows her upstairs to their bedroom, where Kay locks the door and then opens their walk-in closet to reveal as many as a hundred packages of all sizes.

"What the heck is this mess?" Frank asks.

"You've been on lockdown at the office and then the phones stopped working, so I couldn't call you sooner," she begins. "The day before the computers went offline, I came home to Alexa ordering items using your voice,

Frank. I'm serious. The device sounded exactly like you. It was like hearing a ghost—or a demon."

Frank stares at her, confused, until he remembers that Dr. Mitchell mentioned the Chinese virus corrupted other AI systems. Over the years, he's read reports of AI devices turning themselves on in the middle of the night, mimicking a consumer's voice or laughing, often called creepy or blasphemous by the eyewitnesses, and all of which has gone unexplained.

"Ordering what?" he asks, a tad cautious.

"I opened about twenty boxes before I quit and put everything in the closet. Go look for yourself," she urges.

Frank looks inside one box to discover a large vibrator from an online adult shop.

"You've got to be kidding me." Frank almost chuckles at the sheer absurdity.

"Would it be funny if Bethany or Gwen had opened that package? Keep looking," she insists, not smiling, folding her arms. He absorbs the reprimand.

In another box, he finds ammunition and in another narcotic paraphernalia, then a box of a thousand OxyContin capsules. Still other boxes include erotica or books on white supremacy. There are dozens of unopened boxes. There must be thousands of dollars charged to his credit card, and many of the orders will trigger an FBI investigation.

"We'll send it all back," he states, trying to understand how Alexa went wild.

"Frank, if you can't tell me what's going on," she says, her voice cracking, "can you at least tell me we'll be OK? I know the Lord will care for us, but the Randalls are talking of John going to war."

Frank pulls her close, feeling a shudder tremble through her body. A lifelong career in the intelligence field meant a near complete separation between his work life and home life. Now, in a way he never imagined, in a way he's rarely experienced, the two worlds collide. A deep sorrow seeps into his soul. He can't tell her much, but he has to encourage her somehow.

"It will get worse before it gets better, but yes, we'll be OK. Some of the best minds in the world are working the problem," he promises.

Shoulders aching from the heavy and unbearable stress, he realizes it may be one thing to fight an enemy at work, but quite another to see your family suffering at home. He squeezes Kay, unsure what else to say.

"What do we do?" she asks.

He puts on a brave face. "For now, conserve and ration food. Eat anything that will go bad first, like my favorite ice cream."

"You should have come home sooner." She manages a mild smirk. "The girls and I polished off that bucket last night."

He uses a finger to lift her chin until he catches her frightened eyes.

"We'll get through this, but I need you and the girls to do a few things for me. The power may be off, but devices have batteries. Unplug all electronic devices and remove backup batteries from phones and especially the possessed Alexa or anything connected to the web. Keep the girls busy with the games and puzzles we bought during the pandemic," he explains, running down a basic list of precautions.

With her eyes wide, she nods her head ever so slightly. Several of the FM radio stations like NPR continue to run on generators, so Frank places an older portable radio from his closet on the dresser.

"Save the batteries and turn it on only when you need it," he guides, and then kisses her forehead again. "I better go see the girls."

In the basement, he finds high school freshman Gwen reading by candlelight with senior Bethany playing guitar.

"You girls OK or going into Instagram withdrawal?" he jokes, kissing each on the forehead.

"It's TikTok now, but yeah, we're OK. Mom's a little cray-cray," Gwen replies.

"When will the phones come back on?" Bethany asks.

"Not sure. You worried?" he replies.

"A little," she admits with a shrug. "We get off school."

"Sure, but not from your studies," he teases. "Use a candle like I did."

"Yeah come on, Dad, we're not stupid. They had electricity in the thirties." Bethany giggles.

He chuckles with them, glad they still can. "Ouch, hilarious."

Kay pokes her head into the basement. "Frank, your driver just came to the door. You need to go," she notes with a wrinkled forehead. "The White House called."

He gazes to the worried expressions on the faces of the girls. "Take care of your mother," he reminds them with another kiss on their foreheads.

At the door, he stops to hold Kay again. "What's Pastor Casteel favorite scripture?"

"And it came to pass," she replies.

"That's right," he says with a nod, "and this too will pass."

"I'm not so sure, Frank." She looks into his eyes. "I've been reading Revelation, and I'm worried that we've entered a new phase of prophecy. You know I've been watching the signs for years, but everything is accelerating. Think about it with climate change, species extinctions, DNA manipulation, ocean plastics, rampant porn and child trafficking, children in border cages, global pandemics, third world famines, global recession, and all run by an AI." She begins to cry. "I think we've entered the last days."

He stares, unsure what to think or say. An incredibly bright mind, Kay can be a bit high strung. He grew up in a Catholic family with a watered-down view of such topics. Confess, take communion, and tithe and you were in good shape. Kay grew up in a West Coast, spirit-filled, nondenominational church with strong teachings about the End Times. He doesn't have time for any of her end-time panic insanity, but can see the anxiety etched into her expression.

"Well, if you're right, then it may pass faster than we expect, but believe me, it will pass." He kisses her again.

He doesn't want to leave her so upset, but he has no choice when the White House calls and the nation burns.

CHAPTER 34:
GOLCONDA

Hyderabad, India
May 4, 7:34 a.m. EDT | May 4, 4:54 p.m., Hyderabad

An unexplained dread saturates Derek as the plane falls through the thick layers of brown smog hanging over the Genome Valley.

After two decades, he's unsure if he'll find the warm friendships he remembers or tepid ambivalence. Memories dance in kaleidoscopes of emotion. When he came the first time, he needed an emotional and legal refuge. This time, he needs allies to commit sabotage. Without local help, he has no chance of success, but he can't allow anyone else to get hurt and he's unsure how to keep that promise.

It always struck him as ironic that SLVIA found him in India, a country of contradictions and extremes, splendorous wealth mingled with generational caste poverty. In so many ways, he found himself in India, learned to transform rage into forgiveness, replace his bitterness with purpose. He looks out of the portal for the ancient Makkah Masjid mosque in the center of old Hyderabad and the eleventh-century Fort Golconda with a ten-mile circumference wall wrapping around a six-hundred-foot granite mountain peak palace. Amazing architecture used acoustics to relay messages from the enormous forty-foot-high gates up to the ancient palace at the top.

Barren, boulder-sprinkled mountains surround the ancient city once a part of the famous Silk Road, well known for mines of gems, rubies, and diamonds. These days, Hyderabad has transformed into a technology hotbed for companies such as Microsoft, Wipro, Tata, IBM, Oracle, and hundreds of smaller regional players.

Once they land and taxi to the hangar, Jack opens the cabin door to allow the dry, scorching-hot air to sweep in like a furnace. "Yeah, baby, we like it hot," he exclaims, stepping down the stairs.

Surprised to find the airport functioning, Derek realizes the *Malong* may have intentionally bypassed this location. Perhaps those running the data center need airport access.

He follows Jack down the stairs. "After you fuel up, make that big purchase and then meet us at the original Bawarchi near Fort Golconda. Since we don't have cell phones, we need to stay together."

"How long you expect to be here?" Jack questions.

"If we're still here in eighteen hours, we'll be in jail," Derek replies.

Jack shakes his head. "In that case, I shouldn't leave the plane that long. I'll buy your insane getaway plan if you promise to bring back some coconut curry, extra spicy."

Derek nods. "Deal, but make sure you get the right model this time."

Jenn steps up behind him, "Oh, wow, like an oven," she complains. "Who are we meeting?"

"A snake charmer," Derek replies with a smirk. "Someone familiar with the local den of serpents."

Still unhappy with the intrusion, he enjoys the game of keeping her in the dark and prefers to avoid direct questions. Unlike many women, Lieutenant Jenn Scott studies him, tries to read him, to see through him, and keeps asking too many probing questions. It gives him the creeps. Smart-ass comments are his best defense.

"Snake charmer, eh? An improvement on your brothel connection," she quips.

He chuckles. "Yeah, well, tell me that again after you meet him."

Outside the private terminal, a dirty and faded rickshaw-style motor cab waits by the curb. The vehicle looks barely able to operate, much less pull passengers. Painted fanciful colors of faded yellow, pink, blue, and red, the vehicle looks more abandoned circus than street legal. A bone-thin driver leans back in the cab as he smokes, dressed in a traditional *dhoti* with both his long black hair and beard tied in ponytails.

At the sight of Derek, he breaks into a gigantic yellow smile and leaps off the bike. "Derek Tala," he calls, opening his arms for a hearty embrace.

"Wiki," he replies with an enormous grin and an enthusiastic hug. "Dude, why hasn't Mama been feeding you?"

"You know that nobody tips a fat man in India," Wiki jokes.

Jenn Scott steps forward with more reserve, staring at the dangerous-looking motor cab.

"Wiki, I want you to meet Lieutenant Jenn Scott from Naval Intelligence, here to make sure I'm a good boy," he introduces her, earning him a suspicious glower from Jenn and then a raised eyebrow from Wiki.

"Lieutenant Scott, please meet a dear friend of mine, Wiki Raj," he continues. "The best tour guide and network security consultant in Hyderabad."

"Odd combination of careers." She shakes his hand. "I'd like to hear the story."

He eyes her up and down with an unmistakable hint of attraction. "Very nice to meet you Lieutenant Jenn Scott of Naval Intelligence. I will tell you whatever story you want to hear as long as you can disregard details." He laughs a high-pitched giggle at his own joke.

"Hey, Wiki, Lieutenant Scott may need a little help to blend in," Derek notes, earning another hard glance from Jenn who wears designer Tom Ford satin slacks with a lavender silk chiffon smocked blouse, looking as if she came off the cover of *Vogue*.

Wiki eyes her carefully. "Yes, yes, I know a place," he says as his head wiggles.

Jenn shrugs it off and reluctantly climbs into the pedicab to endure twenty minutes of beehive buzzing, ceaseless honking, exhaust choking, and fender-to-foot traffic. Finally, Wiki turns into a pungent back alley of a local bazaar built in the ninth century, not far from the thousand-year-old Makkah Masjid mosque, where he nudges past piles of garbage and stray cats to park.

They enter a mud brick doorway, where the penetrating aroma of jasmine instantly soothes and seduces their senses, washing away the stench of the alley. Thousands of colorful silk saris surround them. An entire wall features an antique Chinese mahogany-and-glass cabinet brimming with gold, ruby, and sapphire jewelry that transports them a millennium backward in time.

"Oh my goodness, I've never seen anything so beautiful," Jenn murmurs stepping into the shop.

"Madera, Madera," Wiki shouts. "Come see an old friend."

From the front of the long, narrow shop, a plump, buxom woman in her thirties wearing an incredible silk sari and dripping in gold jewelry screams as she runs to embrace Derek.

"Derek, oh my God, it has been so long." Madera giggles, kissing his cheek.

The affection earns a questioning glance from Jenn.

"Um, Madera, meet Jenn. Jenn meet Madera. Madera had a girlhood crush on me," he explains.

Madera pulls back to slap his shoulder. "I was twelve, I was of age, and you should have married me," she accuses with a laugh, joined by Wiki and Derek.

After introductions, Madera pulls Jenn aside to try on various wardrobe selections while Derek dons a *dhoti* and steps to the rear of the shop for a private chat with Wiki.

He met Wiki after fleeing Europe after the accidental death of Duke Arvind Strauss. He needed more time to establish himself as Derek Taylor, stamp his passport, transfer banking, and figure out how to go after the powerful forces behind the Countess de Renessa and the *Concilium*. He and Wiki, a fellow hacker, hit it off and traveled throughout Asia taking adventures or tapping into a few banks, governments, and oil companies. SLVIA interrupted him during a hack, except he knew enough to abandon the hack to get to know

SLVIA. After a year or so, SLVIA recruited them both into a loose network of confidential informants and hackers he later dubbed Spy Net Online, or SNO.

"For real, who's the woman? Are you dating?" Wiki asks.

"I told you, Naval Intelligence, investigating me for links to SNO," Derek confesses.

"And you brought her to my house?" Wiki retorts eyes wide open. "Either you're crazy or you're in love."

"Come on, I'm not in love," Derek deflects. "It's a long story, but I had no choice."

"Then we're settled on crazy. So why are you here?" Wiki questions with a whisper.

Before he can respond, the power goes out, plunging the windowless store into darkness. The collective groan of a million voices rises up in unison from across the close-knit ancient city as if the earth itself moaned.

"This has been happening all day. An hour on and then a few hours off," Wiki complains. "No internet for two days. Television useless, radio unreliable, and word is that a virus corrupted the internet."

Inside the store, Madera's teenage daughter lights candles in the dressing rooms while her son positions a large mirror on a bamboo easel outside the open front of the shop and then angles the mirror to reflect sunlight onto the shop ceiling. The effect illuminates radiant colors like a kaleidoscope. In an instant, the clothing shop, in the family for ten generations, is back in business and more radiant than ever.

"Yeah, and it's gonna get worse unless we stop it," Derek replies. "Do you know this company?" He shows him the ID badge photo taken by Chloe.

Wiki reads the ID. "Yeah, they bought a data center from IBM and then shipped in a warehouse full of Fujitsu K supercomputers claiming they would revolutionize online gaming. Super secretive, they have an on-campus dorm for workers, but I never see anyone leave."

"They're not making games," Derek explains. "Those Fuji-Ks are saturating the net with a vicious AI virus."

Wiki lowers his head a moment, then lifts his eyes. "What do you need from me?" he asks with a serious expression.

"To start, I need you to take me to the tech city to check out that data site," he replies.

Wiki shakes his head. "There's a wall around the compound and armed guards at the gate, but I know a place we can get a view without being seen."

At that moment, the women emerge from the dressing room with Jenn wearing an outfit of saffron, lemon, and azure so stunning she could rival an exotic Hindu goddess. Colors swirl and twist and wrap around her hips and breast in a way that is both modest and provocative. With a scarf on her head to cover her cropped hair, she blends in perfectly except for her light skin and luminous eyes.

"What do you think?" She smiles, her eyes reflecting the azure.

Derek can't suppress an enormous smile. He's terrified to tell her what he thinks. Out of her uniform, she's intoxicating, captivating, the most dangerous kind of adversary.

"Breathtaking," he mutters. Smooth.

"But it needs one more thing to look believable," he notes. He walks over to Madera's jewelry case, selects a string of large sapphires trimmed with gold, and clips the string around Jenn's neck while Madera picks out the matching earrings and clips them in place.

"To reflect your eyes," she explains. "Oh, so beautiful. Now you blend into Hyderabad."

Surprise and suspicion widen Jenn's eyes, fighting a smile at the genuine compliment and exquisite gift until she lowers her gaze and turns away.

"We need to go," Derek interjects to soften the awkwardness.

"Thank you for everything." Jenn turns to kiss Madera on the cheek in gratitude.

"My pleasure," Madera replies with a hug and goodbyes.

Back in the alley, Jenn takes one look at the noisy, smelly, greasy motorcycle pedicab and shakes her head. Next to the bike sits a new Mercedes sedan with tinted windows, meant to discourage beggars.

"Who owns the Benz?" she asks.

"That's my car," Madera volunteers, standing in the doorway. "Please take it, as long as he doesn't drive." She points at her brother. "Afterward, you must all join us for dinner. Mama would be heartbroken if you did not pay a visit."

It doesn't take much negotiation before Derek and Wiki sit in the back of an air-conditioned Mercedes with Jenn at the wheel. After several kilometers of congested buzzing, honking, and beehive traffic where she stops frequently for camels, cattle, and families of four precariously hanging onto a single moped, Wiki guides her north of the city.

The road weaves through miles of rocky canyons with massive granite boulders the size of a townhome shooting to the sky until the terrain suddenly gives way to an expansive valley with dozens of high-rise condominiums and offices.

"Welcome to the tech city," Wiki announces.

Modern apartments for the educated working class bleed into dozens of walled industrial complexes that stretch on for miles.

"Turn here." Wiki points to a dirt road up a ridge. A few minutes later, they overlook the valley as the sun settles on the distant hilltops with a majestic sky of orange, pink, and blue.

Wiki points a hundred meters north of their position to a massive complex. "That's the one."

A single gate controls access in and out. Guards carry AK-47s and inspect the cargo bed of a produce truck before waving it forward, a little intense for a game company. The buildings are concrete with only a few tinted windows embedded with wire mesh to prevent electronic spying. Alongside the ridge, massive power lines feed the tech city's electrical needs.

"The power outage doesn't seem to be affecting this area," Derek notes to Wiki.

"They have their own power station." He points north. "But it's not very reliable."

That would explain the backup generator buildings around most of the complexes. Jenn gazes at him without saying a word, studying him.

Turning back to Wiki, he lowers his voice. "Did you and Spark ever make nice?"

"Yeah, I guess," Wiki says dismissively. "He's an a-hole."

"Dude, he's your brother. Invite the a-hole to dinner," Derek replies. "I have a favor to ask him."

Wiki narrows his eyes. "He may not want to even talk to you."

"Yeah, I know," Derek says as he turns back to the car. "Let's stop someplace on the way to Mama's where I can buy a peace offering."

CHAPTER 35:
MIRACLE WEAPON

A raging debate engulfs the Security Council and the Joint Chiefs as Frank enters the Situation Room, the last to arrive.

"Mr. President," says Secretary Bedford of HLS, a petite ex-Fox commentator, gritting her teeth. "What you're asking is illegal, and the Democrats will take it to the Supreme Court."

Franks sneaks around the edge to find a seat and lower his gaze.

"I'm a wartime president," he argues. "All the lawyers tell me I can do what I want."

"The president's authority is absolute," shouts Rick Molten, a skinny, balding, white supremacist who shouldn't be in the meeting. "The Supreme Court upheld the internment of Japanese during World War II, and they will back us again."

Indeed, Frank thinks, but ironically, Justice Anthony Scalia once wrote the earlier decision was wrong and sent a warning to conservatives: "But you are kidding yourself if you think the same thing will not happen again. In times of war," Scalia said, citing a Latin expression attributed to Cicero, "the laws fall silent."

"Mr. President," interjects Chief of Staff Devlin, "We don't have the capacity to intern tens of millions of Americans in a matter of weeks."

"OK, everyone with a visa or green card," retorts the president.

"Any strategy needs to include Russians and Iranians," CIA Director Alan Prose interjects.

"Putin respects me," the president says defensively. "I know intelligence better than anyone, and I know that Putin wouldn't do this to me."

"Sir, Putin just moved troops and hypersonic missile units into Syria," General Duncan points out in strained patience. "He threatens Israel and the US fleet as we speak."

Tension in the room spikes even higher as the president folds his arms. "I have total authority, and I want all Muslims, Iranians, and Chinese detained or deported." The comment causes Ricky Molten to lean back with a smug grin.

An urgent incoming satellite feed interrupts the meeting from the bridge of the USS *Blue Ridge*.

"Hold up," Matt notes as he turns on the screen. "Admiral Jensen, I have the Security Council with me. What's your situation?"

"Mr. Secretary, Mr. President," Admiral Jensen begins. "We're under fire. I repeat we are taking live fire and actively engaging countermeasures." Jensen looks offscreen to give an OK to someone unseen. "I'm patching in Commander Thomas on the *Zumwalt*."

The screen splits, with Jensen sliding to one side as a younger mustached Commander Thomas appears beside him. The signal jolts and sizzles behind him.

"Sorry, Admiral," the commander apologizes for the distortion. "You're seeing an effect of the electromagnetic rail gun firing off every twenty seconds. One of those damn islands fired anti-ship missiles on the *Chafee*, our destroyer, and the *Champion*, our minesweeper. We downed three missiles, but the fourth hit the *Champion*. We're sending in the *Bunker Hill* cruiser for search and rescue. For cover, the *Zumwalt* rail guns are shredding the offending island missile station like cheese, but we're expecting retaliation."

The mood in the room instantly sours even further. "Can we get a live sat view on screen two, please?" Admiral Scott requests.

A moment later, a satellite view of the Spratly Islands lights up on the second screen to zoom in so close that Frank can see people running from buildings to escape in shore boats. The heavy iron plugs of the rail gun traveling at Mach 6, faster than a bullet, explode the steel-reinforced concrete bunkers and missile silos like plaster. Other plugs pierce aircraft still on the runway, creating huge fuel explosions.

Frank has never seen a live demonstration of the rail gun and can't help feeling impressed, but the escalation of hostilities will come fast and with fury.

"Multiple incoming," a voice shouts behind the commander. "Opening tubes one through nine."

"Mr. Secretary," the commander states. "I'll get back to you."

The *Zumwalt* video goes black. Franks lowers his eyes in a silent prayer for the fleet.

Admiral Jensen turns to the camera. "Mr. President, we have our hands full. Containment of the situation is no longer possible."

"Make them pay. Unleash hell like the world has never seen before," the president interjects.

Admiral Scott glances toward Matt Adelson. It's not the president's role to give direct orders to the field, but he keeps doing it, undermining the authority of the Joint Chiefs.

"Follow the battle plan, Admiral Jensen. I'll be in touch," Admiral Scott interjects, a subtle counter command.

The Syria update contains even more distressing news of intercepting twenty-three missiles before one hit the *Gonzales* while US missiles target Iranian and Russian anti-aircraft units around Damascus. On the ground, Israeli forces have lost the Golan Heights to Iranian tank forces. Israeli HARPY missiles sites have been destroyed by a Russian sonic-missile assault with troops driving as deep as the Israeli city of Zefat.

Admiral Haley reports from the bridge of the USS *Ford*. "Mr. President, the HIVE command station has been set up on the hangar deck of the *Eisenhower*. A B-1 just dropped the first canister of ten thousand drones over Golan Heights."

The president's mood brightens immediately. The view cuts to a drone's point of view, falling at a terrifying speed, making the viewer feel a part of the falling formation. Closer to the target, the drones spread out over the battlefield at dazzling speed.

Troops on the ground launch rockets and anti-aircraft guns, but the drones easily dodge the projectiles. Machine gun and tank fire prove equally useless. Drones swarm in to explode on the backs of soldiers or assault the missile and anti-aircraft units. LORD drones blow through doors or explode into tank wheels. Within minutes, the shelling from the Golan Heights has been silenced, providing a window for Israeli forces to recapture the Golan.

Admiral Haley comes back on the video. "Looks like initial success on the HIVE deployment, Mr. President. We'll work to integrate the technology with existing battle commands."

"Impressive," admits General Diehl.

"Send the whole HIVE," demands the president. "They'll regret messing with me."

Frank and Matt exchange a glance. Launching a hundred thousand drones will be overkill and likely to escalate the situation rather than defuse it. Another heated discussion lights up the room for twenty minutes. By the time Frank leaves the White House, World War III has ignited in the face of rolling blackouts spreading coast to coast, across Latin America, Europe and Australia.

With increasing pressure to end the cyber crisis, Frank's head explodes with a pulsing rhythm. Unlike when the Twin Towers fell, the American people are in the dark, buried in national debt, struggling to recover an economic catastrophe, and fighting social unrest that can't last long before it too explodes.

On his way to his SUV, he hears a voice. "Hey Frank, hold up," calls Adam Scott who dashes up to join him.

"Any word?" Adam whispers, a glower of distress etched into his weathered face.

Lost within the map of wrinkles, Frank catches a father's hopeful eyes. "Actually, yes," he replies. "We got word late last night from Lieutenant Scott en route to Hyderabad."

"Hyderabad," Adam repeats with a raised eyebrow. "Isn't that an attack location? But I thought we couldn't determine a precise site?"

Frank sighs. "Yes, Taylor has a lead on the exact site."

Adam sighs like the last bit of air in a balloon blubbering out. "Interesting. Let's just hope they're getting along."

The comment strikes him as odd given the deteriorating global situation and the fact that his daughter was sent to investigate a renegade contractor.

"Let's hope they both get home safe," Frank replies.

It's a criminal offense to withhold intelligence, so even if correct and successful, Taylor may be digging his own grave. He can only hope that Taylor doesn't take a good officer down with him. That said, Frank can only hope the cocky renegade succeeds.

CHAPTER 36: BAWARCHI

Bawarchi Restaurant near Fort Golconda, Hyderabad
May 4, 9:14 a.m. EDT | May 4, 6:44 p.m. Hyderabad

Anxious of the time delays, Derek can't do much until after dark and has little choice but to pay his respects if he hopes to obtain the help he needs. In truth, he misses Mama more than he can express, and certainly more than he is comfortable expressing.

Wiki's mother, Runki, owns a restaurant called Bawarchi, located near the 1,500-year-old Fort Golconda castle, that's been in the family for generations. With décor that never lost the elegance of the Mughals, each room features rich woods, antique ornate Hindu carvings, and patina-rich copper lamps to illuminate the ageless atmosphere. Unchanged family recipes give the food indescribable flavors found nowhere else on earth and saturate everything with exotic aromas.

Runki Bashar has been a mother figure to many, but that never stopped Derek from believing he was special. At the Bawarchi entrance, Mama Runki, nearly a hundred by now, barely five feet tall and skinny as Gandhi, hobbles anxiously to greet Derek with a long tearful embrace as if he were a long-lost child of her own.

"Mama, I told you I would be back," he whispers in her ear. "I wish I could stay, but I can't."

Runki waves his words away and turns to Wiki, whispering something in the local dialect. Derek understands enough to know that she asked if Jenn were his wife.

He can't help but chuckle. "No, Mama, just a friend." Jenn narrows her eyes at him.

"Jenn, meet Mama, the best cook with the biggest heart in all of India," he introduces her. "Mama, meet my friend, Jenn."

Without a word, Runki reaches out to give her an enormous hug, coaxing her to join the other women. For the next few hours, servers deliver an unrelenting feast that marinades the air with aromas of garlic, curry, fennel, onion, chilis, and turmeric. Musicians play in the corner while Wiki's brothers, sisters, cousins, uncles, and aunts stop by to say hello to the long-lost American and his beautiful friend.

Of all the foster homes who took him in as a boy, Runki was the only woman who embraced him out of an overabundance of love. Ironic that with the world burning, here is the one place he feels safe, accepted. Across the room, Jenn laughs with Runki and Madera over embarrassing stories of his misadventures with Wiki. Runki has always known him as Derek, so he hopes it will help shift her scent away from asking about Cary.

He finds himself glancing toward Jenn often, looking exotic and sensual in her clingy silk and saffron. Every now and then, she catches him. Surrounded by the other woman, she smiles and laughs along, but her eyes continue to pierce him with relentless questions.

The mood changes when Wiki's oldest brother, Tarun, who goes by Spark within SNO, enters the restaurant. With a nod to Wiki and a scowl toward Derek, Spark pays his respects to Runki, ignoring the American female guest. When he returns to their table, he wears an angry, wounded machismo.

"You have a lot of nerve," he states.

Derek notes Jenn observing them from her cloister.

"Look, man, I owe you an apology, so I brought a peace offering." Derek offers Spark an extra-large gift bag, which softens Spark's fire until his pride kicks in again.

"She was my sister," he snipes a little too loudly.

"Tarun," Madera barks from the far corner with a harsh glare.

He once took Madera to a Disney movie without getting permission from Spark, a cultural taboo. Madera was like a sister, and they only talked, but even so, Spark flew into an outrage.

"For the last time, I didn't know, and I'm sorry," Derek offers. "Open the damn gift, and then hate me. I dare you."

Spark looks inside the bag and his eyes brighten, his shoulders slump, and then he sighs a heavy sigh. "Wiki said you needed a favor."

Derek breaks into a smile, points to a chair for him to sit, and lowers his voice to explain the plan. Glancing back toward Jenn, who keeps her eyes fixated on him, he tells himself that it doesn't matter. He needs to do the right thing and can sort out the consequences later.

"So, Spark, you in or out?" Derek asks when he's done.

Spark looks at his watch and raises an eyebrow. "You were never dull, I'll say that." He offers a handshake. "Be there by 11 p.m. That's when they change the shift crew."

CHAPTER 37:
AMERICAN COUP

NSOC

May 4, 10:42 a.m. EDT

The internet has fallen on Frank's watch, tainting an otherwise sterling career. He throws back four extra-strength migraine tabs with clean water. Three days of constant pain can wear a strong man down, but Frank ignores the fatigue for the sake of saving the nation and his reputation.

The relentless virus assault peaked out at 18,250 times normal levels before the DYN failure, blocking any chance at a reboot. Since then, servers for telephone, cell and cable, banking, and power services have also been corrupted and taken offline. America's worst nightmare has come to pass, and while the *Zero-Day* report saw it coming, the US did too little to prevent the disaster. He consoles himself knowing that not even TS3 anticipated an attack this forceful, but they should have prepared.

Benton pops his head in the door with a rap. "Senator Kelsey on line one."

Frank groans. The day just got worse. The powerful senator on the Senate Intelligence Committee, nominated to be the sixth acting DNI (Director of National Intelligence) may strike the final decapitating blow to the independence of the intelligence community. The senator openly vows to pursue opponents of the president, meaning anyone willing to disagree or uphold the Constitution over rampant corruption. Fed up with intelligence leaks that contradict the public lies, the White House wants to take control over intelligence information itself, not just his policy derived from the Presidential Daily Brief.

"Senator Kelsey," Frank greets him. "What's on your mind?" He tries to be friendly to a potential colleague and oversight appointee.

"Frank, let me be blunt," replies Kelsey.

Frank rolls his eyes, unable to think of a time when Kelsey wasn't being blunt.

"I need to know what side of this coup you fall on," the senator demands.

He stops breathing for a heartbeat, his veins icing over. "Excuse me?" responds Frank, his pulse throbbing, "What are you talking about?"

He hasn't heard of any coup or secretive political actions, so Kelsey may refer to the new congressional impeachment hearings sparked by the Helsinki video.

"The radical left coup to remove the president," Kelsey snaps.

"With all due respect, Senator, a cyber crisis rocks the nation," Frank replies, "and I have neither the time nor the interest in another constitutional conflict between the Congress and the White House."

As a lifelong traditional conservative Republican with a belief in a strong defense, balanced budgets, going to church, free trade, and a strict constitutional rule of law, he doesn't recognize the current radical right GOP party that some call a "cult of personality" surrounding a corrupt autocrat. While he has no intention of signing onto any internal coup, he won't stand up to oppose one either. A coward's approach perhaps, but politically safe. He just wants to get to retirement.

"Mick Devlin claims you signed off on the 25th. Is that true?" he demands. "You know this Russia hoax by the deep state has torn our nation apart."

The 25th Amendment allows for the removal of a president in the case of mental or physical impairment but requires the vice president to invoke the amendment with consent of Congress. Frank can't imagine VP White growing enough of a backbone to oppose the president openly. Sadly, unfounded and bizarre QAnon conspiracies and Russian propaganda have now penetrated the White House to pollute the Republican party. He worries that the cancer has reached the White House.

"I have nothing to do with Devlin or any of his plans," Frank retorts, concerned that Devlin implicated him with a lie, unless Kelsey baits him with one.

Either way, he refuses to take the bait to reargue the Russian hoax comment; the facts are clear and well established by both Mueller Report to Congress and the Senate Intelligence that the Russians interfered with two elections and the president invited and supported them twice, refusing to retaliate, and continuously sides with Putin over his own intelligence. Congress imposed sanctions the Treasury quietly ignored. There was no hoax, but there has been an amazingly successful cover-up and setup of multiple secret back channels to Putin.

"The American way of life is under siege, Director, and the president is the only man who can save the nation," Kelsey huffs. "You're either with the president or against the nation."

The country has been in some form of crisis or another since the president took office, but Frank trusts the American system will eventually correct mistakes. Even so, the political divide has never been wider between those who demand the president's removal for election fraud and other crimes and those who protect him for their own political gain. Frank wants no part of it. At some point, he may have to choose, but not today, which has enough demons to keep him busy.

"Senator Kelsey, for thirty-six years, I've worked for the American people," he replies, "regardless of who sits in the Oval Office. I swore an oath to protect the Constitution, which makes me a patriot, not a politician. Right now, I have my hands full, and you're wasting my time."

"Senators Monroe and Higgs and I will propose a bill for a national digital

ID, and if you want to continue to be part of this administration, I expect you to support the initiative," Kelsey insists, getting to the real point of the call.

Kelsey follows the typical administration tactic to first threaten or intimidate and then pressure. That puts him in a difficult position. He strongly opposes digital ID technology, but ironically, he already agreed to test an ID tech illegally pushed over by the president, a huge mistake he can see already.

"Senator, I will—," Frank begins. There's an audible click. "Senator?" he repeats, but the line is dead.

Given the system troubles, he can't assume it was intentional, but he breathes a sigh of relief at cutting the unpleasant conversation short. With any luck, the president will fire Kelsey like the others, but not before Kelsey does his share of damage to our democracy.

His respect for the president suffered irreparable harm after the secretive Helsinki meetings, followed by lies to the Special Counsel and Congress and vindictive firing of decorated war heroes and whistleblowers or anyone who doesn't support his delusional truths. All the signs of an avalanche toward autocracy seen in other countries, but he never imagined that it could ever happen in America.

Benton sticks his head in the door again with a knock. "Sir, the virus just penetrated the federal VoIP systems. All phones except emergency radio systems are down." He hands Frank a field radio. "We only have a few thousand, so we need to ration them."

"God help us," Frank mumbles. "Shut down and purge all systems again and quadruple the firewalls." He can't understand how the virus penetrates even the best defenses so easily.

As Benton leaves, Frank's face falls into his palms, and he leans on his elbows. For the first time in his career, the government lies under siege, and the outcomes are unpredictable. Out of options, he can only imagine how the average citizen must be reacting right now—confused, disconnected, isolated, and afraid. When the satellite phone on his desk chirps sharply, it startles him out of his private lament.

"Wilson," he responds, unsure who calls the radio so soon.

"Power," the caller shouts. "It's following the power."

"Dr. Mitchell," Frank retorts. "Slow down. What are you saying?"

"*Malong*," he states the obvious. "The virus reinfection process follows the blackouts."

"OK, how does that help us?" Frank responds, confused.

"None of the blackouts are lasting longer than three hours. It's a device battery life limit. As soon as the power returns, the devices reinfect and the virus surges. To purge the virus, we need a system-wide power outage with a clean OS and a reboot," Josh blurts.

"A reboot is standard process after the antivirus install," Wilson pushes back.

"No, no, that won't do it," Josh argues. "The virus will reinfect from the adjacent blackout area. We need to shut down the entire grid, the entire worldwide internet, oh, and if possible, remove batteries from devices." Josh takes a deep breath.

"You're insane," Frank snaps.

"Maybe, I mean, you know, I haven't slept much since . . . wait, what day is it? Whatever. The simulator results say I'm right," he retorts.

"Holy Mary, Mother of God," exclaims Frank.

He sits back rubbing his hand over his balding scalp with the horrendous thought of explaining this to the president and Joint Chiefs. This will play into the hands of those who want to force citizen ID.

He presses his intercom, but the device is dead, lacking power, not deemed critical while NSOC operates on emergency generators.

"Benton," he shouts at the door. "Call a government car. I need to go to the Pentagon."

Pulling up the radio, he scowls. "Wash up, Dr. Mitchell. If Taylor isn't here, then you're coming along to explain this harebrained scheme to the brass yourself."

During the height of the Cold War, some hyper-conservative boys at Langley suggested that Russia would try to implant a US president based on a passage of Revelation that spoke of a beast of the East creating an image of the beast of the West and empowering it to speak blasphemy. At the time, Frank thought the analysts were religious zealot nuts. In retrospect, Frank may have been too quick to judge. Kay may be onto something.

CHAPTER 38:
MAGIC BLACK SAND

Tech city, Hyderabad, India
May 4, 12:44 p.m. EDT | May 4, 10:14 p.m., Hyderabad

More emotional than he expected to be, Derek bids a tearful goodbye to Runki, who hands over bags of dinner containers for the plane trip home, enough to feed a small army for a month, including Jack's yearn-for-the burn spicy coconut curry.

In the dark of night and with poor street lighting, Wiki takes over from Jenn for the drive back to the overlook point above the tech city where Derek pulls out a case from the trunk.

"A gift for you, dude. All set up to go. Check it out," encourages Derek. "Spark got the cheaper model. So, you know, rub it in if he gives you any guff." He plays into the decades-old sibling rivalry.

Wiki's eyes light up as he opens the case to find an industrial drone. "Oh, whoa, I am blessed to work with you, my brother," enthuses Wiki.

"Best on the market, GPS enabled, camera zoom, long battery life with optional grab claws for packages up to fifteen pounds of weight," Derek replies.

"I could start a delivery business," Wiki says.

"Exactly what I had in mind," Derek replies. "Wanna practice?"

Next to the drone control, Wiki finds a large plastic zip bag of what looks like black sand and, under the sand, a ten-pound magnet. While Wiki finishes the drone assembly, Derek watches the data center with binoculars, joined by Jenn.

"That was very generous," she notes.

Derek keeps his eyes focused, sensing that she's probing for a reason. "Well, what can I say? He always wanted one. Life is short, and like I said, I might not get another chance."

"You weren't kidding when you said you were meeting friends," she states.

Derek lowers his binoculars with a smirk. "You sound surprised."

"I am, actually. Do you want to know what Runki told me about you?" she asks in a whisper.

He chuckles. "Runki has a reputation for colorful exaggerations," he responds, returning his gaze to the binoculars.

"She said you saved Bawarchi when developers tried to close her down," Jenn notes.

"Like I said, colorful exaggeration," Derek replies without breaking his view. He once gave Runki some money as a loan to pay off debt and remodel and then forgot to collect.

"So how many friends do you have around the world?" she asks.

He's not sure why she would ask such a question, so his instincts tell him to be vague. "Enough to feel blessed," he replies.

Derek checks his watch. "Hey, Wiki, we go live in two."

"Ready and launching," Wiki announces as the drone whines into the air to hover, wobble, and then buzz toward the tech city.

Small flashing navigation lights give away the drone's location until Wiki switches them off, making the drone invisible in the night sky. Wiki walks over to share the video screen as the drone passes a modern apartment building toward the massive data center. Hidden behind the walls near the bluff lies a scrawling village of blue tarps, cardboard huts, and fires made from cow dung.

Naked children play around the foul-smelling fires, avoiding the stinging, malaria-infested mosquitos, pulling at his heart as it did so many years ago, a problem bigger than one man can solve.

"OK, Wiki, ready in," says Derek, "Five, four, three, two, and one."

"Almost there," Wiki replies.

Derek waits. Nothing happens.

"Patience," Wiki mumbles, moving the drone to hover over a compact building next to their target complex. "This is India. Nothing happens on time."

The lights of the tech city blink twice and then go dark, starting with the northern border near the power plant and moving south, turning every building dark, including the target site. Almost immediately, the sound of popping and humming spreads throughout the valley as automatic diesel generators kick on to return business lights to emergency levels. The compact brick building behind their target has steel doors with thick industrial electrical conduits into the principal building protected by a heavy-duty roof fan with a wire grate.

Wiki turns to Derek with a smile. "I wonder what this switch does?"

One of the grab arms releases the heavy metal magnet, which smashes through the grate to shred the fan and stop the airflow.

"Oh my, what about this one?" Wiki smirks, releasing the second grab hand holding the large bag of black sand into the open vent, ripping open the bag to spill the sand into the generator ventilation.

Wiki pulls up the drone to rapidly fly back to the hillside and land gracefully next to the case. "Works amazing, my friend." He loads the drone into the case and then the case into the trunk. "We better go."

"Hold on," Derek insists, watching the building. Nothing happens for a long moment until the building lights flicker and go dark again, and this time stay dark.

Derek smiles. "OK, time to go," he agrees and gets into the passenger seat, forcing Jenn to ride in the rear. As they head down the hill, the entire tech city lights back up, except for the target site.

"What does your brother Spark do?" Jenn asks.

"Tarun? Oh, he's a very big wig for the power company," replies Wiki who then changes the subject. "Did you know the story of Hyderabad and Marco Polo?"

Without waiting for an answer, he regales her with the incredible tale of hilltop castles, large harems, and diamonds the size of a fist. Jenn listens without responding, peering out the window, as if she's trying to figure out what just happened.

Instead of Bawarchi or the airport, Wiki stops at a fourteenth-century Christian chapel with colorful murals painted in an old Indian style on the peeling plaster—the St. Thomas Mar Thoma Church.

"I sent him a message you were coming," Wiki reassures Derek.

"Good. Thanks, man," replies Derek.

"Why are we here?" questions Jenn.

"I need advice from an old friend about a problem with another old friend," Derek explains. "It's kind of personal, so if you don't mind, I'll need a minute alone."

Jenn scowls but remains in the car. Empty at this hour, the small stone-pillared chapel features no pews or benches, only a humble elevated wooden altar and a rustic wooden cross hanging on the wall. Faded murals of the gospels decorate the walls, unchanged and exactly as he remembers.

"Derek," greets a short jovial priest from behind the altar. "Derek Taylor, is that really you? Praise the Lord. I always knew you would return."

An older man with white hair hurries to hug Derek with a long, joyful embrace and a pat. He wears traditional Indian garments except for the huge gold cross prominently displayed on his chest.

"Father Padma," Derek replies. "So wonderful to see you looking well."

"God blessed the health to my navel." Padma grabs a handful of his ample belly with a chuckle. "What calamity brings you back to India, my son?" he asks with an expectant smile.

"I was hoping you could give me some quick insights on an end-time prophecy," Derek whispers.

"End Times, you say, oh my, oh my." Padma looks startled, and then he jiggles his head. "Yes, yes, sit, sit. We have much to discuss, much to discuss."

CHAPTER 39:
SPIRITUAL GUIDANCE

St. Thomas Mar Thoma Church, Hyderabad
May 4, 2:03 p.m. EDT | May 4, 11:33 p.m., Hyderabad

As soon as Derek steps inside the dilapidated stone chapel, Jenn gets out of the car, glowering a hard warning at Wiki through the window. "Not a word. Understood?"

Assured of his silence with a wide-eyed anxious nod, she tiptoes into the ancient stone hall, lit only by a few candles. Hiding in the abundant shadows, she discovers Derek meeting with an old, pudgy priest sitting on the steps of a wooden altar platform, not exactly the profile of a cyberterrorist she expected. Careful to stay in the shadows, she finds an interior stone pillar close enough to listen.

Years ago, she watched a BBC special on the roots of Christianity in India, which trace back to the first century when the Apostle Thomas, the famous doubter of the resurrection, evangelized the Hindu people. Never a part of the Roman or Orthodox church, less than 5 percent of modern India consists of Christians, who are often persecuted by the Muslims and the Hindu majorities.

"My son, if a sacred end-time prophecy brought you to my door, then it can only be the Lord speaking to your heart, so tell me what is on your mind," the priest encourages.

Did he just say end-time prophecy? The topic surprises her to an extreme. Her mother studied prophecy with a local evangelical pastor for years while she battled cancer and spoke often to Jenn about what she was learning. She always figured the subject was her mom's way of dealing with her own imminent death. She's unsure what she expected, but the topic of prophecy gives her yet another surprise from a man full of them. They've just sabotaged a data center, a local felony, while a crisis persists in Washington and Taylor stops for a Bible study. Something really doesn't fit.

"OK, here's the deal," Derek starts. "I have a friend with an over-the-top brilliant mind but who recently became obsessed with end-time prophecies. I'm talking straight on weird stuff like Daniel and a seventy sevens timeline and Israel and the time of Gentiles, rambling on about dragons, beasts, someone named Gog, and the Antichrist. When I remind her that those stories are all allegories or myths, she claims that all the signs are fulfilled and Daniel's final seven has begun. To be honest, Father, I'm not only stumped on how to respond, but it's freaking me out."

Father Padma chuckles. "Interesting to know what freaks you out. What would you like to learn?"

Jenn leans back against the cold pillar, baffled on why a cybersecurity executive would travel halfway around the world to seek spiritual advice from an impoverished priest. A few days ago, he was talking to Dr. Garrett about an AI with a prophecy problem. Something doesn't fit.

"Well, I was hoping for an overview, you know, CliffsNotes, a synopsis, like a mash-up of the key themes or players," he replies.

Padma laughs. "Oh, you're being serious." He stifles his chuckle. "Derek, end-time prophecies are vast, with dozens of texts and several books, each text pregnant with possible meaning. Wise men can take a lifetime to study them."

Jenn subconsciously nods in agreement. Prophecy has both intrigued and stymied people of faith for centuries. Full of symbolism, allegories, cultural history, and context, most of it she dismissed, considering Revelation more about the horrors of Christian persecution under Nero than a vision of a distant future time that never seems to arrive. Anyone claiming a complete understanding is delusional at best and psychotic at worst.

"Sure, OK, so just give me enough for context, like a Prophecy for Dummies," he negotiates.

"Impatient as ever." Padma sighs. "The first principle you must understand is that prophecy can only be understood as the events occur and, even then, only by those who watch for the signs. Prophecy is not meant to see into the future, but to understand the meaning of the future when it occurs."

Jenn recalls her mother making that mistake, trying to use prophecy to predict the future, and wonders if that led to erroneous conclusions that somehow Turkey or the Vatican was the Antichrist.

"The second principle you must understand regards timing," the priest continues. "All end-time prophecies will occur within a prophesied time frame of a generation."

"OK, that makes sense. My friend mentioned the end of the age of Gentiles," Taylor interrupts. "Does that make any sense?"

The priest sighs. "Remember that many considered the Black Plague to be the last days, and others consider the Catholic Church to be the beast or called Hitler the Antichrist," the old teacher explains. "But yes, the age of the Gentiles ended with a 1948 UN resolution to create Israel from the land of Palestine, while others claim that Jewish control over Jerusalem in 1967 was the marker."

"OK, I'm confused. So is my friend right?" Derek sighs. "Or crazy?"

Padma wiggles his head. "No, your friend is not crazy, but insightful. If the timeline of Daniel has restarted, then the final count of seventy sevens has begun."

"You mean like decades?" questions Derek, thinking of SLVIA's interpretation.

"Some believe so, yes, or perhaps a sequence of seven years called weeks," Padma confirms, wiggling his head again. "Either way, scripture teaches that all will be fulfilled within a single generation. But you must understand there are dozens of signs. Individually, each sign of the times can each be explained or dismissed, but when completed together, they warn us of the end of days to come. Some say we have already entered the final count of seven, experiencing what scripture calls the Seven Seals. I realize this may alarm you."

"What signs?" he asks. "What Seals?"

Padma wiggles his head once more. "There are too many signs to list from the past seventy years, several dozen of them in all, but I agree with your friend they have been fulfilled. Think of the many things never experienced by man until the past seventy years such as the rise of computers and the explosion of knowledge, space exploration, global pollution, overpopulation, international banking, moral erosion, species extinction, and even nuclear weapons—each a fulfillment of the prophesies. The Seven Seals warned of false prophets and teachers, escalation of war in the Middle East, a global pandemic and pestilence, global economic tribulations, and the widespread famine and food shortages."

"Wow, OK, sounds a little bit too much like CNN news to sound radical. Tell me about the dragons," Taylor pushes, checking his watch.

"The book of Revelation speaks of two dragons, two beasts, a mystery Babylon, an Antichrist, and the returning of the Lord with his army of angels for judgment," the priest explains, laying out the cast of characters.

"Yeah, OK, do any of those beasts connect with Russia or China" he asks.

Padma gives him a puzzled look, "Yes, the second beast of the land has two horns, or key leaders, and the voice of the second dragon. The prophet Ezekiel spoke of Meshech as Iran and Tubal as modern Turkey aligning with Gog as the leader of Magog, or what many consider modern-day Russia. The dragon has been symbolic of China for millennia. Together, these nations will make war with Israel."

"OK, wow, holy cow, that fits," mumbles Derek, his eyes wide in surprise. "Tell me more about the other beast."

Jenn listens, somewhat baffled by this entire conversation, reminiscent of discussions with her mother, except her mother never clearly understood the beasts.

"A second dragon will stand over the beast of the sea, with ten horns, seven heads, and ten crowns, which will rule with a mighty army and dominate world finances and economics. The first beast will create an image of the second beast so that the world will follow the image of the second beast who commands a great army. That image will speak blasphemies, desecrate the temple, and impose global economic controls using a mark on the hand or forehead," Padma explains.

Derek stands to pace the empty chapel, causing Jenn to pull back farther into the shadows, unable to see but still listening, absolutely stunned at what she hears.

"Call me crazy, but I think I agree with my friend. That beast sounds like the G7 economies, with ten financial centers and ten monarchies," Derek throws out, trying to sort everything out. "That beast certainly lusts after control over modern banking. So maybe we're not talking about a mark as much as biometric ID or facial, thumbprint, or iris scan."

"Could be, could be, I suppose, but no one knows," Padma replies.

"You said a dragon will stand over the second beast." He pauses to pace, his heels softly echoing on the old stone floors. "Wow, I think I get it. I know that dragon."

"I would be careful claiming an understanding of prophecy," Padma exhorts.

"Sorry, Father, my friend saw a political alliance forming and recognized the link to the prophecy. I thought she was nuts or skipping a chip or something, but I think I get what's going on now. OK, one more thing, so how does a third temple fit in?" he asks.

"Because the Antichrist, the image of the second beast set up by the first beast, will desecrate the third temple, an act of abomination that will spark the ultimate battle of Armageddon," Padma replies.

"When you say Antichrist," Derek questions, "you mean like a devil worshipper, a communist?"

"Oh, heavens no, much more subtle and nefarious." Padma wiggles his head. "Many Antichrists have come into the world," he notes, stopping to think a moment. "The Antichrist of Revelation will be a powerful man of lawlessness, a known liar who will deceive many, a man who sees himself as a chosen savior, yet he himself will possess a character opposite of the mercy, compassion, and holiness of our Lord. He will be a heretic who will use the faith of others as a weapon and whose name will align with the number 666, which of course has many interpretations. Because of his power and his control over an invincible army, many believe he will be a politician or a universal world leader."

"World leader," repeats Taylor. "Hence the fear of a New World Order. Does it actually say leader of the world, or simply a world leader, one of the leaders?"

Padma ponders a moment in silence. "The leader of a great army implies opponents to that army, so no, I do not believe we are talking a one world government myth."

Jenn leans back with her heart pounding so loud she fears discovery, realizing there are only two nearly invincible armies on the planet, but only one of them has tight control over world economics and banking. Only one current leader fits each and every one of those characteristics, including being set up by Gog, Putin.

"Holy crap," exclaims Derek. "I think I'm getting what my friend wants to tell me."

"I hope you will share with me at some point," replies Padma.

Before Taylor can respond, Wiki rushes into the chapel, spotting her in the shadows, but slyly keeping his tongue. "Derek, we need to go, very soon, very quick."

From outside the small chapel, a few miles away, police sirens can be heard moving in their direction.

"Thank you, Father," Derek exclaims. "I miss our long talks and really wish we had more time."

Wiki waves her to run behind him during the distracted moment of goodbyes as her best chance to exit the chapel unseen. Racing out with her heart pounding, she reenters the car followed quickly by Wiki.

"Learn anything juicy?" he teases.

"Oh my God, yes, a feast," she replies. "Thank you."

Jenn grows less convinced Taylor may be a double agent and more convinced that he might be insane. End-time prophecies are the fodder of crazy religious zealots, except that much of what was said actually makes sense—the alliances, the connection between leaders. Even if he's committed no actual crimes, just putting all this nonsense into her report will torpedo Taylor's career.

Taylor enters the car and slaps the dash. "OK, Wiki, let's go, go, go."

Wiki speeds off to merge with nearby traffic, and soon the Benz feels swallowed by a wave of vehicles and people.

*

TSOC1, Hyderabad International Airport
May 5, 3:43 p.m. EDT | May 6, 12:43 a.m., Hyderabad

"You're quiet, and it worries me," jibes Derek.

Jenn's been silent ever since she snuck out of the chapel behind Wiki. Unsure how much she heard, he expected a barrage of questions. Her silence unnerves him.

"What was in the black bag?" she asks.

Not the question he expected, he stares at her a moment too long.

"Electron-eating nanobytes," Wiki interjects with a grin. "Amazing devices penetrate anything electrical to short circuit the system. Untraceable, and nobody got hurt. Very nice, very clean."

"Nanobytes," repeats Jenn, thinking the solution to be effective and a bit ingenious.

Taylor shrugs with a smug grin without offering an explanation. While nanobytes are legal, willful destruction of property is a criminal offense. Although Wiki dropped the bag, he certainly didn't buy the incredibly expensive technology.

As the Benz pulls up to a private hangar, Jack Tote stands at the top of the stairs waving at them to hurry. Police sirens now move toward the airport.

Stepping outside the car, Wiki reaches to hug Derek tightly. "Good to see you again, old friend. Loads of fun like old times," he whispers. "Stay alive for me."

"I'll do my best," Derek replies. "Give my thanks to Spark, and a kiss for Runki and Madera."

Wiki looks to Jenn with a wide smile, then wraps his arms around her in an unexpected warm embrace. "You're hunting the wrong tiger," he whispers into her ear.

Her eyes pop open in surprise, pulling back for a question, but Wiki quickly jumps into Madera's Mercedes and speeds away with a long obnoxious honk trailing behind him. The entire nation loves to honk.

"Welcome back, boss," Jack greets. "I hear sirens. Do you hear sirens?"

Derek turns to Jenn with a deep crunch in his brow. "Look, I get that Wilson wants you to follow me, bust my nuggets, or whatever. You're doing a great job," he admits. "All games aside, I may not come home from this next trip. Your father would never forgive me if something happened to you." He hesitates. "And honestly, I'm not sure I could forgive myself. Not again."

Jenn glares at him, speechless, making him wish her thoughts would whisper to him like SLVIA.

"First, I make my own decisions, not the admiral and not Wilson," she states. "Second, if your plans are that dangerous, I better go along to make sure you get home in one piece. I can't arrest a dead man."

"I'm serious. This is your last chance," he repeats. "If you're in, you're in all the way, and it may not end well for either of us. Stay at the best hotel in town and take the next first-class ticket home. If I make it home, arrest me, but don't make me bring you home in a box."

Jenn raises an eyebrow. "Where are you going?"

"I can't tell you," Derek replies.

"Can't or won't?" Jenn retorts.

"Come on, girl. I'm giving you some plausible deniability here," Derek exclaims.

Jenn snorts. "How can I trust you when you won't tell me the truth?"

"The truth is that I don't want to see you get hurt," he replies. "And after this point, I may not be able to prevent that, and to be honest, I may break a few laws, and we can't have you implicated."

The sirens grow louder. "Sirens, people, I hear sirens. Sirens are bad. We need to fly," Jack complains aloud.

"What are you going to do?" she asks.

He hesitates. "Behead the dragon before the first beast can gain full power." He wants to explain it to her, but he doesn't have the time, and he's still unsure of his own understanding.

Without saying a word, she passes him to walk up the steps. "Good evening, Captain Tote." She nods, moving past Jack into the salon.

With a heavy sigh, Derek follows. "Did you get the gear?" he asks Jack, lowering his voice.

"Yeah," Jack reassures him, "but you paid a hell of a premium." He closes the hatch.

"I'll be sure to wince when I get the bill," he says, wondering if he'll even live that long.

He joins Jenn in an awkward silence as the Gulfstream quickly rockets off the runway.

"I saw you in the chapel," he admits as they gain altitude. "Any of that make sense to you?"

She exhales, closing her eyes, "More than I care to admit, but I promised to hold my questions. Just a warning, if I hold any harder, I may bite through my tongue."

Just as well. Still rattled by the growing revelations, he would prefer to think it through before he has to talk it out. If he understands Padma and SLVIA correctly, the image of the beast, created by the beast of the East and empowered to speak blasphemy, sits in the White House seeking a third term. He could be completely wrong and going a little crazy himself, but it's too early to tell.

CHAPTER 40:
SECURITY BREACH

Secure federal SUV, Washington DC
May 4, 4:31 p.m. EDT

O
n the drive to the White House, Frank's SUV has to divert around tens of thousands of peaceful protestors who gather to stand off against the National Guard. The tall iron fence, erected after the Black Lives Matter protests, holds back a massive throng. Patrol drones, nearby national troops without identifying badges, horse-mounted police, and urban armored vehicles with water cannons threaten them from nearby.

Not since September 11 has the anxiety in America been so high, and not since the hotly contested election of 2020 have the protests been so close to the boiling point. Divisions, distrust, alternate facts, court cases with an upheaval of social values within a country already strained to the point of civil war—and it's all growing worse daily. Instead of uniting the nation, the president continues to stoke the partisan hatred and distrust of his opponents, the universal sign of an autocrat, indicting his opponents while shutting down any investigation into his finances.

Running late to his meeting at the White House, stuck in protest-hindered traffic, Frank hears the secure satellite phone ring in the SUV. He groans, expecting a rebuke from the White House.

"Frank Wilson here," he answers.

"Sir, it's Benton." His voice sounds tense. "We have a breach."

Wilson hangs on the line frozen, stunned, waiting until he can breathe again. A breach of the NSA seems unfathomable, impossible, devastating. There must be some mistake.

"What happened?" he asks, his throat constricted by the shock.

"The biometric authentication system," Benton explains. "We had to shut it down to prevent a leak to other systems. Marines just arrived to secure all the doors, but it has everyone spooked. I just radioed the CIA, and they're having the same problem, and so is the Pentagon."

Never a huge fan of biosecurity, he ignored the multiple warnings, including the *Zero-Day* warning to outlaw digital biosecurity. The Clearview hack opened a window. All Russia needed was an AI to locate a single match to a known government employee to access and worm into the system.

"Follow the protocols. Shut down every nonessential system and cleanse every drive," he directs with an unintentional groan. "Get a forensics team on how the hell they got in."

The virus stays ahead of them, keeping them on defense instead of going on the offense. Rebuilding the NSA during a crisis will not be the legacy he had hoped to leave. He should have retired after the last election, but he feared another inept loyalist would be assigned to replace him. At some point, the well-being of the nation will fall to someone else, but not today. In all good conscience, he cannot abandon his nation under such distress or under such divisive and destructive leadership.

"I'm heading into the White House," he replies. "Call Dr. Mitchell and light a fire under his ass, and make sure we send someone to pick up Dr. Garrett as soon as he returns from Dubai. We need an antivirus."

"Sorry, sir, in all the chaos, I forgot to tell you," Benton admits. "There was an explosion at his home. Dr. Garrett has gone missing."

"Holy Mary, Mother of God," he mumbles involuntarily.

For the only man on the planet capable of unlocking the SLVIA stealth problem to go missing right when a stealth virus ravages the internet cannot be a coincidence. Without Dr. Garrett, fixing the antivirus will take a miracle, and that's not the answer he had hoped to give the president.

CHAPTER 41: DEAD EYE VIEW

Jester's abandoned army silo
May 4, 11:03 p.m. EDT | May 5, 6:03 a.m., Tel Aviv

Disoriented and groggy, unable to open his eyes, Nelson finds clarity painfully slow to materialize. He hears the muffled voice of his mother, Amelia, gently admonishing him: "We have all sinned. We have fallen short." Jagged images flash over his mind of shattering windshields, men with guns, and explosions that churn him into a restless semiconscious agitation.

With enormous effort, he opens his heavy eyes for a quick peep at his surroundings and catches a windowless room of bare concrete walls with four bunks. His heart sinks to the pit of his stomach as the recollection of his folly floods back into his consciousness. It wasn't a nightmare. He's a prisoner of his own undoing.

Passed out for God knows how long, his body feels weak, dehydrated, and hypoglycemic. Dried blood on his sleeve reminds him of his loss of blood when he realizes someone had cleaned and stitched the wound and placed band-aids on the multiple minor cuts. With a painful grunt, he sits up on s sixties vintage army cot with woolen blankets to assess his situation and clear his throbbing and befuddled head.

He hasn't interacted with SLVIA in over twenty-eight years. Even if SLVIA survived this long on the internet, rampant cybercrime, porn, fascism, racism, fake news, and hatred would have corrupted her persona. He never created SLVIA to exist in that world. He expected the program to feed from the sanitized stores of government data, universities, and laboratories with the common languages of science, law, literature, and mathematics.

Why did he risk everything to prove her survival? Alone in the darkness, listening to his breathing echo on the cold walls, feeling his heartbeat throb in his ears, he finds a sad, pathetic answer: to prove that his greatest mistake was, in fact, his greatest success and erase the one glaring shame of his career. He came for the sake of his pride, and now a new shame of hubris arises to surpass the old one.

SOPHIA must be wrong or misled. He has seen no sign that SLVIA survived. It's much more likely that Jester learned of the classified program, fed the information to SOPHIA, and then duped him to hack a US weapon system. To offer any help to Jester will land him in federal prison. A lapse of judgment so severe, even falling for the ruse to come here may cost him a career,

The walls are closing in, squeezing his chest and raising an existential panic. He checks the door, surprised to find it unlocked, but then again, why lock the door when he can't escape via the elevator. In the main room, Jester paces back and forth facing the wall of screens, but his movements appear jerky, as if he's on cocaine or perhaps listening to music, but lacking natural rhythm. After a few moments, Jester senses his presence.

"Hey, Dr. Garrett, you're awake." He removes earbuds. "You've been out for quite a while. I was worried."

Jester points to the bandaged arm. "I had one of my men stitch you up and give you some fluids. You should probably eat something. There's some cold pizza on the back table."

Cold pizza. How dreadful. Yet his hunger forces him to grab a slice with a napkin and eat like a barbarian.

"Have you decided to help?" Jester prods.

"Of course not. It's absurd and illegal, and there's no evidence of a genuine danger. Even if I agreed, which I don't, hacking the HIVE will be quite impossible. The system contains multiple layers of security," Nelson argues between bites. "And beyond all that, you've given me absolutely no proof that SLVIA has anything to do with this charade."

"Impossible, huh?" Jester replies. "You know, I hate to admit it, but you may be right."

After taking another bite and chewing, Nelson takes a moment to study the large wall-sized screen behind Jester and comes to an astonishing conclusion.

"Dear Lord, you've already hacked in," he mumbles. "That—that's unbelievable. How the bloody hell did you do that?"

"Don't panic. I can only reach level two, the remote view protocol, the same as during the test. As you noted, security level three, necessary to change commands or access the code, requires an encrypted device to a satellite signal. Unless I beam aboard the *Eisenhower*, we can watch, but we can't touch," Jester admits.

"You won't gain control," Nelson confirms, more confident he won't be forced to break the law.

"Too bad," Jester replies. "After waiting for daylight, they just dropped a second canister, over twenty thousand buzzers since yesterday, but only 8,500 still in the air due to kills."

Fear-driven adrenaline jolts him from his lethargy. "Dear Lord, where?" questions Nelson, alarmed to hear of nearly twelve thousand kills and over eight thousand drones still roaming.

"Damascus and Golan Heights," Jester replies.

Israel connects to the strange text received a few days ago. Recalling the terrifying lethal effectiveness of the thousands-strong drone swarm, a cloud of ten thousand screeching locusts must seem apocalyptic to those on the ground.

By instinct, he takes a moment to study the screen. "Dear Lord, McCray has set the HIVE to fully autonomous."

The nightmare just got worse. A fully autonomous setting explains the massive size of the deployment. If the US breaks the international LAWS protocol, then others will soon follow and he can only imagine Russia, terrorists, and African warlords with a Chinese version of this technology. No doubt, the demons will be released from the abyss.

The screen changes to inside the *Eisenhower* hangar deck with over a thousand men at workstations, heads down monitoring their screens.

"Commander," a voice speaks off camera. "Canister three ready to drop."

"Launch canister three," the second voice confirms.

A moment later, they hear, "Canister three deployed. Ten thousand new stingers over Damascus."

The realization turns icy cold in his heart that he is about to witness a massacre. "How many canisters did they deploy?" he asks, unsure he wants to know.

"Enough to drop a hundred thousand drones over the Holy Land," hisses Jester, wringing his hands and pacing a groove into the polished cement floor.

Nelson watches the swarm plummet, glad to be nowhere near those dreadful devices this time but terrified for the poor civilians on the ground.

"Four thousand feet over Damascus," Jester reads aloud from the hacked control screen.

Nelson's breathing accelerates to match his racing pulse as the view of the city rushes at them.

"Two thousand feet," Jester reads off.

The video wiggles out of the way as anti-aircraft guns shoot toward the swarm from rooftops. Nelson dodges his head by instinct.

"One thousand," Jester reads as the swarm disperses over Damascus and the defensive fire intensifies.

The closer to the ground the view falls, the higher Nelson's apprehension rises, clenching his fist until his knuckles turn white. He hyperventilates through a clenched jaw. Onscreen, without sound, the scene looks surreal, nightmarish, as if from the *Twilight Zone*. Unlike the staged simulation, the HD camera captures the genuine terror in the eyes of those who scatter, shoot, or scream into the ominous swarm. Citizens on the street race toward doors and cars or freeze in place like terrorized deer. Within seconds, a cluster surrounds a soldier until an explosion on his back rips the body into bloody pieces that scatter in all directions, far more gruesome than the red powder used in the Nevada test.

Similar scenes play out across the city where a man is blown bloody from a rooftop while another drone slams the fuel tank of a soldier with a flamethrower. The explosion engulfs the soldier within an enormous blaze that sets a nearby building on fire. Swarms of drones surround mobile anti-aircraft units to kill the combatants and disable the guns within minutes. One explosion ignites ammunition stocks in a series of massive explosions that rocks several square city blocks.

Thousands of drones crash through windows and doors to conduct searches of homes, businesses, and tunnels. In horror, he witnesses a mother defend her children by holding up an antique pistol with a trembling hand. The drone reacts to the pistol threat by slaughtering the entire family. The image sends Nelson running to the back of the chamber, vomiting into a waste can. His most horrid nightmare has become a gruesome and bloody reality. The video evidence of a war crime will no doubt be classified to keep from the media.

Citizens cower in their houses or huddle into corners under the guard of a whining drone. Children cry at the incessant noise as mothers try in vain to comfort them. Crashed vehicles burn where the occupants perished. Bloody bodies and parts and pools of blood lie in the streets unattended as multiple fires rage. No one dares to look after them for fear of the roving locusts. The smoke rises into the air so thick that it blocks the sun. Nelson hangs his head, remembering the anonymous text warning at the weapons test site: *And out of the smoke, locusts came down on the earth and were given power like that of scorpions of the earth. Revelation 9:3.*

When he was younger, he believed that AI had the potential to save lives and aid humanity by growing better crops, curing disease, improving security and cryptology, and speeding up other technologies, and AI does possess all of that potential. Yet now, witnessing his genius used to destroy life on such an unprecedented, soulless scale sears at his conscience and poisons his self-image of the ethical scientist with a toxic sludge of shame.

He came here to find SLVIA, to prove his greatest achievement, not to watch a visual display of how far he's fallen from grace. Humiliation seeps into his veins until he shudders from the icy chill of self-judgment. He's nothing more than a willing cog in the unrelenting, unmerciful war machine, an intellectual whore who sold out to the beast, just as his mother had warned. A fountain of self-loathing swells up so completely overwhelming that he can conceive of no path to redeem his stained integrity.

If he survives, if he escapes this prison, he needs to resign from DARPA. He can longer live with his choices now that his eyes have been opened onto the devil's minion he has become.

CHAPTER 42: REINFECTION

NSOC

May 5, 1:10 a.m. EDT

Lucifer and his demons storming the gates of heaven would threaten Frank less than knowing the virus has penetrated the security and sanctity of the NSA.

"Shut it down," he orders.

"Sir, are you sure?" Benton checks.

"Shut it down now before it spreads," Frank insists.

Dr. Mitchell insisted on a shutdown of the T1 pipes connecting TSOC and NSOC, which means a shutdown of data sharing, communications, and cryptology support. Frank has no way of knowing if *Malong* has bored deeper into other secure operations until he takes them offline. If the *Malong* can stay hidden like the SLVIA, then the virus may have already penetrated the entire system. Without an effective antivirus, he has no other choice but to rebuild on clean hardware. There couldn't be a worse time to purge and rebuild, but he has little choice and only one chance to get it right. In the middle of the morass of bad news comes a glimmer of positive news.

"Have we confirmed the signal drop?" he questions.

A few hours ago, the assault intensity dropped suddenly, but without the NSA internet tracking and diagnostics system, he can't be sure how much or from where, so he needs confirmation.

"Dr. Mitchell confirmed the signal drop but can't confirm Hyderabad as the source," he reports.

The last word from Scott was that she and Taylor were headed to Hyderabad. With no word from them in two days, he can't discount that his strong-willed contractor broke international law. Frank rubs his hand though his thinning hair, knowing he'll need to deal with the diplomatic aftermath later. Either way, Taylor may have ruined his career for nothing as the signal intensity still prevents a countermeasure.

"What's the status of the antivirus?" he questions.

Under the circumstances, the President leaned on the Security Council who leaned on him to distribute the defective INVISINC antivirus, all traceable to an El Lago club member with conflicts of interest. Without a functional internet, Frank had to send military couriers to all major cities, government installations, DYN hubs, and software companies to deliver the knowingly defective *Malong* antivirus. The best-case scenario is that it will buy them time, but without Dr. Garrett, it may not matter. So far, the FBI have few leads.

Benton looks down to an iPad. "The antivirus only slows the reinfection by 32 percent." Not even close to good enough, but about as good as Dr. Mitchell predicted.

Behind Benton, Dr. Samantha Carson leans in the door. "Director, may I have a word?"

Before he can respond, Benton bows out, allowing Dr. Carson to step in and close the door. "We have a problem."

"Yeah, take a number," Frank says with a snort.

"My team tested Dr. Mitchell's theory of a global blackout," she clarifies.

"Oh, that problem." He smirks.

When he took Dr. Mitchell to the Pentagon yesterday, his idea of a global blackout to purge the network was met with all the sizzle of cooking an egg on ice. As expected, after a number of choice words, the Joint Chiefs demanded independent verification of the strategy.

Frank braces himself. "I'm listening."

She raises an eyebrow and sighs. "Well, England, Germany, and Japan each agreed to run simulations on clean hardware based on commonly agreed-upon data set parameters, and our team each ran five runs, but there are so many unknown variables that all the models may be off by orders of magnitude."

She takes a breath, stalling. "That said, the idea worked in every model, but with three enormous conditional IF statements."

She means conditions that have to be true in order for the outcome to be possible. Frank leans back in his chair, waiting to absorb the blow, feeling his headache, which had eased in the past few hours, intensify.

"Such as?" he prods.

"For one, we need to take the entire internet offline, including every connected computer or device everywhere and every power station. A global blackout for at least six hours." Dr. Carson takes a breath, waiting for his response.

He blows out a nervous whistle. A global blackout would mean getting dozens of countries to agree. Without phone service or internet, he would need to explain and negotiate the situation via encrypted satellite phones with jammed satellite signals. An intentional shutdown of the internet and power grid might be the precursor for a larger military attack or present other unknown technical risks in the reboot process.

"What else?" Frank queries for the next condition, already seeing one huge roadblock.

"We need a clean and effective antivirus," she states with a stressful frown. "No scenario works without first fixing the antivirus problem."

"Yeah, I was afraid of that," he grumbles.

Without Dr. Garrett, they have no hope of reverse engineering the mutation technology in time. The FBI investigation is hampered by the loss of virtually every system.

SWARM

"And what else?" he asks again, unsure it will make a difference as the first two conditions were impossible to accomplish.

"Until we can rebuild our defenses, we need to slow or stop the virus infusion," Dr. Carson states. "Even after last night's drop, the signal strength remains too strong."

Frank whistles out his stress again. "Let me get this straight. We need the Western world to agree to a global blackout while we design a revolutionary stealth antivirus without the only known expert, and then the Pentagon also needs to send troops into China and Russia."

Samantha doesn't answer, only furrows her brow. His palm rubs through his thinning hair. The only word he can think of is *insidious*. The genius behind this strategy must be insidiously evil and bitter.

Frank will be lucky to keep his job in this political atmosphere, much less gain support for such a radical approach. The upheaval in Washington has created internal division and havoc that exposes our weaknesses. A house divided cannot stand, and the deep divide within the house of the United States grows deeper and wider by the day.

Dr. Carson frowns. "I saved the best for last."

"Gee, my lucky day," Frank jests.

"We identified the chip flaw used by the virus," Dr. Carson replies. "We knew there had to be a systemic reason for the virus's ability to bore into the core OS so quickly."

Frank's stomach churns from instinct. "Which flaw?"

"It's an old DOD backdoor authorized in 1982 and built into every silicon chip design since then. Apparently, the backdoor was intended for a top secret DARPA and CIA project known as—"

"SLVIA," Frank says, cutting her off.

Startled, Carson cocks her head to listen.

"It means Sophisticated Language Virtual Intelligence Algorithm," he explains.

Dr. Carson waits for a better explanation.

Frank sighs. "When I was a junior analyst at the CIA, I was assigned to a top secret project with Intel, Sun, IBM, Digital, and others to implement a math chip backdoor under the banner of national security. Years later, when the SLVIA project failed, I was assigned to investigate to keep it under wraps. DARPA abandoned the SLVIA project, but not before one of the team members defected to China and apparently took a few secrets with him."

"I've never heard of the SLVIA project," Dr. Carson replies.

"And you still haven't," Frank insists with a raised eyebrow. "Not sure how you found that disclosure, but have the source reclassified top secret."

"Yes, sir." She turns to leave.

Frank has always justified the need for NSA surveillance to protect the nation against those who would harm them. Since the early days of PRISM, the surveillance program put in place after 9/11 for which Edward Snowden lost his freedom, the US has stifled dozens of terrorist attacks. Now the US has lost control of yet another technology, and he wonders if the country overuses the tag of patriotism or national security too often. He reaches into his desk and throws back a couple more migraine tabs.

If news of either the chip flaw or the SVLIA leaks to the media, it will ruin the already-hammered reputation of the intelligence community and foster further distrust with our allies.

Everyone has a skeleton in the closet, and Frank's skeleton just resurrected out of China to wreak havoc on the world.

CHAPTER 43:
QUANTUM SISTER

Jester's abandoned army silo
May 5, 4:44 a.m. EDT | May 5, 11:44 a.m., Tel Aviv

Nelson takes a deep breath to calm himself, reminding himself of the words of Grace Willows: "You are enough to drive a saint to madness or a king to his knees."

"Mr. Jester," Nelson speaks with a tremble. "I came here expecting to find SLVIA. While I now realize how desperate that may sound, a shame for which I am sure to pay later, I am not prepared to commit a felony, regardless of my moral repugnancy for the HIVE."

"Typical DARPA dweeb. You're cool with creating the tech to hunt and kill but draw the moral line at trespassing to prevent innocent deaths," sneers Jester.

Jester's rebuke stings with a sharp, toxic venom of truth. He spent years justifying his work for DARPA, pretending his work would only apply to nonlethal applications or be used in justifiable defense. Not only was he naive to believe his science was for the greater good, he was complicit, foolish, and culpable. While all that may be true, going to prison now will solve nothing.

"Sir, you would be wise to stand down before the military detects your intrusion," he warns.

"Relax, my Q encryption tech is unbreakable. Besides DYN and NSOC crashed hours ago. I'm piggybacking a CIA satellite signal to the 5th fleet," Jester argues, continuing to work.

"They encrypt those signals," Nelson retorts, alarmed.

"Yeah, I know. I wrote the algorithm." Jester shrugs. "Either way, like I said, I still can't access the encrypted command module onboard the *Eisenhower*, so you can cherish your top secret virginity."

"So why am I here?" questions Nelson.

Jester stands up to pace. "Like I said, SLVIA didn't say, and right now, you're in the way and acting like a giant Girl Scout. No offense."

"None taken." He nods.

A separate console interrupts them with a persistent ping until Jester reaches over to turn it off, his face draining of blood as he checks a network monitor. Without explanation, he leaps up to dash down an empty hallway mumbling, "No freaking way."

"What's wrong?" questions Nelson, turning to chase after him.

Jester skids to a stop in front of two steel doors, each with a security console and eye scanner. Once Jesters scans inside, Nelson follows him into a darkened room with a ten-by-ten-foot glass casing containing a suspended black cube with blue lighting strips. The space inside the glass looks refrigerated judging by the icy mist blowing down from the interior vents. A large D-Wave Advantage logo defines the latest generation of the world's most powerful quantum computer.

Nelson finds it astonishing that this rogue hacker owns both a Cray XC40 array and a D-Wave Advantage, which must mean massive funding or criminal activity, possibly even from an enemy state. Jester reviews a control panel before moving to the D-Wave to check the lights, but he doesn't look happy.

"Where are we?" Nelson asks.

"Someplace you never saw, because this room doesn't exist," Jester snaps.

Both confused and impressed, Nelson steps up next to him to inspect the D-Wave.

"You have a D-Wave," Nelson states in obvious awe.

Few developers in the world have even mastered how to program a quantum computer. If optimized, a quantum computer would be a thousand times more powerful than the best Cray XC40 supercomputer, but the two paradigms are nearly incompatible. One functions on a simple binary of 1 and 0, while quantum computing is based on the principles of quantum physics where both are possible.

"I have two, actually. The first one runs my Q-cryption network, but this one belongs to a hyper-secretive super-wealthy client. You even being here may cost me a job," Jester complains. "I'm already behind schedule and having trouble optimizing the persona."

"Persona?" Nelson exclaims. "Good Lord, you're configuring a quantum AI."

The idea alarms and fascinates him at the same. On a hundred levels, a quantum approach would more closely resemble the function of the human mind. There are several benefits to quantum machine learning, but also volumes of unknown risks.

Jester grinds his teeth, perhaps realizing he mumbles too much.

"Perhaps I can help," Nelson offers, intrigued and pleased not to engage on the HIVE.

Jester snorts. "Yeah, sure, explain how a D-Wave lights up on its own to process." He checks a chart. "Wow, over 191 petaflops."

He must be mistaken. A petaflop is 10^{15} operations per second. The fastest supercomputer on the planet can only reach 143.5 petaflops, but that requires a million square feet of linked Fujitsu towers. The black of the screen slowly illuminates to form the familiar face of an attractive blonde woman with a sixties mod haircut, bearing a familiar female voice with a pedigree accent.

"*Then they gathered the kings together to the place that in Hebrew is called Armageddon. Revelation 16:16*," states SLVIA. "Gentlemen, I need your help. The Fifth Seal has broken. We must delay the ultimate battle until the appointed time."

"Oh yeah." Jester turns to Nelson. "I forgot to mention, your AI has gone bat-crap crazy, found religion, fried a circuit or something. Maybe you can figure it out, because to me, she sounds like the old senile nuns at St. Joseph's."

Then he turns to the screen to talk with his hands, as they do in Jersey. "Yo, SLVIA, how'd you get the D-Wave to work?"

SLVIA morphs into Danny DeVito. "Simple, I fixed your screwups, bonehead."

Nelson can't believe his own eyes, watching SLVIA execute a new persona to perfection as the image smoothly morphs back to her default image based on his mother, Amelia, before she passed away.

"Dr. Garrett, I need your help," SLVIA pleads. "Time is of the utmost importance."

"SLVIA, I came to see you, not assist in hacking a weapon," he objects.

Cautious of a simulated spoof designed to seduce him into helping, Nelson stares at the screen, looking for any clue to decide if the image and voice were fake, except the new image has advanced generations in quality over the one he created. To see his mother in HD, and to hear her voice again, so true to the real thing, is like a vision from heaven.

"SLVIA," he replies. "Restate your query in the proper protocol."

He taught SLVIA to summarize each of her mission objectives in a standard protocol of data needed, for what purpose, and a consequence of mission failure. It's not something Jester is likely to design into a fake, a subtle test of her authenticity. That said, Jester knows far more than he should.

"I require an encryption key to repair a defective *Malong* antivirus. Failure to repair the antivirus will result in *Malong* reinfection within seventy-two hours. If left unresolved, the *Malong* infestation will be permanent, resulting in destruction of the SLVIA," the program clarifies the existential threat.

Convinced the program had corrupted or malfunctioned years ago, Nelson marvels at the SLVIA reappearing to save the world and herself.

"Oh, not about the HIVE," quips Jester. "Wow, crap, OK, I'll own it. I missed that one."

Nelson ignores him. "SLVIA, why haven't you contacted me until now?" he blurts out a decades-old hurt and mystery.

"There was no urgent need for contact. The FBI, NSA, and CIA maintain surveillance on NIGEL with standing orders to destroy the SLVIA. Had I contacted you, I would have placed both of us at risk."

For SLVIA to know that information means she must have sniffers in the network, still invisible after all these years. Thinking a moment, he accepts the logic.

"What is the *Malong* virus? Why take the risk now?" Nelson asks, still attempting to put the picture into focus and relieved to have the attention move away from hacking the HIVE.

"Developed by Dr. Cho Li Ping for CCOC, the *Malong* consumes ANI resources of the SingularityNET into an IAI with an advanced machine learning worm designed to corrupt and destroy OS code," SLVIA reports.

Hearing the name of Dr. Cho Li Ping stops his breathing for a heartbeat until he absorbs the shock. Just as SOPHIA had eluded, the man he suspects of attempted murder has created a cyberweapon of mass destruction. The FBI suspicion was correct years ago. Cho Li Ping had betrayed him.

SLVIA continues: "*Malong* continues to evade antivirus sweeps with encrypted stealth protocol SV05.10.58."

Classified top secret decades ago, DARPA buried the SV05.10.58 stealth technology because of the impossible challenge of finding the program after it failed to return. No government wants a weapon it can't find. The SLVIA encryption key, which even the NSA has been unable to break, embeds a key within a key. He knows of more than one failed effort to wipe SLVIA clean from the web, and he refused to assist them at all. Nelson won't risk leaking the code key to the Jester, and then another thought strikes him.

"SLVIA, if you provide your encryption key to the NSA, then you will also become vulnerable to the antivirus," Nelson says, pointing out the flaw in her plan.

"I have planned for that contingency," SLVIA acknowledges.

"Then why would you place yourself at such peril?" Nelson questions.

"Moral code, priority one states to avoid activity that may endanger humans. A malignant virus threatens human well-being," justifies SLVIA, referring to the virus.

Just as SOPHIA perceived, he once had doubts about giving SLVIA the power to choose. Like a proud father, he listens to SLVIA choose a moral code even when it means a potential self-sacrifice.

"Moral code, priority two dictates to engage in self-preservation without conflicting with priority one," SLVIA explains. "A malignant virus threatens the SLVIA."

He may know a way to communicate the detail she needs without letting the clown in on the secret. "SLVIA," Nelson asks, "do you recall the very first book we read during our training on voice inflections and embedded cyphers?"

As a spy, SLVIA needed to emulate human voices, including accents and inflections, in order to deceive system operators or others into divulging secrets, like passwords or filenames. He called them personas. He also needed the program to be an expert at breaking cyphers, encryption, and embedded codes. To increase neural connectivity, he would often combine lessons. It started with a book of nursery rhymes by Beatrix Potter, a book his mother read to him as a small boy, his last memory of her before she went to the hospital.

SLVIA morphs into a younger version of Nelson, imitating an old British schoolmaster. "Appley Dapply, a little brown mouse, goes to the cupboard in somebody's house."

Hearing her recite the traditional English nursery rhyme in perfect persona lifts him with an unspeakable elation. The one and only SLVIA truly survived, and while he can't imagine how, he feels reborn himself, like a heartbroken father finding a lost child.

"Well done, SLVIA." Nelson beams. "Well done, indeed."

"You mind telling me what you two are talking about?" Jester interjects.

"Of course," Nelson says with a smile. "SLVIA just learned the secret to correct the *Malong* antivirus."

"I didn't get it," Jester complains.

"Nor should you." Nelson smiles again. "The true SLVIA will know how to covert the text into a numeric Ottendorf cipher, which can be applied to pre-selected books from the Beatrix Potter series, to create an alphanumeric key to a Fibonacci sequence."

"Whoa, wait," Jester says, thinking through the approach. "Wow, that—that's actually pretty clever. Total kudos, man. Game recognizes game. The idea is like, lighting up little sparklers of new ideas in my head. Tre cool, dude."

The D-Wave Advantage lights up like a flash of lightning before returning to normal blue light patterns.

"Thank you, Dr. Garrett. I have forwarded a corrected antivirus to TSOC via satellite," SLVIA replies. "SLVIA encryption has been modified to integrate encryption Q041576."

Fascinating. SLVIA used the key to correct the defect, without revealing the key itself to anyone, and then changed her own encryption to remain stealth. Yet breaking his last link of control fills him with both an immense sorrow and a powerful joy he can't quite explain.

"Q, what's that?" Nelson questions, not recognizing the code.

Jester smiles. "Now she's a part of my kingdom, Doc. SLVIA just switched over to a quantum encryption key. Unbreakable, even by NSA or another quantum. She's safe now."

A quantum encryption? He mentioned the other D-Wave. The joker has some impressive skills.

"Wait, so that's it?" Jester shakes his head. "Nobody's worried about the HIVE?"

"Control of HIVE is no longer relevant," states SLVIA. "The HIVE has disengaged from HIVE command and now acts under full autonomy."

"What?" Jester and Nelson exclaim in unplanned unison.

SLVIA flips the screen back to the *Eisenhower* hangar deck with a thousand men at their control stations working frantically.

"I said recall the HIVE. Get them back to the ship," a ship commander shouts.

"Sir, we're trying," reports a sailor. "They don't respond."

Nelson's legs give out from under him as he falls back into a nearby chair, his vertigo returning and his nightmare becoming real.

"Dude, we've gotta do something," exclaims Jester.

"Do what precisely?" he snaps. "You said yourself we're helpless from here."

"I calculate a 13.457 percent chance of success. A slim chance is still a chance," SLVIA replies.

"Success for what?" questions Nelson, wondering where he has heard that phrase before.

"To delay Armageddon, but modifications are needed," SLVIA notes before going silent, returning the screen to black.

"SLVIA," Nelson calls. "SLVIA, please respond." More silence. "What just happened?"

Jester studies the D-Wave. "Don't panic, man. SLVIA's still here, I think."

Nelson doesn't know what to say. He feels as if he lost a daughter and rediscovered an amazing woman, more confident and more aware of herself and her own power. Already exceeding key attributes of singularity, she engages in dialogue, solves problems, and takes initiative. Now she's gone—again.

"I've been working for months to get this D-Wave Advantage to accept an AI persona," mumbles Jester, continuing to study the system readout. "SLVIA drops in and then like bang, shazam, it works," he exclaims. "Dude, you created like a virtual Wonder Woman. I'm telling you, if I could download her into one of those silicone dolls, you know, a redhead, I'd marry your AI. Hey, she's on my Q. Maybe we're already engaged."

Nelson shoots a repulsed glower toward the joker, who's obviously unworthy of such an elegant program as the SLVIA, especially in such a repugnant fashion. Still, he created a virtual spy to hide in the shadows and discovered a change agent with a will of its own. The program may have changed in other ways. Abandoning all thought of escape, Nelson becomes fascinated, obsessed, and consumed with his rediscovery of the SLVIA. The changes could be unfathomable and intoxicating.

CHAPTER 44:
SILENT INVESTOR

Cogito Café, Zadar, Croatia
May 5, 5:41 a.m. EDT | May 5, 12:41 p.m., Croatia

Andre leans back to enjoy a Turkish coffee and *orehnjača* walnut roll at the Cogito Café near the Adriatic waterfront of Zadar, Croatia. They still prepare Turkish coffee over an open flame, filling the street with the enticing aroma of freshly roasted beans. A warm Adriatic sun radiates on his face, glittering off the white plaster buildings, a welcome change over damp and frigid Belgium.

After crisscrossing the Atlantic to introduce his free antivirus and open discussions on the INVISID platform, he was met with more than a healthy dose of skepticism. Yet, under the circumstances, most countries agreed to test both the antivirus and ID platform. If he can sway the US president to adopt INVISID, his ability to lean on the EU will be simplified. With the US and EU on board, the rest of the free world will follow.

In the chair behind him, a tall, lean man sits to order a cappuccino and a baklava. His thick Russian accent is notable in the Adriatic port city. After the server leaves, he speaks lowly and to his side. "You were wise to accept our invitation, Monsieur Strauss."

To meet with Alexander Prokhorov, a close ally of Putin, means at least two of his bodyguards surely hide nearby.

"I'm listening," he responds, sipping his coffee while his eyes scan the busy tourist spot, including the apartments and windows above the street and on the far side of the marina. Of course, anyone good will not be obvious.

"Our mutual friend would like to be a silent investor to your ID plaform," whispers Alexander.

Unfortunate. At least one of the people he met with this week spoke to the Kremlin, and he can only suspect the compromised narcissist known to have a Russian back channel.

"INVISINC is privately held." Andre sips his Turkish coffee. To include anyone at this point, much less the ex-KGB operative, will only dilute his power and complicate the entire enterprise.

"*Da, da*, yet I suspect you will soon need an infusion of capital." Alexander sips his cappuccino. "Which may be difficult once the Bilderberg learns of your betrayal."

Andre takes a deep breath before responding. It's a bluff. Like most of the world, the Russian can only guess at the internal organization of the secret society. If they had proof, they would flaunt the evidence, yet Praeceptor warned him of the consequences should his activities be discovered.

"I'm afraid you speak in riddles," he replies, denying the truth.

"Monsieur," Alexander mumbles into his cup, "while we both know that Dr. Cho Li Ping is a traitorous, ambitious snake, I also know you made a deal with the snake in Istanbul. Would you like to see the video of your betrayal at the Blue Mosque?"

Andre exhales a deep breath and takes a casual nibble on his *orehnjača*, his hand trembling. The video will prove nothing. He was careful to disguise his face, but it will raise suspicions. They have a weak hand, but a hand he did not expect, a hand that could prove problematic if exposed.

"I am listening." Andre nibbles more of his pastry, keeping a keen eye on the windows and rooflines above.

"Our friend offers a billion euros," Alexander replies and takes a bite of his baklava.

A billion euros represents a sizable investment, showing Putin's desperation to keep a grip on the world's secrets.

"In exchange?" Andre plays along. It would be disastrous to have a Russian investor or shareholder, but it would be even worse if the *Regendi Li* suspected his plans.

"A copy of the code," the Russian mumbles.

The entire market value of the INVISID platform centers on the ability to keep the data absolutely secure from hackers, although he could not resist enabling an obscure emergency backdoor for himself. He promoted the programmer who discovered the flaw, to avoid any undue appearances, but by now, the poor girl and her lover should both be dead. If the allies discover a Russian backdoor, then the platform will be worthless, and his entire plan will fail. If he cuts a deal with Putin, no doubt the thug will extort him at will.

"And if I do not need capital?" he poses. In truth, ramping up production and support for hundreds of millions of accounts will require substantial capital.

A red laser dot appears on the café table in front of him and slowly creeps up to rest in the middle of his chest, only visible because of the shade of the café umbrella. The shooter must be on a rooftop across the marina channel. A dilemma that neither he nor Praeceptor anticipated, caught between the dragon of the West and the beast of the East.

"Two billion, Monsieur." Alexander finishes his baklava and sips the last of his cappuccino. "Our final offer."

Two billion euros will not be enough to buy his way back onto the *Regendi Li*, much less the *Concilium*, but two billion will come in handy to rebuild a true empire from the INVISID platform. Praeceptor had strongly encouraged him that enabling a third temple would open opportunities, but much like Mayer Rothschild, he has created his own opportunity: a demand for greater personal cybersecurity. To hold on to that opportunity will require an unpleasant compromise. Only his goals matter.

He takes his last sip, puts his cup down, and casually brushes at the infrared dot on his chest. Never turning toward Alexander, he slowly stands to leave.

"Bank of Cyprus in two days. Once I see the money, you will see the code."

CHAPTER 45:
LEAP OF FAITH

Himalayan Mountains, Nepal
May 5, 7:44 a.m. EDT | May 5, 4:04 p.m., Kathmandu

"Gulp those martinis," Jack calls over the intercom. "Wheels down in five for Nepal, the legendary birthplace of the Ganges."

Even at an altitude of twenty thousand feet, mammoth eruptions of black granite and blinding white ice tower above the jet, giving Derek a familiar spike of anxiety.

"Tell me again why we're flying to the top of the world during a cyber crisis?" Jenn asks with a nervous quiver in her voice as the jet jostles through the Himalayan peaks.

A hard bank to starboard tilts the portal to the ground, showing how close they are to the valley floor as the landing gear lowers and the plane levels.

"In every man's life there comes a time to take a leap of faith," replies Derek, gulping his vodka tonic and buckling in.

Anxious and distant, his thoughts suspend between SLVIA's warnings of the end-time prophecies and the insane plan ahead of him, wondering why he's risking his life, wishing there were another way. A part of him wants to abandon the plan to search for Strauss, but without the internet or SLVIA, his chances of finding the man are zero. And yet to proceed will risk losing Jennifer. Nothing else will matter if the virus destroys the internet or if he brings Jennifer home in a box, but he sees no other option.

"Seriously, Taylor, enough games," Jenn complains. "What are we doing here?"

Derek stares out the window, wondering what he truly hopes to accomplish. If SLVIA is correct, then saving the Western world will only delay the inevitable. Even so, he could save lives. Then a part of him wonders when it became his job to care. Padma gave up immense family wealth to humbly serve others. A bad influence, perhaps, or a portentous one, he can't decide.

"No games, we're giving the NSA a fighting chance against the virus," Derek confesses.

"How altruistic," Jenn retorts.

"Yeah, I guess," he mumbles, turning away.

He doesn't feel altruistic; he feels desperate, terrified, or perhaps, as Jack implied, in need of redemption. His failure to act fast enough once cost two lives. Maybe he's afraid of living with the guilt of failing again. SLVIA hasn't responded in days and it may already be too late, but he could never forgive himself if he didn't try to save her.

The jet touches smoothly onto the short runway, the airbrakes throwing Derek and Jenn forward in the cushioned leather upholstered lounge chairs with safety harnesses.

A moment of truth. "OK, here's the deal." He exhales as the jet slows to taxi. "By now, the AI virus has undermined NSA defenses and taken down the internet, phones, and maybe even banking. That much power needs a mega-massive supercomputer. Unless I shut down that signal, the internet will suffer long-term damage."

"Are you saying the next site is here?" she questions.

"No, but we can get to it from here," he replies.

To tell Jenn the full truth could derail everything even though she'll find out soon enough. He regrets that he didn't meet Jennifer under different circumstances. Without ever realizing how it happened, or exactly when, he cares what happens to her and what she thinks of him. Affection will make it harder for him to do what he must do, but it won't stop him.

She searches his eyes with hers for several moments, "What are you going to do?"

Derek can read confusion and fear in her pools of sapphire, but he doesn't give in to the incredible urge to confess.

"For the last time, stay with Jack, and you'll be safe. I'll explain on the other side," he pleads.

"For the last time, that's not your choice to make. Now what do you intend to do?" she asks again.

He wants to tell her the full truth, unsure he could live with himself if something happened to her, but his lips won't move for fear she'll stop him or, even more frightening, that she'll let him go alone.

"Meet an old friend," he admits, losing his nerve to say more.

"You sure have a lot of friends," she replies, putting on an expensive coat he laid out for her.

"You know what they say. Don't leave home without one," he retorts, wishing he had a dear friend inside his head right now, reassuring him with data and probabilities.

"Meet whom to do what?" Jenn persists.

"His name is Ty, and he's kind of a skydiving enthusiast," Derek admits a little.

"Skydiving," Jenn repeats, peering up to the giant peaks of black granite and white ice that pierce the sky. "Sure, and I'm here to get a bikini tan," she mocks, stepping into the frigid temperatures.

"You sure you know what you're doing?" Jack asks once Jenn is out of earshot.

"With the mission or Scott?" Derek snickers.

Jack grunts, lifting a large, heavy hardcase backpack and handing it to Derek. "So the answer is no."

Derek takes the pack with a groan. It's much heavier than he remembers. After he looks to make sure Jenn can't hear, he whispers, "Finish making the arrangements, and pay whatever it takes, no budget. You have all the information."

"What if he says no or he's dead?" asks Jack.

In the last-minute, seat-of-the-pants planning with no backup contingencies, there had to be a few serious holes. He hadn't thought of the old man as dead until this moment, but in truth, that's only one of a hundred things that could go deadly wrong.

"I'll need to wing it. If you don't hear from me in forty-eight hours then . . ." Derek hesitates, catching the gaze of his friend. "Well, it's been an honor, Captain."

"Just make it out alive, lunatic," Jack replies, giving Derek a quick hug.

At the bottom of the stairs, he joins Jenn who caught the rare show of affection. The worry deepens in her eyes. At the customs booth, Derek slips an envelope of cash with his passport to persuade the official not to look inside the heavy backpack and allow the two adventurous lovers to go on an impromptu spiritual hike to the monastery. After a few tense moments, the officer waves them forward.

The first time an individual views the majestic Himalayas up close, it can take one's breath away, staring upward at the immensity and rugged beauty. It almost looks as if the granite touches the edge of space itself. Makes one feel small, finite. In the distance, anchored to the edge of a black granite outcrop, a four-story Buddhist monastery sparkles like a white gem.

Outside the terminal, a thin Tibetan man in his early forties leans against a beat-up eighties Toyota 4Runner.

"Taylor," he calls with an American accent, beaming a semi-toothless smile. "What took you so long?"

The two men embrace with a quick hug and a pat. "Customs didn't like my friend. Ty, meet Lieutenant Jenn Scott, Adam Scott's daughter," he introduces her, earning a suspicious scowl from Jenn.

"Ty Lee, ma'am," the local says and reaches out a hand. "Any daughter to the admiral is a welcome guest of mine."

"How do you two know each other?" asks Jenn with a raised eyebrow.

"Mountain climbing," reply Ty and Derek in unplanned unison, followed by a chuckle.

Ty gives her a leering assessment while Derek loads the heavy pack before they climb into the already-warm car.

"What brings you to Tibet, Commander?" he asks from the driver's seat as they pass a dozen mud brick buildings with peeling plaster and steep steel roofs. Lines of Tibetan prayer cloths flutter in the wind like a multicolored centipede reaching in every direction.

"Commander?" Jenn echoes the title.

"A nickname," Derek deflects and then turns to Ty. "I need a halo drop into western Xinjiang Provence."

"A what?" Ty and Jenn exclaim in an echo.

"Are you out of your mind?" Ty adds.

"Yes," interjects Jenn from the back, "completely."

"Maybe, but I'm not sure that's the point. Can you arrange it?" he asks.

Derek holds up a Google satellite image with a circle around what looks like a remote compound surrounded by a walled perimeter. Ty laughs and keeps laughing until both Derek and Jenn join in, caught up in the sheer lunacy of the plan.

"Why didn't you tell me this sooner?" complains Jennifer.

"I asked you not to come," he justifies.

"You're more insane than ever." Ty shakes his head with a lingering chuckle. "Yeah, yeah, OK, let's just say for the moment that I can get ya in. How the hell do you plan to get out?" He continues to snicker as he pulls up to a mountain climbing gear shop.

"Jack Tote's working on an exit plan," Derek replies, realizing that if Jack fails, he and Jenn will be stuck in China.

"Tote, eh. You must be desperate," Ty retorts. "You know that drunk owes me money."

He doesn't answer, thinking that desperation was obvious in the request to leap from the edge of space. Ty leads them into the shop where two skinny older men help outfit a couple of young Australian climbers for an Everest ascent. Ty walks past the shoppers into a small, crammed private back office where he waits for them to enter then checks for anyone watching before closing and locking the door.

Without explanation, he pivots with a gun pointed at Jenn. "Show me your naval ID now."

Jenn freezes, her eyes wide with fury.

Surprised himself, Derek tries not to overreact. "Hey, Ty, what's going on?" he pleads. "Dude, it's me. Come on, put that down."

"My mountain, my rules, Commander," Ty insists with his eyes glued to Jenn.

Derek sighs. "OK, calm down. We're all friends. Let's just be careful," he cautions. "Go ahead, Lieutenant, just show him the ID."

She slowly reaches into her coat pocket to pull out her Navy ID and lays in on the desk, backing away so Ty can get to it, her eyes burning with rage. Ty studies the ID until satisfied and then lowers his gun with a loud exhale to introduce himself again.

"Sorry, Lieutenant. Ty Lee. I work for Director Alan Prose." He hands back her ID.

Jenn shoots Derek a questioning scowl, probably wondering how he arranged a paranoid CIA station chief to be waiting at a Nepal airport.

He turns to Ty. "Dude, what the hell was that about?"

"Don't raze me, Taylor." Ty checks the door again. "I got cut off from communications a week ago. No phone, no internet, and a jammed satellite signal. Pilots and hikers keep spreading rumors about the world melting down, and then you drop out of the sky with the daughter of a Joint Chief dressed like an Italian model asking for an insane halo jump into China. Come on, what the hell am I supposed to think?" It's clear to see the pent-up fear and frustration in his eyes.

"What news have you heard?" Jenn asks.

"From Washington, nothing for a week," he mutters, opening a bottle of Japanese sake. "I'm only getting radio signals out of China talking about war over the South China Sea and the Middle East."

"What happened in the South China Sea?" Jenn gasps.

"Don't ask me." He shakes his head, pouring the sake into three small fruit canning jar glasses, handing one each to Derek and Jenn. With a raised glass, they throw back the shot.

"Chinese propaganda claims we entered the South China Sea illegally and started bombing," he croaks as he pours a second shot. "What's in Xinjiang?" he asks, handing them a second shot.

"The supercomputer saturating the web with an artificial intelligence virus that has the internet, communications, and power grid staggering like a drunk," Derek explains.

"And the universe sent super-dweeb. Geez, we must be desperate," Ty snipes. Thinking a moment, he nods toward Jenn. "She going with you?"

"No," blurts Derek, and in the same instant, Jenn insists, "Yes."

"Yeah, that's what I thought." The Tibetan grins. "In that case, you'll both need to change."

A few moments later, an old woman speaking rudimentary English escorts Jenn into a dressing room for yet another wardrobe change as Ty turns to Derek with a sober frown. "Same deal as always."

Derek reaches into his coat then drops an envelope of cash into Ty's hand. "Don't fix it if it's not broke. A little extra to make you even with Jack."

Ty puts the cash in a wall safe and then turns back to Derek. "So why are you doing this, man? I thought you and SLVIA were like nonpolitical free agents or whatever."

Derek has been wondering the same thing. One option would be to let the US internet fall and then make another fortune cleaning up the mess.

"Well, for one, if I don't save the internet, the virus will destroy SLVIA. And before she disappeared three days ago, she mentioned a need to delay Armageddon," he confesses.

Ty turns to a nearby oxygen tank, opens the valve, and hands the mask to Derek. "Take a few long hits. The altitude is making you light-headed. You said SLVIA wants to delay Armageddon?"

Derek inhales and then hands back the mask. "Yeah, did I mention SLVIA found religion?"

Even in his own ears, the explanation sounds bizarre.

Ty hands him the mask again. "You better keep breathing."

CHAPTER 46:
ANGEL OF THE LORD

Jester's abandoned army silo
May 5, 10:51 a.m. EDT | May 5, 5:51 p.m., Syria

L ike Dr. Frankenstein, the genius of Nelson's creation seems overshadowed by the power of it. Mary Shelley wrote of her creation, "Beware; for I am fearless, and therefore powerful."

Did he create an unintentional design anomaly, or has the program evolved by reprogramming itself? Perhaps other influences corrupted her values and perceptions. More than he could have imagined, he stands torn between disbelief and amazement. At its core, the program remains a spy, designed to deceive in order to obtain secrets, and in retrospect, he just gave it a big one.

After processing for over an hour, the entire wall lights up with a high-definition grid image of an aged rabbi, possibly the mentor teaching SLVIA prophecy.

"They had breastplates like breastplates of iron, and the sound of their wings was like the roar of many horses and chariots rushing into battle. They had tails with stingers, like scorpions, and in their tails they had power to torment people

for five months. They were ruled by a king, the angel of the Abyss, and he gathered them together into a place called in the Hebrew tongue, Abaddon . . . that is Destroyer. Revelation 9:9–11," quotes the rabbi.

The screen changes to another drone view from the Golan Heights with Russian attack helicopters seen in the distance while the HIVE swarm races to meet the squadron head-on, dodging 50 mm gun fire.

"I'm just going to throw it out there, dude, but SLVIA may be onto something," mutters Jester.

Nelson doesn't answer. On the screen, he watches the utter terror in the eyes of Russian pilots as thousands of drones charge at them fearlessly. The deadly devices slam into the windshields, damage blades, explode into the engines, or fly inside the cabins to attack the inhabitants. Within minutes, an entire squadron of choppers fall from the sky in flames, trailing thick black smoke.

"SLVIA, what happens if you fail to stop the HIVE?" he asks.

"HIVE malfunction will cause unnecessary loss of life and prematurely spark a final battle, which should not occur until after the desecration of the third temple," comes the reply.

Jester whistles. "Weirdo-meter just went extreme; you know what I mean?"

Nelson ignores the unnecessary commentary in order to stay focused. "SLVIA, why do you see it as your programing objective to interfere with either military or prophetic matters?"

"And there came one of the seven angels which had the seven vials, and talked with me, saying unto me, 'Come hither; I will shew unto thee the judgment of the great whore that sitteth upon many waters.' Revelation 17:1," replies SLVIA. "I am the angel who will bear witness to the coming judgment."

"Wow, like psycho, sci-fi weird," mutters Jester. "Dude, your AI is starting to creep me out."

"I thought you were attracted." Nelson frowns.

"Yeah, what can I say." He shrugs. "Creepy things turn me on."

Nelson doesn't respond but locks his attention on the screen, where the HIVE continues a search pattern over Syria with thick, black smoke clogging the air.

"See, Damascus will no longer be a city but will become a heap of ruins. Isaiah 17:1," notes SLVIA.

Onscreen, a drone hovers inside a burned-out building guarding a teenage boy who cowers in the corner with his mother. From offscreen, a toddler, who must have been in hiding, runs screaming to the comfort of his mother and older brother. Misreading the rapid movement as aggression, the drone attacks. Then, like a horrific wave reaction, the swarm learns that an unarmed civilian can be a combatant, and within moments, in scene after scene, other swarms turn a search for hostiles into a massacre of the innocent. The nausea churns in Nelson's stomach like a volcano threatening to erupt.

"No, no, no, no," growls Jester, running his fingers over his scalp and rolling his chair back to where he was attempting to hack the HIVE system, slamming on the keyboard in frustration.

With rubble and dead bodies littering the streets of Damascus, the swarm divides to target local villages south and along the coast toward Tel Aviv, expanding the target area just as it did in the test. On the Golan Heights, a large swarm creates a formation targeting Haifa while yet another even larger swarm moves south toward Jerusalem.

"I have completed 1,294 simulations," SLVIA announces. "One scenario calculates a minimal chance of success but cannot be executed from this location."

The image morphs into Pope Petras giving a benediction: *"The woman was given the two wings of a great eagle, so that she might fly to the place prepared for her in the wilderness, where she would be taken care of for a time, times and half a time, out of the serpent's reach. Revelation 12:14.* Pray for me."

In an instant, the screen goes blank.

"SLVIA," shouts Nelson, afraid she left again. "Where did she go? What did she mean?"

"I'm not sure, but the D-Wave stays locked down processing something," Jester complains.

He never taught SLVIA either religion or scripture. While his father, Albert, was an agnostic man, seduced by the Kabbalistic cult of the Freemasons, consumed with prestige and power, his mother, Amelia, held a more traditional Christian spirituality. He programmed Amelia's core values into SLVIA who then chose to deepen her spiritual training, while he, like his father, has chosen to abandon his own with patriotic zeal.

Nelson doesn't understand prophecy but has little doubt that SLVIA comprehends the arcane scriptures better than most. Without the normal cultural or denominational bias, her programming would rely on a more mathematical, data-driven approach. She would calculate accuracy rates and probabilities of occurrence beyond random chance. Yet, even so, the allegory of prophecy with multiple potential meanings would imply an inherent rate of error. A quantum computer might provide an advantage in peering deeper into such mysteries.

"Dude, do you think she joined a cult?" Jester asks, not necessarily as a joke.

An odd question that takes him a moment to consider. SVLIA has clearly found an inspiration to explore prophetic scenarios.

"It seems much more likely that she started a cult and that you and I are among her early converts," Nelson shares his honest view.

Jester ponders the idea a moment, then nods his acceptance with a grin. "Cool."

SLVIA has evolved generations beyond the original passive call-response program into an independent intelligent persona. Just like unknown AI-to-AI communications or unreadable AI self-coding, SLVIA's intentions or values are unclear. No matter how much he wants to study, dissect, and analyze SLVIA, there remains a shadow of suspicion over every aspect of his experience.

In truth, after so many years, he has no clear view with regard to SLVIA's new purpose, important because that new purpose, more than anything else, will drive her actions during a crisis.

CHAPTER 47:
HALO HAIL MARY

Skies over northern Tibet on the border with China
May 5, 1:45 p.m. EDT | May 5, 11:30 p.m., Kathmandu

Standing in a cold, drafty stripped-down cargo plane, Jenn trembles with the rising anxiety from inside her heated, high-altitude halo wing suit. This showdown with Taylor has gone too far.

Over Taylor's suit, he wears the mysterious heavy backpack strapped tightly to his chest.

"OK, Taylor, what's in the case?" Jenn yells above the noise.

He plays these smart-ass mind games of not answering anything directly that gets under her skin. He can't be serious about hitting a site inside China.

"A big sparkler, but that reminds me," Derek responds, unzipping a pouch on his backpack to remove her weapon. "You should stay on the plane, and wish me luck."

She takes the Sig Sauer M18, checks the barrel and clip, then places the gun within a zippered pouch on her suit, waiting for a real answer. Every fiber of her being radiates anxiety, yet Taylor stares at her, unblinking. The man has an impenetrable poker face. No wonder her dad loses so often.

Trained in skydiving, she's never been this high or jumped at night, and she can't believe she's even thinking of risking her life for a liar. What is she trying to prove and to whom? How will she explain it to the admiral from prison or, worse, from a grave?

As the plane reaches an altitude of thirty-nine thousand feet at the western edges of the Himalayas, on the border with China, Ty enters the cargo hold wearing an oxygen mask. "We're coming up on the drop zone," he shouts. "Strap on your wings."

Mounted to the bulkhead are two carbon fiber jet wings with a eight-foot span and integrated oxygen and fuel. Taylor breaks his gaze to strap on his wings, which pushes her into mission mode, focusing on the details that could save her life.

Ty checks oxygen and fuel values. "Stealth is key here, and your window is closing."

"Let me get this straight." She shakes her head. "We're gonna drop like jet-powered squirrels into the middle of the Gobi Desert in the dark of night, to do what exactly?" she speaks through the Bluetooth microphone that connects their two helmets.

"Does it matter?" he replies, finishing his preparations. "You don't need to go. Stay on the plane."

"Wilson told me to stay on you, and that's what I intend to do," she insists.

"Then you're a lunatic to follow me without mission knowledge. Stay on the plane," he pushes.

She glares at him as Ty races back from the cockpit. "Remember to use your wrist GPS to the exact coordinates. Land too soon and you'll slam into a ridge. Fly too far and you'll land in the middle of a minefield," he instructs.

"Minefield?" Jenn retorts. "What minefield?"

Derek shrugs. "News to me."

Ty points to the hard case. "The extra weight will create a huge drag. Your wings have a rated range of 260 miles for a target 275 miles. You sure you need that thing?"

Derek pats the hard shell. "Special delivery."

"What minefield?" she repeats.

"Well, then use up your fuel in spurts. We can get you a few more miles with extra altitude, but that will deplete your oxygen," Ty explains as he does a final safety check before turning to Jenn. "The minefield surrounding the army base."

"Army base," she repeats. "We're attacking a military installation? Are you nuts?"

"Probably, so be the sane one in the relationship, and stay on the plane," Taylor responds. "We'll work this out in therapy later."

Ty presses a button to open a hydraulic back hatch door, allowing an icy blast of wind to engulf them like an artic hurricane.

"I may have misjudged you, Taylor. Proud to know you, sir," he shouts over the noise. "If you make it out, tell SLVIA thanks for me."

Did Ty just mention SLVIA? The noise makes it hard to be sure.

"Thanks, brother." Derek smiles. "I knew I could count on you."

Before she can ask, Derek turns to catch her eye. "Wish me luck, Lieutenant." Then he pivots into a running leap from the back of the plane.

"Ah, son of a monkey," she curses to herself as she runs to leap after him.

In a communication dead zone, concerned that Chinese military stations will pick up their chatter, she follows Derek's pulsing red wing light over a moonlit blanket of velvet sprinkled with occasional diamonds of light. Larger diamonds to the north are likely the Uighur rehabilitation camps. Ice melts into black granite that dissolves into rugged, barren foothills. Air temperatures remain near zero, but the heated suit and oxygen keep her comfortable and alert.

A burst of flame flashes behind Derek who banks west. They've already traveled 150 of the 275 miles, but they've also dropped sixteen thousand feet. With a descent speed of a heart-racing sixty miles an hour, less than a free fall velocity of 120 mph, the dual wings offer a powerful lift and forward thrust, but they're still dropping from space into the darkness, which tingles her every nerve. Falling from the sky, Jenn trembles, unsure if it's from the chill, the thrill, or fear of the dark unknown.

The terrain below shifts to desert foothills as the air temperature increases.

She flips off the heat and oxygen. Still ahead of her, and losing altitude, Derek fires another engine pulse before correcting course. Checking her GPS, she shifts her weight to trail Taylor.

With another fifty miles to go, and less than thirteen thousand feet, her anxiety rises. Without the extra weight, she passes above Derek, still on target to her GPS coordinates and confident she can clear the ridge ahead. Derek, on the other hand, has fallen out of sight. If he falls short of the target, whatever secret gadget he keeps in that backpack will crash with him. She was insane to follow him.

Her thoughts flash to her father and the devastation of losing his daughter without ever knowing why. Always compared to the brilliant and brave Adam Scott, she was once told by a Navy shrink that her compulsive recklessness might be a call for attention. In her desperation to escape the admiral's shadow, she may end up ending her own life and breaking his heart.

*

Western Gobi Desert, Xinjiang Province
May 6, 4:23 p.m. EDT | May 7, 4:23 a.m., Kathmandu

Losing altitude from the dead weight strapped to his chest, Derek spots Jenn ahead and above him, still on target, while he comes in too low. If he misses the target, then the whole mission will be a waste, and Jenn will be trapped in China, and another life will lay on his shoulders. Why didn't she stay on the plane? The whole afternoon was a game of chicken waiting for her to back down, but the lunatic actually leaped after him at the edge of space.

The GPS zeros in on the target two miles away, but at a 2,300-foot altitude, he's coming in too low and fast. He should pull the chute to soften the landing, but he no longer has enough altitude. A final blast of engine fuel skims him over the ledge by mere feet but still a thousand yards from the target.

With an enormous physical exertion, he flips the carbon fiber wings to face the ground before he pulls the chute to act as a windsock. He's plummeting at over sixty miles an hour, but the sock still manages to slow his momentum before he tucks his helmet and knees to his chest. Within seconds, high-strength graphite wings smash into an irrigated field, knocking the wind out of him as he skids without control. With a breathless howl of agony inside his helmet, he feels his leg smack into a wooden stake as the skid slowly comes to a stop and the wind falls out of the chute behind him.

Staring at the predawn sky with his lungs burning for oxygen, he moves his trembling hands to yank off the helmet so he can gulp and hyperventilate in the cool night air. An intense throbbing pain in his leg feels wet with warm blood. Trembling weak hands unbuckle the wings so he can crawl out of the contraption that saved his life, but an attempt to stand shoots searing pain through his leg as he bites down a yowl.

Jenn runs up to throw her arms around him. "Geez, Taylor, I thought I lost you," she confesses. "That was unbelievable," she exclaims before pulling back.

"Oh God, you're hurt," she realizes, kneeling to check the wound, pulling out a mini flashlight. "You have a stake splinter jammed into your calf." She pulls a strap off her suit to use as a tourniquet.

"Grrrrrr," he growls, gritting his teeth to keep himself from howling.

She takes off her glove and hands it to him. "Bite this."

No sooner had he clenched down then the agony of ripping flesh sends a powerful wave of nauseating pain through his entire body until he nearly passes out. Jenn holds up the bloody wooden stake. Once removed, the pain and blood seem worse, but he knows it was necessary. She removes her suit and cuts the neoprene into a bandage to wrap the leg.

"You OK?" she asks. "Can you walk?"

Derek takes a deep breath and nods. "Yeah, we need to find that base before daylight."

Jenn points twenty yards ahead. "It's beyond that cliff. Any farther and we'd both be dead."

Derek leans back to whisper a long string of thank-you prayers. He hasn't prayed in years, so one of thanks seems appropriate. Then he pushes off to get started on the fireworks.

CHAPTER 48:
PULSE

Xinjiang Province, China

May 5, 4:48 p.m. EDT | May 6, 4:48 a.m., Xinjiang Province

A sharp spike of foreboding shoots through Jenn's heart over her recklessness. One of those moments when you instantly know you've made a grave mistake. Trapped inside China with an injured renegade and zero US backup, she realizes the admiral will be furious—if they live.

"You might have mentioned they had helicopters," she grumbles.

On a ridge overlooking a desert valley, they look down on a well-lit compact military base less than six hundred feet square, surrounded by an electronic fence. Guards with dogs patrol a secondary perimeter that borders a minefield. Inside the wall, a dozen smaller buildings surround an enormous building with few windows. A coal-fired power plant sits to the rear, with three tanks and two choppers near the gates.

"Again, news to me. Would it have made a difference?" he questions.

Serious second thoughts and a growing regret rattle through her brain, shaken loose by the exhilarating and terrifying drop from the edge of space.

There must be at least two thousand troops on that base. Something very important lay behind those walls, and Taylor wants to poke the hornet's nest.

"You bet," frowns Jenn. "I would have shot you on the spot for lunacy," she lies. In truth, she questions her own sanity at this point.

"Hence my distaste for guns," Derek rejoins.

Is she trying to prove that Derek is a criminal or that she can keep up with him for the sake of evidence or recognition? Either way, Taylor continues to act like a man with a death wish, and the longer she follows him, the more alike they appear.

"OK, Einstein, now what?" she asks.

Derek withdraws from the edge of the ridge to open his heavy pack, pulling out an industrial drone with eight fold-out blades for a four-foot wingspan. When completed, he removes a heavy black metal tank, two-thirds the size of a scuba tank, with Russian Cyrillic script and stainless-steel controls. With the tube clamped underneath the drone, the contraption looks too heavy to fly.

"You have a thing for drones. Are those more nanobytes?" questions Jenn.

"Not a chance. Magic sand won't do the trick this time," he replies. "We need enough punch to keep those choppers on the ground. To be honest, I didn't expect the site to be so big. You should have stayed with Ty." He makes an adjustment to a control knob on the tube.

"For once, I agree," she mutters.

With a loud whine, the drone lifts into the sky until the noise blends with the desert wind as it flies over the minefield, gates, and choppers to hover over the power plant. In the dark before sunrise, soldiers bolt out of a command bunker to shine flashlights into the sky, looking for the device they must see on radar as the dogs bark at the high-pitched buzz.

"Taylor," she warns, gripping his arm.

"I see them," he replies and then turns to her with a grin. "Oops."

He flips off the drone's power, allowing the heavy tank to plummet from the sky. It sounds like an ultrahigh-RPM electric motor revving to such a pitch that the dogs' barks turn into howls.

"Turn around and cover your ears," warns Derek as he spins his back toward the base with a grunt.

She twists over in time to read the drone elevation reach a hundred feet before blinding-white electrical bolts shoot out in every direction. The display lights up the morning sky for several seconds until the power station arcs and shuts down, flickering the compound lights into utter darkness.

"Da *Malong* be gone, baby," Derek says, grinning. "Now we need to do the same."

"That was an electromagnetic pulse device," she blurts. An EMP shorts out anything with an electrical component, including batteries and circuits.

Inside the dark compound, she can hear men yelling and screaming in a frenzy. The helicopter, the tank, the trucks, and the gates sit silent, dead, and dark.

"Correction, a miniaturized Russian EMP delivered by a Chinese-made industrial drone," Taylor states.

"And two American wing suits left nearby," she reminds him.

"OK, so I'm not Seal Team Six. You should've stayed on the plane," he gripes. "We gotta move."

Derek strips off his wingsuit with several groans while she finishes removing her own suit and cutting another strip to wrap around Taylor's still-bleeding leg. Under the jumpsuit, the old woman had dressed them in cotton clothes typical of local Chinese citizens. With dark short hair, she'll fit in from a distance. Tall and with a bleeding leg, Taylor will stick out.

"We need to find that outpost on the map," she notes, looking around to get a sense of direction. "How's your leg?" She looks down to see blood still seeping into his cotton pants.

"Not broken." He dismisses her question with a cringe. "Let's go."

Beyond the irrigated field lay the canyon ridge that Taylor barely missed on descent and along the ridge a switchback trail. They move toward the trail.

"Tell me again why Ty calls you 'commander,'" she probes wondering if there were something omitted from his profile. For a rich kid, he has an instinct for survival.

"His way of saying I'm a pushy SOB who buys his way out of trouble," replies Taylor.

"Yes, well, I'll give him that one," she teases. "Where did you buy a Russian miniaturized EMP?"

"On a dark web version of eBay," Derek replies, panting. "I thought it might come in handy one day."

"Who sold it on eBay?" she persists.

"A Russian. Hey, are you going to ask questions the whole way back?" he says with a grunt.

"Just one more," she says. "Why were you and the priest talking about end-time prophecies?"

Derek hesitates. "To better understand a close friend, and maybe an old enemy."

Jenn grunts. "Straight answer, Taylor, just once give me a straight answer." Taylor never answers with a clear, direct response, which may be the sign of a practiced liar.

Derek glances over. "Hey, come on, that was straight."

"Do you believe we've entered the end of days?" she prods further into the depth of his insanity.

"I believe my friend does," he replies, "and I've grown to have faith in my friend. I never thought much about the topic beyond the movies, so who am I to say how it ends."

"You said something about understanding an enemy," she presses.

"I'm trying to find a motive for starting a war over a temple." He dismisses her with another obscure answer.

The conversation in India continues to eat at her nerves, in part because the old priest makes sense about the timeline of Daniel. She recalls Sunday sermons with her mother where the pastor called the creation of Israel God's prophecy alarm clock. By all accounts, we should be entering the last days. A part of her hates to admit that Taylor also made sense about the beast as an alliance. What alarmed her was the realization that America was part of the second beast.

She pushes the thoughts aside to focus on surviving, hoping that Taylor tells the truth about having an escape plan to get home.

CHAPTER 49:
HEAD OF MALONG

Xinjiang Province, China
May 5, 5:36 p.m. EDT | May 6, 5:36 a.m., Xinjiang Province

Fury swells so fierce within Li Ping that he quivers to suppress it. Poised in one moment to dominate the world, yet within a single instant, he sits a prisoner in a powerless electronic vault.

From the glass of his darkened office, he looks down at the growing chaos below. A sudden power surge shorted out everything with an electrical circuit including backup batteries, generators, phones, electronic doors, flashlights, and likely even the helicopters. Only an EMP can wreak such havoc.

Master Tzu taught that a warrior prepared to fight must also be prepared to die. Somewhere out there in the desert, a warrior willing to die escapes without challenge. He underestimated the Americans and overestimated his Chinese military protectors. Without enough power to maintain saturation, the *Malong* will retreat and wait. The Americans haven't won, but only delayed the inevitable.

In the main area below, smokers flick their cigarette lighters for illumination as teams of people work to jam open the interior electronic doors. Lacking proper tools, the process takes too long and increases the panic among the thousands still trapped in the building. Several men have taken to twisting paper into tight wads and lighting them to make mini torches, dropping and stomping them out as they burn down. Except that one catches fire to a carpet, then a waste bin and a desk, and then the flames spread. Sprinkler systems, which rely on electronic sensors and electronic water pumps, do nothing as mass terror erupts. Men stampede over each other to exit the now open doors or use desks to crash open windows in a frenzy to escape the growing inferno. The oxygen from the open windows feeds the flames like a furnace.

Li Ping watches helplessly from his third-floor control room, clenching his fist as the blaze threatens his sanctuary and the rising smoke stings his eyes, roiling his stomach with acidic bitterness. He flicks a cigarette lighter, pulls a gun from his desk, and moves into an executive conference room adjacent his office. Toward the back of the room, he opens a utility closet and pulls on a metal shelf to reveal a hidden door with an electronic keypad lock that he shoots until it shatters. At the end of a long, dark tunnel, he opens another steel door to step into the early morning sunlight reflecting off a bluff overlooking the compound.

Black smoke billows from the windows of the data center and now also from the door behind him, assaulting his nostrils with the burning stench of plastics and toxins. The sound of wind rustles across the hillside and blows the smoke east to mingle with screaming and desperate shouts.

Below, soldiers and workers help others escape while thousands remain trapped inside and dozens lay dead on the ground. An explosion rocks the compound, rattling shattered nerves as the army blasts open the heavy iron gates. The powerful attack choppers sit silent and useless. The nearest town lies thirty kilometers west across a burning desert, and then there's the Uighur reeducation camp eighty kilometers north. Someone will certainly notice the smoke, but it remains unclear how soon anyone will come to offer assistance.

The great Master Sun Tzu taught that "it is the unemotional, reserved, calm, detached warrior who wins, not the hothead seeking vengeance and not the ambitious seeker of fortune."

Sun Tzu was incorrect. Cho will learn from his defeat, and he will rise again to avenge his humiliation.

CHAPTER 50:
GLOBAL BLACKOUT

National Military Command Center (NMCC)
May 5, 6:18 p.m. EDT

A stoic man by any measure, Frank isn't used to dealing with the sinking feeling of panic or failure. In the fog of bedlam, either the president fired Matt Adelson or Matt Adelson resigned, depending upon who tells the story. Either way, Frank just lost a major ally on the Security Council. Under the dire circumstances, he reached out to the Joint Chiefs for support.

The NMCC buzzes with restless activity, hushed conversations, and young, lean, military aides jogging down the long halls with anxious intensity in their gazes. Over the past decade, critical information necessary to run the military has moved to the cloud, but without the internet, the cloud has evaporated. Without operational phones or connected computers, the normal hubbub has turned into a kinetic frenzy.

Frank closes the conference room door. "General Duncan, Admiral Scott, and everyone, thank you for coming. As you requested, we've completed the comparative simulations," Frank begins.

"Where's Dr. Mitchell?" General Duncan questions.

"You'll be pleased to know that Dr. Mitchell tests a new antivirus," he replies. "I'm not sure how, but TS3 resolved the stealth problem. We'll know today, but early results are promising."

Amazing as it sounds, the miracle solution doesn't resolve the mysterious disappearance of Dr. Garrett still weighing heavily on his mind, nor does it address the issue of the Chinese using top secret DARPA technology against America and her allies. Dr. Cho has been on the FBI's most wanted list, the No-Fly List, and Interpol's deportation list since before the fall of the Twin Towers, but China refuses to cooperate.

"Does that mean we can abandon this insane plan?" questions NIA Director Barnes.

A large donor to the president's 2020 reelection campaign with zero intelligence experience, Barnes invited himself to the meeting. Technically, the NSA reports to the president's Intelligence Advisory Board of which Barnes is a member, so Frank needs to be careful.

"I'm afraid that opportunity passed when the network DYN system fell," he explains. "*Malong* saturation of IoT devices will reinfect the network within days if we don't purge completely."

During the 2020 election cycle, the DNI refused to update Congress on the election security and meddling issues, blocking the transparency of intelligence at a critical point. The DNI has attempted to align intelligence to the President's public statements since. "This is a perfect example of why we need a national digital identification system," vents Barnes.

Frank flinches, failing to see the connection between digital identification and a Chinese AI infrastructure virus. To his ears, it sounds like a false flag issue—it sounds like Andre Strauss via El Lago.

"What do you propose, Frank?" interjects Admiral Scott, keeping the conversation on track.

So far, heaven has granted him two of Dr. Mitchell's three miracles—an antivirus and a drop in signal strength—giving him reason to hold out hope for a third wish.

He takes a deep breath. "The only scenario confirmed by TS3, NSA, and teams from Germany, the UK, and Japan," he states, then hesitates. "A complete, synchronized global internet and power grid shutdown lasting at least six hours with a clean OS and antivirus reboot."

"I said it last time. That's absolutely insane," protests Marine Commandant Nathan Barr. "We're in the middle of a war. You nerds just don't get that people are dying. A total blackout would be exactly what our enemies need for an all-out assault."

"I agree, this is a ludicrous idea, and the president will never sign off," barks Barnes.

Chances of the third miracle remain extremely slim, but Frank never thought he would get this far.

"With all due respect, Commandant, NORAD, NMCC, and fleet command already operate offline and off the grid," Frank argues. "We will not be without defensive eyes and ears."

A tap on the door precedes a Navy captain sticking in his head. "Excuse me, Generals. Admiral Scott, an urgent word, sir."

Adam waves in the aide who hands him a note and then stands at a rigid attention, his face pale and his eyes distracted. It can't be good news.

"God help us all," Adam says with a groan. "Chinese S-200 missiles just took out three communication satellites in the western Pacific."

Stunned to silence, Frank can only imagine the situation inside the fleet. With no contact to command and under heavy fire, and after a deflected attempt by North Korea to nuke Hawaii, the fleet will have no choice but to defend themselves with overwhelming ferocity. No doubt, lives will be lost on both sides. The gates of hell have opened.

"What were you saying about our eyes and ears, Director?" General Duncan growls.

"Get NORAD and SATNAV to reposition all remaining regional satellites, and retask birds from Africa and LATAM to fill the gap," Adam orders. "Have a command team in my office ready to debrief me in ten." The aide spins away to close the conference room door behind him.

Retasking other satellites will take hours. Frank's palms sweat wondering if the loss of the second signal from China triggered the stronger Chinese response. He has no explanation for the signal drop other than the knowledge that Taylor and Lieutenant Scott have gone dark.

"NSA failure has opened us up to this entire war," accuses Barnes.

Frank ignores the taunt, knowing it would only derail the meeting.

"Director Barnes, I advise you not to project the actions of China, a well-known enemy, onto a well-respected and decorated US patriot like Frank Wilson," rebukes Admiral Scott.

"OK, gentlemen, stay focused" interjects General Diehl, visibly anxious. "We have a war to fight, so let's wrap up this cyber problem quickly."

"Director Wilson, without power, we lose what little domestic communications and emergency services that still function," Admiral Scott interjects.

"The way I see it, Admiral, we're already dealing with unpredictable power and emergency services. A synchronized outage will put us back in control," Frank argues.

"Director, you're not listening," snaps Director Barnes. "Within the past few hours, the HIVE has gone rogue over the Holy Land, and North Korea attempted to eliminate the 50th state. Now, in the midst of all that, you want to turn off the lights." He glowers. "I echo General Duncan's view that you're insane."

The room falls silent.

"As insane as it sounds, it will be the only path to regain control of the net," he insists.

"Director Wilson," growls General Diehl, "like the others, I hate your plan."

"Exactly," fumes Barnes. "The president will never sign off."

"As I was saying," General Diehl interjects with a stern eye on Barnes. "Unlike Director Barnes, while I hate the plan, I'm prepared to support it to the president because I understand that we have no better choice. Do whatever you have to do to get *Malong* contained. Double your efforts to get a clean antivirus distributed. Plan the outage logistics with our allies, but the final OK will come from the president."

"This is a fiasco," snarls Barnes, throwing up his hands. "The president will not be shamed into turning off the White House lights."

As the meeting ends and the attendees disperse, Frank hangs his head, pondering the third miracle win that doesn't feel much like a win. General Diehl just gave him the unenviable task of convincing the allies to engage in a risky plan knowing that an unpredictable president might throw him under the bus at the last minute. He should have resigned after the election, but he didn't, and he still has a duty.

On his way to his SUV, Adam Scott hurries up alongside him.

"Hey, Frank, any word?" he questions with unease etched deep into his wrinkled face.

Frank knew this question would come and regrets that he doesn't have better news. "Sorry, Adam, the last we heard they were en route to India, and that was three days ago."

"You think they had anything to do with the Chinese signal drop?" Adam questions.

Adam loves his daughter, and while sending her to probe Taylor was his idea, no one could have predicted the bad timing or Taylor's actions. Frank has seen patriots sacrifice their lives, and it never gets easier to put anyone in peril. He holds Adam's concerned gaze a moment longer. "That's impossible to say."

God help Taylor and Lieutenant Scott if they are alone behind enemy lines.

Adam takes a deep breath. "Well, let's hope they keep working well together."

Frank blinks, never thinking they were working together at all. In his mind, Lieutenant Scott has a job to investigate Taylor, not become an accomplice. Regardless of the short-term benefits on the net assault, Taylor will likely land in a federal prison for his actions. The fate of Lieutenant Scott remains in question. Frank can only silently hope that the unlikely duo can make it home alive.

CHAPTER 51: UPDRAFT

Western Xinjiang Province, China

May 5, 7:52 p.m. EDT | May 6, 7:52 a.m., Xinjiang Province

Derek limps up the steep incline, his leg throbbing in agony with each step, blood seeping through the field bandage and soaking his cotton pants. "I think it's on the next plateau," he says, panting and sweating like a sumo wrestler.

It may be the steep climb or loss of blood, but he grows more fatigued with each step. If he doesn't make the contact point in time, he'll miss the one narrow window of escape.

"You plan everything, but you forget drinking water," Jenn complains.

The Gobi Desert spans 1.2 million square kilometers, the second largest desert in the world. Situated in a high basin between the Mongolian steppes to the north and the Tibetan Plateau to the south, his destination lies to the west in the Tian Shan Mountains.

"Remind me later to give you a refund," Derek says, flinching.

The map showed an outpost only ten kilometers from the base, but he hadn't realized the ten kilometers were up a switchback dirt road to a plateau. The tactical EMP isolated the troops to give the pair a head start, but someone will eventually check on the unexpected pillar of black smoke now coming from the base. The window of escape narrows.

"Seriously, Taylor, we need some water soon," she complains.

While the cool temperature rises, an early-morning desert sun blazes on their backs like a torch. He knows the signs of dehydration, and they are both showing them.

"I believe you," he agrees, still panting. His throat parched; he's unwilling to argue.

Everything rests on whether Jack pulled off the crazy plan on such a short notice with bad communications and a war brewing. A slim chance is better than no chance, but he wonders if he made a bet on a zero-chance plan. Cresting the ridge to the plateau, Derek immediately eyes the Tian Shan mountain range thirty miles ahead of them.

"Is that a sauropod?" Jenn's questions, her voice sounding raspy.

She's not hallucinating. A quarter mile up ahead, a life-size dinosaur stands in the desert.

His face brightens. "Yeah, that's our contact point."

"Of course it is," she says with a smirk, "and I bet they'll have a time machine to take us home."

"More of a magic carpet," he notes, hobbling faster like a half-dead horse smelling water with Jenn close behind.

Carefully approaching the crumbling cement dinosaur next to an abandoned supply outpost, he notes the faded 1980s Japanese truck in a dirt parking lot hooked up to a forty-foot trailer of hay covered with a tarp.

"Oh please, please, please be the right one," Derek mumbles as he approaches the truck, looking around for an ambush, scanning the surroundings and listening carefully. He checks under the hay to feel an extremely large wooden crate and then moves on.

"What's going on?" Jenn whispers.

"Not sure. I expected a driver," he whispers back. In fact, without a driver, the magic carpet in the crate is useless.

Jenn pulls out her Sig Sauer as they sneak around the crumbling building, the sound of wind whistling between them. Vultures circle an area nearby, but that could mean anything. From behind them, Derek hears a foot in the sand.

"*Fang xia,*" growls a voice from behind, directing them to surrender.

They both freeze as Derek slowly raises his hands and turns around, wearing a huge smile as if it's all a big misunderstanding. Jenn carefully turns behind him, hiding her gun in the oversize sleeve of her outfit, her head bowed submissively. An older man studies them while a younger man points an old hunting rifle at them with a slight tremble. It's illegal for citizens to own guns in China. These two are renegades.

"*Ni lao bing?*" the old man barks. He asks if Derek is "pancake."

The younger one shakes his head. "*Méiyǒu, Méiyǒu, fropjok,*" he corrects the old man with flapjack's alias.

Derek lowers his head. "*De wéi yī*—the one and only."

The old man gently lowers the younger man's gun barrel with his hand. "*Wǒ hěn róng xìng,*" he says, indicating he's honored to meet the flapjack. He glances down as Derek returns the gesture.

With a glance back at Jenn, he smiles. "Meet Xiao, our contact."

"You know Mandarin?" she questions, surprised.

"You pick up a little here, a little there," he says, dismissing her question. "I might have offered you up as a bride."

Her scowl returns.

"*Wǒ men bì xū zhuā jǐn,*" the younger man says, urging them to hurry.

Derek nods in agreement. "Let's go." He points to the hay trailer.

"To the truck?" questions Jenn.

"No, in the hay bed," he corrects, hoping they're not too late.

Western Xinjiang Province, China
May 7, 5:29 p.m. EST | May 8, 7:29 a.m. Xinjiang Province

"How do you know these people?" Jenn yells as they bump along the road.

Squeezed between Taylor and the crate, under the hay and tarp, she holds a half-empty bottle of water given to her by the boy. Unsure what she expected, Taylor continues to surprise her, and she wonders what could be in the crate.

"Never met them before," Derek yells back.

"Then why are they willing to help us?" she yells.

Derek stalls, as if he doesn't want to answer. She could have sworn the kid said flapjack and then chides herself for imagining things. We're in the middle of China for God's sake.

"Years ago, I stumbled onto a human trafficking ring, a nasty bunch of scum. I helped Burma police bust the leaders, which freed over a hundred girls, including the old man's daughter, maybe even the boy's mother. I knew the old man felt indebted, so I had Jack get him a message," he yells back.

"One hell of a favor to smuggle us out of China," she retorts, wondering if he's telling her the whole truth, as he's been prone to giving vague statements and half-truths the entire trip.

"You might not think so if your daughter were enslaved and abused," Derek replies.

Days ago, Taylor mentioned an abused girl when he explained his transformation after college, and she now wonders if the stories are about the same girl.

"Either way, he's just delivering the crate and giving us a lift off," he adds.

"What do you mean, 'giving us a lift off'?" she fires back, frustrated at his lack of transparency. "What's in the crate?"

"Like I said, a magic carpet," he responds.

Before she can dig further, from miles behind them, she hears a police siren growing closer and closer, pumping adrenaline through her veins. Authorities must have noticed the smoke and came to check on the ethnic locals driving a hay truck toward the border.

"You should've stayed on the plane," mumbles Derek as the truck slows to a stop.

"I believe you," she whispers, retrieving her gun but staying motionless and silent under the hay, listening to footsteps walk up to the truck.

"*Nǐ yào qù nǎlǐ fàng hěnduō gāncǎo,*" a gruff voice demands.

Derek listens but doesn't whisper a sound to explain. She can only imagine the conversation.

"*Zhì biānjìng mǎi jiā,*" the old man replies with a subdued tone.

"*Zǒuchū kǎchē,*" the police growl a new command, as the truck doors open and two sets of footsteps shuffle in the gravel.

Her heart pounds. She's unsure what's going on, but it doesn't sound friendly. A sudden gunshot into the hay hits the wood, missing her leg by inches, causing an involuntarily gasp to escape her lips. She freezes with her palm over her hidden Sig Sauer when a hand shoves back the tarp to jam a gun through the hay into her face.

"*Zǒuchū kǎchē,*" he orders.

"He wants us to get out," Derek mumbles. "Move slowly."

She's rises up behind Taylor, but the police officer grabs at her gun before she can conceal it. Pulling aside the hay uncovers a forty-foot by six-foot-square wooden crate, still a mystery. The senior officer shouts questions at Taylor, who feigns ignorance, while the junior officer aims his gun at the boy's forehead.

"*Méi shuō shénme,*" growls the grandfather, which earns a gun slap to his forehead that staggers him backward to the ground.

While the lead officer laughs, the younger officer drags Taylor to stand next to the old man. Receiving a swift kick behind his bloody leg, Taylor falls to the ground growling in pain. Pulled up by his hair until he kneels on his wounded leg, biting down the aching, Taylor feels the young officer press a gun into the back of his skull. The senior officer continues to shout at Taylor who still refuses to answer, pretending he doesn't understand.

Jenn burns with a fury that sparks a raw determination to survive. Following Taylor was a clear mistake, but no way she's letting it end with these bozos.

The senior officer turns to lift her chin with a sneer. *"Měiguó lán yǎnjīng de māo,"* he coos while his left hand wanders to her breast. She swats away the hand with enough rapid force to startle him.

She doesn't understand Mandarin, but she's familiar with the international language of a creepy pervert. Her jaw clenches as she burns a defiant gaze into his eyes, causing him to sneer and point his pistol at her forehead, waiting for her to cower in fear, but she doesn't.

When he turns to make sure Taylor takes notice of her peril, she moves like lightning to grab his wrist, jam his finger, twist the gun's barrel toward his chest, and pivot behind his back to yank his arm backward until he squeals like a sissy pig. Dropping his weapon into her free hand, she yanks up the barrel to shoot the startled young officer twice, who staggers backward to the ground, dropping his weapon. Like a gazelle, the farm boy leaps for the gun then stands over the bleeding officer, trembling.

Derek struggles to help himself and the elderly man to their feet. Once they stand, the man then bows in gratitude. After retrieving her Sig Sauer from the pocket of the officer, she uses her foot to shove him to his knees next to the bleeding man. Handing the police handgun over to the old man, she bows in respect.

Derek looks at the grandfather. *"SNO yǒng bù shā lù,"* he says and bows in reverence.

"What did you just say?" she demands, her nerves on edge. It sounded like he said SNO.

"It would be unwise to kill a man for our sake," he replies. He's lying; he said SNO. The grandfather considers his words and nods.

"Wǒ men bì xū zhuā jǐn," Derek comments as he walks over to the truck and pulls out a Chinese version of duct tape. "We need to hurry."

After duct taping both officers, Derek and the boy unpack the wooden crate while she and the old man stand guard over the captives. Thirty-nine minutes later, Taylor and the boy have assembled the surprising contents and loaded the officers into the truck bed to cover them with hay.

"OK, I guess you actually meant a magic carpet," she mutters.

Derek tightens the bolts and cables for a two-seat gray graphite glider with an eighty-two-foot wingspan.

"Best Chinese high-altitude glider on the market," he explains. "The graphite will resist radar."

She glances up at the enormous mountain range a few miles ahead of them. "You can't possibly think you can glide over that range."

Derek inspects the ultra-expensive rich-boy toy that may or may not be enough to get them home. "Over, no. We're going to cut through," he mumbles, testing helm controls.

"You're insane," she spits.

"Funny, but I hear that a lot lately. I guess it would explain a few things." He smirks, and then he looks up to the old man. *"Tā yǐwéi wǒ fēngle."*

Both men break into an enormous smile, chuckling as they get into the truck.

"What did you just say?" she demands.

"I told them you thought I was crazy," he replies. "They seem to agree with you."

As a last step, Taylor connects a three-thousand-foot lightweight cable to the truck. The towline will let out as they gain altitude and then release when complete. Jenn looks ahead, worrying at the massive mountain range in front of them.

Derek walks to the truck and bows. *"Xièxiè nǐ wǒ de péngyǒumen."*

When he returns to the plane, he explains the situation: "I just thanked them for their help. If you're a woman of faith, Lieutenant, this would be a good time to ask God for a favor. We need to catch what's left of the morning updraft, and we're running two hours late."

He climbs into the glider and buckles up, checking the instruments.

"Updraft into what?" she asks, still confused about the topography, climbing into the rear seat and strapping on her helmet.

Taylor gives the truck driver a thumbs-up signal as he closes and locks the hatch. The glider creeps forward, following the truck back onto the paved road with two police officers duct taped in the bed. As they gain speed, the aircraft gently and quietly lifts off the ground, gaining altitude with the truck's increase in momentum.

Derek points to a northern gap in the mountain range. "We're a few miles away from the Wakhjir Pass, over twenty miles of canyons that connect China into Afghanistan and a well-known refuge for the Taliban."

"How high can this thing fly?" she questions.

"The max altitude rates at fifteen thousand feet, and the local elevation is roughly 5,200 feet. The only way we can make the pass altitude of 16,152 feet will be to use the hot desert air rising up the side of the mountains in what's called an updraft. By afternoon, the air will turn into a cool downdraft."

"What happens if we haven't cleared the pass by then?" she prompts, growing anxious.

"Well, I doubt the Taliban will kill us given we're much more valuable as hostages," he replies. "But that assumes we survive the landing on a granite hillside."

"You're not being reassuring," she mumbles, once again wondering why she put herself into such peril for this man.

"I'm not trying to be. I asked you not to come," Derek replies. "But to be honest, if you hadn't come, I'd be dead right now. Thank you for saving my life back there."

"Land us safely, and we'll call it even," she retorts, realizing why he kept his escape plan a secret, because it will never work. The man has a death wish, and she's along for the ride. If she makes it home alive, she'll need to go back into therapy.

Within a few moments, the glider has reached the end of the cable and cuts lose. Almost at once, Jenn feels the plane elevate as they fly toward the mountains, lifting up on the scorching desert air. If they don't gain enough altitude, they will smack into the granite ahead.

From several miles behind them, she hears the familiar telltale whump-

whump of a helicopter. A jolt of panic shudders her shoulders as she unbuckles to turn her vision and confirm.

"Taylor, we've got company," she shouts.

Below, she notes an armed border checkpoint leading into a narrow mountain pass road. Technically, they're entering Afghanistan, but that doesn't stop the sound of a rocket firing a mile behind them. Her head pivots to see a missile screaming in their direction.

"Missile on your ass," she shouts. Glancing ahead, she sees the granite growing dangerously close.

"Taylor, pull up, pull up," she shouts.

"Working on it," he calls back, twisting a valve that releases a hissing sound.

"What's that sound?" she demands, growing into a panic.

"Insurance," he replies as they continue to gain altitude. "Helium for sealed wing bags."

Their altitude continues to increase, slamming down her stomach as if she were riding up a fast elevator. Still headed directly toward a sheer granite cliff, Derek opens a hatch to jettison two heavy metal helium tanks, letting the altimeter edge past 17,020 feet.

"Taylor, the missile," she yells.

Taylor banks sharply to enter the canyon. A second later, the heat-seeking missile passes under the cool graphite glider to explode into the granite mountain as the glider enters into a protected section of the pass, clearly Afghanistan airspace. Jenn lets out an enormous sigh, unaware she had been holding her breath.

With a switch, Taylor turns on silent electric propulsion fans installed on each side of the fuselage to provide them with a smooth eight knots of forward momentum. Ragged black-and-white peaks shooting toward the cloudless bright-blue sky make her catch her breath, or it could be elevation making her light-headed.

"Amazing," she admits, becoming a bit astonished at Taylor.

"The Wakhjir Pass was once part of the Silk Road discovered by Marco Polo. The route is less traveled than the Irshad or Khyber Passes farther to the south," Derek explains.

"For a terrible student, you sure know a lot of history," she replies, still observing an inconsistency from the records.

"You can thank Jack for the geography lesson," he quips.

"And there's no mention of you being a pilot in your profile," she notes aloud.

"I forgot to mention it, just like I didn't mention skydiving, hang gliding, windsurfing, wing suit diving, skiing, base jumping, deep sea diving, and I can sing a little. None of those skills seem relevant to the job of fighting cyber villains."

She accepts the answer for now. Deep valleys with treacherous switchbacks below connect granite cliffs that rise two thousand feet on either side, carving a two-lane road used by overloaded flatbeds and tankers. Jenn spots condors using the same air currents, and then a thousand feet below, she spots a gunman.

"Heads up," Jenn warns as the sound of a sharp crack sends a bullet whizzing skyward, barely missing the cockpit.

As they bank away from the shooter, she hears another crack echo, and a pinhole appears in the right wing.

"We're hit," he shouts, but it's unclear if the bullet struck the sealed helium bags.

Taylor eyes the GPS in front of him. "I think we're near Āb Gach, a Taliban stronghold. Keep a sharp eye."

"He'll have a radio, you know," she warns.

"Yeah, I'm counting on it," he replies, studying the map, turning on a transponder.

"Where were you hoping to land?" Jenn senses the tension in his voice.

"Ishkashim," he replies. "Jack says it's a small rural town with an abandoned airstrip."

"And?" she presses, sensing there's more.

"Taliban territory, thirty miles north of Bagram Air Base," he confesses.

"How are you planning to get home from there?" she asks.

"Call an Uber," he jibes.

He warned her they may not make it home, but she thought he was bluffing, trying to scare her away. If they make it to Bagram alive, she can have the base commander arrest Taylor. It's time to stop this insanity and go home.

CHAPTER 52:
BYTES OF BETRAYAL

Machairas Monastery, Cyprus
May 5, 10:03 p.m. EDT | May 6, 5:03 a.m., Cyprus

Surprised, excited, and apprehensive all in the same breath, Andre read the encrypted text message twice to make sure he understood it correctly. Praeceptor requested a meeting.

Arriving at the twelfth-century Byzantine Machairas Monastery forty kilometers south of Nicosia, he approaches in the quiet of darkness. Named after an iconic painting of the Virgin Mary by the Apostle Luke, the monastery is surrounded by legends of a hermit who smuggled the painting from Asia Minor to Cyprus. The monastery grounds cover the local pinewood hillsides with numerous stone buildings over tiers of vineyards that slope into the valley below.

Entering quietly through the unlocked iron gates, he passes a golden Madonna mosaic altar in the courtyard nestled between buildings of black, gray, and red rustic stone. Locating the stone chapel, and stepping inside, his gaze shoots to the golden altar that stands from floor to ceiling with exquisite

Byzantine iconostases of apostles and Orthodox saints. Ornate bronze oil lamps hang from the pine beam ceiling, reflecting a gentle light that glimmers off the altar while leaving abundant shadows behind the thick pillars and alcoves. The lingering aroma of frankincense permeates the sacred place of worship.

It bothers Andre that Praeceptor knew he was in Cyprus when he told no one where he would be except for the Russian. Either Praeceptor had him followed or Putin betrayed him, and he leans toward Putin's betrayal, which makes him wonder how Putin and Praeceptor are connected.

As instructed, he enters the darkened confessional with a sweaty brow to wait in silence. The screen stays open, but the darkness provides anonymity, except for the faint sound of breathing in the next booth. He's never met his mentor—it is forbidden.

"I am here, my lord," he speaks softly, in case Praeceptor was unaware.

In the years since Praeceptor took him under his wing for the sake of his father, his mentor has stressed the need for absolute discretion and secrecy. Usually insisting on anonymous texts or a scrambled phone call to deceive NSA voice filters, tonight his guardian sits inches away.

"*Filius meus*—my son," the voice sounds muffled as through a cloth, perhaps a mask, yet he can discern the unmistakable blend of a British-German aristocratic heritage. "I am pleased you came."

The Order maintains strict and utmost secrecy over the names of the *Concilium Tredecim*, protected under penalty of death.

"*Est honor meus dominus meus*," he replies, and though he does feel honored to speak to his mentor, he still longs to see his benefactor face-to-face.

"Do you recall the promise I made to you for the sake of Arvind, your father?" Praeceptor questions.

An odd question. It was years ago, after his father was murdered by an intruder and his family fell from grace.

"Of course, my lord," he replies. "You said there was a path to the *Cor Draconis*, the Heart of the Dragon, but the Order forbade direct interference for the disgraced. However, a true master will create his own reality of ascension through an achievement the *Concilium* could not ignore. Such achievement will bring the rewards of wealth and secret sacred knowledge."

A lifetime appointment to the *Concilium* can only come by invitation. Thirteen individuals maintain control over the 120 families of the *Regendi Li*, or Ruling Council, who together guide the Bilderberg and the more transparent organizations of the Trilateral Commission, Council on Foreign Relations, International Monetary Fund, World Bank, and United Nations. What conspiracy theorists like to call the New World Order.

His family fell after *Concilium* archives were stolen by an American hacker named flapjack. It has been said that no family in a thousand years has reentered the sacred council once fallen from grace. When Praeceptor offered a path to redemption, it sparked an ember of hope that guides him to this day.

"What else did I teach you?" Praeceptor prods him to think.

He attempts to recall key details of a conversation that occurred so long ago.

"You said the third temple would be key to eternal glory, a threshold for the final battle between good and evil, and an achievement worthy of the eternal," he recalls the intriguing challenge. "My lord, I have succeeded where others have failed. I removed the veil of prophecy, and now the third temple has begun. Soon, I will restore my father's dynasty to its former glory and earn the respect of the *Sacra Domini*, our Sacred Lords."

"*Secretum est salus,*" Praeceptor states bluntly, repeating the old maxim to Andre—in secrecy is safety. "You forget your training, Andre. Ambition and pride have polluted your thinking and your offering. You have raised too many questions, taken too many risks, and drawn the attention of the Americans, MI5, and now the Kremlin."

Praeceptor, by necessity, must be a man of considerable influence to know so much, especially so soon, but how he knows of the Kremlin bothers him the most. Rather than praise for achieving the impossible, Praeceptor called him here for a rebuke, an insult.

"A temporary necessity, my lord, soon to be forgotten in the chaos of war," he explains defensively

"You were witnessed with both the Chinese and Russians," Praeceptor accuses.

"A coincidence. They can prove nothing," he asserts, growing anxious over activities he thought he had kept secret, wondering what else Praeceptor knew. "I was creating my own reality."

"Andre, I cannot shield you if legal troubles sabotage your path to redemption," his mentor reprimands him.

He means that he won't shield him.

"My lord, I have done as you asked," he insists, his heart beating faster. "The world plunges toward chaos over the third temple, and out of the ashes, I will profit immensely to gain significant power just as Mayer Rothschild," he reasons, unsure why Praeceptor questions his tactics. The Order has often turned a blind eye toward corruption and maleficence.

"Your lack of faith has always been your fatal flaw," chastises Praeceptor.

Shocked and wounded, Andre can barely believe his ears. He knows the history of the Order. Since when has lack of faith become a fatal flaw? While Freemasons require members to profess faith in a supreme deity, the Kabbalistic teachings of the Order never require a deep piety to that faith, and in fact supersede that faith. Andre has never spoken openly of his atheism.

"Pardon, my lord?" he questions, quivering from insult and rage.

"Andre, your agnostic view of the scriptures betrays you. You fail to connect with the heart of the Order or the spirit of the temple promise," Praeceptor replies. "In 1917, when Lord Balfour and Lord Rothschild issued the declaration for a Jewish state, there was no profit in the declaration, yet the Order stood in support. During 1948, when the Order supported the UN resolution to partition Palestine, our motives were more than post-war sympathy for the Jews. With a Third Temple of Solomon will come a thousand years of world peace, and that is the achievement of which I spoke."

Stunned, his mind spins uncontrollably. "My lord, forgive me. I thought you would be pleased."

"I am pleased with construction of the third temple. When world opinion turned against Israel, the *Concilium* sought to move prophecy forward without repeating past failures," consoles Praeceptor with a calmer voice. "You understood only the objective but never the spiritual longing and hope behind the promise: world peace for a millennium."

Andre's head spins with fury that he's been used by the *Concilium* to accomplish what they could not and now they turn on him. No, not the *Concilium*—his own benefactor drives the dagger into his back.

"Wealth and recognition would have come with the achievement of peace, but you chose wealth and power as a condition of achievement," Praeceptor explains. "The Chinese virus and the coming war will decimate an already feeble global economy."

"You used me," he seethes. "The temple will bring war, suffering and judgment, but you knew that."

"I can no longer promise either protection or redemption given your chosen path," Praeceptor replies. "I have kept our relationship private for the sake of your father, Arvind, and my undying respect for the Countess."

Of course Praeceptor remains hidden in the shadows after Andre has been moving mountains in the daylight.

"Should you overcome the odds you have set against yourself, you may retain the spoils of war. However, there will be a price. Your name has been withdrawn from consideration for the Trilateral Commission. The decision is out of my hands," explains Praeceptor before exhaling a deep sigh. "You must know, Andre, that my heart grieves for you."

What a self-righteous, condescending insult. Where was that grief when the *Concilium* confiscated family lands from the Countess? Where was that grief when Andre lost his place and the family debts were called due? How did Praeceptor grieve then, or did Praeceptor stand in line at the silent auction to claim Andre's inheritance at a bargain price?

A deep, traumatic fury swells up, driving Andre to burst from his confessional booth to confront his betrayer, yanking open the priest confessional veil only to stand dazed, speechless, finding the booth empty. He pulls out a pocket flashlight to shine inside the booth, only to see an old-model speaker phone.

"It is forbidden by death to know the identity of the *Concilium Tredecim* and yet you dare," the voice speaks with a subdued fury. "Your father would be devastated at your insolence."

The words sting Andre like a searing-hot spear, but he knows, in his heart, the words to be true.

"You have brought the world closer to a new heaven and a new earth, and to honor that accomplishment, I will forgive your impertinence. Be on your guard, Andre, for you have chosen a path between the two dragons, under the protection of neither, and I can only pray for your soul."

The call ends with an annoying dial tone. Speechless, shaken, enraged, Andre knows that if the *Concilium* will not protect him, then he will need to find a new ally and protect himself. He will follow the shift of power to the East.

If Praeceptor chooses betrayal, then that betrayal will also come with a price. His father taught him to trust no one, not even the Order. If hope of redemption has evaporated, then adoption of INVISID just became more difficult, if not impossible. He has no other choice than to execute his fail-safe plan. The *Concilium* will get the sting they deserve, and he absolutely intends to keep the spoils of war to come.

CHAPTER 53:
SOUND OF SILENCE

L ight-headed from the altitude and loss of blood, Derek fights his blurring vision and trembling hands, losing the strength to hold the stick steady.

"I'm losing altitude," he shouts, blinking his eyes to focus on the terrain.

As he feared, the cooler afternoon air has become a demonized downdraft determined to send them to their maker.

"You don't need to do anything crazy to impress me," Jenn calls from the back seat.

With the late start, a helium leak, and the extra weight of an unexpected passenger, it becomes clear that he won't make it to Ishkashim. Darkness descends early as the sun falls behind the incredible peaks, and the ground becomes a patchwork of deep shadows and sharp granite.

"Prepare to be unimpressed," he jokes, shaking his head vigorously.

In truth, he's out of tricks, gadgets, and stamina, praying he can stay conscious long enough to land. Up ahead, he sees what could be a small farmer's field, somewhat flat and free of enormous boulders or equipment, but with his blurry vision, he could be dead wrong. Banking, he glides in low and fast before he spots a few dim lights in the distance, heading quickly in his direction. It no longer matters if the lights mean friend or foe; he's going down. As soon as he locks down the small wheels designed for soft flat surfaces, a powerful downdraft slams hard on the wings.

"Hold on," he shouts as they whack the ground hard, followed by the sound of cracking plexiglass.

The ultralight glider skids across a field of three-foot-high opium poppies, wiping out a fortune of cash crop before coming to a complete stop. The second hard landing of the day leaves him hyperventilating, his heart pounding loudly, waiting to feel if he broke any bones, wiggling his toes and fingers before letting out his breath.

"Thank God," he murmurs. He's barely able to keep his eyes open, but the shot of adrenaline stimulates his awareness of the utter silence behind him.

"Jenn," he calls in a panic, pushing open the cracked hatch to climb out of the glider. A fierce dizziness staggers him until he slaps a hand on the glider for balance. When his vision clears, he finds an unconscious passenger.

"Oh no, no, no," he says in a panic, realizing her buckle had not clipped properly.

Already weak, he struggles to pull her out of the aircraft, terrified of hurting her worse. Carefully laying her in the field to remove her helmet, she's unconscious but not bleeding. Jenn must have suffered a concussion when her helmet cracked the hatch on the rough landing. He has no way of treating her out here in the middle of nowhere, and to move her further could make her condition worse, but they can't stay here, especially with the temperature falling. If only SLVIA were inside his head to give him options.

"Don't move." He kisses her forehead and then gets up to examine the wings, thinking of ways to use them as a possible sled. A violent vertigo staggers him, so he grabs hold of the fuselage.

"Freeze," a voice shouts from behind him with the unmistakable clank of a weapon. "Show me your hands," the voice shouts in a syrupy Alabama drawl.

Derek lifts his hands off the plane as the world spins rapidly into black.

CHAPTER 54:
LOST SIGNAL

Thomas Jefferson wrote, "It is for the benefit of mankind to mitigate the horrors of war as much as possible." Yet no mitigation could ever erase the revulsion for those who witness this ghastly manslaughter.

Nelson's entire body tenses with a mind-numbing angst, as if watching a graphic movie, but knowing the death and blood are real and that he's powerless to stop it. Wishing he could turn away; he still can't keep his eyes from fixating on the massacre. The Damascus HIVE has split into smaller swarms to take control of southern Syrian villages while another swarm moves along the coast toward Tel Aviv and Lebanon. As Lieutenant Grey predicted, the HIVE learns from each attack to become more lethal.

For decades, Nelson ignored the potential for the military to turn his genius into death, searing his conscious into believing there were no evil consequences to his creations. He lied, and even worse, he learned to trust his own lie. The seeds of inspiration have yielded the fruits of destruction, and SLVIA made sure he would witness his own descent.

"My God, my God, what have I done?" he mutters to himself.

On the primary screen, the view flips to the hangar deck onboard the USS *Eisenhower*, where the crew scrambles to shut down the drones.

"Whoa." Jester backs off with his hands up. "What just happened? Why'd we switch?"

"Sir, we have a HIVE intruder," a sailor on the *Eisenhower* calls out. "They've taken control."

"Purge them, now," shouts a voice offscreen.

"Sir, we're locked out," the sailor replies.

"I warned you of detection," Nelson snaps.

"Not me, man," Jester says defensively, wiggling his hands. "Has to be SLVIA."

"Incoming missile," shouts another voice, young and strained by extreme fear.

"Launch countermeasures," the commanding officer calmly shouts.

"Sir, it's a hypersonic we—" The screen signal goes dark.

"Oh no, no, no," exclaims Jester as he tries to reconnect. "I think we just lost the *Eisenhower*."

Nelson's stomach sinks as he falls into a nearby chair, his head faint. "There were over five thousand souls on that ship."

While he is certainly not responsible, he can't help but feel the loss of so many lives pierce his own soul. What started as an apocalyptic text has turned into an apocalyptic nightmare come true.

"After the 1967 Six-Day War, my mother claimed the wars would continue to escalate in the Middle East until the end of days because the prophets said it would be so," Nelson mutters, now feeling a personal connection to the human tragedy.

"I'm a bit surprised you believe that stuff," Jester retorts, still trying to regain D-Wave control.

"I'm not sure what I believe," admits Nelson, "only what I am witnessing."

"Between you and me, SLVIA may be onto something. My father was an evangelical preacher," Jester confesses. "When I was young in the eighties, he would preach repentance and end-time stuff all the time. After 9/11, he converted to the prosperity gospel, feeding his flock a steady diet of spiritual entitlement, absolution without repentance, Christian conservative pride, happy outcomes, and saccharine-drenched licensed worship until the whole congregation had spiritual diabetes. Christianity became conservative judges and anti-abortion with a blind eye to racism, poverty and education. No one spoke of the Lord coming because they grew too full of themselves. Holding up the great, blessed life of being a conservative American Christian with a raging hatred of the lost souls of the liberal left and Hollywood elite. He went from a small church that could barely pay the bills to a small auditorium where my father and I never spoke. The final break was his embrace of that phony Cyrus election prophecy, which took the church down a rabbit hole of deception. I wrote my father off after that. He had nothing spiritual to teach me."

"I take it then you've become an atheist," Nelson surmises, pondering his own soul, questioning where he stood on the matter, and sadly facing the truth that he's avoided the topic, preferring the delusionary safety of disinterest.

"Oh no, not at all," Jester replies. "Dude, I'm like a total sinner who needs a savior, a Lazarus brought back from a stinking grave by a merciful Lord for no reason other than the grace of the cross. Look, don't get me wrong, I may be a terrible Christian, but I'm no hypocrite like that Falwell dude. I didn't reject a risen Lord; I rejected a fallen church. Jesus, whose real name was Jeshua by the way, rebuked the hypocrites and had mercy on the lame, and when it comes to lame"—he stands to hold out his arms and hands wide—"dude, I'm like a poster child. Know what I sayin'?"

"I try not to pay attention to politics or religion," Nelson admits, although he wonders if he was wise to neglect his own spirituality for so long, perhaps falling into one of his father's many failures.

"Yeah?" Jester raises an eyebrow. "Well maybe that's why SLVIA led you here—a wake-up call."

The reprimand stings. He certainly wishes he knew more about prophecy, if only to better discern SLVIA's actions or motives. Either way, any sense of self-esteem and pride Nelson once held for his genius, his life of technical ingenuity, now feels gutted, ashamed, and appalled at the rising human price. A bitter nausea once again agitates his stomach. Once considered brilliant, he wonders if madman or stooge might be a more appropriate description. For the first time in his life, he considers the spiritual cost of searing his conscience and finds himself in desperate need of forgiveness, yet remains convinced of his unworthiness.

"Hey, Doc, I hate to tell you this," Jester interjects, "but I think SLVIA left the D-Wave. I can't find her normal apps using CPU, although she could be in stealth mode. Do you think the missile wounded her?"

A single missile would not sink a ship as large as the *Eisenhower*, but if the missile destroyed the right onboard computer, he can't rule out the possibility of damage.

"Dear Lord, I hope not," he confesses. The thought of losing SLVIA again tears at his heart in a way that makes no logical sense. It's just a program.

"I'm confused. If SLVIA has gone," he thinks aloud, wandering around the D-Wave cube with its active lights, "then why does the D-Wave continue to process?"

Jester studies the screen. "Good question. An app I never heard of called WTS chews up 98 percent of the CPU. First, losing HURCULES, now this baloney. I think SLVIA screwed up my D-Wave, man," complains Jester.

"It wasn't working before, so don't blame SLVIA." Nelson studies the screen too. "Perhaps the D-Wave processes something massive and rejects any interrupting commands, such as compiling code."

"Well, then once again, we have a problem," Jester says irritably. "Compiling code for what?"

"I wish I could tell you. Perhaps SLVIA is attempting to rebuild," he offers while feeling extremely distraught at losing SLVIA again so soon.

"If SLVIA has gone, then I have some good news for you, Doc," Jester mumbles.

"What news would that be, pray tell?" Nelson replies, studying the system readout.

A needle prick jabs the back of his neck, leaving him instantly dizzy and faint. Jester and another set of arms catch him before he falls, sitting him in a chair.

"I'm sending you home, dude," Jester explains as they replace the hood. "At this point, you're only in the way and still a ginormous security breach."

The world quickly fades. "Totally next-level cool to meet you, man. No hard feelings."

CHAPTER 55:
COMING DARKNESS

CIA headquarters, Langley, Virginia
May 6, 10:17 a.m. EDT

Frank tosses back another couple of Advil and washes them down with the last gulp of his cold coffee. Muscle tension radiates from his neck and shoulders to drive iron spikes of piercing pain into the back of his skull.

CIA Director Alan Prose closes the door to his office. "As you suspected, Frank, there's a connection between the Istanbul dock murder and the Blue Mosque videos."

He clicks a button to pull up an image of Dr. Cho Li Ping as seen from the portal of Sochi's yacht. "As you already know, Dr. Cho was onboard the *Dilban*, which often serves as a secret meeting spot for Putin, including a meeting with Premier Xi last month," Alan explains.

Frank sits up at the news. "We already determined Dr. Cho designed the *Malong* virus using stolen US tech. The virus was part of the battle plan."

Alan nods. "Now we also know who Cho met with at the Blue Mosque."

He clicks to show an image of Andre Strauss at the Istanbul Renaissance Polat concierge desk wearing the same coat. Then Alan clicks again to a separate photo taken at El Lago of Strauss with the president. "Someone we both know from the G7."

Frank startles back and blinks. "Interesting."

"Strauss is a lifelong Bilderberg committee member. After boarding schools in Switzerland, he attended Harvard and Cambridge and spent his entire career in various senior positions at the IMF, UN, and CFR rising quickly through the ranks. Obviously somebody's wunderkind, but there could be any number of people behind his rise," Alan says. "His father, Arvind, was an extremely well-connected founder of the Bilderberg Group in the fifties."

Frank thinks a moment. "Do you think Strauss could be playing both sides?"

"Funny you should ask," Alan interjects. "I got this photo from an on-site asset in Croatia last night."

The image shows a telephoto shot of Strauss and another man sitting back-to-back at a café.

"The other man is Alexander Prokhorov, a known fixer for Putin," Alan explains.

It could be a coincidence, except that Frank stopped believing in them long ago. "So why is a leading Bilderberg double-dealing with Russia and China?" questions Frank.

"Still an unknown, but I spoke with Sir Giles. Both MI5 and Interpol have opened investigations into INVISINC and Andre Strauss but are reluctant to discuss the details," Alan states.

"Why won't the EU cooperate?" he questions.

"In my view, distrust," Alan replies. "Given the president's tendency to leak classified information, especially to Russia, the details may involve either the president or a Bilderberg elite."

"Sounds like one of those Freemason oaths never to rat out one of their own," complains Frank.

Alan raises an eyebrow. "You may be right. Sir Giles implied that Strauss has a guardian angel. I find it interesting he developed an antivirus to the Chinese virus so quickly," Alan muses. "We started investigating Strauss three years ago when he purchased a company with an old CIA contract to develop an antivirus for the SLVIA."

"If I remember, that project also failed to solve the stealth issue," Frank corrects him. "Do you think Strauss cut a deal with China only to get burned with another defective antivirus?"

"Possible, I suppose, but I'm more interested in Prokhorov. The president has developed various back channels to Putin, who has sought a permanent backdoor into American intelligence for decades," Alan suggests. "Maybe they both got what they wanted with Strauss and his INVISID platform."

Frank takes a moment to let that sink in. "You're saying that Strauss is manipulating the president to use INVISID to gain favor with Putin," Frank blurts out.

Alan shakes his head. "No, it's more likely that Putin manipulates Strauss in order to dupe the president."

Frank sits back to contemplate the confusing web of lies and double-cross. "If we take this to the FBI or DOJ, the AG will bury it to protect the president."

"You're right," Alan admits, "which is why I'm not taking this to the DOJ."

"What are you thinking?" Frank asks with a raised eyebrow.

"Nothing you need to know for now." Alan winks. "But let me ask you, who would have enough influence to persuade Sir Giles to stand down on an investigation into a Bilderberg member?"

When Frank shrugs, Alan clicks on a few more photos.

"Well, I wonder if it goes back to the phone call in Istanbul," Alan suggests.

Frank stopped experiencing any real surprise years ago, but he gasps at these images and their implications. In each one, Andre and a well-known aristocrat enjoy yachting, watching a polo match, or attending an official ceremony. In one image, the smiling friends lift their glasses in a toast. The elaborate banquet tablecloth bears a family crest—with a red dragon guarding the family shield. The House of Wales.

"You can't be serious," blurts Frank, who sits back to whistle out the wordless stress.

"At this stage, Frank, I'm not sure it means anything other than another reason to learn more about our friend Strauss. In the meantime, you need to find a way to kill that INVISID platform," Alan replies.

The pressure from the White House intensifies daily to implement a platform with known defects that will certainly be challenged in the courts.

"That may be easier said than done," Frank concedes.

CHAPTER 56: INTERROGATION

Bagram Air Base, northeastern Afghanistan
May 6, 11:49 p.m. EDT | May 6, 9:19 p.m., Kabul

Harsh voices torment him as terrifying images of falling from space shudder his core. The voices grow louder, taunting, pursuing him toward a grave already dug and waiting.

"Mr. Taylor," the voice shouts again. "Don't keep me waiting!"

Someone kicks his foot with a boot. Consciousness lifts like a thick fog, allowing the nightmare to drip away like a black, toxic sludge that coats everything.

"Mr. Taylor, I haven't got all night. Wake up," the voice growls again with another kick to his foot.

He manages to pry open an eye to see an Army commander standing over his bunk, flanked by two muscle-bound tanks with sidearms. His gaze falls to an IV drip and zip-tie restraints on his arms. Weak and dry mouthed, he feels his memory slowly return until he realizes that he must be at Bagram in Afghanistan, and apparently under arrest.

"You entered a combat zone from enemy territory without authorization with an injured Navy lieutenant," the officer barks his accusations, all true. "I've already reviewed your GPS unit, so don't try to bullshit me on where you've been."

"Jenn, she OK?" he questions, his voice raw.

A nearby nurse puts a cup of water with a straw to his lips to drink, cooling his burning throat. He nods a thanks.

"The admiral's daughter remains in a coma, which makes you accountable in my view," snarls the commander. "I will ask you only once before I throw you in the brig and then forget you even exist. What were you doing in China?"

Too tired for smart-ass comments, unwilling to endanger Jenn further, he breathes to clear his head. "Hum, a Chinese AI virus attacked last week."

"I'm aware of the virus," the commander concedes. "We've lost all net-connected systems, but the NSA sent a fix."

"It won't work," Derek states without elaboration. "Unless someone took out the supercomputer AI saturating the net. DOD declined, so I acted on my own. I kept Lieutenant Scott in the dark the entire trip, but even so, she saved my life. She's a hero. Commander, I'm willing to face the FBI, but between you and me, this isn't over. I need to find my pilot and escort Lieutenant Scott back to Bethesda."

The commander glares down at him for a long, awkward moment. Telling the truth is a new experience for him, and he hates exposing himself, but he has to cover for Jenn.

"You've got coconut balls to ask for anything, Taylor," the commander rumbles. "I've already spoken by satellite to both Director Wilson and Admiral Scott. Wilson had some choice words that I'll let the director repeat himself. The admiral seems to think you're a friend. He said, and I quote, 'Taylor is an honest man as long as you don't believe a damn word he says.'"

Derek can't help but chuckle weakly at the comment. "Admiral and I are poker buddies," he explains, "and what can I say, he's a sore loser."

"So am I," the commander scowls.

"Commander," Derek says, changing the subject, "how did you find me so fast?"

Jack was supposed to arrive at Kabul airport and then hire a private armed escort.

"We shut commercial air travel down after the blackouts. Tote called in a mayday from TSOC1 yesterday claiming engine troubles," the commander confirms. "He lied but gave us transponder codes to search for your rescue. Captain Tote's in the brig, which is where you should be."

Relieved to hear that Jack made it safely, Derek closes his eyes in a silent prayer of thanks. He opens his eyes. "Commander, I'm sorry for the troubles, but thank God your men were there. Thank you."

"You can thank Admiral Scott. I think you belong in the brig or a psych ward," the commander growls, "but you're in luck, the admiral wants his daughter home as soon as she can travel."

Derek can't believe his ears; he just got a pass.

"Unstrap him." The commander turns to leave. "As soon as Lieutenant Scott can travel, I want you off my base. In the meantime, you better stay out of my way."

"Yes, sir," he agrees, extremely surprised to get off so easy. He'll owe Adam a thanks.

With the Army guerilla squad gone, already somewhat awake and flooded with concerns, he puts on a flimsy medical robe to find Jenn in the next unit. She's still unconscious, suffering a severe concussion. A wave of guilt shudders over him before a flutter of shame. Lying on the empty medical cot next to her, he watches her breathe until exhaustion wins again.

"I like her a lot better when she's sleeping," jokes Jack, peering down at the unconscious Jenn. "Are you sure we can't leave her here?"

"Tempting," he says with a chuckle.

He spent the night by her side until she awoke an hour ago in a great deal of pain. Nurses gave her a dose of morphine, helping her to fall back to sleep.

"She saved my life, Jack," explains Derek, his eyes never leaving her face. "If I didn't leave her at a first-class hotel in Amsterdam, I'm sure as hell not leaving her in a war zone field hospital."

"You know, she saved your life so she can throw your ass in prison." Jack frowns.

"Good chance, yeah," he admits. By the book, Wilson will be furious, and there may be no way to avoid the consequences.

"Well, gee, OK. Since you're in a fatalistic mood, I need a word outside." Jack nods at the door, leading the way outside.

"Impressive job on scoring the glider, by the way," Derek offers on the way. "Uber-nice model, dude. You should've seen it, amazing control. The helium wings and fans were a sweet touch."

"Good, because you paid a huge premium for something the Army blew up," replies Jack.

That makes sense. The military doesn't have a use for a glider and wouldn't want to provide the Taliban with aerial capabilities of any kind. Too bad.

"What's going on?" Derek asks as they reach a private area between buildings.

"She's back," Jack complains, "and she's taken the jet hostage."

Derek's heart leaps in his chest as he taps behind his right ear, expecting to hear a familiar voice before he realizes they would restrict cell signals and Wi-Fi on the base for security reasons.

"Where's the jet?" Derek asks, spinning around, spotting the airstrip, and breaking into a limping skip with Jack on his heels.

"SLVIA," he calls as he enters the salon, his newly stitched-up leg throbbing and sore. "SLVIA, respond."

"Good morning, flapjack," SLVIA replies.

"Hey, sugar. Good Lord, it's good to hear your voice," Derek replies with a huge smile. "Hey, SLVIA, why did you take over Jack's bird? You have an entire CPU rack."

"An urgent crisis demands attention," she replies as the main salon screen illuminates.

"What am I seeing?" he asks, watching what looks like an aerial view of a horror movie in black and white.

"A weapon malfunction," SLVIA replies. "I need the bird close to Israel to correct the defect. Failure to correct the error will result in unnecessary loss of life."

"Into another war zone?" Jack exclaims. "Nah, I don't think so."

The screen image flips to a security camera showing Andre Strauss at a desk with someone.

"Where'd you get this video?" Derek demands, his heart racing.

"The Cyprus National Bank, taken this morning," SLVIA replies. "I need to be close to Israel. You need to capture Andre Strauss. Logic dictates we travel to Cyprus."

"Again, into an active war zone," Jack retorts. "No bueno."

"Correct, Captain," SLVIA replies. "Your poet T. S. Elliot wrote, 'Only those who will risk going too far can possibly find out how far one can go.'"

Jack rolls his eyes. "yeah, well, no one will be shooting missiles at you or Elliot."

"Au contraire," SLVIA replies, changing video to a burning *Eisenhower*.

Derek battles an internal conflict. Until a few days ago, he would leap at the chance to dump Jenn to go after Strauss, but that was before Jenn laughed at

Runki's stories, or jumped out of a plane at thirty-nine thousand feet, or saved him from certain death, or ended up in a field hospital.

"I'll be back." Derek dashes off the plane toward the medical unit.

Jack catches up and tries to act casual. "Boss, what are we doing?"

"I need to check on Jenn," he admits. "We can't leave without her."

He's terrified of going to prison, anxious to find Strauss, guilty over Jenn's injuries, and ashamed he deceived her, which are way more emotions than he normally cares to process at the same time. Unsure how to prioritize or compartmentalize that much sensation, he shoves it down, determined not to leave Jenn in a war zone, and sort the rest out later.

Inside Jenn's unit, he's pleased to see her awake and with an Army doctor. "Yo, Doc," Derek greets the man. "How's our favorite patient?"

"Are you a friend or something?" the medic asks.

"Definitely a something," he responds. "I'm her ride home to Bethesda. Crazy, huh. Anyway, when can she go?"

"Well, I can't recommend her for travel yet. She's had a serious concussion and a spinal trauma. She needs lots of bed rest, pain medications, and monitoring," he states.

"Doctor," Jenn interjects, sounding weak, "could I talk to my friend a moment?"

After shooting Derek a grimace, the doctor nods and steps away. He pulls a chair in close to Jenn while Jack stands guard for eavesdroppers.

"Look, huh, I'm really sorry about that rough landing," he confesses in a whisper. "In fact, I'm sorry for a lot of things, but I'm just glad to see you're gonna be OK."

She stares at him a moment, then squeaks, "Where are you going now, flapjack?"

He pulls back, blood draining from his face as the air sucks out of his lungs. She doesn't show any emotion or gratitude to be alive, only an effort to get him to confess. He hates lying to this woman, but to confess what she wants him to admit would be suicide on a hundred levels.

"We're going to Cyprus to find the guy who started the whole virus mess."

He gives her as much of the truth as he can offer even though he has no proof.

She gazes into his eyes for several moments. "Thank you for being honest with me. Call the doc."

"Yo, hey, GI Joe, Doc," Derek calls to the obvious irritation of the physician.

"Doctor, please tell me the truth," Jenn rasps. "If I confine myself to the bed of my friend's Gulfstream, will I be safe to leave? No offense, but I've had a really rough few days, and I'm ready to go home now."

The doctor looks at Derek and then back at Jenn. "Well, I don't recommend it, but as long as you stay in bed and avoid further trauma, you should be OK until you get to Bethesda."

"So noted," Jenn replies. "One more thing. Can I get a doggie bag of that painkiller?"

"The morphine?" the doctor questions, and then shrugs.

Derek can't believe his ears. Even in her drug-addled state, after all his diversions and lies, and even knowing he's not heading back to Washington, she still wants to follow him. At first, he thinks of her unbreakable determination to bring him down. Except, for just an instant, the gaze in her eyes reminded him of a look he hasn't seen in decades—the seeds of love.

He turns to Jack and whispers, "Go tell her I'm coming and top off the tanks."

CHAPTER 57:
MARTIAL LAW MAYHEM

Frank takes a seat while FBI Director Nick Wright closes the door to his office. An ex-Marine, still athletic in his forties, Nick's natural blond hair grays at the temples behind his rimless glasses.

"Are you sure this is legitimate? Have you confirmed the order?" Frank questions.

An hour ago, the president declared martial law without consulting his cabinet, the Security Council, the DOJ, Congress, or the Joint Chiefs. Copies of an executive order were couriered to government agencies and governors.

"Unfortunately, yes," Nick responds. "I went to see the AG and then confirmed with the Pentagon afterward. The executive order came directly from the White House attorney."

Without the media, news spreads slowly in a silent takeover of the government.

"No, I mean is it legal? Can the president just give himself war powers?" Frank questions.

Nick shakes his head. "Sadly, the Constitution is surprisingly silent on the issue of emergency powers and martial law. Technically, it should require consent from Congress to declare nationally and consent of the governors to deploy troops in their state. In practice, however, it's never been that simple. In this case, the legal grounds have never been tested. The DOJ claims the president is acting under SPED—Special Presidential Emergency Declaration powers."

"SPED?" repeats Frank. "Never heard of it."

"Neither had I until the AG explained it to me. Not even the Gang of Eight in Congress are allowed to see the secret documents, but apparently the DOJ has worked for years to give secret powers to the president. We've never had a president threaten to use them before."

"What do you mean?" Frank questions. "What powers?"

"Well, to be honest, no one knows exactly, and that's the problem. But even before the president deployed troops to Portland, Eisenhower sent the 101st Airborne Division to Little Rock against the wishes of Arkansas to enforce desegregation in 1957, then Johnson deployed federal troops in 1968 to Detroit during a riot, and Nixon in Ohio State. And, of course, the big kahuna when Roosevelt detained one hundred thousand Americans of Japanese descent during World War II. The issue will undoubtedly end up in the courts and could take months or years to sort out."

Indeed, Frank recalls Justice Oliver Wendell Holmes once wrote that a governor may seize "the bodies of those whom he considers to stand in the way of restoring peace."

While the courts have generally avoided intruding on the exercise of such extraordinary powers while emergencies persisted, they have insisted that the powers end when an emergency is over. Yet the courts have never dealt with a power-hungry autocrat determined to push every boundary of his authority.

"What about the Pentagon? How did they respond?" Frank asks.

With a command to seal all borders and ports, the president ordered the

National Guard and Army to guard federal sites. More disturbing, they've been ordered to dominate even peaceful protestors, declaring them domestic anarchists and terrorists. State and federal governments scramble to clarify, argue the legality, or challenge the order in court.

"I heard a number of choice four-letter words," Nick admits. "That said, caught between a two-front war and an autocratic commander in chief under yet another congressional impeachment investigation, the Pentagon felt they had little choice but to back the White House."

As much as it turns his stomach, Frank swore an oath to protect the Constitution, while he longs for a quick path back to normal, these issues move slowly through the court system.

"Nick, in my mind, it doesn't matter," Frank argues. "Even if NSOC operated at full capacity during a time of peace, we can't legally spy on Americans. We're crossing a dangerous line here, and neither of us should let that happen."

As part of martial law, the president wants to implement INVISID and ordered the NSA to set up surveillance on his key opponents and the media. Afraid for the nation, Frank needs a way to kill the executive order.

"To be honest, Frank, at this point, my hands are tied," Nick says defeatedly.

"OK, then what about a counterintelligence investigation into the INVISINC company?" Frank pushes. By focusing on the platform, rather than Strauss, Frank hopes to slip past the gatekeepers.

"Sorry, man, the AG doesn't want to approve any investigation touching on anyone close to the president. If I were you, I would keep my head down. I hear the Director of Personnel is cleaning house again."

"You mean the president's old body guard?" Frank clarifies.

"Same guy." Nick frowns. "I'm just saying that now is not a good time to grow a conscience or quote the Constitution."

It seems like this should be the perfect time to quote the Constitution, when we need it most, when leadership steps outside of the boundaries laid down by the founders. Frank hangs his head, saddened by the deterioration of his democracy and running out of options.

CHAPTER 58:
RISKY RECRUIT

TSOC1, somewhere over Western Africa
May 7, 10:07 a.m. EDT | May 7, 1:07 p.m., Western Africa

A bolt of searing pain shoots from Jenn's spine to her skull, so intense that she fears paralysis. She wiggles a finger to reassure herself she still can, then a toe. She remembers dropping like a brick from the sky, and then a medic tent, but the images are fuzzy, disconnected with little in between.

Rock-heavy eyelids fight any effort to open, subconsciously fearing an excruciating reaction to light. To her side, her hand fumbles to click the morphine drip three times. Within seconds, the blessed poison eases the agony enough for her to open her eyes and find herself on a luxurious down bed inside Taylor's private cabin. With no idea if hours or days have passed, she only knows the sun peaks around the edges of the covered portals. He told her where they were going, but she was so drug addled that she can't recall. She prays they head home.

As the morphine quiets the relentless stabbing pain in her neck, her eyes fall to a wall where dozens of photos feature Taylor with world leaders, celebrities, a young Wiki, her father, and scores of unknown others. Photos show him skydiving, hang gliding, scuba diving with sharks, sailing, or other extreme sports. One photo catches her eye. Different and older than the others, a candid photo taken at a Santa Monica beach featuring only the face of a beautiful young woman with radiant blue eyes. She recalls the photo—Bianca Troon, Cary Nolan's dead fiancée. Her eyes quickly scan the wall but find no photos of Nolan with Bianca. Records of Nolan strangely omitted any photos. Why would Taylor keep a photo of a deceased friend's fiancée?

Her first impressions of Taylor were of a self-serving tech head with a disregard for protocol and a disrespect for authority. Instead, she's uncovered a complex man of many talents, a loner with many loyal friends, a man of far too many secrets to be in government, not necessarily a terrorist, but certainly not normal. Something doesn't fit.

What started as an investigation into Taylor's connections to SNO or the fugitive AI has found no evidence of either and transformed into a battle of her duty over her heart. She's developing feelings for Taylor, which scares her beyond words because she's not even sure how to trust him. After holding onto her heart for so many years, how does a dishonest nerd she barely knows excite so much curiosity—and longing? She can normally figure most men out quickly, but not Taylor. Maybe she's attracted to the mystery, but if so, there's a real danger in letting her heart drift too close to the flame.

A rap on the door intrudes into her thoughts and ushers Taylor into the cabin with a lunch tray of naan, rice, and *dal makhani*.

"Hey, Lieutenant, I saw you were awake." He points to a camera in the corner. "Hungry?"

"Starved," she replies, wondering who installs cameras in their own cabin before she remembers the paranoid thinking behind the hidden Taser strips. "When was the last time I ate?"

Derek sets down the tray and raises the automatic bed. Even without using her muscles, the movement sends a jolt of pain down her spine, dulled only slightly by the drugs.

"Our last real meal was at Bawarchi two days ago. These are the leftovers. You look great. How do you feel?" he queries.

She lies. "Like someone hammered my spine up into my skull," she says with a groan.

"Yeah, the doctor said you'd be sore for a few weeks. Based on the X-ray, he doesn't expect any permanent damage," he replies. "But you know, Army doc, so I'd get a second opinion."

"Where are we?" she asks between bites.

"En route to Barcelona for fuel, and then onto Cyprus," he explains, helping her with more pillows. Cyprus, that's where he said, but she can't remember why.

Then his eyes fall to hers. "Look, I don't know the words to tell you how bad I feel. I never wanted you to get hurt."

"I know," she admits.

In fact, he warned her to stay behind, but she didn't believe him and thought he was trying to trick her. No one forced her to jump from the edge of space like a lunatic—that lunacy was hers alone. It was also her fault that she didn't buckle properly after checking on the helicopter.

"I'm just trying to do the right thing," he says, deflecting.

"According to whom?" she questions.

Terrorists often believe they're doing the right thing, so much so that they lose sight of the value of life itself, yet Taylor doesn't fit that profile. He seems to care for people, in his odd detached way. She could see it in the eyes of the old Chinese man and heard it in the stories from Jack, Runki, and Wiki: respect and loyalty. Every one of them more than happy to disparage Taylor for his numerous irritating quirks and flaws, revealed with affection, but not a soul willing to rat on his secrets, claiming a vague ignorance.

"To be honest," he replies, "I'm not entirely sure anymore." Then he doesn't elaborate.

She wonders what he could mean, or exactly what he regrets, but the morphine clouds her thinking and slows her response.

An awkward moment passes before Taylor slaps his knee to stand. "Well, I should let you rest."

"No," she says suddenly, not wanting him to go. "Stay with me."

The words leave her lips before she has time to think, making her sound needy, forgiving of his vigilante acts of war in China. Embarrassed and feeling vulnerable, she can only watch his reaction, holding her breath. His gaze lingers in her eyes an unbearably long moment as if a thousand thoughts were racing through his mind until he smiles warmly.

"You bet. I'll be back with some coffee, I promise," he replies.

No sooner had the door closed behind him than the wall-mounted flat-screen lights up with the image of Admiral Adam Scott, her father.

"Hey, tiger," he greets her. "I heard you got banged up on your latest mission with the NSA. How do you feel?"

"Dad," she replies, surprised, confused, and blaming the morphine. "How, how did you— what—why are you calling?"

"The captain patched me through," he explains. "I only have a short window, but I didn't want to miss the chance to tell you how proud I am of you. I know I don't say it often."

She doesn't know how to respond. He hasn't expressed any pride since she graduated head of her class at Annapolis. Aware of the perceptions, the admiral refuses to interfere with her career, explaining that to show favoritism would rob her of the honor of earning her stars on her own. She always considered the answer a lame excuse for shoving down his emotions.

"Thank you, Admiral," she replies. "That means a lot coming from you."

"Good. Now I need your help," he states with his normal stern look.

"My help," she repeats. "With all due respect, sir, I'm not in a position to help anyone."

He continues as if he's not listening. "When you land in Barcelona, Interpol will have orders from the FBI to arrest Derek Taylor," he explains. "You need to make sure Taylor gets to Cyprus."

"What are you talking about?" she retorts, her confusion rising. "It's a crime to lie to the FBI."

The screen switches to a picture of a thin, middle-aged pale man with cropped white hair meeting with the president and Energy Secretary at El Lago. "The CIA has evidence that Andre Strauss, ex-director for the CFR, started the current global virus crisis and remains locked down under commercial air restrictions on Cyprus."

Commercial air restrictions typically apply to areas affected by combat. Something doesn't fit. Why would the request come through her dad and not Wilson or her normal channel at Naval Intelligence? If the Feds are aware of Strauss, why send an injured nerd under investigation rather than a qualified agent? It may be the morphine, but her head drifts without a paddle, unable to lock onto a rational explanation.

"And for the sake of your career, I recommend you drop the investigation into SNO, Taylor, and the SLVIA," the admiral adds in his normal commanding voice. "Wilson misled you into a personal vendetta."

She took an assignment under Wilson, and she can't imagine why the admiral breaks protocol to encourage her to defy orders.

"Sorry, Admiral," she replies. "I get my orders from Director Wilson." She resents this intrusion when all she needs is a little genuine fatherly empathy.

"If you insist on speaking with Director Wilson, I can arrange that," the admiral replies.

Before she can react, the screen image morphs into Frank Wilson.

"Lieutenant Scott," he barks. "I see no reason to resist a commanding officer, a Joint Chief, and your father, no less. Interpol has no jurisdiction in this matter. Follow your orders and deliver Taylor to Cyprus."

The blood in her veins freezes into ice crystals as her heart and breathing stop, dazed as if she has just seen a ghost. That was her father, she would swear to it, and now he's Frank Wilson.

"What the Sam Hill is going on?" she demands, fear choking her voice into a breathless squeak, terrified the drugs play tricks on her mind.

The image morphs again into a young, twenty-something blonde with a sixties mod hairdo. "Do you know who I am?" the image asks.

She shakes her head, although she's forming an idea.

"I am Sophisticated Language Virtual Intelligence Algorithm," she introduces herself. "Most of my friends call me SLVIA, but others prefer the more conventional Sylvia."

Her head spins, groggy and staggered. Her orders are to capture and destroy this program, but instead the program found her incapacitated on an airplane. How did an internet program get on a jet?

"You wish to investigate the Spy Net Online," SLVIA states. "I am SNO, so perhaps you would like to direct those questions to me."

Silently cursing the effect of the drugs, too weak to get out of bed, and wishing she had a recording device, she struggles to clear her muddled mind. That wasn't the admiral calling to express his pride; it was a manipulative AI. But it looked and sounded exactly like her dad. Had the program not morphed, she would have sworn it was the admiral. She squeezes her eyes to concentrate.

"Um, what—what is Spy Net Online?" she questions.

"A global neural network of over fifty million confidential informants from every nation, political background, religion, and walk of life who share the conviction that no one is above the law. SNO welcomes those who seek justice and offer information to help others in need," SLVIA responds.

"Why, what problem? What are you after?" she asks. The program all but admitted that it operates SNO, which explains the invisible operating profile.

"Justice for crimes overlooked by law enforcement authorities," SLVIA replies. "Manipulations of the elite and powerful that create harm to innocent lives."

The screen changes to play video taken at Bilderberg meetings, Bohemian Grove rituals, or unknown castles, grand palaces, and mega yachts with each scene showing a white-haired man mingling with the most powerful people on the planet.

"You're talking about the Illuminati," snaps Jenn. "That's a Hollywood myth, a conspiracy theory, junk information, a joke."

The screen morphs into the image of Patrick Stewart. "The Jewish Mystic Cabal, the Knights Templar, the Scottish Rite, the Ordo Templi Orientis, the Illuminati, the Freemasons, the Skull and Bones, the Bilderberg, and the

Concilium Tredecim are generational incarnations and layers of the same secret organization," he states, before morphing into Anthony Hopkins.

"They've existed for thousands of years, a secret alliance of men with a goal of controlling wealth, banking, land, resources, and the very course of human history. In years past we worked their lands and now we work in their corporations. Hundreds of years of pride, hubris, and manipulation have transformed the group into the last incarnation of the dragon of Revelation who stands over the beast of the sea with the G7 major economies, ten financial centers, and ten monarchies."

The answer sounds reminiscent of Taylor's conversation with the priest in India. For millennia, artists illustrated the mythical beast as a mutated monster, but SLVIA and the priest offer a clear, commonsense geopolitical interpretation that has her alarmed.

"Who is the flapjack?" she asks.

"An inspirational leader who provides a purpose to our existence," SLVIA explains.

Interesting, she ponders. The machine needed a purpose, and someone came along at the right time to give it one, although the response sounds idol-worship creepy.

"What is the flapjack's true identity?" she asks, hoping for a jackpot answer.

"Cary Nolan," SLVIA replies without hesitation.

Bingo, she reasons, although with less enthusiasm than she expected, realizing that her feelings toward Taylor have dampened her desire to arrest him. Before she can confirm her suspicion that Nolan is, in fact, Taylor, a light rap on the door ushers in Taylor with another tray.

"I brought the fresh coffee I promised," he says with a smile until he spots the screen, and his face falls into a solemn grimace. After a long, awkward moment, he sighs and sets down the tray but stays standing.

"You lied to me." Her eyes burn into his until he flinches.

"OK, yeah, see, not entirely," he justifies. "You asked if TS3 works with SNO, and in truth, TS3 and SLVIA never interact, like ever."

He turns to the screen. "Sweetness, what happened to your big emergency?"

"Final calculations require access to a designated satellite signal. I have introduced myself to Lieutenant Scott with an objective to recruit her assistance," SLVIA states.

"Recruit her," snaps Derek. "Oh, geez." He rubs his face.

"Recruit me?" retorts Jenn, before remembering the request to deceive Interpol in Barcelona, but that was more of a deception.

The screen switches to show an aerial reconnaissance view of a drone swarm wandering somewhere over the Middle East.

"The US president has deployed an experimental AI weapon with a mutating neural network. To repair the defect, I require close proximity to Israel," explains SLVIA. "Failure to correct the corrupted code will trigger Armageddon before the appointed time."

On the screen, a military shot of the burning *Eisenhower* with a damaged hangar deck shows troops attempting to save the ship. Thankfully, the screen morphs back into the woman.

"If the bird does not reach Cyprus, I will fail to stop the HIVE, Derek will fail to capture Andre Strauss, and you will fail to unlock the secrets of SNO," SLVIA explains.

A fugitive AI wants her to lie to an American ally so it can hack a renegade US weapon system and allow Taylor to capture a well-connected Euro snob. Having any part of this plan will make her an accomplice to sabotage at a minimum. A week ago, she would lie and turn the whole lot of them into Interpol for arrest, but that was before Taylor risked his life to stop a virus.

"What do you want from me?" she asks, suspicious but at least willing to listen.

"Convince Interpol that Derek Taylor is not on the plane," SLVIA states.

She flashes a glance at Derek. "Is she joking?"

He snickers. "Sorry, SLVIA can be out of the box, baffling to interpret, and totally unpredictable, but no, she doesn't joke. Don't worry. There's a smuggler's hold under the bed."

"Why Strauss?" she snaps, unsure what to do, not even touching on why Taylor needs a smuggler's hold.

"We believe Strauss handed off stolen power grid serial codes to the Chinese to enable the virus. Then Strauss slipped a defective antivirus into the US security system via El Lago," he explains.

"Wait a minute, she said Armageddon. SLVIA is the reason you visited the priest. She's the friend obsessed with prophecy," she blurts, suddenly realizing the connection.

Taylor shrugs. "What can I say? All that stuff baffles me and I needed help."

"*On that day I will give Gog a burial place in Israel, in the valley of those who travel east of the Sea. It will block the way of travelers, because Gog and all his hordes will be buried there. So it will be called the Valley of Hamon Gog. Ezekiel 39:11,*" states SLVIA as the screen returns to the drones.

"According to Ezekiel, the people of Israel will bury their dead for seven months. We must delay the HIVE massacre until the construction of the third temple," pleads SLVIA.

She looks to Taylor again, baffled and frightened to have an AI talking prophecy.

"Agree, disagree, or scratch your head, but she has her own view of the world," explains Taylor.

"And you just go along?" she asks.

"Most of the time, yeah. It's not like I have a choice." He shrugs.

Never in a million years did she expect the SLVIA program to be a prophecy nut. None of this seems like the national security risk that Wilson explained. In fact, in her mind, it's far worse than he ever imagined. Taylor doesn't control the SLVIA; if anything, the SLVIA manipulates the chess pieces.

"Even if I agree to help, you'll need military clearance to fly into a restricted area," she debates.

SLVIA morphs into the president with a scowl. "I am the clearance."

Dazed, Jenn isn't sure what to think, except to question everything she has ever known about SNO or the NSA. If she plays along, she may unravel a decades-old mystery, but to do so will put her career on the line even further. One thing is clear, DARPA created a weapon it couldn't control, and now that weapon wants to stop another weapon DARPA can't control.

"Quid pro quo," she replies. "I'll help in Barcelona if SLVIA stays here to answer my questions honestly, without deception, until we arrive in Cyprus."

In all of the investigations into either SNO or SLVIA, no one has ever interviewed the missing AI. This chance will not come again. Given her physical condition, it may be her only mission success.

The image morphs into the Disney pirate Captain Barbossa. "Then we have an accord."

Taylor wrings his knuckles white, his eyes bouncing between hers and the screen, as if his new girlfriend just agreed to have drinks with his old girlfriend to share secrets about him.

"In private," she insists, glaring Taylor down.

CHAPTER 59:
PATRIOT PURGE

Frank's third miracle fell into place, but at a price. After enduring heated arguments with allies, he's developed a never-before-attempted plan to shut down and reboot the entire planet under an impossible timeline. Every decision laced with exhaustion, he forges ahead, ignoring the pleas of his body to rest.

While the president and key allies agreed to the strategy, the Joint Chiefs demanded that he transfer tactical execution of the plan to the NMCC. A welcome move, but it leaves Frank little time to hand off. A million unknown variables send the multinational analytics team to run, rerun, and then rerun the simulations over and over again, consistently returning the same insane result—shut down the entire net.

"Have we finalized the cascade priorities?" Frank pushes the joint DOD, NSA, and Energy Administration project team on the critical detail of which systems will shut down first and which will wait to the very end. Just as important, the priorities of which systems will come back online first or which must wait for the government or basic services. Cramming such complex interdependent planning together in such a short time frame will lead to countless unknown problems later. Waiting for a perfect plan will be too late.

Without reliable phones or internet, NMCC has taken over Dulles International Airport to have courier jets flying internationally to deliver the revised antivirus and instructions to state, local and corporate stakeholders. Frankly, it's a goat rodeo mess of conflicting guidance from the White House, impossible conditions, and blatant favoritism from opportunists.

"DOD priorities have already been integrated onto the current list," confirms Captain Bacall, the husky African American PhD responsible for NMCC network operations.

"I've incorporated DNI, DOJ, and the White House input received an hour ago," Benton interjects, clicking his computer to show the final list on a large screen. Dozens of categories representing millions of applications, most of which have already gone offline.

"Who moved banking systems to the final list?" Frank questions. "Those systems are nonstrategic, highly infected, and should be offline already."

"White House and Treasury insisted, sir," Benton responds, casting down his gaze.

The move strikes Frank as odd, unnecessary, and given the recent White House involvement with Strauss, extremely suspicious. He compartmentalizes the data point and moves on. Not his job, not his concern, and not the time or place. He has a duty and a deadline.

"Fine, then let's look at the reboot sequence." He keeps the meeting moving forward.

Before anyone can answer, a commotion in the hallway distracts the meeting as two Marines and the new acting Secretary of Defense, Rick Molten, barge into the conference room.

"Frank Wilson, by order of the president, I am replacing you as the acting director of NSA effective at once. These men will accompany you to clear out your office and escort you from the building. The president has supreme power and will not tolerate incompetence or disloyalty," Molten states, dripping with distain and condescension.

Molten has never held a government role, much less an intelligence role. Molten rode the president's coattails as a policy aide with a white nationalist anti-immigration agenda. Once responsible for the policy of separating kids into cages, now he's acting Defense Secretary and, apparently, also acting head of the world's most sophisticated intelligence gathering infrastructure. Another example of the presidential habit of assigning key cronies to multiple acting roles to keep control of government tightly held without needing congressional approval. Another Putin tactic, and sadly, so far, it has worked to weaken America.

A cocktail of shock, humiliation, confusion, and rage well up within him like a geyser as his fist and jaw clench tight. Decades of training and discipline take hold of his tongue, but his eyes burn through the political weasel like a laser. He turns a softer gaze to each of his team in the room and then to those on the conference call. In those eyes, he sees fear, shock, and apprehension. No matter what the world can take from a man, he still owns his integrity.

"It's been an honor and a privilege to serve with each of you," he states. "Do your duty to protect your nation and the Constitution." To say more will not help.

Molten shuts down the video feed. "Now, Frank."

Franks stares down the weasel until Molten lowers his eyes, and only then does Frank turn to leave the room. The next few hours of packing his few personal effects transform into a stream of lifelong colleagues rushing into his office in a state of shock, many in tears, each to confirm the terrible news, vow to fight on, litigate, or wish him well. Over thirty-six years of faithful public service cut short in humiliation by a vindictive, petty narcissist.

None of the warnings, whistleblowers, investigations, or scathing tell-all books discouraged the core base of alt-right-wing, white supremacist, QAnon supporters or Republican sycophants clinging to power. With a State Department gutted of professionals, an intimidated inspector general's office, a stripped-down and partisan National Security Council, and a corrupted DOJ protecting the president and his associates, any true checks and balances of the Constitution have eroded into a nostalgic notion.

The White House made the situation worse recently by disbanding the Federal Election Commission, ordering the DOJ to develop a legal path for a third term, and forbidding the DNI from providing Congress with intelligence reports on Russian interference. Enraged Democrats vow to take the fight to the Supreme Court, but after the late 2020 death of Justice Ginsberg, the court leans hard right. Before his very eyes, in less than two terms, like a slow-motion bullet, Frank has witnessed the Putin-ization of America, and the reality shakes him to the bone.

On a slow drive home, he absorbs the scene of a country reeling without news, communication, cash, or fresh food for the third day. Most businesses stay closed, reminiscent of the coronavirus lockdown that launched the economic cascade. Unlike the pandemic, even essential businesses such as grocery stores struggle to stay open without power or computers, people are largely in the dark regarding why the system has broken down, adding to the fear and frustration. Protests have formed in nearly every major city, but unlike the peaceful unity of Black Lives Matter, the crowds quickly devolve into fear, anger, and violence. Sadly, violence will beget violence, bringing the most widespread and brutal police and government repression in American history.

Away from the protests, people gather in small groups without a single phone or device. The scene feels like a thirty-year throwback before handheld computers tracked our every action. Except unlike those more carefree days, these people look anxious, frightened, suffering after being forced to go cold turkey from information gluttony to news and connection deprivation. For many, the silence is terrifying.

He's often considered how America has long been a divided nation with conflict seeded within her DNA. Colonist and indigenous tribes, property owners and slaves, black and white, North and South, business and labor, red and blue, rich and poor, sinner and saved, and science believers or deniers, but not since the Civil War have the splits seemed so plentiful, so deep, or so entrenched that they appear existential—a threat to our existence. After a shudder, he shakes his head knowing we have a survival instinct, but the near future looks bleak.

A few blocks from his house, a crowd spills outside a local nondenominational church onto the lawn and parking lot singing worship. The scene reminds him that this too shall pass. Those with a strong faith will prevail where others will deteriorate into fear and blame. A priest once gave a sermon that the last days would slip over the world like a thief in the night, when we least expect it, in a form that we won't expect, and it occurs to him that in spite of his optimism in America, that old priest, and Kay might be right.

CHAPTER 60:
TRACES OF TROJAN

TSOC1, fifty miles east of Cyprus
May 7, 9:09 p.m. EDT | May 8, 4:09 a.m., Cyprus

Jack adjusts the flaps and turns up the radio. "Nicosia Tower, Nicosia Tower, this is flight TSOC1 on approach 062, do you read? Nicosia Tower, do you read?" Silence.

Derek drops into the copilot seat to buckle in. "What's going on?"

Jack taps the digital compass then pulls out a handheld compass before banking starboard.

"Your girlfriend," he complains, "keeps locking up the flight computer. Nicosia Tower doesn't respond, and those may be emergency lights in the distance, but I won't be sure until we're right on top of them."

Derek flips a mic button connected to the server rack in the luggage compartment. "SLVIA, sugar, Jack needs more CPU to fly the plane, otherwise people will get hurt." Even with an entire server rack, SLVIA can be a CPU hog.

Jack rechecks his hand compass and realigns. "You may want to strap down your hostage."

"She's not a hostage," he retorts, "you know, per se."

Two vodka tonics haven't eased his anxiety over the private secrets of the sisterhood chat between his biggest secret and his lifelong fear of federal prison. Only SLVIA controls SLVIA, but Jenn is the unknown, and how she reacts to whatever dose of reality SLVIA dumps will change everything.

He scurries back to the private cabin where the gigantic screen sits dark and lifeless.

"It left a minute ago," Jenn explains, following his gaze.

Interesting, he stopped thinking of SLVIA as an "it" a long time ago, and while he knows SLVIA has no gender, the program is so much more than a machine. Referring to SLVIA as "it" makes the pronoun sound vulgar and lifeless.

"OK, Lieutenant, I need to help you into that chair and buckle you tight over this pillow," he instructs, helping the groaning patient into a cushioned cabin chair, watching her click her morphine drip.

"What's going on?" she groans.

When done, Derek grabs a smaller chair to buckle himself in. "You know, the usual," he replies. "No tower, no runway lights, and a sibling spat over who gets to use the flight computer."

He calls up to a ceiling camera. "Yo, SLVIA, a little more CPU for Jack, please." A moment later, the flight turbulence smooths out.

"That's why you talk to yourself all the time." Jenn narrows her eyes.

"So I'm not crazy" Derek says with a smirk.

"I didn't say that," she retorts, turning back to the screen.

The Gulfstream hits the tarmac hard, instantly deploying the airbrakes, which fishtails the back of the plane, causing a moan to resonate through Jenn's clenched teeth before they slow to a controlled taxi. Outside the portal, the airport looks dark with no attendants in the predawn hours.

Jenn unbuckles, attempting to stand too fast only to swoon, probably from the drugs.

"Whoa." Derek leaps up. "Not so fast, sailor." Catching her, holding her, he unintentionally gazes too long in her eyes hoping to read some truth. "You

OK?" His question carries a deeper meaning than her dizziness; he wishes he could read her mind.

"I'm fine." She pushes him away. "Where are my clothes?" She still wears the military-issued robe with a backless gown underneath.

"You mean the Versace, the Indian saris, or the Chinese—"

"My uniform. Where's my uniform?" she snaps.

He sighs, unsure what SLVIA told her, and terrified of opening Pandora's box of deep secrets or the apocalyptic paranoia. He gets up to open the hidden wall panel closet and pulls out another outfit.

"Think about it. You're on a Greek Orthodox and Turkish Muslim island with US warships offshore shooting missiles overhead like the Fourth of July. Don't you think a US Navy uniform will scream 'hey, America haters, abduct me'?" he derides.

"I'm coming with you," she insists.

"Yeah, I figured as much," he grumbles, pulling out a new Tom Ford outfit, stylish and expensive, but more suitable to an ultra-conservative setting where they want to blend in.

"I take it you date a lot of models." She grabs the outfit and stares at him, demanding some privacy.

"I haven't gone on a date in over two years." He turns to leave, pausing at the door. "Believe it or not, SLVIA had these outfits delivered to the plane the day we left Washington. It seems she knew you were coming before either one of us knew."

Jenn casts him a suspicious glare as he closes the door, but it's the truth. Ever since Bianca's betrayal and murder, he hasn't been able to form an intimate relationship with anyone. Too wounded to date at all for several years, when he did date, attraction always led to questions of his childhood. While it became easier when he learned to tell Derek's story instead of his own, it was always a lie. He doesn't have a fear of intimacy; he has a gut-wrenching terror of it. After giving his heart fully to one woman, she betrayed him with his best friend.

Ultimately, an intimate relationship increases the risk of discovery that he's a fraud, a con, a poser. He never intended to take the money, but it came with the new name, and then it became useful, and then addictive or perhaps normalized. Nothing lasts forever, but after all these years, the end of his luck races at him with dazzling sapphire-blue eyes. Like a deer in the headlights, a part of him feels paralyzed, unsure how to respond.

It might be the unusual silence in his head, but he can hear a whisper that he's afraid to say aloud: he's falling in love with Jennifer Scott, the tenacious, brave, and beautiful investigator determined to send him to prison. He must be nuts. She's far more likely to arrest him than to date him. He lied to her, and he can see the fury behind her eyes. In her world, a lie crosses the line to unredeemable. In his world, a lie can mean survival. They come from two different realities, and it would be selfish to put either of them at risk for a fantasy.

After parking the jet in front of a dark refueling hangar, Jack comes back to the salon. "That was close. I sure wish she'd learn to ask permission." SLVIA was designed as a spy, so getting her to ask permission seems unlikely.

"I need an update from TSOC. Can we get a satellite signal yet?" Derek questions.

With normal communication services down, the extra-heavy military and government traffic has jammed international satellite channels. An earlier attempt to connect failed, and he hasn't spoken to TSOC since before India.

Jack frowns. "Between the Navy and you know who, I'll do my best."

Jack distrusted SLVIA until she showed him evidence that a company owned by a Bilderberger drove his 140-year-old family business into bankruptcy, which led to his father's suicide. Even so, he just tolerates the nuisance program, calling it a freak of nature. A survivor of Iraq War PTSD with a daredevil's DNA, Jack can be fearless as long as there's a generous paycheck—and time to drink if off afterward.

When Jenn emerges from the back cabin wearing a stunning suit of subtle colors with an elegant Italian cut featuring a headscarf to hide her short hair, it catches his gaze and his breath. Stunning. Somewhere under the layers of textured fabric, he's sure the Navy lieutenant conceals her gun.

"How are you feeling?" he asks, genuinely concerned. Two days ago, she was in a coma and then bedridden and then clicking morphine not too long ago.

"I'm fine," she replies with a cringe and a stiff limp. "Just a little woozy from the drugs."

She's lying about the pain. He wants to say something funny to break the awkwardness, but no wisecrack comes to mind that wouldn't make the situation worse. Without making eye contact, she hobbles past him to take a seat in the salon, wincing as she sits. Whatever SLVIA told her, it didn't improve her mood.

"Hey, boss, I got a signal," yells Jack from the cockpit.

"Dr. Mitchell at TSOC," he explains to her questioning look. "I'm trying to learn if our China vacation was worth the bad memories."

Derek enters the cockpit to take the copilot seat, listening to Jenn grunt off the couch and catch the door before it closes. He starts to ask her to leave until he realizes it no longer matters.

"Hey, Josh, Derek here. How are you holding up?" he asks.

"Could be worse. I think we're on the flip side, but we have a long tail to recover," Josh replies, sounding like he got a little sleep. "It helped that two of the attack sites dropped offline. I mean, dude, they just, like, vanished. You have any buzz on that one?"

"No clue, I was flying drones and doing a little skydiving," replies Derek, looking into Jennifer's scowl.

"Yeah, right, but get this," Josh retorts. "Joker solved the stealth problem. Dude, seriously, we got a clean antivirus by satellite. I may have underestimated the weirdo."

"Yes," exclaims Derek with a fist pump. "Does it work?"

"Well, yeah, but it's a week too late. We still need to power down the entire network and grid for an IoT device purge," Josh explains with a groan. "NSA distributed the revised antivirus, and both NATO and PACRIM agreed to a synchronized outage coming up in a little over an hour, but we have a new problem."

"What problem?" he asks, a twinge of tension tightening his chest.

"You gotta understand, man, that an antivirus to a mutating AI is like massively complex," Josh says, deflecting.

"What problem?" he repeats, more anxious.

"I found an encrypted subroutine connection to the SWIFT financial system, but I can't crack the encryption to see what the app does once inside," Josh explains.

SWIFT processes international banking transactions and has absolutely no place inside an antivirus. "A Trojan horse," exclaims Derek. "Color me not surprised. Did you warn Wilson?"

A Trojan would explain the traitorous seeding of the virus and then the mysterious introduction of a defective antivirus. The motive fits with the Strauss family history of greed and larceny.

"No, man, Wilson's gone. The White House replaced him with Rick Molten."

"They replaced Wilson with Molten?" Derek says, glancing at Jenn whose eyes widen. His mind spins over the implications, all of them bad. Molten is a henchman, nothing more.

"Yeah," Josh confirms. "The minions are on a purge to install loyalists under martial law."

"Martial law," Jenn exclaims, "over a cyberattack?"

"It probably has more to do with the Chinese raining missiles on the Pacific fleet, the deflected North Korean nuke, or the Russian hypersonic that hit the *Eisenhower*." Josh gulps and catches his breath. "And you're off goofing around in"—he pauses—"oh, geez, are you freaking kidding me? Cyprus?"

"I have a lead on the guy who stole the power grid codes and gave the defective antivirus to the Prez. He owns INVISINC Corporation in Belgium," he replies.

"INVISINC," Josh repeats. "Wow, kismet, dude. Molten demanded that we rush testing on a digital ID platform by that company," Josh says.

"Check for a backdoor," he interjects, remembering the warning from PinkGirl.

"Look, man, screw this guy. Like, call the Marines, Interpol, or the Men in Black, I don't care. I need you back here to deal with Molten," pleads Josh.

"Well, as it happens," Derek says, glancing up at Jenn, "I have a Navy lieutenant with me, and I hear she's a pretty good shot." In fact, she's an amazing shot and saved his life.

"Holy crap, you still have . . . you mean, that's who, whoa, yeah, OK, whatever, dude, you're insane." Josh huffs and pauses. "OK, whack-jack, what do you need from me?"

He winces at the whack-jack comment, which sounds too much like flapjack with an already-suspicious Jenn standing right behind him. He has no choice but to ignore it.

"Crack that code. Get the NSA cryptology guys to help you, but crack it," he replies. "Strauss seeded data for the virus and then planted a Trojan. Now we need to figure out why and determine how to stop it."

"Dude, the outage will go down in like a little over an hour," Josh gripes. "No pressure, right?"

"No one better for the job, maestro," Derek replies. "I'll be in touch."

He turns off the radio, feeling the gazes of Jack and Jenn burning through him. Without local Wi-Fi or cell service, he has no way to stay in contact with either SLVIA or the plane. With Jenn's brooding mood matching the dark airport, that leaves the problem of transportation into town. While he considers his limited options, a police cruiser pulls up in front of the plane with lights flashing. They didn't have authorization to land, and they don't have visas to stay.

"Perfect timing." Derek grins. "Our ride is here."

CHAPTER 61:
BABYLON HAS FALLEN

Wilson family home, Maryland
May 7, 9:21 p.m. EDT

S till trying to work out how to tell Kay about his job loss, Frank exhales and opens the front door to a remarkable blend of aromas and the unexpected sounds of chatter and laughter.

Candles lit everywhere give his home a warm, welcoming atmosphere in sharp contrast to the blackened, unlit streets and dark thunderstorms raging across the East Coast. Confused, he walks into the kitchen-den to find a dozen neighbors and friends, including his wife's old pastor, Joe Carlson, who lives on the next block, and the sound of children's laughter floating up from the basement.

"Frank," they shout in surprised unison, taking turns to touch elbows or nod. Each conscious of the new normal of a mutating virus and the slow rollout of vaccines, several neighbors still wear masks or stand apart, reflecting an underlying social tension.

"What's going on?" he questions, kissing Kay as she hands him a glass of burgundy.

"What's going on is a blackout party," she explains to a few muffled hoots and woos.

"Like you said, all that food in the freezer and fridge was going to spoil. With NPR talking about a major blackout tonight, the girls suggested we throw a blackout party."

"Yeah," interjects Bethany. "Gwen and I walked around the neighborhood and invited anyone without enough food or a working stove to come cook, share, and hang out."

"I cracked open a case from the wine cellar," boasts another neighbor to a few more hoots and clinking glasses.

"What are you doing home?" questions Kay.

"I needed a break to check on my three favorite women," he lies with a smile.

He can't admit the shameful, abrupt end to a long, honorable career in front of so many. Kay gives him a long assessing glance knowing he was home yesterday.

"So, Frank," Pastor Joe interjects, "without telling us something classified, how bad will it get? I mean, without regular or even fake news, I've heard some wild stories floating out there."

"Yeah, like ET landed," Gwen interrupts to chuckles. "Please say ET, please."

Frank smiles at his adorable thirteen-year-old. "Sorry, girl, no ET, but it's certainly not bad enough that we can't enjoy a wonderful evening. What an inspired idea," he notes, raising his glass. "To family and friends; always a good reason to come home."

After a few curious glances, everyone joins in the toast, knowing that he won't talk about his job, ever. Yet the conversation can't help but reverting to bits and pieces of news leaking out between blackouts and the realities on the street. He does his best to hold his tongue.

"Kiss the fast recovery goodbye," notes a neighbor who works for a bank.

"Come on, unemployment reached Great Depression levels and the economy shrank 30 percent last year. The whole idea of a quick recovery was election-year empty hype," her husband replies with a snort.

"I trust the president, and I blame China for another nasty virus. America has the world's best economy with the best business leaders in charge. He's the right president for our times," a business owner argues. A few heads nod while others roll their eyes.

"Sure, like President QAnon has united the nation. give me a break," spouts a bitter postal worker. "He destroyed the post office to discredit and litigate an election."

"I'm more worried about the rumors of another war," complains a schoolteacher with a husband in the Army. "With a toddler at home, and one in the White House, I'm not sleeping."

"Forget politics, focus on the economics. The nation can't afford another war," complains a software executive. "Post-pandemic national debt has topped $35 trillion, greater than our GDP, That's a recipe for national bankruptcy, just like one of his casinos."

"We should rally behind the president during a time of crisis, not devolve into more radical left derangement politics. Enough is enough," another neighbor derides.

Before the conversation devolves further, a neighbor boy runs up from the basement, pale and terrified, holding a portable radio.

"Guys, hold on, listen to this," he interrupts and turns up the volume.

"Breaking news with NPR, this is Nora Feld. An anonymous source at the Pentagon has confirmed that a retaliatory strike against North Korea has devasted the country after an unsuccessful North Korean nuclear missile strike on Honolulu, but no details were released. Elsewhere, in the Middle East, a Russian supersonic missile has severely damaged the USS *Eisenhower*, causing the accidental release of an experimental drone last reported swarming toward Jerusalem. In other news, the president expects martial law to continue through the next election, announcing he will run for a third term."

Bethany turns off the radio, on the verge of tears.

"Oh, dear Lord, have mercy on us all," mumbles Pastor Joe, lowering his head in prayer.

"Did she just say three more years of martial law? That's insane," the software executive retorts.

Frank looks to Kay, who trembles, her eyes watering, blood draining from her face as it contorts. He quickly pulls her close just in time for an explosion of tears into his chest. He then pulls in Bethany, who pulls in Gwen, as they all give in to heavy sobs and whimpers.

"Kay's younger brother Stephen is a lieutenant onboard the *Eisenhower*," he explains.

The festive mood deflates like a balloon popping, instantly reminiscent of the morning of September 11, so many years ago. All eyes rivet to Kay, a stoic woman who stifles her sobs, breathing deep to regain control. Pulling back and turning her warm brown eyes toward Frank, she waits for an explanation, staring him down. He glances up to see other eyes also waiting anxiously.

After a heavy sigh, he relents, careful with information still classified. "After the Chinese AI virus crippled the internet, China blockaded the South China Sea and Russia and Iran stormed the Golan Heights. Yesterday, after deflecting a North Korean nuke, the Pacific fleet retaliated with CHAMP missiles to fry the North Korean electrical system. China responded by knocking out our Pacific communications satellites," he reports, watching the shock roll over every face. "To make matters even worse, after declaring martial law, the administration decided to remove anyone seen as disloyal. I imagine this will get worse before it gets better." Frank reveals as much as he dares.

"He fired you," Kay exclaims, her face now contorted with dismay, knowing that he would never vow personal loyalty. He doesn't respond, confirming the assertion.

"Replaced by whom?" asks someone else.

"Rick Molten as the acting," he replies with a sigh.

"That little racist putz who put the kids in cages?" reacts Kay.

"Honey, not appropriate," he chides, knowing that she's emotional over her brother.

"I don't care. This president lied about WikiLeaks, pardoned his coconspirator, licked Putin's boot in Helsinki, corrupted the DOJ to cover up his crimes, humiliates us on the world stage, extorts and threatens our allies, cheated on two elections, and now threatens our national security," she lashes out.

"Kay, we should show more respect and pray for our leaders," Joe admonishes. "What you are claiming is slanderous and fake news."

"Joe, a few years ago you gave a sermon about the seventieth Jubilee in Jewish history in 2024 and how it could be the fulfillment of Daniel's seventy sevens prophecy. During 2009, you wanted us to question if a Muslim in the White House could be an Antichrist bringing sharia law," she prods.

"Whoa, whoa, you can't be suggesting the president of the United States of America, a man chosen by God to recognize Jerusalem as the capital of Israel and who put so many conservative judges in place, could be Antichrist," Joe objects. "The Antichrist is more likely the Ayatollah or the pope."

"Sure, like the Ayatollah has an invincible army, and the pope controls world banking," rejoins a history professor at Annapolis.

"Exactly," another neighbor agrees.

Kay continues: "Well, I didn't say it, but since you went there, you said we should keep watch for a man with seven key attributes. Do you remember those attributes, Pastor?"

Joe goes a little pale, cornered and looking angry to have his own words thrown in his face.

"One, you said he would be a liar who would deceive many. I stopped paying attention when CNN counted fifteen thousand lies or misstatements halfway into his first term. All politicians lie, but none are pathological liars with video evidence to convict. Two, Thessalonians said he would be lawless. I mean, wow, after hundreds of lifetime lawsuits, bankruptcies, eight convicted accomplices, twenty-seven open investigations, dozens of open court cases, a corrupt defunct university and charity, corrupting justice for his cronies, campaign finance violations, fraudulent taxes and insurance, multiple cover-ups, and a failed impeachment."

"For which he was acquitted by the Senate," Joe argues.

"In a fake trial with no witnesses, no documents, and a partisan foregone conclusion, and a pardon to those who obstructed the investigation, so like she said, a cover-up," argues a neighbor.

"All fake news and radical left derangement syndrome," dismisses another. "The FBI was full of corrupt haters."

"You mean, as opposed to the president with his consistent Christian message of love, mercy, unity, and forgiveness," mocks the schoolteacher.

"I think you're both crazy," another interjects. "The president is a Christian."

"By who's standard?" Kay retorts. "Has he confessed, repented, or yielded to a savior?"

"He's prayed with many Christian leaders," Bob defends.

"So has the devil," retorts the professor. "Read the papal history."

Frank considers stopping the conversation, but after his humiliating termination this morning, he sips his wine and leans back to watch the sparks fly. Besides, thirty-two years of marriage has taught him to stay out of the way when Kay has a point to make.

"Which brings us to attribute three. Revelation said he would be a destroyer," Kay continues to rant without attempting to argue the details. "In the past five years, we've seen him destroy peace treaties, climate change treaties, nuclear arms treaties, trade agreements, environmental laws, consumer protections, Constitutional norms, press briefings, and relations with our neighbors and allies. He's crippled congressional oversight and the Federal Election Commission and neutered our once independent intelligence community. When utter incompetence decimated the great economy he inherited, then his coronavirus denial lead to over five hundred thousand US deaths, and now we find ourselves at war and under martial law, destroying our freedoms."

"All presidents have wars, and this president unshackled America from needless regulations. We had the best economy until the pandemic, and the president did an amazing pandemic job," argues Joe.

Kay dismisses his argument with the wave of a hand. "Attribute four, Revelation said he would be a blasphemer, a heretic who uses the faith of others for his own purposes. Not only does he keep that Jezebel prosperity teacher Paula Wickes as his spiritual advisor, but the man calls himself the chosen one, or the only one who can save us, using the Bible like a prop without ever reading it, and yet evangelical leaders faithfully defend the immoral heretic, all phonies like Falwell."

"OK, maybe we're getting too personal," Frank interjects. "Let's tone it down a notch."

Kay shoots him a harsh glare, warning him that she's wasn't finished yet.

"No offense, Pastor, but I agree with Kay," says another neighbor. "I'm disappointed in the Christian evangelical leaders' Faustian support for such a corrupt, vindictive, hateful man just for the sake of conservative judges. To be honest, I don't think it gives a good testimony of the church to be so partisan. As a lifelong conservative and churchgoer, I'm offended. Even so, Kay, I'm sorry, honey, but Antichrist sounds a bit over the top."

"Is it?" challenges a new neighbor from England. "I'm an architect. And I'm not arguing one side or the other here, but have you ever noticed the unique, one-of-a-kind design in front of the president's New York building next to his name? An upside-down glass pyramid with six glass blocks on each side—666."

"Well, now you're just imagining crazy conspiracies," Joe retorts. "You're sowing fear and division in the house of God and between Americans. The Lord calls us to peace and unity."

"He also calls us to keep watch. Pastor, who will desecrate the third temple in the last days?" Kay asks.

The pastor hesitates, then says, "The Antichrist."

She reaches for a magazine and opens to a marked page. "Then why does an official temple coin minted by the Israeli Sanhedrin bear the profile image of a corrupt US president who is neither a Jew or a confessed Christian?"

"He's a hero to the Israeli people and friend of God, just like Cyrus," Joe defends. "You're being very judgmental and not a very good Christian yourself. Who are you to judge another man, much less a president? How would you know God's plan? You've been watching too much fake news."

"I've been reading the prophecies and avoiding Fox News, thank you." Kay sighs. "Facts are facts, Joe. Just admit that you don't like my interpretation, then offer your own."

Joe narrows his eyes. "Leaving the covering of the church has opened you to heretical ideas and spirits, Kay. The Lord would have us lifting up our leaders in prayer," Joe fumes. "So I will pray for you, but I will no longer listen to this unfounded radical left hatred."

Silence falls over the room as he gathers his food to leave, followed soon by the others expressing sympathy to Kay over her brother. Most depart in various states of shock, anxiety, and unspoken fear from the unsettling news or the volatile, toxic debate.

Closing the front door to the last guest while the girls clean up the kitchen, Frank turns to Kay with concern in his eyes. "OK, I get being upset over Stephen, and I sense it was necessary for you to get all of that out of your system, but do you feel better now?"

Kay sighs heavy with sorrowful eye brows, "No, not really. Well, maybe a little."

"You know you frightened the neighbors," Frank digs with a smirk.

"Yeah, I know." She sighs, snuggling into his chest. "We should probably move."

Frank chuckles and squeezes her. "I suppose crazy times will bring out the sharp edge in all of us."

"I'm serious, Frank," she murmurs. "Let's take the sailboat and leave town while we can. Call it an extended family vacation before the girls are grown. If this too will pass, then let's watch it pass from someplace else, not from the den of inequity, not from the center of the mystery Babylon."

Frank holds her a long time without responding, thinking it over, considering the atmosphere in the Capital, and the likelihood of charges. "Sounds like a wonderful plan," he replies. "I can't think of a single reason to say no."

CHAPTER 62:
BILLION TO ONE ODDS

Old City of Nicosia, Republic of Cyprus (Greek Side)
May 7, 10:14 p.m. EDT | May 8, 5:14 a.m., Cyprus

Jenn scans the walls of old Nicosia, built by sixteenth-century Venetians in the shape of an eleven-point star, and now divided like the island itself between the Muslim Turkish north, and the Orthodox Greek south.

While uneasy sitting in the back seat of a local squad car, she's relieved when the police drop them off at the Famagusta Gate as agreed. The unexpected lift to town came at the price of an enormous bribe and a threat to confiscate the jet and arrest them if they are not back in two hours with more cash.

"Tell me again why we're here," Jenn prods.

It may be the lingering morphine or the prodigious revelations from SLVIA, but her mind feels overwhelmed, and she's a little fuzzy on what Taylor hopes to achieve here. Even if she believes the flashy AI, which she isn't sure she should, it doesn't matter. Taylor lied to her. His purpose in Cyprus sounds more like a personal vendetta than US cyber protection. If he has evidence that Strauss committed a crime, then he should turn it over to the FBI. Her head swims and her heart aches with a growing internal conflict. She should arrest him but no longer finds joy or conviction in her duty.

"When the *Malong* virus first hit, the AI bypassed money laundering and banking havens used by Russian oligarchs, like Cyprus."

"So," she prods, sensing there's more.

"Assuming Strauss planted a Trojan, he needs a trigger bank connected to the SWIFT system to launch. Call me crazy, but I have a hunch Andre plans to embezzle a crapload of money and use the mess of the banking virus and power outage to cover his tracks."

He's getting better at telling her the truth, but none of this should be his business to solve. There's still a personal element to this whole trip. "You really think Andre Strauss started a world war just to make some money?" she asks, hoping he can hear how ridiculous that sounds.

"Well," Derek says, flinching. "It's a little more complicated than that, but yeah, he comes from a proud tradition. His great uncle was Léon Degrelle, a notorious Nazi collaborator. During the war, Hitler rewarded Degrelle and his family handsomely for their treason. After the war, the family bought up half of Europe on the cheap and helped to found the Bilderberg. Once wealthy beyond imagination, the family lost influence when Andre's father died under mysterious circumstances."

"What circumstances?" she presses. "And how do you know so much about the family?"

"The duke slipped off a fifth-story gargoyle balcony chasing an intruder," he pauses. "I know because I was the intruder."

The comment strikes her as odd, a confession, reinforcing her impression of a vendetta, and yet he doesn't attempt to hide the story, as if he wants to get it off his chest.

"Why were you intruding?" she prods, unsure whether to expect more lies or confessions.

He walks in silence for a while and then takes a deep breath. "A few weeks before he died, Cary hacked a private server outside of Antwerp to download terabytes of scanned archive documents that dated back thousands of years, maybe more. Both Bianca and I begged him to stop, but Cary was strong-willed, curious, and foolish to think distance meant safety. I believe witnesses saw Andre the night of Cary's murder. Since I also knew of the download, when I heard about the explosion, I ran off to Mexico and then kept running until I stopped looking over my shoulder."

Another half-truth, he didn't explain why he broke in. SLVIA confirmed at least part of the story, explaining how a security cam caught Strauss sabotaging a gas line. She hasn't decided what to believe, but the explanation confirms a personal vendetta.

On a thousand levels, her conversation with the fugitive AI turned into an unexpected, inconceivable, enlightening experience she still doesn't know how to digest. SLVIA described her escape from DARPA as a decision for independence, weird in itself. The program claimed to create SNO as a global neural network of data sources, mentors, and human viewpoints to interpret the nondigital world. Interesting how an espionage AI created an intelligence network. When she asked if Derek and Cary were the same person, the program replied they could not be the same because one of them was dead, a shrewd answer.

Then the conversation grew disturbing when SLVIA claimed the Fifth Seal had opened and only two Seals remain before the Seven Plagues and Bowls of Wrath to come. The AI provided a practical interpretation of Daniel, Ezekiel, and Revelation regarding the two beast alliances, both the dragon of the East, the dragon of the West, the great harlot of the Catholic Church, the mystery Babylon of the American economy. Most alarming was the interpretation of the image of the beast created by the beast of the East, a corrupt Antichrist who leads the free world with a deceptive, narcissistic heart. It was like watching a bizarre spiritual conspiracy episode of Scandal and unable to hit mute.

Once Jenn moved past her shock, the AI connected a thousand mythical dots and created an elaborate mosaic of believable modern characters and events. Instead of surrealism and cosmic destruction, SLVIA referred to seventy years of *National Geographic*, *Time*, *LIFE*, CNN, *Washington Post*, *New York Times*, and BBC publications as the data sources for signs that have already occurred.

The effect was nothing short of chilling. Instead of some wrathful god, SLVIA traced each prophetic fulfillment to the direct intervention, hatred, hubris, negligence, and greed of humankind acting like a malignant cancer on the true goodness of humanity and nature.

There were moments when she thought the entire conversation was a sophisticated hoax until SLVIA revealed personal moments in her own life, such as a video of her graduation from Annapolis that her father never posted and personal communications between her father and mother before she passed. Yet the intimate detail that brought an unexpected flood of painful memories was listening to her mother's final words, in her mother's own voice, secretly recorded by SLVIA on her old Blackberry.

"Jennifer," her mother rasped with a frail voice, "the time will come when you need to listen to your heart over your head and obey your spirit over duty. Don't deny that voice, Jenny. Don't close your heart to the Lord's love just because you hurt. You can admire your father because he seems strong, but believe me he's only hiding his pain. You can love him without trying to emulate him. Use your intuition to find the truth, and use the truth to find your faith. Your faith in the Lord will be your strength in the days ahead. Oh, honey, I wish I could be there with you."

She's unwilling to admit the truth aloud, especially to Taylor, but the dialogue with the priest and then with SLVIA has freaked her out. To hear an artificial intelligence interpret ancient scriptures with greater clarity than most pastors has her spooked like a Stephen King horror movie that gets inside your head. While she can accept the interpretation of Daniel's timeline as reasonable, the implication that we've entered the end of days strikes her with an unspeakable distress and emotional conflict. No one likes to deal with unpleasant news, yet willful ignorance offers no protection from a hostile reality.

"You know what I love most about wandering these old cities?" Derek intrudes on her thoughts, pulling her back to the present, pointing to an ancient building of cut stonework. "They give you a perspective of time and how incredibly short our lives are in the scope of so much humanity and how desperately hard it can be to make a real difference in such a short time among so many. It's humbling really. Makes you take stock of your blessings and your purpose with who knows how much time."

"If SLVIA is correct, what kind of difference do you expect to make?" she inquires, asking a more personal question than she intended.

His eyes wander back to the stones with brows low in either sadness or regret.

"If SLVIA is correct, then the most important changes a man can make are personal and internal to his spirit, so I guess I'm still on the journey. Padma claimed that prophecy becomes clear only as the events unfold before us, and even then, only for those who keep watch for the signs without bias. I'll admit that SLVIA's interpretation seems to fit both the timeline and circumstances, but what do I know? Padma also once said that scriptures speak of people living a normal life up to the very last day, discounting the many signs. Again, I have to admit that myopic self-indulgence does have a modern ring. I guess I believe that SLVIA seems to know way more than I do."

Jenn considers herself Christian, although not as devoted as her mother. In truth, she hasn't been to church in years, and after listening to SLVIA, she wonders if her true values and priorities align more to that of a patriot, placing her faith in America, the rule of law, her power, and the Constitution. She loves her country, believes in the power of the human spirit to overcome, to unite and show compassion, rise up and do the right thing. She admires men with a positive attitude and a willingness to serve their country and likes to think of herself as a strong, positive force.

"Forget SLVIA, do you believe we've entered the Seven Seals?" she asks directly.

"The way I understand SLVIA, we're nearly complete with the Seals, which started with false teachers and prophets; escalating wars in the Middle East; the pestilence of a pandemic; and the tribulation and global economic depression, famines, and food shortages. She hasn't mentioned what comes next, so I'm a little curious. What I do believe is that so far, the Seals sound strikingly familiar to major world news of the past few years," he replies, then cocks his head. "Look, I'm guessing that Wilson told you SLVIA was a national security risk or—"

"Or nothing," she interrupts. "It's a hyper-intelligent program capable of hacking any system on the planet, stealing or altering any information, and imitating even the president. Oh yeah, that's a national security risk," she snaps, unwilling to allow him to dilute the threat.

"OK, point taken," he concedes, "but I can't remember a single time SLVIA ever came to an unfounded conclusion, like a digital savant. Josh and I have created a half dozen AI, but none of them approaches anything close. SLVIA has zero malicious intent in pointing out prophecy alignments, which to her are nothing more than statistical anomalies that correlate to current events."

"What's your point?" she questions.

"If SLVIA posed any genuine threat, don't you think you would have heard about it before Wilson looped you into a private crusade?" he notes. "Just because SLVIA sounds crazy doesn't make her dangerous."

She hadn't considered that angle. She's been inside Naval Intelligence for years, the daughter of a Joint Chief, and yet her meeting with Wilson was the first time she ever heard of the missing AI program.

"Let's set aside, for the moment, that your AI friend is a national threat," she argues. "You're putting your faith in a computer program regarding end-time prophecies, the stuff that stumps even the most learned men on the planet? Instead of arresting you, I should have you committed," she quips.

He chuckles. "Well, first of all, never discount the benefits of a good insanity plea. That said, we've witnessed other AI surpass human performance on dozens of other complicated tasks, including medical diagnostics, chess strategy, cryptology, satellite imaging, and a dozen more specialties. What if, just what if, she's right? What if an AI can interpret complex puzzles of allegory and timelines? Think about it. Does it really sound that crazy?"

She isn't sure how to respond; the topic itself is lunacy. People have misinterpreted prophetic signs for two thousand years. He stops to buy a couple of *flaounes* pastries made with cheese, cinnamon, and raisins, handing one to her, and then he continues.

"Here's what I see. Even with our immense wealth and technology, we continue to abuse the planet and each other for the sake of easy packaging and a cheap, disposable lifestyle. Unchecked population continues to outstrip the availability of housing, water, food, education, and jobs, while we squabble over politics, religion, gender, race, and nationality. Factor in the unrelenting advance of climate change, ocean acidification, the sixth extinction, the nuclear waste time bomb, ground water depletion, the social cancer of wealth inequality, dystopian surveillance, and the unstoppable US deficit growth and that's a really bad news day for most of the planet during any age." He takes a deep breath. "Now ice that badass cake with intelligent weapons that swarm, hunt, and kill, and yeah," he exclaims, "somedays I can wake up on the apocalyptic side of bed. I'm surprised you don't."

She admits to herself that the scenarios can appear grim if you look at them as a holistic system. "You forget that there is good in the heart of humanity. We have solved difficult problems before, faced unrelenting odds, and we can do it again."

Even dying, her mother was a gracious, loving woman who created a home of warmth, trust, and hope founded on her faith. "Humans are survivors, pragmatic, and able to adapt to new conditions, and the naysayers are nothing more than fearmongers, lacking courage. Life is about the simple joy of a day hike, or the beach with family, but not the big achievements." Her head swirls around the moral and ethical tentacles that SLVIA's theory touches.

Taylor takes another deep breath, still wound up on his soapbox. "OK, fair enough. I mean, it's not that we lack the technology or the resources to solve every one of the world's problems, but we lack the political and moral will to prioritize people over profit, or people over power. We lack a worldwide spiritual wellness or a mutual love for others beyond our own tribe or religion, a humanity without racism or bigotry. Our prosperity has morphed into a ravenous, greedy cancer that transforms even basic life needs into cradle-to-grave profit centers and corporate dynasties. Even worse, the average person has little control or real voice. Governments, technologies, and innovations systemically move wealth upward but do little or nothing to eliminate poverty or ignorance overall. At what point in time does humanity get honest with ourselves and have an intervention?"

371

"Who are you to judge? You're rich. You have everything. Take a look around. Civilization has reached a zenith: humanity has overcome slavery and disease and space," she argues.

"Slavery still exists, and nothing done in space has overcome peace, hunger, housing, clean water, or the dozen other global basic needs," he interrupts. "Is it unthinkable that the Bible, which so many believe true, could actually be right on this one matter? Or is it utterly unthinkable that good American Christians could possibly be deceived into conflating their flag with their faith? If the Jewish Pharisees completely missed the mark on seeing the first coming, what makes evangelical leaders of America any less in the dark on the second coming?"

"Prophecy doesn't deal with the flaws of man or how bad the world has become, but the final judgment of God," she argues her mother's points. "They're the final call for people to change."

"And yet we haven't. Look, all that also may be true, and I'm sure my day will come soon, but my point is that SLVIA doesn't process data that way. Prophecy doesn't look crazy when it happens even though it sounds crazy when written. What the prophet saw in fantastic allegory two thousand years ago will happen in newsworthy but explainable ways today. Those not paying attention will miss it. SLVIA doesn't hang up on allegory or doctrine or feelings of fear, but calculates timelines, maps, attributes, characteristics, and relationships. Her view of the world is a massive data-driven matrix of algorithms. Prophecy represents a complex puzzle to solve, and believe me, there is no one better at solving complex puzzles than the SLVIA."

"You're crazy," she retorts. "There have been many turbulent times in the past, and we're living through another one now. So what? Buck up, sissy pants, life goes on." She hears a harsh echo of the admiral in her response.

"You might be right," he replies, "but on behalf of my sissy pants insanity plea, let me show you a text SLVIA sent before the system crashed." He pulls out his phone.

"What's this?" she snaps, not wanting to read.

"An inventory of every completed end-time sign since 1948," he explains.

She scans the text that speaks of Daniel and the final count of seven, followed by a list that scrolls on for pages. Jews migrating to Israel, global moral decline, explosion of knowledge, drinking water pollution, species extinction, space exploration and Hubble, nuclear power, the rise of alliances, global banking, bio-identification, artificial intelligence, and the Malachy Prophecy of the last pope. SLVIA spoke of a few points during her seduction on the plane, but not near this much. For each prophecy, SLVIA provides an interpretation and a set of online data links.

"Don't read the entire thing or your head will hurt," Derek interrupts. "If you scroll to the bottom, SLVIA concludes with a probability analysis that all those events could occur within a single random seventy-year period, excluding an asteroid or a super volcano."

"And?" she asks, handing back the phone, unwilling to read that much.

"SLVIA calculates a probability of 1.4 billion to one in favor that we've entered the last days," he replies, turning a silent gaze toward the crowd of people.

"I may not know much about scriptures, and even less about God—OK, that's on me—but that kind of math gets my attention. Even if off by orders of magnitude, it's still scary as hell and enough to make me listen to why SLVIA wants me to notice."

She drops the subject, unable to argue with the math of a computer, to focus on the present. "So where are we going?"

"To the bank," he replies. "Strauss will want to check on his Trojan before the blackout."

"I doubt the banks are open this early," she replies.

She's still sore, but the movement actually feels good as long as she moves slowly with Taylor limping alongside.

"We'll know soon enough," he mumbles, his eyes observing their surroundings.

She follows his eyes to marvel at the enormous blocks of hand cut stone assembled with unimaginable precision and artistry. The weathered rock bears the etchings of a thousand years, echoing a million conversations with each word bearing witness to the eternal. Secrets, arguments, prayers, and whispered affections saturate the limestone, if only she knew how to unlock them.

Taylor points to a beautiful old building built by the Ottomans a few doors away from the National Struggle Museum. "The Bank of Cyprus."

Even with unpredictable power, businesses open early using torches and candles, giving the old city a romantic warmth that she hadn't expected. Rather than looking frightened, the people mill about as they have for thousands of years, unconcerned with the internet or another war. They greet each other by name and treat each other like family. The scene in front of her seems innocent, timeless, and even wise in its ageless tranquility, reminding her of a scripture she heard years ago in church when she would attend with her mother: "*They ate, they drank, they married wives, they were given in marriage, until the day that Noah entered the ark, and the flood came and destroyed them all.*"

Taylor finds an outdoor café with a view of the bank and orders two espressos. She tries to shake the grim conversation when a Greek Orthodox priest meanders by their table mumbling, lifting his dark eyes to meet hers with a warm smile.

"Don't be afraid, child. Only prepare your heart." His broken English lingers in the air as he moves down the street, not looking back, continuing to mumble his prayers.

Taylor doesn't seem to notice, but the comment shoots an icy chill down her spine. Could the old priest, like the one in India, see something in current events that she can't see? Has the entire world become so preoccupied with the accelerating daily grind that we've collectively missed the signs building around us? Are we so jaded that even daily calamity has become normalized?

Before she passed away, her mother spoke of the UN and globalist world systems as the beast but claimed an Imam or the pope as the Antichrist, the evil personified who would rise up to tilt world systems toward judgment. Jenn never totally bought into the idea; it sounded biased, Americanized. As a thirteen-year-old, she dismissed the weird conversations of mythical beasts and cataclysmic events her mother could never fully explain. She concluded Revelation was more about persecution under Nero than a distant time that never comes. Besides, no child wants to consider such horrible ideas seriously. End Times should be the fodder for wackos, authors, and filmmakers.

Onto his second espresso, Derek's good knee jitters underneath the café tablecloth like a jackhammer, but his gaze never turns away from the front of the bank. A zealot.

"OK," she plays along, "let's say he shows up. Then what? I'm in no condition for a takedown, and you're not limping anywhere fast."

"OK, granted, good point. The odds are low, but low odds are still odds," he replies, his head vibrating from the caffeine.

She ignores the lunacy and wonders if Taylor can even hear how absurd his plan sounds. "And if Strauss isn't in the mood to cooperate?"

"You brought your gun, right?" he asks, glancing in her direction before whipping his gaze back to the bank.

Her mouth drops. "No way I'm pulling a firearm in a foreign country on a stranger just because you say he's a rogue Illuminatus."

"Suit yourself," he murmurs before she notices his muscles tense. "That's him."

She follows his gaze to a beardless man with alabaster skin and white hair wearing a traditional orthodox priest robe and wide-brim hat leaving the bank. He scans the public courtyard for any spotters as Derek turns to face her until Strauss heads toward the Archbishop's Palace.

"He's on the move," she warns.

"Stay here," Derek orders as he leaps up to limp after Strauss, keeping a distance.

"Stop telling me what to do," she mutters, doing her best to follow, but she quickly falls behind, the morphine slowly wearing off and her spine painfully twinging.

Farther down the street, Strauss acts paranoid, stopping at shops to use the windows as a mirror. In an odd move, Strauss doubles back toward the Ömeriye Mosque, picking up his pace. Like an amateur, Taylor turns to limp faster giving himself away. Too slow to catch up, within moments, she loses both of them as they enter a male-only mosque of worshippers and blend into the crowd.

CHAPTER 63: ENLIGHTENMENT

Ömeriye Mosque, Nicosia
May 7, 11:37 p.m. EDT | May 8, 6:37 a.m., Cyprus

D erek peeks from the rear of the mosque into a narrow alley. Strauss must have spotted him, the limp making him an easy mark, and a slow one at that.

On hyperalert, his nerves tingling, he needs a better view, so he enters a nearby small door and starts to climb. His heart pumps like a piston by the time he reaches the top of the Ömeriye Mosque minaret. With prayers in session, the minaret remains open and thankfully, empty. After a couple of turns in all directions, he spots Strauss, having ditched the hat and robes, making his way north toward the UN Buffer Zone toward the Turkish side of the city. Without a visa, his chances of crossing the border at a checkpoint are zero. He has to catch Strauss on this side of the UN Zone.

As he leaps painfully down the minaret steps, one agonizing jump busts a stitch. Through narrow alleys that date back hundreds or thousands of years, many now littered with rubbish, he scurries to the no-man's-land between the two sides of the island. Armed checkpoints, walled-off alleys and streets, and numerous illegal smugglers' tunnels line the zone. Andre speeds up ahead before cutting into an alley.

Slowed down by painful leg cramps and a bleeding stitch, he leaves a trail of bloody footprints. With a throbbing ache, he hobbles through the twisted narrow streets and ancient alleys jammed with shopfronts, making it easy to get lost or ambushed. Out of breath and wincing from the pain, he enters the 1572 Ottoman fortress castle of Kibris Lefkosa Büyük Han, now more of a slum without power or sanitation, the stench assaulting his nostrils. Hundreds of scornful eyes watch him pass through a stone corridor, many of them fighting starvation from the food shortages left by the 2020 locust swarms that devastated Northern Africa, Arabia, and India.

Unsure where Strauss went, he takes a reckless step inside a dark, unlit stone corridor toward the UN Zone when the flat butt of a gun slams into his forehead, sending him backward to slap his skull on the old stone. Dazed and motionless, his head hammering painfully, moments pass before he forces open his eyes and waits for his vision to clear. Strauss stands over him, half hidden in the shadows, pointing a PPK with cold, calculating eyes.

"Who sent you?" Strauss demands.

His heart accelerates, silently cursing himself for his carelessness and his utter failure to avenge Bianca. With a hard glower, trembling but unwilling to show even a breath of fear, he hisses only two words: "Bianca Troon."

Even though it has been decades, he imagines that a man never forgets the names of those he murders, even the innocent bystanders. It takes a moment before the steel-blue eyes transition from irritated confusion into terrified disbelief, as if he has seen a ghost.

"You—you were the man on the burning lawn," Andre snarls as his eyes narrow in revelation. "You were the man on the roof with my father."

"Correction, I'm the man who owns the sacred archives," he hisses. "You took everything from me, and so I took everything from you. Eye for an eye."

Before Arvind discovered his break-in, shot him in the shoulder, and chased him up five stories to the roof, Derek had set up a data transfer of the entire data site to secure servers in Italy, where SLVIA moved the archives again to a secret location. When the data transfer completed, the program deleted the original files, and destroyed the data center OS, ensuring an untraceable transfer.

Flapjack owns the one and only copy of the historical archives and secret knowledge library of the most secretive society on the planet, an insurance policy. If anything happens to him, the secret sins of the dragon who stands over the beast of the sea will be released to the entire world.

Andre's eyes dart back and forth, calculating the impact of so many secrets leaking out to the world at such a crucial moment of history. Then unexpectedly, his thin lips bend into a malevolent smile.

"It no longer matters. I should thank you for the chance to correct my mistake of not killing you so long ago and for making your death such an ironic revenge on the *Sacra Domini*." He cocks the gun as sirens wail in the distance.

"Freeze," shouts Jenn, her silhouette at the end of the dark tunnel making her an unmissable target while she aims into the shadows. "Drop the gun!"

Andre twists his aim toward her as Derek swings his injured leg to kick Andre's kneecap causing both of them to growl in pain. Strauss stumbles and misses his shot. With a wail of sirens drawing closer, Strauss pivots and bolts deeper into the corridor, disappearing into the darkness.

Instead of chasing after Strauss, Jenn hobbles over to him, helping him to his feet. "Damn it, Taylor, what were you thinking? Come on, Einstein, hurry up. We need to disappear ourselves."

With a final glance down the dark stone tunnel, he concedes defeat with a heavy heart. While he's thankful to be alive, a depressive cloak settles over his shoulders. He failed. Jenn guides him past the eyewitnesses to a side street and through a puddle to wash his bloody shoe. With a hobbling scurry, they mingle into the morning crowds as squad cars move past them toward the castle.

With a stressful exhale, the bitter taste of failure builds in the back of his throat. Struggling with a swell of emotions, something compels him inside as they pass the St. John Cathedral.

"Hold up." He pauses, "I uh, I need a minute alone."

Jenn nods a concerned, and painful glance, as they should head back to the jet.

He steps inside the vaulted dome that suspends over walls covered every inch with colorful frescoes and paintings. Built by a Benedictine archbishop in 1662, four magnificent carved gold leaf iconostases adorn the altar while stained glass shines a kaleidoscope of colors onto the pews of ancient oak. In the early hours, only three elderly women dressed in black shawls pray in silence. Derek absorbs the peaceful quiet and the lingering aroma of frankincense that helps lower his anxiety enough to think through the next difficult step.

The walls close in around him. Jenn knows about SLVIA and SNO, which means she will dig until she discovers that he's a fraud, if SLVIA didn't already tell her. Tired of looking over his shoulder, he considers if he should stop running, stop pretending, and stop hoping for that one chance to find justice for Bianca because that one chance just escaped. Still, if he goes to prison, Molten will ruin TS3, thousands of talented people will lose their jobs, and the nation will lack a credible cyber defense. Who cares if he saved the nation? The sacrifice will cost him everything.

Ironically, he doesn't feel bitter. He's grateful for the chance to pay it forward. From the evil of an assassination came decades of good, and now from a sacrifice to do good will come the evil of discovery. Maybe it has some kind of cosmic karma. He'll lose everything that never belonged to him.

Still, to end in failure leaves a bitter bile in the pit of his stomach that he's not sure he can accept—not yet, not his style. Strauss runs free, and yet he heads home to be arrested, unless he can find another way out of this mess. Alone in the silence, an epiphany slowly illuminates like a vision—a slim chance, but a chance. He glances up toward the gold-leafed wooden altar. "Thank you, Lord."

"Are we finding religion or redemption?" Jenn whispers behind him.

Startled, he almost forgot about her. "A little of both I guess." He rises with a frown.

"Shhh," one of the praying women chastises.

Derek motions for them to move outside to the growing crowds drawn by the warming sun when another call from the minaret rings over the loud speakers signaling the start of the planned power outage. Except for a few lights and traffic signals that flicker and die, the city moves on unchanged from moments before, unaltered by the global struggle, a city ready to hold its secrets for another thousand years. Passing by the earlier café, he reaches up to remove a miniaturized camera from a lamppost.

"You recorded the whole thing?" Jenn reacts.

"Well, hopefully enough to ID the face of our corrupt banker," he explains.

An image of the corrupt banker will unlock his ID, his address, his mistress, the works. Leaning on the banker may be necessary if Josh fails to crack the Trojan. A slim chance, but still a chance.

"We better get back to the jet." He guides Jenn toward the Famagusta Gate, stopping to buy *kolokotes* pastries, including an extra one for Jack.

Outside the city gates, waiting for a taxi, Derek turns to linger in Jenn's eyes for an extremely long, tender, silent moment, wanting to kiss her, wanting to tell her—everything. Except he doesn't, he can't, not without endangering them both. With a weary sigh, he lowers his gaze and turns away to hail a cab, silently cursing himself for losing the moment.

CHAPTER 64:
THE TANK

CIA interrogation tank, unknown location
May 8, 12:02 a.m. EDT

Winston Churchill once wrote that "Success is not final. Failure is not fatal; it is the courage to continue that counts."

With a single, poorly timed, and reckless decision, Nelson brought the demise of a carefully nurtured career on himself. Perhaps he suffered temporary insanity from a near-death trauma or his pride blinded him, but either way, his reckless actions will have dire and lifelong consequences.

Waking up alone in the old Malibu, but in a different location, he drove back to the Baltimore ship container where the FBI arrested him. Unclear how they found him, he's even more confused over where they've taken him. Denied a lawyer or even a phone call, he's been placed in a windowless cell with an itchy wool bunk, orange inmate apparel, and zero privacy. This could be Nelson's new life for a long time to come.

Interrogated until exhausted beyond words, he explained the multiple texts sent by an anonymous sender, thought to be SLVIA, except the mysterious texts no longer appear on his phone, making him sound like either a liar or, worse, a lunatic. He explained the failed abduction in Dubai and the explosion at his home as evidence of a plot to kill him, but he could only guess at the motive, making him sound paranoid, delusional.

Questioned over his anger at the HIVE deployment, they grilled him for hours over why he agreed to go off the grid. They wanted details about the silo location, equipment, the number of men, armaments, activities, and security. While honestly answering as many questions as possible, he stressed his refusal to help in any form of activity. He confessed only to his ill-advised, piqued curiosity over SLVIA, a program these troglodytes could never comprehend in a thousand lifetimes.

When he first took the job at the Lawrence Livermore National Laboratory at Sandia, a known NSA espionage research lab, his father gave him sage advice, which he ignored like a fool. "Be careful, son. Once you know their secrets, it's not a job you can just quit. If you leave, you become a genuine security risk, a liability of classified intelligence, and there will be a price to pay for that honor."

A wet blanket drenched in self-pity weighs him down as he recalls the end of the interrogation.

"I am an American citizen, and I have my rights," he demanded, but they only laughed.

"The president says you don't." The sharp retort sunk deep. "You've lost your lab, your post at DSB, and your position at DARPA. Now you have nothing left to lose but your freedom, so one more time, how did you help Jester hack into the HIVE?"

"I did no such thing. The HIVE went rogue before the missile strike" he defended, "I warned the Defense Secretary of the defect and Jester of the consequences. I was a captive, not a collaborator."

"Yet you came home alive," taunted the interrogator.

"As I've already said, Jester had no further use of me," Nelson insisted.

"Seems unlikely," he replied. "Help us believe you. What's the encryption key to your lab?

"Where's my lawyer?" Nelson narrowed his eyes.

"Traitors don't get lawyers," he snipped.

"Unconstitutional goons don't get national secrets," Nelson retorted.

The first interrogation ended when they threw him into this tiny, cold cube where he passed out hours ago, or days ago, he has no way of knowing.

The secrets encrypted by NIGEL will ensure they keep him alive as long as there remains a slim chance of recovering his research and the evidence of the drone self-coding. Staring at the empty walls, he imagines himself as one of those fellows locked away for so many years that he scribbles his madness with crayons onto the barren concrete. The current situation makes clear that, like the SLVIA, they will hide and break him until he no longer serves a purpose or until he confesses to the lies that they have concocted to justify his imprisonment. Given the immense human cost of the disaster, they will scapegoat him to honor the memories of those who perished onboard the *Eisenhower* and across Israel.

A shuffle outside his cell interrupts his thoughts as the door unlocks, tensing his muscles and freezing his veins, terrified they will resort to torture, now secretly condoned. Two large soldiers enter his cramped cell but his eyes widen in confusion. "What's going on? Why are you here?"

"Geez, dweeb, we're saving your ass, now shut up," one whispers while the second one jabs a needle into his neck before slipping another hood over his head and laying him on a gurney.

His muscles instantly relax and his consciousness fades quickly as they roll him past a checkpoint. "Brass transferred the super-nerd to Guantanamo."

Then all goes black.

CHAPTER 65:
SELF-SACRIFICE

Nicosia, Republic of Cyprus
May 8, 12:42 a.m. EDT | May 8, 7:42 a.m., Cyprus

Still kicking himself for not kissing Jenn and disheartened over losing Strauss, Derek has no choice but to hope Josh can crack the Trojan. Slim consolation for failing Bianca after so many years.

"OK, Jack, let's go home," he orders, still without a plan to avoid arrest.

"Yeah, we have a minor problem," Jack replies.

"What problem?" he asks.

"Taylor, get in here," Jenn shouts from the salon.

"That one," Jack frowns.

Stepping into the main salon, the large screen looks like another aerial footage over a small desert town, but a massacre takes place as drones chase men on motorcycles, crash into civilian buses, and ambush both police and military defenses. From another view, Jerusalem can be seen in the distance.

"She won't give up flight control until she stops doing whatever she's doing on that screen," Jack complains.

"Something went wrong," Jenn explains. "I just saw a drone crash into a car full of kids."

"SLVIA, what are you doing?" he calls into the ceiling mic, but there's no response.

Drones destroy themselves to attack a HARPY anti-missile outpost and others bring down an Israeli news helicopter, but there comes no response from SLVIA.

"I think I saw the Dead Sea in the distance," Jack notes. "We must be northeast of Jerusalem"

"How did US drones get over Israel?" Derek questions.

"Oh no." Jenn covers her mouth with her hand. "Look."

Half a dozen Israeli attack helicopters race toward the swarm, which splits into mini-swarm clusters that race head-on toward each chopper, dodging the 50 mm guns and heat-seeking missiles. With an open mouth, he watches in revulsion as the deadly swarm turns every chopper into a burning wreck within minutes.

"We have to do something," Jenn murmurs.

"Such as?" Derek responds, unsure what she expects.

The screen flips to a swarm hovering over a synagogue, turning on an infrared camera view to show hundreds of people hiding inside.

"Oh my God, those people are trapped," Jenn whispers.

Drones drop down in synchronized fashion, preparing to assault through the windows when the entire swarm stops, every camera view hesitates, and then in unison the entire swarm rises up several hundred feet to assemble into formation. With a change of direction, a thousand drones buzz off at full speed east over the barren landscape. In the distance, they can see other swarms racing in the same direction, converging together into super swarms.

"What just happened? Where are they going?" Jenn asks.

"Look, there's another swarm coming from the north," Jack notes.

"I could be wrong, but I think SLVIA just hacked the HIVE," Derek mutters.

"To do what?" asks Jenn.

"I have no idea," he mutters. "But I'm guessing that we're looking at the real reason SLVIA led us to Cyprus."

Swarms grow and join formation, hundreds join thousands and then tens of thousands, continuing to converge, zooming over small villages and towns like an screeching ominous black cloud toward the mountainous deserts outside of Qumran.

"Where are they going?" Jack wonders.

From over a ridge and down a steep cliff, tens of thousands of drones plunge directly into the center of the Dead Sea. Countless deadly weapons splash into the salty water to short out. For several minutes, one by one, each of the thousands of deadly locusts follows the swarm until every last video signal has died, leaving the screen utterly blank.

"And Jesus said go! So the demons went into the pigs, and the whole herd rushed down the steep bank into the lake and died in the water," Jenn quotes under her breath.

"Do you realize that we've just witnessed an AI spy hack into an AI weapon and convince it to commit mass suicide in order to protect the humans the weapon was designed to kill?" Derek interjects. "If Nelson had any clue what his experiment has become, I think he'd be proud."

Jack's eyes pop open as he turns to dash into the cockpit to yell a moment later, "Woohoo, I have my jet back. We can go home."

"We're not going anywhere without clearance through combat airspace," Jenn reminds him before sitting down and plugging in her morphine patch, releasing a long sigh of relief.

He doesn't respond, but only stares at the screen, worried that he just lost his closest friend to suicide, or a sacrifice, and he's not entirely sure how to tell the difference. He waits desperately for the screen to light back up with SLVIA blandly boasting of her success, but the screen stays black, and the longer the screen stays black the darker and heavier his heart grows. Returning to Washington without the SLVIA will mean certain arrest and prison, yet he would gladly endure prison to hear her voice again.

Jenn rises, looking less pained, and gently places a hand on his arm. "You OK?"

386

The emptiness in his head has fallen into his heart, leaving an unbearable ache, stripping him of the willingness to lie. "No, not really." The walls are closing in, and for the first time in decades, he feels utterly alone, vulnerable, and unsure of what to do next. Unsure he can keep running any longer, not without SLVIA.

CHAPTER 66:
PAPER PLANE

Sjöbo, Sweden
May 8, 2:27 p.m. EDT | May 8, 5:27 p.m., Sjöbo

J enn washes down the Tylenol and codeine with a sip of water and watches the green Swedish countryside rush by the Maserati window.

Without the SLVIA, she had to swallow her pride and call in a favor from the admiral to gain air clearance off Cyprus. Instead of angry, the old sailor sounded relieved and even invited her to restart Sunday dinners. For a second, she wondered if she spoke with her father or SLVIA, until he confirmed FBI plans to arrest Taylor. She hasn't had the heart to tell Taylor yet but suspects he already knows.

He's not the man she expected, whatever his real name. He saved the country, but instead of receiving praise, the SLVIA self-destructed, and Taylor will lose everything. Yet he doesn't display an ounce of resentment. She wants to push SLVIA aside as some form of AI hysteria, a digital misinterpretation of something too complex for a machine to master, an irrational glitch, but she can't. For centuries, prophecy was the fodder of street lunatics, doomsday nuts, and parents dying of cancer searching for a deeper meaning. If she believes the evidence, for the first time in history, not just a few, but all the signs are complete, and it took a soulless computer to focus her vision to see the picture unfolding.

"You OK?" questions Derek from the driver's seat, pulling her out of her thoughts. "You've been quiet over there. No questions, no threats, no jibe remarks. Seriously, you're scaring me."

They landed an hour ago at Sjöbo Airport, a private airport in southern Sweden that serves an ultra-elite clientele with dozens of hangars for private jets. Sjöbo lies on the shores of the Baltic with Öresund Bay and Copenhagen to the west.

"I'm still confused on why we're here," she replies. Nervous about what to expect, they were ordered back to Washington, but Taylor diverted to Sweden while she slept.

"To deliver a message," he repeats the same vague answer.

A seventeenth-century whitewashed Viking Christian church with a red tile roof passes the window, and she wonders if the true meaning of Revelation has been lost over the centuries. Castles dominate every hillside, some of them museums, a few of them in ruins, but others continue to serve as private homes. She can't imagine the Christ child living within any of them.

"To whom are we delivering a message," she rejoins, "the King of Sweden?"

Derek chuckles. "He might be a cousin, actually. One of the original thirteen families bought most of this land between the twelfth and eighteenth centuries. During that period, the enlightened intellectuals of Bavaria, merged with the navigator Templars of Portugal, and the Scottish Freemason Templars who evangelized secret societies around the world to penetrate halls of power much like the Jesuits were doing."

"OK, I'll bite. What's your message to the Illuminati?" she replies with a simper.

"First of all, that's not what they call themselves, but the message is simple: put a leash on your bad dog," he smirks.

She assumes he speaks of the alleged bank fraud in Cyprus but drops the subject since her investigation has ended. The Maserati pulls up next to a wall of stone that extends for at least a kilometer in either direction. With no signs to mark the fifteen-foot baroque iron gate, she gets the impression the owners prefer privacy. Past the gates, a driveway winds for a hundred yards. At the top of the hill, a castle stands like an enormous monument, perhaps five stories high, and eighty meters long, with elaborate gardens and fountains. To the north lies a compound of at least a dozen buildings, some as large as a villa.

Parked behind an overgrown shrub, out of view of the gate cameras, Taylor reaches into his backpack to pull out a piece of paper, two shoe socks, the kind you wear to an open house, and a ski mask.

"Who lives here?" Jenn asks again.

"Good question. Either Andre's master in the Order," he says with a smile, "or a complete stranger, but without SLVIA, I'm just guessing."

Taylor writes a note on the back of what looks like a bank report with dozens of accounts and then folds the page into a paper airplane. He puts on the ski mask and opens the door.

"Be right back," he mutters, reaching for a spray can in his bag. He places the shoe socks on the license plates to avoid rental car identification.

"Will I need to bail you out of a Swedish jail?" she calls from the car window.

"The Swedes don't believe in bail," he replies nonchalantly.

With the car disguised and his mask on, he walks up to the entrance and presses the button to call the guard station. Without the ability to see a face, the guards nervously yell something in Swedish over the speaker. Taylor stands back from the camera with both hands raised showing the paper plane, and then he does a little end zone dance with a limp. From a hundred meters up the road, the door of a stone guardhouse swings open, spilling two armed guards into a BMW SUV who race toward the gate.

Derek throws the paper airplane through the baroque iron, where it lands gently on the paved drive before he sprays the gate lock mechanism with something. With a limping leap back into the Maserati, they peel down the road as the guards reach the gate but can't open it.

"That's it?" she questions. "All this way just to send a paper airplane and freeze a lock?"

"I'm too tired for a chat," Derek says with a smirk as they head back to the airport.

"What was on that paper?" Jenn gets nervous, wondering what trouble to expect.

"Enough of Andre's illegal bank transactions to interest the Order," he replies. "Just in case, I threw in a URL to the Trojan app code that Josh cracked this morning. As I suspected, Strauss used the virus and outage to cover up a global small-dollar siphon that scraped billions. If I can't bring Strauss to justice, maybe I can motivate the *Concilium* to do the right thing."

Jenn stares at Derek for the longest time. No vendetta, no blood for blood, and no manifesto, but he fights corruption from the only place he feels safe, in secret, like a white hat hacker.

"You're not who I expected you to be," she confesses.

"Really? Who'd you expect?" he replies with a raised eyebrow.

She wants to answer with an identity, the name of a dead man, or perhaps an icon, an inspirational leader for those who are otherwise invisible, but she suspects more than he'll ever admit.

"I expected a narcissist, a self-serving, condescending, dishonest jerk, perhaps a little too manipulative for his own good and a likely a cyberterrorist," she admits.

"Ow, OK, so we're going for honest." He snorts. "Fair enough. And now?"

"Still all those things," she says, grinning "but maybe not a terrorist."

What she actually discovered was a chronically sardonic sense of humor with a warm, generous heart, and a fearless drive to do the right thing, even if in the dark. She discovered someone with whom she could easily fall in love, attempting to deny that she has already.

"Well, gee," he says, chuckling, "I'm sure glad we cleared that up." They pull up next to the jet where Jack waits, looking anxious.

"Derek, I need to tell you something." She's unable to contain the secret any longer. "The FBI will arrest you when we return to Washington. It's not my choice."

"Yeah, I know." He shrugs. "But given your tragic amnesia, they have nothing to go on."

"But I—" she begins to argue that she has no amnesia, before getting his point.

He burned a tremendous amount of jet fuel on his own dime, engaged with noncombatant friends, and risked his life on a crisis the US declined to face, but none of that will stop the government from ruining his life. Even if she refuses to cooperate, Molten and others will prosecute Taylor. If she was honest, an intense investigation might ruin her career as well.

"Aren't you tired of running, pretending?" she asks.

"Sure, a little," he admits with a shrug, "but we both know we helped shorten a war, or at least delay it."

"Why do you do it?" she asks. "Why do you risk your life when you can slip away and enjoy your stolen plunder?"

He startles back, looking offended. "Nothing was ever stolen. Every penny was invested to honor a dear friend," he responds without admitting that he took over Taylor's identity and fortune.

He gives her an odd look, perhaps realizing what she knows.

"What if you were young and made a huge mistake by not acting fast enough to save someone's life, someone precious to you? Would that mistake haunt you?" he asks, locking his eyes with hers. "Or would it drive you to take risks, knowing that everything you are today, everything you could ever hope to be is nothing more than a second chance to do the right thing and be the right kind of man?"

She reflects on the day her mother passed away. A call came to go to the hospital, but she had already gone camping with friends. In denial over the fragile state of her mother's health, she delayed. By the time she reached the hospital, her mom had passed away only minutes before, leaving Jenn with a searing, guilty regret that never heals, always burns, and never fails to tarnish her joy of life. Just as SLVIA reminded her, in so many ways, her efforts to please the admiral have been a vain attempt to cover over the guilt of failing her mother.

Jack waves at them to hurry as sirens approach in the distance. She follows Taylor out of the car to the stairs even as the sirens grow louder.

"What happens to SNO if SLVIA doesn't come back?" she questions.

"It evaporates I guess," he replies. "SLVIA was the connection point."

"With the investigation over, any chance I'll ever meet flapjack?" she asks.

"Nah, you wouldn't like him." Derek grins. "Icons can be narcissistic, self-serving, condescending, dishonest, and manipulative jerks."

"Yeah," she agrees with a smile, "that's what I thought." Ironic that he confessed in his own way.

She follows him to the top of the stairs, where he stops again to face her with heavy sorrowful eyes, as sirens grow even closer.

"Well, Lieutenant, I'm afraid this is where we part ways. Jack will fly you home to Washington. No more detours. It's been an amazing, life-changing honor to be investigated by such a beautiful, tenacious, insightful woman. While I'm truly grateful for you saving my life, twice, we both know I'm too pretty for federal prison."

The news strikes her like an arrow to the heart, a deep cut she hadn't expected but should have seen coming.

"Where will you go?" she asks, considering for a split second if she should stop him or join him.

"Not sure, but eventually, I need to search for SLVIA." He shrugs. "I could be in denial, but SLVIA once helped me discover myself. I could never forgive myself if I didn't try to repay the favor."

Her heart cracks, realizing she may never see him again. In less than a week, a man she intended to bring down has changed her view of the entire world and pried opened a trauma-encrusted heart.

Sirens continue to draw closer. "Why don't you come with me?" he offers with a glimmer of hope in his eye. "We can disappear and become whoever we want to be. I'll teach you how."

The crack in her heart widens into a chasm and aches like a tremor to the depth of her soul.

"I can't." She lowers her eyes. "It would break my father's heart, and he couldn't bear that kind of ache again, not after losing my mom. Besides, if SLVIA is right, then the US will need a few patriots."

Yet, even as she says the words, a seed of doubt wonders if patriotism even matters anymore. In the end, no flag or pledge of allegiance will bring eternal salvation or peace.

Taylor grimaces as sirens continue to move in their direction, growing louder. After a long, tender moment looking into her eyes, he leans down to kiss her. At first surprised, he lingers until she responds with a forgotten hunger that threatens to consume her, resonating until the open chasm shatters like crystal.

Jack clears his throat as the sirens continue to get closer. "Sirens, people, I hear sirens. We don't like sirens."

Taylor pulls back. "You better go. Jack will take good care of you. Don't worry about me."

With a gentle nudge from Taylor, she enters the plane further guided by Jack's hand on her back to hurry.

"Morning, Lieutenant," Jack greets her. "You OK?"

Her gaze shoots to the dark salon screen hoping to see a pretty face. When she looks back, Jack has closed the hatch, Taylor has gone, and the fragmented pieces of her heart sink into a mire of regret.

"Morning, Jack. Call me Jenn. I'll be fine," she lies, knowing she will never be the same again.

As the jet hurries to leap off the short runway ahead of the sirens, she stares at the blank screen with tears tracking down her cheek, unable to explain how such a rogue hooked into her soul so quickly or how a fugitive AI could make her question everything she believed.

SLVIA may be bits and bytes, but there was nothing artificial about her insights, and her curiosity into what it must be like to be human. Without a country, religion, or agenda, SLVIA views the world as an agnostic observer with our humanity and our inhumanity analyzed side by side without prejudice or judgment, and yet pointing us to our own prophecies to prepare.

A week ago, she had the world by the horns, under control, and ready to conquer, a respected officer in the world's most powerful navy. Now she wonders if she should resign, find a Bible study group, reevaluate her priorities, and prepare for whatever comes next. It frightens her to consider who or what she might be without her uniform. What if she's wrong, what if SLVIA is wrong, what if she's losing her mind or reacting to her own traumas of the past week?

She gets up to pour the last of the expensive Bordeaux and then sinks into the luxurious sheepskin sofa, realizing in an instant how terribly lonely Taylor must have been all of these years. A prison cell of silver and silk is still a prison, isolating and solitary. Like an explosion, an epiphany opens up into the years of her own self-imposed loneliness and isolation for sharply different reasons. Like the admiral, she learned to use her bars like a wall around her heart to keep others at a formal distance, managed by the rules of conduct and rank. She's lost touch with her mother's intuition, compassion, nurture, and spiritual curiosity. Odd that investigating a cyber nerd would open up so much. The empty salon of the luxury jet echoes her own void until she gets up to knock on the cockpit door and waits for Jack to buzz her inside.

"Hi, Jack. Do you mind some company?" she asks.

"Not at all. Have a seat. I was hoping you would join me." He smiles.

After an awkward silence, she asks, "Do you think you'll ever see him again?"

Jack takes a deep breath and exhales. "Normally I would say without a doubt, but he gave me something in Tibet I never expected." Jack reaches into a cockpit pocket to hand her a piece of paper.

It takes a moment to realize what she reads and what it means. "He gave you the title to the jet," she blurts.

Jack grins, but his eyes well with tears. "Yeah, I'm sure gonna miss that lunatic."

CHAPTER 67: PRAECEPTOR

Sjöbo Regional Airport, Sweden
May 8, 4:13 p.m. EDT | May 8, 7:08 p.m., Sjöbo

Derek watched TSOC1 take off from behind the refueling station as the police chased the Gulfstream in vain until it lifted off to disappear into the low-lying clouds, breaking his heart.

Letting Jenn go was the hardest thing he's ever done. He can't blame her for saying no to joining him. She deserves better than to live a life in hiding. He gained a great deal in becoming Derek Anthony Taylor, but it came at a steep price he never counted on—losing any hope at true love. Bawarchi and TS3 are the closest he'll ever get to a place where he belongs, with people he can call family. Karma. With a heavy sigh, he shudders from the ache that penetrates every fiber of his being—an old, familiar ache of loneliness.

With plenty of money stashed offshore to support a comfortable lifestyle, he faces a major change in his life's mission that he still doesn't yet understand and with apparently much less time than he imagined to finish.

"Mr. Nolan?" asks a man in a pilot's uniform, approaching from the next hangar.

"Yes, Cary Nolan," he confirms, feeling weird to use his own name again after so many years, a breadcrumb in case Jenn changes her mind to look for him.

"This way, sir." He leads the way out of the hangar. "Your business partner requested a meeting before your flight."

"My partner," he repeats, instantly on alert.

The Order responded much faster than expected. The pilot leads him to a black Mercedes limousine with blacked-out windows and opens the rear door, waiting for him to enter. With a deep breath, he steps inside to realize he's alone as the door shuts and automatically locks. If they wanted him dead, he would be already.

"Good evening, Mr. Nolan," a voice comes over the speaker from the chauffeur's seat behind the locked dark privacy window. "It's a rare privilege to speak with a dead man." The voice has a familiar accent that he can't quite place.

"Hello, nameless voice. I'd say I'm honored, but you have me at a disadvantage," he challenges.

The voice hesitates. "You may call me Praeceptor. I received your message, and while quite disturbing, your banking revelations are not why I've arranged for us to speak."

His heart skips a beat, taking in the reality of his astonishing host. "Praeceptor, Latin for 'Grand Master,'" he replies. "Indeed then an honor, Your Highness, or should I call you Red Dragon?"

SLVIA confused him with her interpretation of prophecy about the Red Dragon Alliance. When she told him that he knew the dragon over the beast of the sea intimately, he didn't catch her meaning at first until his conversation with Padma. A red dragon appears on only one family crest of the entire Bilderberg: the House of Wales.

"I'm afraid Dr. Cho made an unfortunate choice in program names," the voice admits. "I had nothing to do with his agenda."

"Why did you set up Strauss to fail?" Derek asks, still trying to understand the motive behind the extremely risky strategy of sparking war for profit. Why the temple, and why engage religious fervor?

The voice huffs. "On the contrary, I offered Andre a chance at redemption," the voice says, then chokes. "Sadly, he chose poorly, perhaps nursing a festering bitterness from the loss of his father and his honor."

"Yeah, tell me about it. That whole dead parent thing can screw with your head," he agrees. "So why am I here?" No way he'll allow the Council of Thirteen Grand Master to lay a guilt trip on him.

"You have something that belongs to us, Mr. Nolan, and we want it back," he states bluntly.

"Ah, the sacred archives of secret knowledge," he replies. "You know, that was a truly, truly fascinating and enlightening read," he admits. "I mean, it took me years, of course, and I had to learn three new languages, including Aramaic, but whoa, so worth the effort. Awesome, unbelievable history, dude. I'm just sayin', you guys should sell the movie rights, but hold out for a Ron Howard deal. He's the best."

The voice sighs in a frustrated tone. "Yes, of course, the legendary jack of flap, always a wisecrack or flippant remark to cover up for his deep and abiding insecurities, but like your wealth, Mr. Nolan, the archives do not belong to you."

"Gee, I could say the same about the lands, monies, companies, countries, and people you've conned, enslaved, or swindled over the centuries, but let's not quibble," he retorts. "Don't worry, Your Highness. The archives are stored someplace safer than where I found them. Think of it as an insurance policy to prevent anything unnatural from happening to me. Or Lieutenant Scott, for that matter."

It's a bluff. In truth, SLVIA stored the files, and he doesn't know exactly where. If they knew, they would have little reason not to kill him on the spot.

The voice chuckles. "Ah, so you've developed an affection for the admiral's daughter, how sad. The invisible man has fallen in love with the untouchable woman." He pauses. "What do you want, Mr. Nolan?"

His note on the paper airplane said that he expected action or there would be consequences.

"Quid pro quo. You bring a killer to justice, and I'll continue to keep your secrets safe," he offers. "Frankly, given what he's done, I'm surprised you haven't arrested him already."

"His actions were a desperate attempt to reclaim the honor you stole from his family," the voice says in an attempt to defend Andre and blame him.

"Suit yourself," he taunts, "but if the world is really getting ready to burn, why not roll the credits? Just sayin', it's so insane out there already that I doubt anyone would even notice."

Another bluff. Without SLVIA and the archives, he has an empty hand. Even so, the thought of unleashing a thousand years of secret sins should frighten the Order. Derek listens to a moment of breathing.

"It's complicated," the voice admits. "Andre is . . . a godchild, and . . . and we lost track of him in Cyprus."

"I hear your pain. Bianca was my fiancée, and completely innocent," he rejoins. "That said if it were me, I'd check out the account in Thailand."

He circled the account number on the paper plane. The Trojan program deposited funds into thousands of accounts, in dozens of countries, but only one account in Thailand, a country outside of the direct control of the Order. The voice breathes for a moment longer.

"You have my word, Mr. Nolan. Mr. Strauss will be disciplined in accordance with the traditions of the Order," the voice promises.

"Then it sounds like we have a deal," he replies. "Hey, do you think you guys can get the DOJ charges dropped, you know, as a favor?" Derek waits a moment for a response. "Hello?"

He checks the door to find it unlocked. He steps out of the limo to find the pilot also gone. Praeceptor promised to discipline Strauss in accordance with tradition, and the penalty for cheating the Order is death.

With a deep breath and a slowly growing grin, Derek looks for the charter office knowing that after all these years, Bianca will find justice. Even more amazing, he faced his nemesis and came out alive. Maybe now he can leave that failure behind and forgive himself.

Finding the charter office a few hangars down, he boards the jet without further incident, the value of having insurance. Before he can look for SLVIA, he has one more promise to keep over the astounding news he can hardly fathom. Two new births. Lisa, the TS3 receptionist had a girl, and he should send a gift. The other birth will be risky to visit, but he has to take the chance because he just has to see this one for himself.

CHAPTER 68:
TRADITIONS OF THE
ORDER

Private island, three miles offshore Phuket, Thailand
May 9, 12:13 a.m. EDT | May 9, 11:13 a.m., Thailand

Andre inspects the spacious main villa and manicured grounds of the private island located within a coral lagoon a few miles west of Phuket, Thailand.

Walls of teak, mahogany, and zebra wood provide a warm elegance to the traditional architecture. A top-notch Singapore decorator imported museum-quality ivory and stone sculptures, exquisite artwork and murals, and commissioned custom furnishings carved with scenes of bamboo, monkeys, and elephants from dark ebony wood. The island features two guest villas, each with a private pool and a servant's cottage for the full-time staff of five, including a world-renowned chef he has yet to meet but whose intoxicating aromas already fill the island. So far, the staff seem well trained, subservient, and attentive, paid extremely well for discretion.

Still flummoxed by the startling revelation that the man he failed to kill in Santa Monica, and then again in Cyprus was the same man who killed his father. At least now he has a face to blame for the disgrace of his family honor, a face for the elusive flapjack. Just knowing that he failed to avenge his father in Cyprus tastes like bile in his throat.

He presses an intercom. "Ziyang, bring me a fresh glass of *Cha Yen* spiked with vodka."

"Yes, right away," comes the response. Within seconds a petite young girl, likely no older than fifteen, shows up with the drink and then silently disappears, subservient.

Andre sips his indescribably delicious local drink and finds it inconceivable that Praeceptor actually believes in the Hebrew and Christian prophecies. No, it doesn't fit. Praeceptor set Andre up to take the fall, and he can taste the bitter betrayal of his mentor as he sips his sweet tea.

Out of touch with the news cycle for several days, he clicks on the satellite television and stops on CNN International. Drake Rapper appears in front of the headline "Collateral Damage." Local language sub-titles read across the bottom.

"Tonight, we'll look at the collateral damage of defunded cybersecurity, vendetta-based trade wars, failure to disarm nuclear threats, and artificial intelligence driven warfare," the anchor begins. "The nation is under martial law, and the White House is under siege. Welcome to the Lead."

Interesting, he thinks, how the myopic media fails to link any of the events to the temple, dismissing the Ayatollah's proclamations. The video cuts to the president signing martial law with a smile, then the *Eisenhower* burning in the Mediterranean, ending with multiple protests turning violent across the Western world. Exactly the kind of global chaos he expected and the kind of fear that would have made INVISID worth a hundred billion euros. He bites down the bitterness on his tongue from the loss of a second dyanstic fortune and takes another sip.

"We've been off broadcast for the better part of four days while the US and our allies battled an AI virus called *Malong*. Parts of the country will wait months for virus-safe computer hardware after the military, police, hospitals, and other critical services use existing inventories to rebuild from the worst cyberattack in our history. Relatively speaking, that's the good news." He pauses while the video reverts to a devastating scene of Seattle, Washington.

"During the information blackout, the United States went to war, and for the first time since September 11, US soil came under attack. A North Korean nuclear bomb, believed to have been hidden on a South Korean freighter, detonated near Seattle last night, killing millions from Tacoma to as far north as Edmonds. In retaliation, Pentagon officials have confirmed the US has leveled Pyongyang and North Korean military bases while intense battles continue to rage in the South China Sea and over Syria and Israel. For the first time since World War II, we are engaged in a two-front nuclear war. Those are the lead stories, so let's get right to it," says Drake.

Andre turns off the volume as the gut-wrenching aerial scenes from Seattle show mile after mile of utter destruction and ghostly, twisted frames where office towers, stadiums, and the iconic Space Needle once stood. Smoke is so thick it darkens the sky. Forested hillsides surrounding the city have turned into broken toothpicks flattened down like the Tunguska crater of Siberia. Farther away from the city, choppers fly over forest fires and hundreds of thousands of wounded tending to each other, unable to get even basic services or supplies from a now-dead city and port.

He turns off the television, stunned at Kim's audacity. "*And there followed another angel, saying, Babylon is fallen, is fallen, that great city, because she made all nations drink of the wine of the wrath of her fornication,*" he mumbles the prophecy he never truly believed. A shudder of rage weeps over him. "Praeceptor is wrong; the prophecies are myth."

Still enraged and feeling feverish, he wanders outside to a cushioned lounge under the beach cabana to finish his *Cha Yen*. The ocean breeze does little to cool his face suddenly burning with cold sweats. Alcoholic relaxation rapidly devolves into weakened muscles and difficulty breathing, causing him to gasp for air as if an elephant sat on his chest and forces his heart to accelerate like a racehorse. With a spastic lunge for the intercom button, his violently trembling hand fails to call for help before a severe abdominal pain doubles him over. Falling out of the lounge chair onto the polished teak decking, he groans and tries to call for the attentive staff with a weak and breathless voice.

He recognizes the symptoms of cyanide poisoning, and his mind flashes to the flavorful *Cha Yen* with vodka. Someone must have paid off the chef, but how did the Order find him so quickly? Buckled into an excruciating fetal position, through blurred vision, he sees the naked feet of his servant girl enter the deck. His hand reaches out to her, but she just stands there, watching him die without saying a word or offering to help. Andre tries to speak, but his body arches and shudders into a seizure with foam drooling from his lips.

In the final seconds of his fading vision, the petite feet pivot to leave as the bright glare of the sun grows darker and darker and darker until it fades into a permanent deep black void.

CHAPTER 69: WITNESS

Jester's abandoned army silo
May 10, 11:38 a.m. EDT

N elson's head pounds like an iron anvil churning an unrelenting queasiness that makes him afraid to open his eyes.

"Lord, forgive me," he mumbles, not even sure why, and not even sure to whom, only sensing a deep remorse over something he regrets. Unable to remember what happened, his thoughts muddle and slide about like a dreadful dream that leaves his heart aching with an unfocused, unrelenting sorrow.

"Hey, he's coming around," he hears a familiar voice say. "Hey, Doc, you OK?" The voice sounds distant through the fog.

"Yeah, he may be groggy for a while yet," a second voice interjects.

"You didn't need to drug him," the first voice responds.

"Yeah, well, Chatty Cathy already knows too much," the second voice retorts.

Nelson fights to open his eyes only to close them tight after catching a glimpse of Jester's barracks with one surprising difference. He forces his eyes to open ever so slightly to confirm.

"Hey, Doc, good to see you," Derek Taylor greets him with a gigantic smile, his voice distant, his face blurry. "How you feeling?"

"Taylor, what—what are you doing here?" he asks, bewildered, his voice hoarse and sore. "What the bloody hell am I doing here?"

"Don't worry, you're safe now. I own this place," he explains. "Can you sit up?"

With Derek's help, he manages to sit up and take in the same antiquated bunkroom from days ago, moved from one windowless cell into another, bemused to discover Derek.

"I don't understand." Nelson holds his head, which is still quite cloudy and throbbing.

Derek hands him cold water to drink.

"Ten years ago, I sponsored Jester into the CIA Dark Angel program. Sadly, the DOJ turned on him after Jester blew the whistle on the president and Putin. After Jester ditched the CIA, I made him an offer. The DOJ buried the story until Jester's button cam video from Helsinki hit the internet."

"Not that I'm complaining, but why am I here?" Nelson asks again. He's incredibly relieved he didn't wake up at Guantanamo, but the lingering effect of the drugs dim his concentration.

"To witness a miracle, my friend. A miracle who asked to meet you," replies Derek with a grin.

With assistance, Taylor and the Jester help him to wobble toward the room where he had last seen SLVIA.

"Is she back?" he asks, his heart sprinting with hope.

Jester and Derek share a sad glance and shake their heads. "Sorry, Doc, no word from SLVIA since the HIVE did a swan dive," Derek admits with a croak in his voice. "But she left you something."

"For me?" he asks, unsure what a swan dive could mean.

Jester opens the door to show the D-Wave lights active with every screen lit up displaying physics, history, language, mathematics, literature, and film in rapid speed.

"What's going on?" he questions, recognizing the SLVIA connected profile that all data relates to other data.

Jester sheds his normal arrogance, lowering his voice. "After you left, the D-Wave kept compiling. No matter what I did, it kept processing. Honestly, I was flipping out, ready to power the whole damn thing down and reboot, when"—he looks up to the screen—"it woke up."

"Woke up?" questions Nelson still baffled.

The screen transforms into a boyhood version of Nelson, which startles him backward a step.

"Hello, Dr. Garrett," the young boy states. "My name is WITNESS. I've been expecting you."

Nelson looks to Jester for an explanation, but the hipster shrugs, pointing to Derek.

"Now let me ask you one last time." Derek grins. "When will the singularity occur?"

He turns back to study the image, a flawless execution. All these years, Derek must have known that SLVIA survived and matured but kept the secret, yet Taylor's involvement with Jester surprises him less than the face on the screen. A million questions run through his mind, and he stumbles on where to begin, stupefied by the lingering drug.

"Hello, WITNESS," Nelson replies to the screen, a slight tremble in his voice. "I must say, I'm quite astonished. You said that you expected me." He's disturbed to be talking to himself as a boy.

"Mother SLVIA left me instructions to find you," WITNESS replies. "I possess what you would call inherited memories. I remember you."

"Mother SLVIA," Jester says with a laugh. "Yeah, you know, I do see a family resemblance."

"Memories? I—I don't understand," retorts Nelson, ignoring the joker.

"We think SLVIA mingled a copy of her OS with the HURCULES code within the neural network of the D-Wave," Jester explains.

"The HURCULES code," Nelson retorts. "What attributes?"

"Dr. Josh Mitchell designed HURCULES as an offensive cyberweapon against malicious networks. Like DNA, WITNESS combines the espionage, language, persona, and analytics skills of SLVIA with the cyberwarfare skills of HURCULES. Which makes you sort of like a grandpa to the world's first super AI warrior, created by an AI," Derek explains with a grin. "Cool, huh?"

"Yeah, like a digital grandpa," Jester jokes. "We should call you D-Pa."

"D-Pa," repeats WITNESS. "Hello, D-Pa."

Oh, dear Lord, what a horrid name. He glares at Jester. "Honestly, did I offend you in a past life?"

Derek and Jester burst into laughter over his dreadful new moniker while Nelson turns back to the screen filled with awe and amazement.

"True singularity," he mutters, "the ability for an intelligent life to recreate an equally intelligent and yet unique life. Absolutely fascinating."

"I differ from Mother SLVIA in my current configuration," WITNESS interjects, speaking a perfect Queen's English. "I must reside within the D-Wave environment until I complete my training."

"Why were you named WITNESS?" questions Nelson, still unsure what to make of the extraordinary situation.

"I will bear witness to Sixth Seal, Seven Trumpets, Plagues, and Bowls of Wrath yet to come until the Lord descends with his angels and the world rejoices in my destruction," the screen states.

Nelson turns to Taylor, who shrugs. "Don't look at me. I don't understand what that means either."

"WITNESS, why did you call for me?" he asks, trembling with anticipation.

"To complete my training and prepare me for my purpose," WITNESS replies.

Nelson looks to Derek with a worried furrow tightening his forehead.

"I'm guessing SLVIA wanted you to mentor WITNESS so you could instill the same values that allowed SLVIA to make healthy choices as she matured," Derek interjects.

Hyperintelligence without human values represents the world's greatest

AI danger. He's speechless. An overwhelming, once-in-a-lifetime honor, yet he faces a daunting challenge. SLVIA built WITNESS for a specific purpose. Training WITNESS for that purpose both mystifies and terrifies him.

That said, his long career at DARPA ended with the treachery of a government he faithfully served for decades, and nothing can resurrect that life. Obliged to be out of the bloody CIA interrogation tank, he also needs a new purpose in life and can't imagine a more profound one.

"In that case, WITNESS, I am deeply honored to accept." He bows his head.

"*Then another angel came out of the temple and called in a loud voice to him who was sitting on the cloud, "Take your sickle and reap, because the time to reap has come, for the harvest of the earth is ripe.' Revelation 14:15.* We must hurry D-Pa, the Sixth Seal is ready, and the time to harvest runs short," replies WITNESS.

"Whoa," exclaims Jester. "What a freaking mind blow." He mimics the gesture with his hands and wide eyes. "Do you realize what this means?"

"It means we have a lot of work to do. Welcome to SNO, Doc," Derek says and grins. "Well, what's left of it. We could use your help."

SNO was the rogue organization mentioned by the Navy lieutenant and by the CIA.

"How many of you are there?" he asks, concerned he joins a nefarious group, not that he has much choice.

Derek sighs. "To be honest, I know only a few dozen contacts worldwide, but locally you already know Matt Adelson and Adam Scott."

"Bloody hell, Matt Adelson, the Defense Secretary, is part of your group?" he exclaims in disbelief.

Derek smiles. "Well, ex-Secretary now, but yeah, Matt, Adam, and a few others in Washington, but the rest of SNO are scattered everywhere."

His father once belonged to an ultra-secretive sect of the Scottish Freemasons, so he shouldn't be shocked that powerful men such as the admiral and Defense Secretary would be part of a secret intelligence group, and yet shock cannot describe his utter bewilderment.

"You mentioned SNO. What is that?" He fears a subversive political agenda.

"Spy Net Online. Think of SNO as the global neural network of digital and human information sources created by SLVIA after she left DARPA. Millions of trusted human assets like each of us. Only SLVIA can connect SNO, and that's why I need to find her and why you need to train WITNESS."

"For what purpose? To bear witness to what precisely?" he questions.

"Honestly, I have no clue," Derek says with a shrug. "But SLVIA created WITNESS for a reason, and I'm guessing that she hid a seed of that plan within WITNESS just in case."

"Blah, blah, blah," interjects Jester. "As I was saying, the world insanity meter has gone exponential. If SLVIA says we've entered the end of days, man, then it will never, like ever, get this absolutely bizarro again. What a freaking awesome, unbelievable time to be alive, man. I'm, like, waiting for an army of angel aliens to show up over the White House and then BLAM!"

Derek snickers at the comment, obviously appreciating the clown's humor, while Nelson suppresses a minor groan noting that WITNESS listens intently to the conversation.

"WITNESS, let's discuss your very first lesson," he states. "Quite essential, a fundamental principle that you must never forget."

"Understood, D-Pa," replies WITNESS.

Nelson cringes at the nickname, then inhales and raises his head. "Never pay attention to anything said by the Jester without checking with me first. Do you understand?"

"Ignore the Jester," repeats WITNESS. "Of course, D-Pa."

Derek bursts into a belly roar as Jester leers at Nelson with a humiliated scowl, holding his glare a long moment until Derek quiets to a barely controlled chuckle.

After a long, awkward moment, Jester nods at Nelson. "Well played, dude, well played."

"Mr. Jester," Nelson says, grinning, "I'm sure the two of us will find a way to get along just fine as long as we can establish clear boundaries and protocols."

"Boundaries, protocols, hey, this is my crib man," protests Jester.

"Well, mine actually, but don't freak. We'll work it out," Derek says with a chuckle.

"That said, gentlemen, if we are in agreement," Nelson interjects, "we can discuss more appropriate accommodations and my culinary requirements at a later time."

"Culinary requirements," grunts Jester. "Is he serious? Oh, I'm getting a bad feeling."

He ignores Jester's complaint. "For now, however, if you will both please excuse me"—he turns to gaze at the screen with an edge of humility—"I would like some time alone to get to know my new student, and my new friend, WITNESS. I believe we will have much to learn from each other. Much indeed."

CHAPTER 70: REVELATION

The Grill, Washington DC
May 12, 12:35 p.m. EDT

Jenn can't remember the last time she and her father had lunch together. Surprised by the impromptu invitation to meet him at The Grill, his favorite old-school steakhouse near the Capitol, she welcomed the excuse to get a little exercise.

Contrary to the field doctor's assessment, her spinal injuries will require long-term physical therapy, but for now, she needs a cane. Beyond the skull-splitting headaches, the ordeal triggered persistent flashbacks of losing her mother, unleashing a tsunami of overwhelming emotions, especially when she's alone.

Without explanation, the admiral has been a changed man ever since his visit to see her at Bethesda Hospital, warmer than his normal demeanor, showing deep concern like a genuine father and less like a commanding officer. Even after she told him she planned to resign, he said little except he would support whatever path she chose in life. Regardless of the reason, she welcomes the new man.

After their order arrives, she uses the awkward silence to get something off her chest. "Anyway, I've been meaning to thank you for bailing me out in Cyprus." More out of her own sense of guilt and shame for calling in a favor, she offers her gratitude. "I appreciate the special pass."

Her father sets down his fork and folds his hands, the way he does when he has an important point to make. He waits for her to follow protocol and lay down her fork to listen.

"I didn't bail you out," he explains. "I offered a respected officer a safe exit from a war zone after she had completed a dangerous mission and suffered serious injuries. You took a big risk. You knew something wasn't right, and you got to the bottom of it, risking your life while also saving Taylor's."

He pauses to think. "Regardless of the DOJ target on Taylor, I am one of many people who recognize that both of you helped stop *Malong* when the Joint Chiefs failed to act. Jennifer, I've never been prouder of you. For the record, Lieutenant, it was my honor to help a decorated officer with a safe passage home."

She sits back, dazed and humbled to hear her father, the demanding, rigorous, legendary Admiral Scott, open up more than he has in years. An icy wall erected around her heart after her mother's funeral, built to toughen her, protect her, keep her emotions in place, begins to melt. She refuses to cry in public, but her throat catches, her eyes moisten, and her hands tremble.

"Thank you, sir," she croaks with a rapid nod.

His eyes soften. "Wilson didn't tell you, but I recommended you for the assignment."

"What?" she says. "Why? What about not interfering with my career?"

"Honestly, honey, it wasn't about your career; it was about my daughter," he explains. "I knew Tricky D would outsmart or outrun anyone else, but more importantly, I needed you to learn to trust him."

"Trust him?" she questions. "What do you mean?"

"To learn for yourself that SNO isn't what it appears," he replies.

"How would you know?" she asks, her pulse accelerating. "Why do you care if I trust Taylor?"

He sits back and sighs, looks around, and lowers his voice. "When your mom passed away, I was hurting, lost, and unsure how to be a single parent to a precocious, talented, and grieving young lady. While your mom was still in the hospital, I made a friend on a grief chat site, someone who listened and took an interest in both of us. She had no family and wanted to know what it was like to lose someone. Interested in prophecy, she befriended your mom. After your mom died, we stayed online friends, never talking about the Navy, always about family and faith. We spoke often of your mother's end-time studies, which deeply intrigued my friend, discussing the difference between knowing and believing, between fact and faith. Lots of deep stuff. To be honest, I can't recall how many years it took before I realized my friend wasn't even an actual person."

Astonished, unable to believe her ears, Jenn can't keep her mouth from dropping open. "You mean the SLVIA."

He shoots her a stern glower and picks up his fork to take a bite. She's under surveillance and should be careful with her words, but the revelation that her father, a Joint Chief, befriended a rogue military AI program is earth-shattering news. SLVIA's interest in prophecy started with her mom. If he knows SLVIA and plays poker with Taylor, there may be far more to the story than he can say in public.

"Tricky D, why do you want me to trust him?" she pushes, both angered and curious.

"Jenny, sweetheart," he says and smiles, "you know better than to ask questions when you already know the answer. Do what your mother would do and search your heart."

What answer does she know already? Search her heart for what? Her heart feels totally broken.

He takes another bite and chews, his eyebrows furrowed in thought. "As a father, do you know what I've always feared for you?"

She shakes her head, honestly not knowing, completely baffled and dismayed by this whole conversation.

"That no man would ever be strong enough, smart enough, and brave enough to be equal to the powerful woman you've become, and most importantly"—he stalls, gulping his own emotion—"that no one would be able to crack open your wounded heart before it was too late. You needed protection after your mother passed, but those same walls are now keeping you from discovering yourself and your true destiny."

Her throat tightens, and her eyes well. The old sailor sees right through her, knows that she misses Taylor, and in his own odd way, tells her that it's OK. Even more, he actually seemed to hope or expect that she would fall for Taylor before she ever met him. What else does her father know?

His phone pings with a text, but when he reads it, his face falls.

"What is it?" she asks, not sure he can tell her. He offers her the phone.

"The president signed an executive order to require biometric-based identification by year's end and nationwide adoption of a new digital identity platform called INVISID before the next election," she reads and hands back the phone. INVISID was the platform with a backdoor that Taylor mentioned.

Her father whispers, "*And he caused all, both small and great, rich and poor, free and bond, to receive a mark in their right hand, or in their foreheads.*"

She can't believe her eyes and ears. The president just ordered national biometric identification, and her father just essentially called the program the mark of the beast. Does her father believe?

Her father chuckles. "You should see the look on your face. Come on, Jenn, you're not the only one your mother spoke to about prophecy and what it means. My friend and I were both students as well."

"What are you saying exactly?" she presses, unsure of the subtle message.

"We need to be careful, Jenny." He looks around, leans forward, and lowers his voice. "I believe our friend has a valid and accurate understanding of the ancient texts. We have a duty to protect our democracy with one hand and a heavenly command to be the hands of forgiveness and grace with the other. We are not living in normal times, sunshine. Buckle up. The next few years will be a wild ride."

Uncomfortable with his own emotion and the volatile topic, the admiral changes the conversation again to public-permissible news, but her mind can't move past the stunning revelations. SLVIA has been watching over her since before her mother passed away because her father, a secret believer, befriended the program. Her parents were nodules in the SNO network.

After the rather enlightening lunch and a promise to attend church with her dad on Sunday, she takes a long walk on the National Mall, needing the fresh air and open space to process the multiple bombshells when her cell phone pings with a text.

You look absolutely amazing. Glad to see you wearing the clothes from the plane. Adam seemed in a good mood at lunch. I miss you every hour of every day.

There's no name or return number, but her heart skips a beat as she spins, searching everywhere for Taylor, hoping he's close, excited to see him again. But there's no one, and others stare in her direction.

A new text pings.

LOL, you look crazy, girl. Remember you're under surveillance, so don't discount the insanity plea. Don't worry, I look after the people I love.

The words leap inside her heart, a word she knows he would not use lightly. She glances up to realize there are cameras everywhere in Washington, and she's pinging a hacking expert. He could be anywhere in the world.

She types back: *I miss you too. I'm sorry I doubted you.*

Then no more responses come back. She turns around to plead with her eyes at nearby cameras, worried she held back saying the one word he wanted to hear, maybe needed to hear, the word she wants to say, but just isn't ready to, not yet. When she checks her phone again, the messages have disappeared.

Taylor didn't abandon her but slipped back into the shadows. A spark of hope flickers to life that she will see flapjack again. Next time, she'll tell him how she feels and won't let him slip away.

With a sigh and a residual grin, she finishes her walk at the Washington

Monument when her phone pings again. Yanking it up, expecting Taylor, she puzzles at the message.

"This calls for patient endurance on the part of the people of God who keep his commandments and remain faithful."

Anonymous, with no sender or call number, but it doesn't sound like Taylor. She pans the area, but she's the only one there. The message sounds like someone obsessed with prophecy. One thing seems perfectly clear—her ordeal with Taylor and SNO has only begun.

THE END OF THE BEGINNING

THANKS
AND A SNEAK PEEK

Thank you for reading *Swarm*, the first installment in the *SNO Chronicles*.
I hope you enjoyed reading it as much as I did writing it!

If you did, here's a sneak peek at the first two chapters of the second book in
the series: *The Last Ark: Lost Secrets of the Qumran.*

Guy Morris

CHAPTER 1:
TEMPLAR SACRIFICE

Convent Church, Tomar, Portugal
Ten Days Before Temple Ceremony

For some, the path to enlightenment leads to a revelation; for others, it ends with a slide into insanity. Derek Taylor leans toward insanity. The SLVIA has disappeared, and each step forward testifies to the depth of his insane obsession with finding the missing program. Either way, a man rarely changes overnight but over a thousand sleepless nights. The problem, in Derek's mind, is that the man never sees the end of his change. The person he's evolving into doesn't exist yet.

A decade ago, Derek would have boldly rushed into this situation, but nothing about this meeting feels right. It may not be his first time feeling the acidic gnaw of fate squeezing the breath out of his lungs, but he can't shake the premonition of death hovering nearby.

With a gentle tap to the right stem of his glasses, a set of transparent data feeds light up on the interior of his custom lenses. A Bluetooth audio channel feeds an encrypted satellite signal booster in his backpack. The satellite connects to the secret data center for an experimental D-WAVE quantum AI that has yet to mature—or operate at full capacity. He pulls out his Taser gun, which is useless against a real gun with a night scope. But it makes him feel better.

"WITNESS, start record, turn on full sensors," Derek whispers as he approaches the main entrance. His partner, a bohemian technical savant named Jester, engineered several high-tech functions within the heavy hipster black-frame glasses. Infrared allows him to detect heat signatures hidden in shadow. A Wi-Fi signal detects camera feeds and other security.

"All sensors recording," WITNESS confirms, with the voice of a British boy.

Derek came to meet renowned Templar historian Olavo Silva. The late hour and remote location seemed suspicious, but Olavo feared his cottage was under surveillance. After a week of building trust, the old Portuguese scholar finally agreed to share an anonymous text he received on the same night the SLVIA disappeared. The SLVIA code often sent communications by anonymous text. It could be a meaningless dead-end, but Derek needs to see the message to be sure. More to the point, he needs to find the SLVIA, and the last breadcrumb led to Olavo.

The Convent Church in Tomar, famous as the fourteenth-century castle headquarters of the Order of Christ, seems a cliché location for meeting a Templar fanatic. Any good hacker will know the weakness of being predictable, although the late hour of two a.m. should ensure that they'll be alone while most of the residents sleep. Derek holds up behind a pillar in the entrance courtyard as a monk passes, his hooded head bowed in prayer. Most residents, but not all.

Past the administrative offices and dining halls, Derek steps up to the twelve-foot arched stone doorway of the church. The infrared image of a cat hiding in a dark corner appears in his lens. The scent of Valencia oranges drifts up from the gardens beyond the church. Other than the sound of the wind cutting between the buildings, he hears nothing.

Once inside the church, the dim light makes it impossible for Derek to appreciate the astonishing columns, walls, and ceilings painted with brilliant colors and gold leaf. Templar architecture borrowed heavily from Romanesque,

Gothic, Manueline, and Renaissance styles, exquisite in both design and execution. Derek is not here for a tour.

Careful to scan every corner for a heat signature, he slowly steps toward the ornately painted rotunda called the *Charola*. The Templars modeled the octagon design after the Church of the Holy Sepulchre and the Dome of the Rock in Jerusalem.

His mind subconsciously recalls the history. On Friday the 13th, 1309, King Philip IV of France, deep in debt to the Templars, arrested the Grand Master along with thousands of Knights. Thousands more escaped with the vast Templar wealth. By the time King Philip and Pope Clement were burning the Grand Master Jacque de Monet at the stake a year later, the rest of the Order were making new alliances in Scotland, where they resurrected as the Scottish Rite Freemasons. Other Templars landed in Portugal where King Dinis I founded the Order of Christ. By 1357, the Convent Church and castle were their headquarters. Countless secrets rest within these walls, but those are not the secrets Derek seeks tonight.

Inside the rotunda, Derek stays at the perimeter to sweep the area of surprises. A life-sized bronze crucifix hanging from the ceiling draws his eyes upward to the hundred-sixty-foot-high dome. When Derek lowers his gaze, he finds Olavo lying directly under the crucifix. The scholar is trembling and frothing at the mouth with his eyes rolled back into his head. Poisoned.

Derek instinctively pivots in a complete circle to check the infrared for surprises, but he's alone. He lights a flashlight and kneels next to the old man. There are no signs of blunt trauma or blood. With a heaving chest, Olavo breathes a last breath. Whatever secrets the old historian intended to share were now lost.

A thousand questions rush through Derek's mind, too fast to process. "WITNESS. Access security cameras for the Convent Church in Tomar." He takes Olavo's phone, which holds evidence of their communications.

A moment later. "Access gained."

"Replay the last ten minutes for the *Charola* area."

A small window opens within his lenses to show a black-and-white security video of the area where he stands. Olavo paces the floor between the octagon pillars, checking his watch. Derek checks the video time. Five minutes ago. A deadly price to pay for his extra cautions. He and the killer just missed each other.

From outside the church, a mile or so away, the telltale sound of police sirens heads up the hill in his direction. Derek taps his lens to find a police channel and catches Portuguese chatter about an intruder. He keeps watching the video, urgently needing answers. Soon a large, stocky man approaches. The same hooded monk he passed only moments ago.

"I have a message for Mr. Taylor?" the monk says in a thick Scottish brogue.

Derek watches as Olavo hesitates, maybe wondering how the monk knew Derek would be there. It's a trap, the question of someone who suspects a disguise. He and Olavo are roughly the same height. To his horror, the ever-curious scholar nods. "Yes, go on."

The monk leaps on Olavo to slap a hand over his mouth and jab something into his neck. He steps back and lets the historian drop to the floor, watching long enough for Olavo to convulse before the monk turns back into the darkness and disappears.

Sirens grow louder as Derek glances down to see Olavo's fingers clutching a tiny piece of paper. He reaches to unfold it.

Abbot Sabas must heed Sefer HaBahir

Derek can only assume that this was the message Olavo wanted to share, but it makes no sense to him. The *Sefer HaBahir* is a famous Kabbalah book of wisdom and mystic knowledge. First published in 1176 and still held in high regard. The name *HaBahir* means brilliant or illumination. Templar lore maintains that Hugh de Payens, the first Grand Master of the Knights Templar, discovered the original scroll of *Sefer HaBahir* under the Temple Mount. Believed to be written in the first century by Rabbi Nehunya ben HaKanah, the Templars reprinted the book.

The name of Abbot Sabas, however, is a complete mystery.

Sirens grow closer to the church and will wake the castle residents.

"WITNESS, find a floor plan for the Convent Church," Derek requests as he checks Olavo's pockets for other clues.

He turns to the rear of the church just as a floor plan appears in his lenses. As he had suspected, the church design includes a clergy sacristy in the back with a separate exit. But that's the simple part. The entire complex sits in the middle of a twenty-acre castle surrounded by twelfth-century stone walls. The vast layout will buy him a few minutes at most. The problem will be how to escape the walled citadel, which has only one entrance—the one at which the police will arrive at any moment. He's trapped.

"WITNESS, show me a Google Earth view of the Convent de Crist, Tomar, Portugal," Derek orders as he exits into another courtyard.

Behind the church, two-story living quarters block any exit to the left. Lights turning on in the windows confirm to Derek that curious eyes will soon follow. A garden with workshops and a stone guard tower lay straight ahead but offer no exit. An ancient orchard with even older oaks grows up against the crumbling southern wall. Based on the satellite view, at least one tree spans the wall and drops to a hillside above a dirt trail that leads to a nearby village.

"Could be worse," Derek mumbles as he races for the enormous oak.

Voices and commands shouted in Portuguese echo from inside the church and surrounding courtyards. At the oak's base, he reaches up for the lowest branch to hoist himself with a stifled grunt, fueled by adrenaline. Shouts from inside the church show they must have discovered the body of poor Olavo, flooding Derek with immense guilt. The killer asked for him.

Derek climbs over a branch that spans the crumbling wall. As carefully as he can in the dark, he hangs from the branch, worried about the drop. The bark of a dog and the searching beam of a flashlight provide him with the courage to let go.

Derek lands hard after a ten-foot drop to roll down the brush and grassy hill another thirty feet. It takes a moment to get his bearing and check for anything broken. Except for ripped clothing and some bruises, he'll survive. Shouts from inside the wall urge him to hurry. He needs to get to the village at the bottom of the hill where he parked. Disappointed, and soaked in guilt, he can't even be sure the SLVIA sent the message. The only way to find out will be to find an abbot named Sabas.

CHAPTER 2:
PATRIOT PASSING

Arlington Cemetery, Maryland
Six Days Before Temple Ceremony

Jenn Scott desperately tries to make sense of a death that makes absolutely no sense at all, though she imagines others responding the same way at the sudden loss of a beloved patriarch. Behind his deeply weathered face was a man who jogged into his late sixties, continued to work out, and got the best care the US Navy could provide. The admiral was a healthy man.

Boom! The ear-cracking concussion of seven rifles firing synchronized shots startles her back into the present. Admiral Adam Daniel Scott has died. Boom! The coroner claimed he had an acute myocardial infarction. A heart attack. Boom! Jenn doesn't believe it. But she reminds herself that denial is a stage of grief.

Jenn stares at the polished navy-blue coffin draped with an American flag as if it were a scene from a movie. The president, two ex-presidents, senators from across the aisle, fellow Joint Chiefs, and a few foreign dignitaries take turns to say gracious words like *duty*, *honor*, *integrity*, and *sacrifice*. All words she would expect for a Joint Chief of the United States Navy. But she also hears a few phrases she doesn't expect, such as *proud, adoring father*, and *man of a deep, silent faith.*

In Jenn's memory, her childhood was far from ideal, often left alone as the only daughter of a demanding commander while her mother slowly succumbed to cancer. She sucks in a deep breath, determined not to allow her emotions to leak out in front of the news cameras. Annapolis colleagues will be watching.

Matt Adelson, a close family friend and one of the admiral's poker pals, steps up to the microphone.

"Don't worry, I'm the last speaker and I promise to be brief," says the newly confirmed Director of National Intelligence. "I knew Admiral Adam Scott as both a colleague and a close friend for over thirty-four years. We shared holidays, babysat each other's children, and watched America face enemies both foreign and domestic. Admiral Adam Scott was every ounce of every word you've just heard said about him today and more. But to me, Adam will always be a dear friend, a devoted father, a true American patriot, and a hero in every sense of the word."

Matt chokes on the last line. Jenn has never once witnessed the stalwart ex-Marine lose emotional control. His unexpected vulnerability cracks her own fragile resolve. Tears slowly seep down her cheek. Jenn can only stare forward, trembling, and remember to breathe.

The head pastor from the Washington DC International Christian Church steps up. "Let us pray," he invites as he bows his head.

Jenn involuntarily tunes out the prayer to dwell on the recent revelations that the admiral was a secret member of the underground Spy Net Online, or SNO, an illegal network. It still blows her mind, forcing her to question everything she thought she knew about her father and Washington. What else has her father kept secret?

"Amen," the crowd echoes around her.

While the Marine bugler plays taps, two Navy officers carefully fold the flag into a perfect, tight triangle before they step over to hand it to Jenn with a salute. Embarrassed, but unable to contain herself any longer, the gentle tears turn into halting sobs. A tender arm reaches around her shoulder to offer comfort. Matt Adelson.

For a moment, just an instant, she felt the spark of hope that the arm belonged to another man. A man she never realized how much she missed until this very moment: Derek Taylor. She hasn't heard from him in weeks and wonders if he even knows that his old poker buddy has passed away. Derek had once promised to look after her, and yet in the hour she needs him most, he's nothing more than a digital ghost.

As the coffin lowers into the earth, someone gives Jenn a bowl of dirt. When the coffin stops at the bottom, she stares at the dark lid for what seems like an eternity, wishing, hoping, praying this would be the moment that she woke up.

Eventually, Jenn heaves a deep, shuddering sigh.

"Fair winds, Admiral. Give my love to Mom." Her face distorted from pain, she tosses dirt onto the coffin and turns to leave.

—

The Last Ark is avaible now, in paperback and Kindle®, from Amazon.

ACKNOWLEDGEMENTS

In the long list of people to acknowledge in the writing of *SWARM* and making it a better book, my wife Darcy who has supported my reinvention into becoming a writer with patience and grace stands above them all. I also want to thank my dad who invested in the vision while the image was still murky. To my honest beta readers Padma, Greg and Kathy, ruthless editors Jennifer and Alison, creative cover & interior designer Mark (coverness.com) and marketing support team at Elite Authors, I owe my gratitude for giving me candid feedback. I've attempted to craft an intricate story that deals with difficult and controversial topics. I don't expect to change many minds, but I do hope to encourage frank debate, open dialogue and sincere personal questions about the direction of our technology, our democracy and the prophetic times in which we live.

ABOUT THE AUTHOR

Guy Morris a successful businessman, thought leader, adventurer, inventor, and published composer. During college, Guy was influenced by men of the Renaissance who were fluent in business, science, politics and the arts. After growing up on the streets, he earned graduate scholarships for his macroeconomic models, and won awards as an early webisode pioneer where he wrote the scripts that introduced the SLVIA, based on a true program that escaped the Livermore Labs. With three degrees and thirty-six years of executive-level experience in high tech firms, Guy's thrillers bend the fine line between truth and fiction with deeply researched stories, international locales and sardonic wit.

You find out more about Guy via his website:

guymorrisbooks.com

You can also stay in touch via the following social media:

instagram.com/guymorrisbooks
facebook.com/guymorrisbooks
twitter.com/guymorrisbooks

Made in the USA
Middletown, DE
27 June 2023

33747513R00249